THE LOST GOLD
OF SAN FRANCISCO

Other books by Michael Castleman

Fiction:
Death Caps

Nonfiction:
Great Sex: A Man's Guide to the Secrets of Total-Body Sensuality

The New Healing Herbs: A Scientific Guide to Nature's Medicines

Blended Medicine: How to Combine the Best of Mainstream Medicine and the Alternative Therapies for Optimal Health and Wellness

There's Still a Person in There: The Complete Guide to Preventing, Treating, and Coping with Alzheimer's Disease
Coauthor with Dolores Gallagher-Thompson, Ph.D., and Matthew Naythons, M.D.

Nature's Cures: A Scientific Guide to 33 Natural therapies to Improve Your Health and Well-Being

An Aspirin A Day: How the Familiar White Pills Help Prevent Heart Disease, Stroke, and Cancer

Before You Call the Doctor: Safe, Effective Self-Care for 300 Common Medical Problems
Coauthor with Anne Simons, M.D., and Bobbie Hasselbring

The Healing Herbs: A Scientific Guide to Nature's Medicines

Cold Cures: The Complete Guide to Prevention and Treatment of the Common Cold and Flu

The Medical Self-Care Book of Women's Health
Coauthor with Sadja Greenwood, M.D., and Bobbie Hasselbring

Crime Free: The Community Crime Prevention Handbook

Sexual Solutions: For Men and the Women Who Love Them

THE LOST GOLD OF SAN FRANCISCO

A Novel

By Michael Castleman

Last Gasp

San Francisco

THE LOST GOLD OF SAN FRANCISCO

Copyright © 2007 by Michael Castleman

Published by
   Last Gasp
   777 Florida St.
   San Francisco CA 94110
   (415) 824-6636
   (800) 366-5121
   fax (415) 824-1836
   lastgasp.com

ISBN: 978-0-86719-674-0

Cover design: Scott Bieser
Book design and Production: Rachelle Rivers

Printed in the United States
First Printing April 2007

Michael Castleman can be reached at michael@mcastleman.com or at
www.thelostgold.com

For Ira Kay
and the Lynbrook Coin Club
1963

April 17, 1906

Orange hair flying, Patrick Reilly guided his winded mare through the throng crowding Mission Street—pedestrians, bicyclists, push-cart peddlers, horse-drawn wagons, and the occasional horseless carriage, which, in the new century, people were calling "cars." He spurred the horse up Mint Street, turned down Jessie, and reined in at a reeking puddle of horse piss by the loading dock of the Granite Lady, the San Francisco Mint. Dismounting, he threw the reins to one armed guard, while another pushed on the heavy iron doors. Reilly stepped into the dim chill of the loading dock, known at the Mint as the Shipping Gallery, or "Ship Gal." Against the far wall sat seventeen bulging canvas sacks. Perched on top of them, four more guards played poker, their rifles leaning against the wall.

"Mother of God," Reilly snapped in a thick County Cork brogue, "put the damn cards away! You're guarding gold, lads. Act like it." Quickly, the guards did as they were told.

Reilly satisfied himself that no one had tampered with the bags, and that they were not visible from Jessie even with the iron doors open. Then he strode past the Assayer's Room and bounded up the stairs into the cool stately foyer of the Greek temple that struck the coinage for the West.

Mint Superintendent Herbert Walther met him in the hall by Stamping Room Number One—"Stamp One"—the larger of the pair of cavernous halls where enormous coin presses ingested smooth gold and silver blanks at one end, and at the other, spat out finished coins that moved along newly electrified conveyers to be washed, polished, and bagged. "Well, Red?" Walther asked his second-in-command. He tried to sound composed, but could not conceal an edge of anxiety in his voice.

Reilly sighed. "The General's gone to the Opera."

The Opera. I might have known, Walther thought. The irony was not lost on either man. Reilly had spent the better part of the day on a round-trip ride all the way up to the Presidio on San Francisco's northern bluffs only to discover that the Army commander, General Frederick Funston, was just one block from the Mint at the Grand Opera House in the boisterous throng waiting to see the great tenor, Enrico Caruso, sing Don José in *Carmen*.

"Thank you, Patrick," Walther sighed. "Get cleaned up, then go home. I'll handle things here."

"But it's my night to stay," Reilly reminded his boss. For the previous 10 days, with round-the-clock Double Eagle production, the two men had alternated supervising the night shift. "I slept at home last night. I'll stay tonight. You need the rest more than I do. And if you don't mind my saying so, you could use a shave." The afternoon was turning into evening, and the Mint's new electric lights came on, casting elongated shadows down the lengthy corridor.

"Do I look that bad?" Walther asked, stroking his chin, finding prickly stubble. The two men had worked closely for eight years, and despite their difference in rank and age—Walther was 15 years older—their relationship had transcended professionalism to friendship.

"Frankly, you do," Reilly said with a mixture of sympathy and concern. "But whether you stay or go, I won't be able to rest anywhere but here until the misstrikes are in armored wagons on their way to Oakland." Then Reilly added, "And you know I've got a dead eye with a Winchester."

"So you've told me … several times." Walther felt too weary to argue with his Production Supervisor. If anyone knew the fix he was in, Red did.

"All right," Walther sighed. "But since the Army's not going to take the bags off our hands tonight, let's move them from the Ship Gal up to Stamp One. Then wash up and get some supper. And don't shoot me when I check to see how you're doing."

Reilly smiled. "So you'll be going home this evening?"

The question hung in the air unanswered. Reilly descended the stairs to supervise moving the gold.

Thank God for Patrick, Walther thought. Both men were widowers, but unlike the childless Walther, Reilly had four daughters who kept house for him near Mission Dolores. Walther was godfather to two of Red's girls. Reilly's friends joked that he worked too hard and drank too little, which was precisely why Walther valued him so highly. The Mint Superintendent had no doubt that Patrick would gladly lay down his life before letting any hoodlum get near the misstruck Double Eagles he was moving up to Stamp One.

Walther entered his office to find two of his men closing the folding iron shutters mounted inside the windows that looked across Fifth Street to Brunswick House. It was a large, wooden, three-story tenement for working men and their families, and like much of the rough-hewn neighborhood south of Market Street—South of the Slot, in local parlance—it was in sore need of a paint job. A dozen Brunswick residents, many of them longshoremen, were smoking and drinking beer on the wide front stoop, unwinding after the day's labor. Their wives were pulling dry clothes off lines into the windows above, chatting with neighbors, and shouting to their husbands on the street below. A group of boys played baseball in Jessie Alley. Pushcart vendors hawked cabbage and sausages. Then everything went black as the iron shutters closed with a resounding thud.

The Mint men worked the hasps and secured the shutters with large padlocks, then proceeded to the windows that looked across Mission Street to a similar tableau, the Cosmopolitan Hotel, another dingy workingman's residence, most of whose denizens toiled in the fish markets near the Ferry Building or in the slaughterhouses of Butchertown by South Beach. A few were leaning out of their windows watching the line of fancy carriages carry the cream of San Francisco society down Mission Street toward the Opera. Walther's gaze shifted to the line of carriages. He thought he recognized James Phelan, developer of the magnificent new Phelan Building, but the iron shutters clanged shut before he could be certain.

In the shuttered twilight, Walther padded across the thick Chinese carpet that his late wife, Helen, God rest her soul, had persuaded him to buy to mark his ascendancy to Superintendent. He would have preferred a blue rug, but Helen insisted on dusty rose to complement the enormous rose marble fireplace that dominated the room. Helen, the artist, had strong feelings about color, feelings Walther found incomprehensible. But when Helen decided he should have a rose-colored rug, rose it was.

Walther leaned over his rolltop and opened the production ledger.

The West's economy was booming. The entire region was starved for coinage, especially ten-dollar gold Eagles and twenty-dollar Double Eagles. Naturally, in the face of unprecedented demand, the geniuses at the Treasury Department had decided to replace Denver's presses. They'd thrown all Eagle and Double Eagle production to San Francisco. Washington had cabled him three weeks earlier with the news that two freight cars of Double Eagle blanks were en route from Denver, and that he was to run San Francisco's presses round the clock to strike them. Walther wired back saying that his presses needed overhaul as badly as Denver's and couldn't handle nonstop production. Besides, even if he could strike the Double Eagles, he had nowhere to store them. The vault could hold only so much, and Department regulations prohibited off-site storage. Never fear, Washington wired back, General Funston has been ordered to dispatch the Twenty-third Cavalry with armored wagons to pick up the extra production and transport it to the federal railhead in Oakland.

Walther noted that, except for the misstrikes, all the extra production had been completed miraculously on schedule. He closed his ledger and cursed under his breath. Damn that Funston. The little Napoleon was so busy spouting in the *Examiner* about Mayor Schmitz's corruption (in preparation, rumor had it, to run against him) that he didn't give a rat's ass about the Mint's security problem. The General's staff had assigned the gold transport to one Major Wendell Legget, who was supposed to have arrived that morning. But some incompetent at the Presidio got his dates mixed up. Legget was in Monterey on maneuvers and was not expected to return for a week. Now Walther was sitting on a vault filled with $200 million in gold, twice his regulation limit. The vault was so full, the huge doors barely closed.

To make matters worse, the previous day, while stamping out the last of the Double Eagles, an alignment screw failed, allowing the blanks to wiggle in the press bed. Before any pressmen noticed, they'd struck 6,491 Double Eagles with serious errors on the reverse. The words "United States of America," and "Twenty D." looked fine. But instead of the eagle-and-shield in sharp relief, the graphic was blurred and the San Francisco Mint mark "S" had been stamped twice, "SS," in Mint argot, "double die." Such errors were totally unacceptable. Those coins could never be allowed to circulate. So all the misstruck Double Eagles—$129,820—had to be culled, bagged separately, and specially marked for melt-down back in Denver. They filled the seventeen bags being moved up from the Ship

Gal. With no room in the vault, they could not be secured, which was a violation of all Treasury Department storage regulations. But Walther had no choice. There wasn't so much as a cubic inch of space left in the vault. Of course, those bags would have been long gone had Legget's armored wagons picked them up that morning as Walther had been assured. But—damn them both to Hell!—Legget was in Monterey, and Funston was at the Opera.

Walther considered his predicament. Since the Mint had opened in 1874, no one had ever attacked it. No one had even tried. But the vault usually held just a small fraction of the $200 million now residing there. That sum was certain to tempt the hoodlums of the Barbary Coast, who'd made San Francisco the roughest port north of Panama—if they got wind of the treasure. That was why Walther had sent Reilly to the Presidio in person. He couldn't risk using the telegraph or telephone. The gangs bribed the operators to tip them to anything worth stealing.

Walther trusted his own men. But he couldn't be sure about the roustabouts at the Presidio. Soldiers' pay was low, so low that Funston and other heroes of the Spanish War were urging Congress to raise it substantially. In the meantime, some soldiers in San Francisco were bound to be on the take. But once Legget had given him a transfer receipt for the misstrikes, underpaid soldiers were *his* problem.

The Mint had iron shutters on its windows, and iron doors on the Ship Gal and Receiving Dock. The metal looked impregnable, but Walther knew better. After almost thirty years, the hinges and hasps were worn and rusted. He'd requisitioned replacements, but the bureaucrats were dragging their heels. If some gang with ladders and crowbars, or worse yet, dynamite, breached the iron, Walther had all of two dozen men, maybe ten rifles, a half-dozen pistols, and perhaps two thousand rounds. Against an assault by, say, twenty armed men, they wouldn't stand a chance, and several of the city's gangs could easily muster twenty men or combine forces to field even more. As for the vault, its eight-tumbler German combination lock represented little deterrent. Any decent railroad or mining man could drill it or set charges and blow its doors clear across the bay. For all he knew, the gangs were at that very moment huddling in basements along Pacific Avenue or Morton Alley planning the attack.

Funston was a block away at the Opera. Helen loved the Opera. They'd subscribed for years and had a box that Walther kept after his wife's ship disappeared in fog on the way to Seattle. He still attended regularly, and sometimes caught himself talking to the empty chair beside him. His box was among a group reserved for ranking federal officials. Funston's was nearby.

The April evening was raw with a wet fog that precipitated droplets on Walther's face as he hurried down Mission Street into the boisterous crowd of Opera-goers. The appearance of the fabled Caruso was the event of the new century, and *tout le monde* was there, dressed as if San Francisco were Paris. Walther nodded to several acquaintances, wishing he'd shaved and feeling woefully underdressed in his work suit, high boots, and long coat. He'd been so preoccupied waiting for the army and Reilly all afternoon that he'd forgotten to dispatch a man to Mei-Lin to fetch his Opera finery. Helen would have been scandalized by his appearance. But Helen was gone, and this was an emergency.

Walther pushed through the crowded lobby with its immense crystal chandelier, the largest west of Chicago, the size of the average workingman's cottage South of the Slot. With a nod here and a handshake there, he threaded his way up the sweeping staircase to the Grand Tier and around the horseshoe past his box to the general's. He drew the heavy velvet curtain aside and in a voice that mingled urgency with contempt boomed, "General Funston? Is the general here?"

A paunchy colonel appeared, filling the doorway, the curtain draped over his shoulder, a burgundy velvet cape. "And you are—?"

Walther identified himself and tersely explained that a situation at the Mint required the general's immediate attention.

"I'm sorry, but the general's not here."

Walther's pot boiled. "And where in damnation is he?"

The colonel did not expect this tone or vocabulary and took a moment to compose himself before answering testily, "At home. Mrs. Funston took ill and the general escorted her home."

"What's his address?"

The colonel glared at the vulgar wild-eyed man standing before him. He did not comport himself with the dignity his office demanded. "I'm not at liberty—" and turned back into the box.

But Walther was in no mood to be dismissed. He clapped a big hand on the man's shoulder, yanked him around until they were nose to nose, and hissed, "Your Major Wendell Legget was supposed to move a large shipment of gold for me this afternoon, but never showed up. The general's staff sent him to Monterey to play games. Now, unless General Funston takes immediate action as promised in this wire from Washington—" he shook the paper in the colonel's face "—the Treasury Department will have him busted to private despite his holy Medal of Honor and I will personally run his balls through a coin press."

The colonel blanched and shook Walther's arm off him. "Are you threatening the general?"

"He's threatening himself—and the economy of the entire West."

The colonel eyed the mint superintendent. "The cable. Let me see it."

Walther handed it to him. All around them, gowns swished and voices buzzed with excitement about *Carmen*. In the afternoon papers, Caruso had promised the performance of a lifetime, raising the anticipation level higher than Twin Peaks. The lights dimmed. The audience hushed. From inside the general's box, a woman called, "Robert! The curtain!" The colonel handed the telegram back to Walther. "Russian Hill." He muttered a number on Pacific.

Helen never would have forgiven him for missing the incomparable Caruso. But as the curtain rose, Walther was bounding down the magnificent, now deserted staircase, modeled on the one in the Hapsburg Palace in Vienna. He crossed the empty lobby and burst out into the foggy night. Half the hansoms in San Francisco were lined up along Mission Street, which smelled strongly of horses. Walther jumped into one and roared the address, promising silver if the man drew blood with his whip.

The cab took off, clattering up the cobblestones of Third Street and across Market, slicing through fetid piles of steaming horse shit.

"I could skirt Morton," the cabbie yelled above the clatter of hooves, "but it'll take longer."

Morton Street off Union Square was the most sinister two blocks of San Francisco outside the Barbary Coast. Two days earlier, a cab had been waylaid at Morton and Kearny, the passengers robbed, the driver beaten.

"No time!" Walther called. "Straight up Kearny!"

The cabbie whipped the horse and the carriage hurtled past Morton. Walther caught a glimpse of the garish rooster sign that adorned The Crowing Cock whorehouse. A knot of men loitered under it, maggots on rotting meat. What were they doing? Something flashed in the fog-softened light of a street lamp. A knife? Then Morton disappeared in the mist as the cab rattled up Kearny, turned on Pacific, and ascended Russian Hill.

Below them on lower Pacific, the Barbary Coast's night life was already in full swing. Walther saw the lights of its grimy brothels, where the dregs of womanhood could be had for a few coins, and its saloons, where, when he was younger, many a hapless lad had been shanghaied to work the ships bound for the Far East. He caught the distant strains of the bands playing ragtime, and then the sharp crack of the Coast's signature sound, a gunshot. The only police who ventured down there—or into Morton Street—were on the take, which was one of Funston's themes in his diatribes against Mayor Schmitz.

Walther tipped the hack a shiny new Barber dime, and climbed the steep stairs to the General's stately Victorian. A Filipino servant, surprised at the unexpected bell, asked his name, then asked him to wait. When he returned, he bowed and ushered Walther into the parlor. Walther and Funston had been introduced at a few functions, but had never exchanged more than social pleasantries. Neither was pleased to see the other.

"The hour is late, Walther," Funston snapped. "My wife is ill. And you look like hell. Don't you shave?" Funston had a notoriously short temper and treated his subordinates, which to him meant everyone other than the President of the United States, with disdain.

Walther had collected himself during the ride and succeeded in holding his temper, but barely. He handed Funston the cable and explained his twin problems—$200 million in gold secured in his vault that had to be moved immediately, and almost $130 thousand in misstruck Double Eagles that had to be moved even sooner.

Funston studied the cable and rubbed his eyes. "No one informed me of this. ..." It was as close as his temperament allowed to an apology.

Sensing an advantage, Walther demanded that the General immediately send troops to remove the misstrikes and, as soon as possible, more troops to lighten the vault.

"Laiken!" Funston bellowed.

A young officer appeared from the kitchen, and snapped to attention. "Sir!" Funston introduced First Lieutenant David Laiken.

"Do we have a company that could get to the Mint tonight with a decent freight wagon?"

"An *armored* wagon," Walther interjected.

Lieutenant Laiken had dark, wavy hair and a large mustache that was unable to hide a boyish face only a few years out of West Point. He pondered a moment. "I don't know about an armored wagon, but the

Sixth Infantry is at the Customs House. They'd have a freight wagon."

"Do they have a telephone?"

"No phones," Walther insisted, reminding the general of the need for utmost discretion.

"All right. Run down there yourself, Laiken. Take my bicycle. Then lead a company to the Mint. Make sure you have the stoutest wagon available and the best teamster. Oh, and Laiken, until Mr. Walther arrives in the morning, you and your men are under the command of—" Funston looked quizzically at Walther. "—What's his name?"

"Patrick Reilly, my production supervisor. Everyone calls him Red."

Funston fixed his gaze on the young lieutenant. "Got that?"

"Yes sir." Laiken saluted smartly, pivoted, and left.

For the first time all day, or maybe in weeks, Walther began to relax. As he did, weariness crashed over him like breakers on Seal Rock.

"You really do look like hell," Funston reiterated, almost tenderly. "When was the last time you got a good night's sleep?"

"It's been a while. …" Walther considered relating the story of Denver's press overhaul and the round-the-clock production that had him and Reilly living at the Mint, but his lips were too weary to move.

"Go home, man. Get some rest." The general clearly meant it as an order. "Laiken will have a dozen men at the Mint in an hour, and by the time you arrive in the morning, my teamsters will be hauling that gold to the Ferry Building. By tomorrow afternoon, I'll have a battalion with armored wagons to relieve your vault. You can count on it."

Exhausted, Walther stumbled down Funston's stairs to Jackson Street and looked for a hansom to take him to Nob Hill to his home on Pine. But there were none. He had to walk. The fog was thicker now and the streets smelled of horses, onions, and sewage. Dogs barked, which wasn't unusual. But they didn't stop, which was. He passed the big stable at Pine and Taylor. The night was calm, but the horses were agitated. He heard the liverymen cursing them.

"What's eating Blackie and Orville tonight?" one said.

"Beats me," came the reply. "Damn horses."

A block away, a cable car ascended Powell. It was all Walther could do to climb his stairs and undress. Mei-Lin was already asleep. The quilt rose and fell over her. Walther stood at his bedroom window gazing down into the blanket of fog toward the Mint. Outside, dogs continued to bark. For a moment, the fog cleared and he could just make out the new electric lights illuminating the dome of the Opera House. He wondered what the papers would say about Caruso, but felt too spent to regret missing the performance. The Opera felt distant and unreachable, like Helen, a chimera in fog. He tried to make out the Mint, but could not. The misstrikes were in Stamp One by now under Army guard. Reilly was there, God bless him. If a contingent from Fort Mason didn't arrive first thing, despite regulations, he would have the soldiers move the misstrikes to the Wells Fargo vault at Powell and Market. Everything would be all right.

April 18, 1906

Before dawn at 5:12 a.m., an angry God grabbed Herb Walther's four-poster bed and shook it hard, the way a growling dog shakes a rag doll. The first shake lasted 40 seconds, but those who survived it were united in the opinion that it continued much longer. Dogs howled hysterically. Horses panicked, smashing their stalls. A deafening roar filled the air as wooden buildings shuddered and cracked, some toppling in heaps of splintered boards, while more brittle brick buildings quivered, then shattered, collapsing into piles of cloudy rubble. Adding to the crazy din, every churchbell in San Francisco suddenly chimed, convincing the rudely awakened city that it was Judgment Day.

The first shock knocked Walther's wooden Victorian off its foundation. Listing to one side, the floors became steep slopes. The furniture slid downhill, the heavier pieces smashing into lighter ones, breaking them into kindling. Most of Walther's windows shattered, covering everything in broken glass. His huge armoire fell over, crushing the wash stand and hurtling porcelain shards everywhere. Then Walther's chimney crashed through the roof, burying his bed under a half-ton of brick, fractured rafters, and ceiling plaster. The weight of the fallen chimney brick buckled the bedroom floor. Plaster dust fogged the room, dyeing everything ghostly.

Fortunately, neither Walther nor Mei-Lin were in the big mahogany bed when the temblor struck. Mei-Lin had padded down to the kitchen moments earlier to draw water for her Master's coffee. Walther had spent a fitful night—damn those barking dogs! He'd awakened for good a few minutes before the quake when a milkman yelled at his agitated horse. Walther dressed and paced the bedroom, fretting about the misstrikes, cursing the Army's incompetence, and recalling that when he returned from Funston's, he'd found his China girl sound asleep. He lifted the quilt and climbed into bed beside her. Her nightgown had come unbuttoned, revealing the swell of a breast and the delicate raspberry of a nipple.

• • •

Walther's wife had been lost at sea three years earlier on her way to Seattle to visit her sister. Shipwrecks bring a peculiar grief: no body, no burial, none of the grim finality of witnessing the return to cold earth. Walther had lost loved ones before, but none he adored as much as Helen, and the manner of her passing left him not only bereft but thoroughly disoriented. Nob Hill had plenty of socially prominent widows and daughters hoping to wed. After a decent interval, several discreetly signaled their availability. But Walther wasn't interested. No one could replace Helen. He buried himself in work at the Mint, but otherwise lived in a lonely daze.

As the months passed and he slowly adjusted to the solitude of his large manse, Walther realized he needed a housekeeper. His next-door neighbor, Gracelia Carter, had a young China girl, Betty. Carter referred him to the smelly dockside shack of a buck-toothed Australian. The shingle said Foster Berryman, Servant Broker. When a woman appeared at his door, Berryman assumed she required a kitchen maid. When a man appeared, he assumed something else.

Technically, the Exclusion Acts had cut off all Chinese immigration. But the Acts were haphazardly enforced, especially in good times when cheap labor was in demand. Or when the brothels needed merchandise.

Berryman winked at Walther, flashing a smirk that revealed rotted teeth with several gaps. The Australian lined up his inventory, a dozen terrified skin-and-bones China maidens. Walther's heart broke. He realized with a start that Berryman was a slaver. He'd heard the stories: Young Chinese women were tricked into leaving their world by glorified pimps who promised a Golden Mountain and delivered a lifetime—a short lifetime—of misery. Any girls Berryman couldn't deal in a few weeks to decent people who needed servants, he unloaded to the brothels of the Barbary Coast and Morton Street. The girls wound up under armed guard in rat-infested cowyards on filthy cots. Even if they serviced 20 pawing drunks a day, they could never pay off their indenture. For China girls, the whore's life meant beatings, syphilis, tuberculosis, opium addiction, and usually within a year or two, a pauper's grave.

Walther looked the group up and down. Some of the watery eyes that met his were imploring, still vital. Others were vacant, their spark already extinguished. From among the imploring, he selected a rail-thin apparition, Mei-Lin, because she did not have any obvious festering sores, and because she called out, "Me, Ma-tah! Wuh hah!" *Me, Master. I work hard.*

Walther pointed at the girl. Berryman yanked her arm, standing her atop a stool, and before an embarrassed Walther could protest, ripped her rags from her, leaving her naked and mortified. "A fine li'l gal, matey."

"What in damnation are you doing?" Walther demanded, doffing his coat and wrapping it around the pathetic waif's shoulders.

But Berryman was not finished with his pitch. He poked Mei-Lin between the legs with his cane. "Haven't had that meself, matey, but I guarantee you'll like it."

Walther pushed the cane away, paid the leering slaver in gold, and marched the terrified girl to Chinatown, where he bought her decent clothes, then lifted her onto the cable car for the ride up the steep eastern slope of Nob Hill to her new home.

Mei-Lin was 22 at the time. She'd never ridden any land vehicle other than a mule cart. The cable car, with its jerky ride, screeching, and clanging bell, terrified her. Her face contorted and tears fell from her big eyes. Walther tried to calm her with a pat on the shoulder, but she shrank from him into a bony ball on the hard wooden bench and held a pole for dear life.

The horror of the cable car gave way to wonderment when Walther pointed up Pine Street to his hillside home. In all her life, Mei-Lin had never seen such a palace. She'd grown up in a two-room mud hut near Canton. Her new Master's mansion had more rooms than she could count, and it was filled with riches beyond her imagination. Walther ushered her open-mouthed into the kitchen and offered her bread, fruit, and tea. She ate like an animal, shoveling the meal down her throat, barely stopping to breathe. She'd eaten little of the swill on the freighter and Berryman had given her next to nothing.

While the girl ate, Walther stepped next door and fetched Gracelia's China girl, Betty, to train his new servant. Betty had been in San Francisco for four years. She spoke to Mei-Lin in her native tongue and introduced her to her duties.

It was a difficult day. Mei-Lin spoke almost no English and Walther's ability to communicate by pantomime was not much better. The girl was terrified and Walther wondered if he'd made a mistake. He might have done better with a washerwoman from Irishtown. At least they spoke half-decent English.

But Betty showed the girl how to cook a stew of chicken, potatoes, carrots, and onions, and by the time Walther turned on the electric lights, another unimaginable marvel to Mei-Lin, he'd decided to keep her.

Then he realized that he'd neglected to set up a bed for his new servant. Of the three bedrooms in the house, only one held a bed. Helen had used the other two as her sewing room and watercolor studio. Since her death, Walther hadn't had the heart to disturb them.

Walther felt no physical desire for Mei-Lin. He was still grieving Helen and the half-starved child was emaciated, hipless, and flat-chested, definitely not a woman, hardly even a girl. Sheepishly, he tried to pantomime that she could sleep in the painting studio on a pallet of blankets, and that he would convert it into a proper bedroom as soon as possible.

But Mei-Lin did not understand. Her eyes told her that in her Master's huge palace, there was only one bed. She knew what that meant. One white devil was better than many, perhaps, but he would certainly breech her Jade Gate … unless—

Walther tried to usher Mei-Lin into the bedroom to collect the blankets for her pallet. She pulled one of his steak knives out of her apron and slashed his arm the way her mother had decapitated rats. Thunderstruck, Walther drew back, clenching the wound as his butchered shirt sleeve turned bright red. Mei-Lin glared at him, holding the knife aloft.

"No ficky!" she cried. "Aykill!" *No fucking. I will kill you.*

Walther staggered back against the armoire, dripping blood. Did this little wisp of a girl actually mean to kill him? Then he noticed where Mei-Lin was pointing the knife—at her own neck.

"No, don't!" he cried, thinking as much of his investment in her contract as of her life. He clutched his arm, which was beginning to hurt. "It's all right," he reassured her. "No ficky." Mei-Lin remained frozen, a wildcat cornered by dogs, her eyes ablaze.

Walther staggered to the wash basin to attend to his arm and to take a few tablets of the new century's miracle pain pill, Aspirin. By the time he bandaged his arm and changed his shirt, Mei-Lin had taken some blankets and set up a pallet in the pantry off the kitchen, as far from the bedroom as possible. When he appeared at the pantry door, she brandished the knife, again pointing it at her neck. Walther held up his good arm in a gesture of surrender, and reiterated, "No ficky," then went to bed.

The next morning, Walther awoke to the aroma of fresh coffee, eggs, potatoes, and bacon. He took the back stairs down to the kitchen and found Betty showing Mei-Lin how to prepare an American breakfast. Mei-Lin was getting the hang of frying potatoes. Walther sat and Mei-Lin served him, bowed and deferential, as Betty jabbered at her in China talk. After a few bites, he signaled his approval by pointing, nodding, and smiling.

Betty said, "Mei-Lin have sahm-sing say aporo-gee." *Mei-Lin has something to say, an apology.*

The girl stepped forward and pointed at his bandaged arm. "Solly, Ma-tah," she whispered, eyes downcast with contrition and fear. "Solly cut." *Sorry, Master. Sorry I cut you.*

"That's all right," Walther replied. "No lasting damage. Sleep in the pantry if you like. No ficky. Good breakfast."

Betty smiled and translated for Mei-Lin, who heaved a sigh that could have cleared fog from the Golden Gate. Then the girl opened her mouth. She had something else to say, but her English failed her. She turned to Betty and spoke in Chinese.

"She say: Tank you bing her. She no wan Moe-tun." *She did not want to wind up on Morton Street.*

Walther smiled at Mei-Lin. "That's quite all right." Then to Betty, "Tell her I won't hurt her. And tell her to be more careful with my knives."

Betty translated, and for the first time, Walther saw the corners of Mei-Lin's chapped lips curl tentatively upward. That evening, Walther wrote to his brother in Sacramento: Anyone who thinks China girls are submissive has never lived with one.

Mei-Lin carried the steak knife for six months, but never again brandished it. Under Betty's tutelage, she quickly learned to cook and clean, wash, iron, and mend. She ate with the gusto of those who have known starvation, and gained weight. She remained slender, but her figure grew more womanly and her long black hair acquired a lustrous shine.

Mei-Lin had a facility for language and soon spoke better English than Betty. Walther invited her to join him for dinner in the dining room instead of eating by herself in the kitchen after she'd served him. She introduced him to Cantonese foods: bok choy, chow fun, spring greens, and steamed pork buns she made from ingredients purchased down the hill in Chinatown. He was dubious at first, but grew to enjoy them, which pleased her.

One evening, Mei-Lin announced that she wanted to learn to read and write English. Walther considered hiring a tutor, then decided to teach her himself in the evening after she cleaned up from supper. They sat at the dining room table, poring over a primer he borrowed from Lincoln Elementary, across Jessie Alley from the Mint. As the weeks passed, and Mei-Lin progressed from the ABC's to reading simple sentences, their chairs moved closer.

Across Pine, a friend of Helen's, Sonja Bagensie, took ill. Her husband, Big John, a vice president with Southern Pacific, asked Walther if Mei-Lin might help out part-time. At the end of her first week, she presented her earnings with a flourish—two dollars. Walther told her to buy herself something nice. Her eyes widened. She had never known such riches. She went to Isaac Magnin's on Market near Lotta's Fountain, one of the few stores outside Chinatown that admitted Chinese, and bought a pair of sturdy American shoes, which worked better on San Francisco's steep hills than Canton slippers.

The Bagensies had four children. The eldest, 10-year-old John, Jr., known as JJ, spent much of his time riding his treasured bicycle up and down Pine Street with a gang of neighborhood kids. One afternoon, Walther jumped off the cable car to see Mei-Lin shrieking with delight as she pedaled JJ's two-wheeler shakily toward him. "Lookee me!" she cried as she recognized him. Walther shouted encouragement, then realized how much he enjoyed the sight of her. Helen was gone. But there was still life in him.

As the months passed, Walther took to bringing Mei-Lin little presents purchased from the street vendors at the cable-car turnaround at the foot of Powell: licorice, Italian pastries, spools of satin ribbon, and her favorite, bottles of the fizzy new drink from Atlanta, Coca-Cola.

The girl reciprocated, using money earned at the Bagensies to buy Walther his favorite treat, dark chocolate from the Ghirardelli shop on the northern waterfront.

"Such an extravagance!" Walther exclaimed when Mei-Lin first presented him with the red tin.

Smiling broadly, she replied, "Good sweets. Good man."

Then, in the wee hours one raw February night as a howling Pacific storm pelted San Francisco with sheets of icy rain, Walther had a dream that he heard Helen calling him, but could not pick her out in a roomful of women. He awoke, and thought he heard a noise downstairs. He found Mei-Lin awake and shivering under her blankets, frightened by the storm. "Too coe pantee." *It's too cold in the pantry.*

Walther took her by the hand, and led her upstairs. In the big four-poster, she pressed her back against his chest, a teaspoon nestling into his tablespoon, thankful for his size and warmth. A moment passed and they both became aware of his arousal.

Walther enfolded her in his arms, cupping her small breasts in his big hands.

"You wahm." Mei-Lin nestled closer to him, no longer shivering.

"I could make you a lot warmer."

She giggled as he rolled her over to face him. She never slept in the pantry again.

● ● ●

At the temblor's first hard jolt, Mei-Lin shrieked and Walther feared for her life. As he slid down the littered slope that had once been his tidy bedroom, his father's old leather chair smashed into his hip and some chimney bricks spilling down from the roof hammered his shoulder. He staggered out of the room, and stumbled down the dark stairs twisted all askew like the Tilt-A-Whirl out at the Chutes. In the foyer, he heard soft moaning and whimpering in Chinese. He picked his way toward it crunching through broken glass and plaster rubble, and found Mei-Lin crouched in a daze by the parlor door. Even in the dark, Walther could see a gash on her temple and blood streaks on her long black hair. He helped her up and embraced her. She clung to him as though she were drowning.

"Are you all right?"

She burrowed her head into his chest like a puppy. "Sink so."

Walther caressed her hair and back, silently thanking God for her deliverance.

The house was a ruin. The windows were shattered. The floors inclined steeply. The furniture was upended, much of it destroyed. An ominous groaning came from the living room ceiling. The collapsed chimney had buckled the bedroom floor above it. Cracked joists poked through the ceiling, creating a cloud of plaster dust. The ceiling seemed on the verge of disintegration. Walther pushed Mei-Lin into the foyer as one massive joist snapped, then another, spilling half the chimney—and what was left of their bed—onto the living room floor.

Walther held Mei-Lin by her arm and, with his other hand, grappled his way in the dark along the wreckage of the hall into the kitchen. It was ankle deep in shattered crockery, flour, potatoes, and onions.

He grabbed a rag and turned on the faucet to wash Mei-Lin's wound. Gritty brown sludge trickled from the tap, then nothing. Damn, Walther thought, the main must have snapped. Then he became aware of an ominous odor—gas. One spark and the house might explode. Frantic, he lunged for the pantry and excavated a wrench from the debris. Then he pushed Mei-Lin down the hall and out the front door into the foggy dawn. The house, leaning like the tower in Pisa, was no longer connected to its brick front stair. Walther and Mei-Lin jumped from the porch to the top stair, and then Walther crunched across an expanse of broken glass to the gas shut-off valve.

Mei-Lin screamed. Walther turned to find her pointing at the Carter house next door. Nothing was left of it, just a mound of bricks obscured by a cloud of chalky dust. Gracelia, Captain Pete, their three children, and Chinese Betty—all buried alive. Mei-Lin scrambled over the knee-high wrought iron fence that separated the two properties, and began hurling bricks sobbing, "Beh-tee! Beh-tee!" But no sound came from the pile of brick. It was a futile endeavor. Walther pulled the flailing girl away.

Pine Street was a shambles. The Carters had the only brick home on the block. The rest were wood-frame Victorians. They hadn't shattered the way brick does, but like Walther's, many had been hurled off their foundations and stood twisted like dishrags. A few had collapsed. Everywhere he turned, Walther saw shattered glass, fallen roof slates, broken furniture the earthquake had tossed out of windows, and cracked retaining walls. In the middle of the street, a milk wagon lay overturned, a white rivulet burbling from its tank. Neither the driver nor the horse that had awakened him—and saved his life—were anywhere in sight. Church bells continued to ring, and everywhere, dogs barked as if rabid. Walther's neighbors slowly stumbled from their homes, dazed, most barely dressed. No one said a word.

Walther pressed a dry rag into Mei-Lin's scalp wound. She wept into his shoulder, moaning, "Beh-tee. Beh-tee."

Just then, movement down Pine Street caught Walther's eye. At first he thought he was hallucinating. The Street itself seemed to be undulating like a wave approaching Ocean Beach. There was no time to react. The aftershock swept under them, a geologic trickster pulling a rug from under their feet. Walther fell hard, smacking a shoulder on what was left of his front stair. Mei-Lin landed on top of him howling, and held him in a death grip.

The shock wave passed. Pine Street was still again. Walther and Mei-Lin struggled to their feet. She grabbed his hand. A piece of broken glass had sliced it open. She tore the sleeve from her robe and tied it around the wound.

"Herb! Mei-Lin!" Someone called from across the street. It was Big John Bagensie, wearing a robe thrown over his nightshirt, shepherding his children out of their home. JJ and his brothers looked sleepy and frightened, but unharmed. "Sonja's still inside!" His invalid wife had trouble getting around in the best of circumstances. "Can you help me carry her out?"

Walther and Mei-Lin picked their way across the rubble-strewn cobblestones. Past Powell, a fountain shot up from a crack in the street. The break in the water main, Walther realized. The water mixed with debris, forming globs of muck.

Mei-Lin huddled the Bagensie children around her. The youngest one, Jenny, was whimpering, calling for her mommy. Mei-Lin lifted the child and sang her a Chinese lullaby in a squeaky soprano.

Walther clapped a hand on Bagensie's shoulder in silent affirmation of his willingness to help. John was a mountain of a man with an enormous potato-shaped head, but in the foggy light of dawn, he appeared stooped, diminished. He touched Walther's arm in return, then turned and plunged into the ruined house with Walther close behind.

"Sonja!" Bagensie yelled up the mangled stair case.

"Johnny?" Sonja calling weakly from her sickbed above them. "Johnny, honey?"

"We're coming, darling! Hold on!"

As the two men grappled their way up the twisted stair, the building groaned. Then something snapped, and the house shuddered with a horrible roar.

"Sonja!" Big John called.

Silence.

The two men clawed their way up to the second floor and through a haze of plaster dust toward the couple's bedroom. They never reached it. The hallway ended in a precipice. The back half of the house had sheared off. It lay in a heap of boards and rubble in the yard below. From the wreckage, a ghostly hand protruded, dust-covered yet dainty. John's face went ashen. He turned and vomited. Walther gazed at Sonja Bagensie's outstretched hand. On her finger, he could still make out her gold wedding band.

The gold! My God, Walther thought, *the Mint*!

He helped John outside. Bagensie reeked from the vomit covering his robe. The children had never seen their father cry.

"She's dead, isn't she?" JJ whispered, and the children began wailing.

"Stay here," Walther told Mei-Lin. "Help John. I've got to get to the Mint."

• • •

At the corner of Pine and Powell, a cable car lay on its side, wrecked, one big steel wheel still lazily turning. The tracks had been wrenched out of the street. Steel rails pointed skyward, bent this way and that, giant pipe cleaners. Nearby, a broken water main had carved a sinkhole in the street. Water poured down Powell, creating a stream of muddy debris.

Walther slid and stumbled down the water-slickened hill on a treacherous carpet of broken glass, splintered boards, and loosened bricks and cobblestones. Everywhere he looked buildings were twisted, cracked, collapsed. Sloven's Produce Market, where Mei-Lin shopped, was gone, its display cases collapsed, its stock—lemons, apples, carrots, lettuces, everything—littering the street, already rotting and attracting rats. Alan Spielman Liquor, where Walther bought brandy, was no more than rubble reeking of alcohol. From every doorway, a stream of dazed humanity emerged, most in nightclothes and slippers with coats or blankets wrapped haphazardly around them. Few spoke. Several knelt and prayed.

From halfway up Nob Hill, Walther surveyed the city. Both of the enormous onion-topped minarets of the Israelites' Temple Emanu-El had collapsed, turning the skyline they dominated into a dreamscape, familiar but transformed. Looking downtown and south toward the Mint, everything appeared eerily normal, at least from a distance—except that here and there, pillars of black smoke rose skyward.

Fire. San Francisco was a city constructed mostly of wood. It had burned several times in its brief history. As a child, Walther barely escaped one of those conflagrations with his life. If his kitchen sink and the broken water mains were any indication, few hydrants, if any, would still hold water. First damnation, he thought, then the flames of Hell. He quickened his pace down the hill.

In Union Square, by some miracle, the new Dewey Monument to the Navy's victory in the Philippines stood intact. A bedraggled throng milled around it, drawing comfort from its unlikely survival. Bankers, sailors, bartenders, seamstresses, undertakers, shopkeepers, beggars, society matrons, priests, Chinese, gamblers, and whores—the entire city, it seemed, was streaming into the vast open space toting whatever effects they could carry: babes in arms, framed mirrors, photo albums, candelabras, bags of clothing, fur coats. Dogs raced around crazed, chasing rats that scurried amid the ruins. Horses snorted, balking at pulling carriages through the rubble-strewn streets. Wisps of smoke wafted through the foggy haze, sticking hot pins into Walther's nostrils.

Across Post Street from the Square, half of the red-brick Catholic church, Our Lady of Peace, lay collapsed in a pile of rubble. A tall, thin, ghostly figure in a long brown robe emerged from the wreckage dragging a heavy sack. Walther recognized him as the baker-priest, Father James LaSalle, well-known around San Francisco for feeding the poor, even Chinese and Indians. He reached into his sack and handed long loaves to any upraised hand.

As Walther passed Union Square, the crowd parted and a short fat man in a silk nightshirt and black tophat waddled past carrying a framed portrait of Teddy Roosevelt and jabbering in a foreign tongue. He was trailed by a valet who tried to wrap him in a gray greatcoat and two porters pushing suitcases stacked in a wheelbarrow. Walther recognized him—Enrico Caruso. He blubbered at his entourage in Italian as they tried to calm him. Could it have been only ten hours since he'd throttled that colonel for Funston's address?

Someone grabbed Walther's arm. A hooligan! The Mint Superintendent whirled, balling a fist to brain his assailant, then became dimly aware that the man was calling his name. "Mr. Walther! It's me, Rocky." It was Alfred "Rocky" Humphrey, one of the Mint's pressmen. Humphrey was shorter than Walther, but broader and tough as leather, with Indian, Mexican, British, and African blood in his veins. He ducked to avoid Walther's blow, but it never came. Walther recognized him in time.

"Rocky!"

"Red sent me to fetch you, sir."

Walther grabbed the man by his lapels. "How's the—?"

"Tight as a drum, sir," the wiry Creole replied. "We lost some windows, but the shutters all held. The Old Girl come through fine."

"And the vaults?"

"All secure, except—"

"Except what?!"

"The doors got knocked off plumb. Red says we'll have to drill."

"And the misstrikes?"

"Safe in Stamp One, under Army guard."

So that Lieutenant, Funston's aide, what was his name? Larkin? No, *Laiken* had arrived with a company from the Customs House. At least *someone* in the Army had his head screwed on straight.

Across Union Square on Post, a building groaned, then its timbers snapped and its facade sheared off and fell into the street, drawing gasps from onlookers nearby. The building's collapse shook the street enough to pancake a nearby building, which threw a cloud of dust into the morning fog. All around, people caught between shock and panic pushed their way west, away from downtown, away from the billowing smoke that was starting to get thick.

A company of police in blue uniforms materialized around Union Square. They blew whistles in an effort to herd the dazed multitude west past Van Ness to the Western Addition. More police appeared, blowing more whistles, and suddenly, the crowd lurched into motion. Walther and Humphrey were swept up in the human tide as it surged out Geary. They clawed their way out of the swarm, and headed down Powell to Market.

It was morning now, but unlike any San Francisco had ever witnessed. The fog hung thick with the chalky dust of broken buildings and the black smoke and papery ash of the growing fires. Everything seemed covered in a ghostly shroud. Walther and Humphrey strode past the Columbia Theater. Its marquee had come unhinged and hung at an odd angle, like a man with a broken neck. The title of the play had fallen off, but the young star's name was still legible, John Barrymore.

At Market, the magnificent new Flood Building was still standing, but its windows were gone and its sculpted facade looked like it had taken cannon fire. Great clots of plaster littered the sidewalks around it. At ten stories, the Flood was one of the city's tallest buildings, and one of the busiest. Now it was a tomb. Walther saw just one person in the lobby, a janitor who appeared unaware of how ridiculous he looked sweeping up with a broom and long-handled dustpan.

At Powell and Market, Walther and Humphrey encountered a hot plume of smoke blowing up the city's main thoroughfare from downtown. It stung their eyes. They looked down Market, but could see no fire, just twisted fallen buildings and a huge bewildered throng moving their way. Before them the domed roof of the Wells Fargo branch had caved in, burying the interior under rubble that stood shoulder-high. In front of it, a broken water main had turned the intersection into a lake, ankle deep. With a sinking feeling, Walther realized there was no chance of moving the misstrikes into that vault, or most likely *any* bank in the city.

They turned up Market and down Fifth. Walther held his breath and peered through the fog past the school and across Jessie to the Mint. As they approached, it came into focus. Humphrey was right. Aside from broken windows, the Granite Lady appeared intact. God bless whoever designed her foot-thick walls. They approached the Ship Gal doors, where a half dozen soldiers menaced them with bayonets. Some had bandannas over their noses and mouths for protection from the gathering smoke.

"It's all right," Humphrey said. "Remember me? Rocky? And this here's the Superintendent."

The bayonets turned aside. The line of uniforms parted.

• • •

"Your girls?" Walther asked Patrick Reilly as they stepped into his office.

"All safe, thanks be to God," the Irishman replied, crossing himself. "Megan ran down here to check on me. The house got knocked about, and the shed collapsed, killing a few chickens, but the girls are all right. They're with the O'Learys." Neighbors.

Two soldiers approached. One was the young lieutenant, David Laiken. The other was his second in command, a man who looked about 30, Sergeant Joseph Alta.

"All right, men," Walther addressed the group, unable to suppress an anxious quiver in his voice. "How bad off are we?" He already had a pretty good idea, but he wanted to give Reilly and the soldiers a chance to talk out some of their tension, before announcing his plan.

"Well," Reilly began, "the Old Girl's solid. I went through her from the cisterns to the rafters and couldn't find any structural damage. But she's an awful mess." He swept his arm around Walther's dim office: The new electric lamps lay fallen and smashed. The big bookcases had toppled, splintering several chairs and raining ledgers and Treasury directives all over the rug. A piece of marble had broken off the fireplace. And everything was covered with a film of gritty white dust shaken loose from the cracked plaster of the walls and ceiling.

"We lost most of the windows on Mission and Fifth," Reilly continued, "and some on Jessie and Mint. The vault got thrown off plumb. The doors won't open without drilling. The press in Stamp One survived all right, but in Stamp Two, a conveyor leg snapped and mangled things pretty bad. Of course, with no electric, the presses are useless—"

"What about water?" Walther interjected.

"The cisterns held, thank God, they're still full—"

"The flood in the courtyard?"

"Broken pipe. It's being capped—"

"And the pump?"

"Dead—with the electric out."

"Dammit to Hell," Walther spat. How long had it been since they'd replaced the old steam-driven pump with the new electric? A month? Two? Electric is the future, everyone said. Got to embrace the new century. Now they couldn't draw the one thing they needed most, water. "The old engine?"

"Dismantled. But Jess thinks he can rig up some bicycles, give us a pedal-powered pump." Jess Thompson, one of the press mechanics and the Mint's only colored employee, was a wizard of a tinkerer.

Walther pursed his lips. "Give him all the help he needs."

Reilly nodded.

The four men were gathered around Walther's grit-covered desk, their faces illuminated by the feeble glow of a kerosene lantern. Little daylight entered the room, or for that matter, the rest of the Mint. For security reasons, Laiken had forbidden anyone to open the iron shutters more than a crack to allow the sentries lookouts. The Lieutenant's order also helped keep smoke out of the building. It was getting thicker now, roll-ing up Mission in great sooty billows from the docks and Butchertown, carrying with it papery black ash that rained down from the sky. Through the shutter opening behind him, Walther peered through the black haze at several pillars of flame in the distance. Fires were chewing through South Beach and Rincon Hill.

"The building's secure," Laiken declared, "at least for now. I've de-ployed armed squads at the front entrance, Shipping, and Receiving, with sentries around the rest of the ground floor and first floor. They have orders to shoot anyone who approaches. So far, no one has."

"Good," Walther nodded. "I want the iron opened up enough so people on the street can see the sentries, see their rifles. A show of force."

"Easily done," Laiken continued, "but it means we eat more smoke."

"Better smoke than lead," Walther replied.

Laiken nodded. "Beg pardon, sir, but we have a serious problem with your iron shutters. I took the liberty of inspecting them. They look solid from a distance, but I must tell you they wouldn't stand up to a mob with crowbars. They're old. Some of the hinges are about rusted through. And the wall anchors are loose. They won't stop—."

"I know," Walther interrupted, pursing his lips. He cursed all Wash-ington bureaucrats under his breath, though loud enough for Laiken and the others to hear. Then he cleared his throat. "But they still look impreg-nable from a distance. That's something."

Just then, the floor beneath them began to tremble, only slightly at first, then more so until it was shaking. The lantern danced on the desk and an awful clatter rose from the direction of Mission Street, punctu-ated by hideous inhuman groaning.

"Earthquake!" Reilly shouted.

"No!" cried the sentry at the window. "Stampede!"

Reilly and Walther exchanged incredulous glances.

"That's cattle," Sergeant Alta concurred. "I'd know that sound any-where." Alta was a big man, square jawed, with beefy hands and a chest that strained his uniform's buttons. He'd grown up on a ranch in East Oakland and was familiar with stampedes.

The four of them stepped over the fallen bookcases to the sentry post and swung the iron open to get a better view. Through the dust and smoke, hundreds of beef cattle were rampaging up Mission Street. Several tripped over debris and fell, breaking legs, unable to get up. They brayed in dim-witted agony. After the herd passed, several men loitering by the Cosmopolitan stepped from one animal to the next. Some had pistols, others shotguns. They put the fallen beasts out of their misery.

"Jesus, Mary, and Joseph," Reilly whispered. "Who would believe a stampede up Mission Street?"

"Butchertown's in flames," Walther said, pointing east toward the waterfront. "They must have broken out of slaughterhouse pens."

The Butchertown fire was still a distant glow, but it was working its way up Mission. Meanwhile columns of smoke and flame rose elsewhere South of the Slot. Walther counted nine fires, some large, others larger, all spreading. A stream of refugees hurried past the Mint, fleeing the flames—longshoremen, washerwomen, slaughterhouse stiffs in bloody aprons, and families pulling wagons full of household goods.

But not everyone was on the move. Outside the Cosmopolitan and the Brunswick, the men who executed the injured cattle loitered in sullen knots, staring listlessly at the Mint, fondling their weapons.

"I don't like the look of those men," Laiken said.

"Me neither," Walther agreed.

"You recognize any of them?" Laiken asked no one in particular.

"Not a one," Reilly replied softly.

"I'll bet gold they don't live at the Brunswick or the Cosmopolitan," Walther observed. "Look at all the people leaving those buildings, taking their things, helping their neighbors, hardly glancing our way. Those men aren't doing that. They're just watching us, sizing us up, biding their time."

"Surely if the fires approach our position, they'll be forced out by the heat," Alta ventured.

"Maybe," Walther replied, "but there's no telling for how long. First comes the fire, then the looting. That's how it works, like spring floods after winter snow."

Walther knew all about fires and looting. When he was a boy, his father owned a jewelry store on Broadway below Telegraph Hill. A hooligan gang demanded protection money, threatening to torch and loot the neighborhood if they weren't paid off. The merchants banded together and refused to pay, so early one morning, the gang set fires. The owner of the liquor store next door to the Walther place broke out barrels of red wine and all the merchants filled buckets and doused their roofs. The neighborhood soon smelled of warm wine, and it looked like the merchants might beat back the flames. Then the police arrived and ordered everyone out, saying the fire could not be stopped. Walther's father was convinced they were on the take. But they had guns and insisted on evacuation. Walther's father filled a satchel full of watches, rings, bracelets, and necklaces, and stuffed his pockets and his young sons' as well. He crammed everything else into the safe moments before the police prodded them down the hill toward the waterfront, yelling assurances that they would protect any property that didn't burn. The next day, when the embers cooled, Walther and his father returned to the hole in the ground where the store had been. There was nothing left. The safe was gone.

"How are we fixed for rifles and ammunition?" Walther asked.

"We brought a dozen rifles and maybe a thousand rounds," Alta said.

"That gives us around twenty-five rifles, a few pistols, and three thousand rounds," Reilly declared.

No one spoke. They all understood their predicament. They could hold out for a while, but with only three thousand rounds, eventually a determined mob would overwhelm them.

"All right, men," Walther began, still recalling the aroma of burned red wine, "we have to assume we're on our own. We have no idea if the Presidio survived, and even if it did, we can't count on Funston to send a battalion, or even a company, to our aid. With what's happened, we can't even assume he'll remember he promised to."

Lieutenant Laiken stiffened. He considered Funston a brilliant, albeit difficult, general, and bridled at hearing him criticized. But he had to admit that Walther was probably right.

"The way I see it," Walther continued, "we have three problems: the hoodlums, the fires, and the misstrikes." The others nodded. Smoke snaked its way into the building and stung their eyes. They could taste it in their throats, feel it tighten their chests. Coughing echoed along the central corridor. Out of the gloom, Rocky Humphrey appeared with a bucket of water and some rags. Walther and the others moistened cloths and placed them over their mouths and noses. They didn't help much.

"Laiken, I want you to keep your men at the doors and windows, with their rifles at the ready," Walther declared through the rag over this face. "I want a show of force. I don't want ammunition wasted. But I don't want hesitation either. If anyone approaches the building with what looks like hostile intent, I want him shot."

"Make the rounds, Joe," Laiken told Alta. "Give those orders."

"Yes sir." Alta marched out. His footsteps crunched on the plaster and glass littering the floor.

"Next," Walther continued, "I want that broken press from Stamp Two torn apart and piled up at the top of the stair leading to the vault. If a mob storms in, we can fall back and use it as a rampart."

"We can move the ammo behind it," Reilly offered. "Stockpile it there. Be ready for them."

"Good," Walther replied. "Then I want as much furniture as possible broken up and piled against the vault doors. When the area is packed, I want it doused with kerosene."

Laiken could not believe his ears. "What the hell for?" he demanded. His lapse of military formality flew like a battle flag in the smoky air.

"To protect the $200 million," Walther snapped. "That's our mission, and I intend to see it through. If the mob is too much for us, I want our last man to light it."

"Begging your pardon, sir," Laiken pressed him, "but how does—" he paused to consider his choice of words—"how does *arson* serve this objective?"

Walther looked him in the eye. He spoke slowly as one might to an obstinate child. "The blaze should keep them away from the vault for a while, and with any luck, it'll heat the doors so hot that they won't be able to get close enough to drill them or blow them for a while longer. By then, the police might have restored order or Funston's troops might have arrived."

Laiken pulled at his mustache. Militarily, the plan made perfect sense. But he was twenty-five years old. He had never seen combat, much less room-to-room fighting with hooligans hardened by the viciousness of the Barbary Coast. This was not the baptism in fire he'd imagined. And now his commanding officer, who wasn't even Army, was ordering a suicide defense. Laiken was well aware of their mission. But he had difficulty recalling why he should risk his life for it.

"Maybe it won't come to that," Reilly ventured. "With the shutters open just a crack, the air's better in here than outside. If the fires get much closer, the heat and smoke should drive the goons away."

"Or drive them to attack," Walther countered. "Which brings me to our second problem. I doubt the fires can be stopped. The quake knocked out the water to my home. I'd be surprised if many mains survived. By this afternoon, everything around us could be burning."

"And roast us like pigs on a spit," Laiken whispered, shaken.

"Pull yourself together, man." Walther's voice was a stew of sympathy and contempt. It brought Laiken back to the smoky present. "I doubt we'll roast. The granite is a foot thick. It won't burn. But the roof is vulnerable. So are the rafters under it. If the roof catches and collapses, we have a major problem."

Alta crunched back into the group with another soldier who joined the sentry at the window. "All quiet so far," he reported, "but we're looking at two gangs, one on Mission, the other across Fifth. The men have them in their sights."

"Good," Walther said. "Patrick, until that bicycle rig gets working, I want the men to form a bucket brigade from the cisterns, and wet down the roof, the rafters, and anything else up there that might burn. If everything is really wet,"—he glanced at Laiken—"we just might make it."

"Right away," Reilly replied, and turned to leave.

Walther stopped him. "Wait. We still have our third problem, the misstrikes. We can't leave them in Stamp One. It's too exposed."

He's right, Laiken thought, the gold would be difficult to defend if a gang—. Suddenly, he felt nauseous. Then he recalled old Colonel Jenkins, who taught Strategy at the Point. As a young man at Gettysburg, he'd taken a ball in the thigh. What was it he'd said about fear? Every soldier shares the fellowship of terror. The key to command was deceiving your men into believing you didn't. Was Walther scared? If so, it didn't show. Laiken pushed his panic into a little box in the pit of his stomach. Then he took a deep breath. "You're right," he said. "Stamp One is too exposed. We should move the misstrikes to the vault area. Pile the broken furniture on top of them. Hope the blaze protects them until help arrives."

"I considered that," Walther replied, "but I have a better idea. I want the bags loaded into your wagon. I want a small squad to run them up to the Presidio and return with help."

Silence. Reilly, Laiken, and Alta glanced at one another.

"I know it's a risk," Walther continued, "maybe even rash. But consider our situation. The odds are against us. We need help. Two mobs are gathering. Other hoodlums could be on the way. We can't expect Funston to send troops on his own. But if we send the misstrikes up there, we might get some attention."

"But why send the gold?" Reilly asked. "Why not just send a man on horseback?"

"Because one man or even a few won't command as much attention as a wagon carrying $130 thousand in gold. The Army was supposed to take possession of it. Let's give it to them."

"But can we spare the men?" Alta asked. He was seven years older than Laiken. He'd seen action in Cuba and had risen through the ranks. He had a rancher's perspective on long odds: There's always green pasture somewhere. You just have to find it.

"Obviously, I'd rather not deplete our forces. We're spread pretty thin. But if the mob breaks through and we have to fall back, it's going to get mighty crowded down at the end of the hall. It's a calculated risk, but we're better off sending a squad for help now, than—" He looked at Reilly and the two soldiers. "Laiken, you want to lead the wagon?"

Laiken gazed into the flickering lantern light. His stomach ached. He raised his eyes to meet Walther's. "No. My place is here. Joe, you lead the wagon detail. Pick some men."

Alta nodded. "How many?"

"Your teamster and one other," Walther interjected before Laiken could speak. "We'll send a couple more."

Laiken and Alta left to move the wagon into the Ship Gal and supervise the loading.

"Patrick, I want you with the wagon."

"Isn't my place here, with the gold? With the men? With you?"

The Irishman dipped his rag in the bucket and covered his nose and mouth. Either it was warm for April or the fires were getting close. The smoke seeping into the room was thicker and hotter. The sentries coughed and rubbed their eyes. Had it been just eighteen hours since his ride in search of Funston? It felt like a lifetime.

Walther stared hard into his production supervisor's deep blue eyes. "I need someone I can trust with the wagon. I don't know Alta or his men. That much gold might tempt even good soldiers. If they get tempted, if they make any move for the gold, I want you to shoot them."

Walther's words made sense, but his tone was more telling. He was a father sending his son out of harm's way. "This isn't just about the gold, is it?" Reilly ventured.

Walther sighed. "Dammit, Patrick, you have four daughters. I'm thinking about them, too. You have a better chance of surviving if you go."

"But—"

Walther cut him off sharply. "No argument. Even if we weren't"—he paused a moment—"*friends*, I'd still want you with the wagon. You're the number two man here. I need you to survive, to get the gold to the Presidio safely, and take over here if—" He fell silent.

Reilly knew he was right. "I'll be back with help as fast as horses can run."

They covered the seventeen bags of gold with a few blankets. John Anderson, a Mint press mechanic, sat on top of the load, holding a rifle. Reilly, Alta, and Corporal Leroy Allen mounted horses. They held pistols and had holstered rifles hanging from their saddle horns. The flames were closer now. One fire marched up Mission. Another chewed its way up Fifth. And several were spreading along Howard. The sky was orange with flame. The fires did not just burn, they howled, monsters unleashed from a nightmare. Hordes of people streamed up Mission, gazing blankly at the dead cattle, stumbling over other debris, choking on the smoke and ash, trying to calm their whimpering children. In all the commotion, few people outside the Ship Gal noticed the teamster snap the reins. "Yah!" The horses leaned into their traces. The wagon lurched out to the street with its four-man guard, Anderson in the wagon, and on horseback, Alta on one side, Allen on the other, and Reilly behind.

"Good luck!" Walther called grimly from the doorway.

"God keep you!" Reilly yelled back as the party clattered up Jessie, turned down Mint, and disappeared into the smoke and chaos of Mission Street.

"Sir," a soldier addressed Walther through a wet bandanna, "a man to see you."

The man wore a San Francisco Fire Department uniform and introduced himself as Captain Jack Brady. "I've come to help."

"One man?" Walther almost laughed.

"That's right," came the testy reply. "You don't want me, I can fight plenty of other fires. Did your cisterns survive?"

"Yes. We're running a bucket brigade up to the roof."

"Good. What about your window sills?"

"What about them?"

"They're wood," Brady said. Walther regarded the fireman dubiously. "Fire can come in through the windows just like through the roof."

"What do you suggest?"

"Douse them. Lucky your sills haven't been painted in a while. Exposed wood absorbs more water."

Great, Walther thought, finally some good from Treasury's neglect of maintenance.

Just then a dark, colored man appeared. "Got three bikes rigged to work the pump."

Walther clapped a hand on his shoulder. "Great work, Jess. Let's run the hose to the roof."

"Cain't. Even wit' three men pedalin', cain't get water above the second floor."

"All right. Use the hose to douse every windowsill you can reach—and anything else that might burn. We've got water. Let's use it." Walther turned to the men who loaded the gold into the wagon. "You men! Help him!"

Walther and Brady inspected the bucket line that snaked upward from the cisterns. Full buckets up, empties down. It was tedious backbreaking work and the air was thick with smoke. Through the narrow opening between a pair of iron shutters, Walther glimpsed the dome atop the Grand Opera House catch fire and burn, illuminating the blackened sky. Thank God Helen didn't live to see this.

• • •

The gold would have arrived safely at the Presidio, except that the teamster holding the reins was Private Ellis Bohman. He had joined the Army in Carson City six years earlier as an alternative to a stretch in prison. He'd killed a man who'd used a marked deck in a poker game. The judge, a poker player himself, didn't see anything wrong with shooting a cheat, but Bohman had plugged him in the back, which was frowned upon in Nevada, even if the victim deserved a bullet. The judge was ready to lock Bohman up, but at the time, the state prison was bursting with IWW agitators who were raising hell in the silver mines, and the Nevada Chamber of Commerce, which the judge chaired, was up in arms about how much the good citizens of the thirty-sixth state were paying to house and feed that bunch of no-account radicals. Bohman had the good fortune to hire a lawyer who was a friend of the judge. The lawyer said his client would be happy to repay his debt to society by serving his country and would never set foot in Nevada again.

Private Bohman knew horses and worked the stables at Army posts from Seattle to Monterey. He was surprised how much he enjoyed Army life. As a stableman, he was left pretty much on his own, which allowed him plenty of time for gambling, debauchery, and pilfering and selling supplies. He served at various forts up and down the West Coast, and wound up at the Presidio, where he prospered by trading stolen Army supplies to several Marin County ranchers who sold the Army horses. He became the stableman at the small outpost the Army maintained at the Customs House at the foot of Market Street. Here, Bohman turned larceny into an art form. So many goods passed through the Customs House— Scotch whisky, Mexican leather, Chinese silk, Panama cigars, Australian gems, Russian furs—that the wily stableman had to rent a warehouse on lower Broadway by East Street to store his booty. He traded it for gold and whores in the dives of the Barbary Coast and Morton Street.

When Lieutenant Laiken showed up at the Customs House, riding a bicycle, of all things, and looking like a schoolboy with a pasted-on mustache, the stableman slipped into the shadows. Bohman had just finished his evening chores and was looking forward to a night of drinking and harlotry at the Crowing Cock. He wanted no part of whatever the young Lieutenant was selling. Then the rogue of a clerk Bohman occasionally paid to cover his thievery by altering ships' manifests whispered that the young officer's mission was to protect a fortune in gold at the Mint. Bohman sensed a potential opportunity and stepped forward to volunteer.

On Alta's order, Bohman pushed the horses. The Sergeant figured the faster the wagon rolled, the less it invited attack and the sooner they would arrive at the Presidio, and return with help. But Mission Street was covered with debris and choked with dazed refugees. Alta and Corporal Allen screamed, "Out of the way! Army business! Move aside! Let us pass!" But their shouts were drowned by the roar of the fires around them and the collapse of teetering buildings. Meanwhile, the smoke, dense and acrid, rendered them ghostly, their uniforms virtually invisible. Those who glanced their way wore vacant expressions and shuffled west with a sullen listlessness no prodding—not even pistol shots in the air—could hasten.

The wagon and its three-horse escort inched past Seventh Street and the new Post Office. Alta looked up Seventh toward Market. Visibility was poor. It was mid-morning, but the smoke and steady rain of ash made it seem like dusk. He peered into the black haze. It cleared for a moment, allowing him to see a fire north of Market and a stream of refugees crowding the city's main thoroughfare.

"Market's mobbed!" he shouted to his men. "We'll stay on Mission!"

"But Market's wider!" Reilly yelled back. "Easier for the wagon!"

"Maybe one of the alleys is clear!" Anderson shouted from the back of the wagon, struggling to retain his perch atop the gold.

The alleys! Anderson's words warmed Bohman like a bearskin coat. A plan formed in his mind. But for it to work, he had to get the wagon off Mission Street, out of the surging throng.

"Wider's better!" the teamster called to Alta. "More room to maneuver! Let's head to Market! We can check the alleys on the way!"

"All right," Alta decided. "If we don't pick up speed by the next corner, we'll try Market!"

If anything, the long block from Seventh to Eighth was even slower going. A row of tenements had collapsed on the south side of Mission, spewing wreckage all over the street. On the north side, a stable and blacksmith shop were listing precariously, about to topple, with a fire gathering strength toward the rear of the building. The refugees gave the tottering stable a wide berth, which pushed all traffic into the quagmire of tenement debris on the other side of the street. It was tough going for the horses and worse for the wagon. "If we get stuck—!" Bohman shouted to Alta.

"I know!" the Sergeant replied. "Turn up Eighth! We'll take our chances on Market!"

Bohman smiled. Just as he hoped. He rolled the plan around in his mind like dice. Eighth Street was coming up. If it were deserted or close to it, he just might be able to make his move. The thicker the smoke, the better.

The party reached the corner and turned toward Market. Along Eighth, a long, deep gash split the roadbed in two. It was filled with brown muck reeking of sewage. On either side, the tenements had pancaked, leaving only a few posts and lightpoles standing. Unlike Mission and Market, Eighth was deserted. Everyone was heading west, out of the fire zone. But Eighth ran north-south and offered nothing but flames at either end.

Bohman rejoiced. This looked promising. Deftly, he piloted the wagon to the left of the giant crevasse, and whipped the reins, "Yah!" The horses, skittish from the smoky chaos, jumped, hurling Anderson roughly to the wagon bed as the wagon bounced over piles of dislodged cobblestones.

City Hall loomed before them a block north of Market Street, towering above what was left of the surrounding buildings. A twenty-year construction project, the building had opened only six months earlier, the pride of San Francisco and the largest building west of Chicago. Now it was writhing in flames. Refugees scurried past, none slowing to pay their respects.

Jessie Alley was impassable, a jumble of broken buildings and wreckage. But by some miracle, Stevenson was wide open. Its tenements had fallen, but they'd collapsed backward, away from the street, and nothing was burning. Bohman reveled in his good fortune. In a few minutes, he was now confident, the Army would be minus one teamster, and he would be rich.

"Sergeant!" Bohman called. "This one's clear! Let's take it as far as we can, then cut up to Market!"

The teamster's suggestion made sense to Alta. The alley was clear of fire and debris. A deserted street meant speedier passage than they could manage through the crowd dragging up Market. "Take it!" he ordered and swung his horse hard to the left.

Bohman ran the wagon half a block up Stevenson, then suddenly reined the team. "Whoa!"

"What's wrong?" Alta demanded.

"Damn linch pin's loose," he informed his commanding officer.

"Can't it wait?" Alta asked impatiently. The sergeant's mare refused to stand still. Snorting, she stepped sideways, then around in agitated circles.

"Not if you want to keep the team," Bohman explained, jumping down from the box. He stuck his head under the traces, then announced. "I can fix it. Just take a minute."

"All right," Alta replied, as his horse reared. He called to the others: "Face outward! Backs to the wagon! Weapons ready! If you see anything you don't like, fire!" Anderson, Allen, and Reilly did as they were told. A great billow of hot smoke wafted over them from the direction of City Hall. It stung their eyes, singed their throats, and reduced their visibility to only perhaps ten yards. Weapons poised, they peered into the dark haze, certain that if attackers were tracking them, this would be the moment to strike, when they were stopped.

Bohman reached under the wagon seat and extracted the rifle he'd hidden there. When he stood up, four backs were turned toward him. Fish in a barrel, he thought. Calmly, he aimed at the spot between Alta's shoulder blades. His shot ripped a gaping hole in the Sergeant's back. The impact blew him out of his saddle. Blood spurted from his back and chest. He was dead before he hit the pavement.

It took the other three a moment to realize that the shot came from the wagon and not from hooligans lurking in the smoky ruins. That moment was all Bohman needed to put a bullet through the side of John Anderson's head. He tumbled off the back of the wagon in a hail of brains and skull fragments.

Reilly and the soldier horseman, Corporal Allen, yanked their mounts around to face their attacker and opened fire. But they wielded pistols, difficult to aim under the best of circumstances, and impossible from horseback, with their animals spooked by gunfire and smoke. Their shots went wild, taking jagged chunks out of the wagon's side walls.

Bohman fired again, and Reilly's horse dropped to its knees, then disappeared from the teamster's view.

Allen fired several more rounds. Some hit the gold and ricocheted with loud pings. One hammered the wagon bench, showering Bohman with splinters, forcing him to duck. Allen used that moment to dismount and reach for his rifle. But Bohman popped back up faster than the horseman anticipated. As Allen's boot hit the pavement, Bohman dropped him with a shot through the chest. Four shots, four hits, he mused with a marksman's satisfaction. He laid the rifle in the box and climbed up to what was left of the bench.

Behind the wagon, Reilly's horse lay on its side, blood spurting from its neck, gasping, straining deliriously at the bridle, dying. When the horse went down, Reilly's lower leg was pinned underneath it. He worked his foot out of the stirrup. Every wiggle felt like a nail being driven through his ankle. The leg would not support his weight. He rolled over the whimpering horse and Anderson's body, and latched onto the side of the wagon, pulling himself up to draw a bead on Bohman. But as the teamster seated himself and reached for the reins, the wagon lurched forward a foot, throwing Reilly off balance. He groped for a new hold and his hand found one of the bags of misstrikes, its canvas ripped open by Allen's wild barrage. Reilly grabbed a handful of canvas to steady himself, aimed at the middle of Bohman's back, and squeezed the trigger.

The shot knocked Bohman off the bench and onto his hands and knees in the box. A sharp pain shot through his side and something warm and wet dampened his hip.

Bohman's fall yanked the reins and the horses started, lurching the wagon a few more feet forward, throwing Reilly off balance again. He fired another round, but missed. He tried to steady himself. He balanced on his good leg and grasped for a more solid hold. He groped inside the bullet-ripped bag of gold. The misstrikes felt cold and oily. They'd never been rinsed or polished, having been diverted off the conveyor before those final steps. He leaned on his elbow, trying to will his arm still, and fired again. The shot hit the front wagon wall, but missed Bohman.

Wounded but coherent, Bohman grabbed his rifle, and swung it over the bench. He aimed for Reilly's chest. Reilly fired again, but was off-balance and missed. He watched Bohman sight down on him and noticed a crescent-shaped birthmark near the corner of his eye. Then Bohman's rifle flashed. The force of the shot spun the Irishman around and he fell hard on his dead horse.

Bohman peered into the smoke. Reilly didn't move. None of them moved. Then he looked around. Not a soul nearby, just a silent black snowfall of ash. He set his rifle down and dropped his pants to examine his side. It hurt badly, but it looked like a flesh wound just above the hip bone—no fun, but not serious. He cut the sleeve from his jacket and stuffed it into his pants to stanch the bleeding.

The gold was his—almost $130 thousand. He was set for life. He limped to the back of the wagon and rearranged the blankets over the bags. The Irishman lay still. His head was covered with blood.

Bohman turned the wagon around, then urged the horses down Stevenson back to Eighth, hoping to run down the alley for a few blocks, then cut through downtown to his warehouse. But across Eighth, a collapsed tenement made Stevenson impassable, forcing him to turn north toward the wall of flame that had been City Hall. A company of police ringed Civic Plaza, herding refugees past the blazing landmark.

Bohman whipped the reins, bursting suddenly from a cloud of smoke at the top of Eighth. He turned down Market against the human tide fleeing the inferno.

"You there!" a police officer bellowed, blowing his whistle. "Wrong way! Turn around!"

Bohman ignored him and plunged deeper into the smoky inferno.

Every time the wagon jounced, he felt a sharp stab in his side. Smoke stung his eyes, burned his throat, and clawed at his chest. He was beginning to feel woozy. He fought to clear his head, thinking: You're rich, man, *rich* beyond your wildest dreams. Hold on.

Market Street was a vision of Hades—dark smoke everywhere punctuated by hot orange flames, with ghostly beings moving about.

At Sixth Street, he passed a knot of soldiers watching helplessly as the building housing the Army's downtown offices went up in flames. They noticed his uniform.

"Hey soldier!" one of them called as the wagon clattered past, "Where the hell—?!"

"Funston!" Bohman yelled as if to pull rank, and snapped the reins to keep the horses moving.

At Stockton, Market was blocked. Buildings on both sides had collapsed, covering the boulevard with a large mound of rubble. A man on foot might scramble over it, but not a wagon, and certainly not a wagon with such a heavy load. Bohman cursed and yanked the reins left, turning north toward Union Square. With any luck, he thought, he could skirt the Square, bypass Chinatown, and head for his warehouse or, better yet, the docks. The piers would be deserted, or undermanned. It shouldn't be that difficult to steal a boat and make for Oakland, and from there, live out his days in wealth, whiskey, and whores.

A block up Stockton, a man emerged from the wreckage of a watch-repair shop balancing a heavy box on his shoulder. Two policeman stepped from the shadows.

"Drop it, looter!" The officers aimed rifles at him.

"Looter?!" the man cried. "I'm the *owner*!"

Too late. A rifle cracked, and the man fell. Under him, the sidewalk turned crimson. Timepieces spewed from the box. The policemen fell upon them, stuffing their pockets, ignoring Bohman as the wagon clattered by. He had no idea how long he could keep control of the horses before the smoke, fires, and gunshots made them bolt.

At Union Square, the teamster turned down Geary and confronted a squad of approaching police about a block away.

"You there! Halt!" Several of them drew pistols. "This area is off limits! Halt!"

Bohman yanked the reins and the wagon rattled back to Stockton with the police chasing on foot. "Stop or we'll shoot!" Bohman whipped the reins, "Yah!" and bounced up Stockton. His side burned. He heard shots. Something whizzed past his ear. Ahead of him was a wall of flame. The horses balked, refusing to get any closer. Fortunately, the smoke parted briefly, revealing an alley to his right. He urged the horses down it.

Where was he? For a moment, he had no idea. His eyes watered badly from the smoke. He could hardly see. His side throbbed. He breathed in labored gasps. He felt dizzy, faint. Then he spied a large painted sign hanging awry from a doorpost that appeared to be all that was left of a collapsed building. The sign was shaped like a bird, a bright red rooster. The Crowing Cock brothel! He was on Morton Street. Before him, San Francisco's most notorious alley stood eerily quiet. He'd never seen it deserted before. Behind him, more gunshots. A bullet ricocheted off a street lamp near him. "Looter! Halt! Surrender!" Bohman whipped the horses, putting distance between himself and his pursuers. But ahead, a burning building collapsed into the street, and the horses stopped, refusing to take another step.

The teamster spun around and fell on the gold. Frantic, he hurled the bags into a black pit beneath the wreckage of a ruined building. A brothel? A saloon? An opium den? No matter. The bags were heavy. His side ached.

Once the wagon was emptied, Bohman rolled painfully off it. He slapped one of the horses' rumps. "Yah!" The team wheeled around and trotted up the street toward the police.

"Here's his wagon!" he heard them say. "Now where is that bastard? Get him."

Bohman scrambled down into the pit. Above him, he heard the approaching clip-clop of boots slapping cobblestones. He held his breath. The officers ran past him, then drew up short before the collapsed burning building.

"Where the hell did he go?" one asked.

"Work the wreckage!" another one ordered. "You see him, arrest him. He resists, shoot."

"Son of a bitch disappeared!"

In a dark alcove ten feet below them, the teamster crouched surrounded by bags of gold. The building that sheltered him had been a cowyard, and like most Morton Street establishments, it boasted a basement where the liquor was stored and opium smoked.

"Shit! Where'd he go?" He heard the police poking at the debris. After a while, their voices faded away up the street.

The cellar was dark, but not quite pitch black. As his eyes adjusted to the gloom, Bohman noticed two legs sticking out from under several cases of something … whiskey from the smell, most of the bottles smashed. Beyond the body, behind the remnants of a brick wall that had shattered, he found an alcove big enough for the bags. Slowly, favoring his injured side, he picked his way through the wreckage, hauling the gold to his hiding place, then covering it with debris. Ordinarily, the job would not have taxed him. But by the time he finished, he was breathing hard, dripping sweat, and feeling faint. His chest ached. His side burned.

Dazed and wobbly, he stumbled over something and landed hard on his knees. A hideous smell assailed him. He was kneeling over the head and chest of the corpse. To stink that badly, the man must have been dead a while. He wore an apron. He was probably a bartender who'd been down fetching whiskey when the earthquake hit. Poor bastard must have been crushed when the quake hurled cases of liquor off the shelves.

Barely conscious, Bohman stared at the dead man. Slowly, an idea bubbled up through the pain in his side. He coaxed the whiskey crates off the crushed corpse. Rats had already gotten to part of his face. His eyes were gone and the flesh of his lips and jaw had been eaten away, giving him a sickening, skeletal grin.

Bohman was overcome by a wave of nausea. He stripped off his Army uniform. He would never need Uncle Sam's rags again. Then he undressed the dead man, and donned his clothing. He poked among the crates until he found a bottle intact. He opened it, poured some liquor down his throat and over his head, then doused a rag and stuffed it into his new pants against his wound. It stung fiercely. For a moment he thought he might collapse. But the thought of the fortune in gold—*his gold*—kept him from fainting. With liquor in his hair and the whiskey-soaked rag dripping down his leg, he reeked of alcohol. Holding the bottle, he grappled his way back up to the street.

Not a moment too soon. The fire that stopped his team was churning his way. He limped toward Stockton, counting the number of paces he took so he could retrace his steps back to the gold.

As he approached Union Square, he launched into his act. He swung the whiskey bottle, making circles in the smoky air, and began braying off-key: "Oh, m'darlin,' Oh m'darlin,' Oh m'*darlin*' Clementi-i-i-ne…"

A knot of policemen noticed him.

"Jesus!" one exclaimed approaching him. "Been on a bender?"

Bohman gazed at him wild-eyed, incoherent, and kept on singing: "You are lost and gone *fore-e-ever*. ..."

"Come 'ere, John Barleycorn." Bohman staggered into the officer's arms. The policeman called to his comrades, "He stinks of liquor. And he's bleeding."

Bohman kept singing and rolling his head. The officer slapped his cheek. "Christ, man, you're hurt! Do you even know there's been an earthquake? The city's burning. Christ Almighty!"

Bohman made no reply except to belch loudly.

Another policeman approached and relieved the drunk of his bottle. The two officers grasped him under the arms and dragged him to the grass by the Dewey Monument. They lay him down to wait for an infirmary wagon.

Bohman's cheek pressed against the lawn. Despite the rain of ash and debris, it was cool and damp. Ninety-seven paces. He concentrated on fixing the number in his mind. Ninety-seven. He felt sleepy and closed his eyes. Ninety-seven paces. The last thing he remembered was the dead bartender's hideous grin.

April 20, 1906

Angels. They had to be angels, those luminous beings dressed in shimmering white robes. God's own angels. They floated by him on gossamer wings, just as the nuns had described so long ago. I must be in Heaven, Patrick Reilly decided. A wave of tranquillity washed over him. I died and went to Heaven.

It made sense. He remembered Stevenson Alley, deserted, except for the wagon detail. He remembered trying to balance on his good leg while grasping one of the canvas bags so he could set himself to aim his pistol at that teamster son of a bitch. Funny, he mused, you could swear in Heaven. And he remembered looking down the wrong end of Bohman's rifle, then seeing it flash. Now he was in Heaven. Another angel floated by. Reilly felt pleased. He hadn't been detained in Purgatory. He'd gone straight to the Lord. He didn't deserve such grace.

Slowly, Reilly became aware of his head. It felt uncomfortably warm, as though he were wearing a wool cap in the sun. He reached up to touch his hair. His hand took forever to make the journey. No hair. Instead, his head was bound in cloth of some kind. They wear turbans in Heaven.

Another silvery angel floated by, and in its wake, he caught a whiff of something vaguely familiar … rubbing alcohol. Why would there be disinfectant in Heaven? He inhaled deeply and smelled something else … smoke. But not the homey fragrance of a hearth. It was the acrid stench of the fire he'd died fleeing. This was not the Heaven the nuns had described. The fabric of his serenity began to fray. If he were truly in Heaven, where were his parents? His wife? The Apostles? Christ?

He tried to call to one of the angels, but his tongue was petrified. His lips wouldn't move. His head ached. His whole body felt leaden. He became aware that he was lying on his back gazing up at what appeared to be clouds, except that they were black. Smoke?

He tried to roll onto his side, but something stopped him, a weight attached to his leg. His breathing was labored. He tried to lick his lips. Sandpaper on rough wood. With an effort, he rolled partway over. Something hard and white entered his field of vision. It had the texture of stone ... marble ... and it looked like some sort of monument ... a tombstone? In Heaven? This made no sense at all. Slowly, carvings in the rock came into focus: "Jose Jesus Bernal" followed by Spanish gibberish. Then "1870. ... 39 años." Definitely a tombstone. Reilly's head hurt more now. Bernal ... Bernal. ... He knew the name. Wasn't he the rancher who first settled Bernal Hill, the grassy rise at the end of Folsom Street where he took his girls for picnics? This was not Heaven. Reilly groaned.

"Ah, so you're awake, lad. Welcome back to the land of the living."

Reilly looked up at an angel in white. Only it wasn't an angel. It was a nurse, a nun in a white habit with a winged cap.

"You were in bad shape when the soldiers brought you in yesterday," the nun explained cheerfully. "Head covered with blood. But when we cleaned you up, it was just a scalp wound. Nothing serious. You're one lucky fellow. A scalp wound and a sprained ankle."

Reilly tried to speak, but all that emerged was a croaking sound.

"I bet you're thirsty," the nun said. "Sister Mary Agnes!" she called to another nun. "Give us a hand?"

The two nurses pulled Reilly up to sitting and held a large ladle to his cracked lips. He sipped some cool water, gagged on it, spat it out, then tried again, and was able to suck some down.

Reilly was sitting on a cot ... in a jumble of cots ... in a graveyard. His head hurt and so did his ankle, which was also tightly bandaged. With a huge effort, he managed to whisper, "Where am I?"

"Mission Dolores," the nun, Sister Mary Louise, replied, "in the cemetery. The new church collapsed. The Mission is full of injured. We had to move the overflow out here, in spite of the smoke."

So it was smoke. Reilly coughed.

"For a while this morning, it looked like we might have to evacuate—us and everyone camped in Dolores Park. The fire was charging up from Happy Valley. But then, praise God, a miracle: A hydrant on Twentieth Street held water and the firemen stopped the blaze at Dolores. But the air's still thick as a smokehouse."

Reilly had to strain to understand the nun's words. Everything east of Dolores burned? His face contorted. "My girls!" He tried to stand up, but didn't get far, and fell back in a heap. Tears welled up in his eyes.

"Where do you live?" Sister Mary Louise inquired sympathetically.

"Shotwell near Fourteenth." Reilly sputtered. "My girls! Oh, God!"

"I'm sure they made it out all right," the nun comforted him. "People been streaming out of that neighborhood since yesterday morning. They're probably camped in Dolores Park."

Reilly tried to stand again, grabbing at the nun's habit. "Got to find them. …" He almost made it up this time, but lost his balance and plopped heavily back down on the cot.

"Sure, go look for them," Sister Mary Louise explained, "but don't expect to be nimble. You lost a fair amount of blood. You have a sprained ankle. You haven't eaten. And we dosed you good with morphine."

At the mention of food, Reilly felt ravenous. A billow of black smoke blew overhead. Papery ash drifted down on them, big black snowflakes. Nearby, on other cots, the injured were sleeping, dazed, moaning. Nuns moved among them offering water and comfort. Here and there, they pulled a blanket over a head and crossed themselves.

Reilly had to get to Dolores Park, find his daughters, then get to the Mint. He clutched Sister Mary Louise's arm and hoisted himself to his feet. His head felt light, his legs shaky. For a moment, the cemetery whirled around him. He teetered, but with the nun's help, remained standing.

Sister Mary Louise reached into the folds of her habit and produced a small apothecary bottle, Dr. Wylie's Excellent Morphine Elixir. "You've had a fair amount of this already, but you'll need more." She slipped the vial into his pocket. "Make it last. It's all I can give you."

Reilly mumbled his thanks, then pushed away from the Sister, intent on getting to the Park. But he forgot about his sprained ankle. He took a step, stumbled, and almost crashed down on a cot occupied by a doe-eyed young woman with a heavily bandaged arm. She was pregnant and looked about ready to pop.

"Whoa now," the nun clucked, grabbing his arm to steady him. "Hold your horses." She turned and called, "Father Kennedy!"

A short rotund priest appeared, and grabbed Reilly under his other arm. Reilly recognized him as the kind but slovenly priest at St. Joseph on Tenth Street. "Patrick, me boy! You're up and around. How do you feel, lad? The doctor said you were shot!" The priest's breath smelled of whiskey.

"Father, my girls—"

"All safe, praise God. I saw Mary Elizabeth … oh, must have been around sun-up, though you can't hardly tell with the damn smoke." The priest coughed. "She and her sisters are in Dolores Park."

Reilly tried to take another step, and crumpled into the priest's arms. Then Sister Mary Louise shoved a makeshift crutch under his arm. Reilly leaned on it heavily. The priest took a step back. Reilly swayed a bit, but didn't fall.

With an immense effort, Reilly took a tiny step. He wobbled and almost went down, but recovered in time. His head pounded. His ankle throbbed fiercely in its tight swaddling. He felt famished. He staggered another tiny step, still shaky, but better this time. "Got to find my girls, then get to the Mint."

"The Mint?" Father Kennedy exclaimed. "You'll not be getting anywhere near there. Soldiers have everything cordoned off. You can't cross Dolores."

With that, the priest and nun turned and padded off to attend to an elderly woman groaning like a rusty hinge on a nearby cot.

Reilly hobbled toward the cemetery gate. Seagulls soared among the smoky clouds overhead. Everywhere he looked, the injured stared vacantly into the gray haze as hot ash rained down on them: a man with both legs bound to splints; a woman in a ripped dress that bared a shoulder covered by a reddened bandage; a mother hovering over a child whose arm was in a sling.

Someone touched his shoulder. Sister Mary Louise. "I almost forgot. When they brought you in, you were clutching these. Here. Your lucky charms." She handed him two shiny, oily, golden disks. Double Eagles. For a moment, Reilly had no idea why he would have been holding them. Then, overcoming a wave of dizziness, he remembered the wagon, the shootout. To steady himself, he'd grabbed a coin bag that had been ripped open by gunfire. He recalled touching the cool greasy misstrikes, but not grabbing any. He gazed down at the coins. The obverses were perfect, the starred border framing Lady Liberty's head, her golden curls held in place by a magnificent tiara that proclaimed "Liberty." But the reverses were an embarrassment. The lettering "United States of America" and

"Twenty D." looked fine, but the eagle and shield were hopelessly blurred, and under them, the "S" mint mark was double-die, "SS."

Reilly thrust the coins into his pocket. He prayed that someone—anyone—had caught that double-crossing whore's son of a teamster. Otherwise, what could he possibly tell Walther?

Reilly tottered gingerly out of the cemetery to Dolores Street. Father Kennedy was right. Across the palm-studded boulevard stood a line of soldiers brandishing rifles with bayonets, and behind them, nothing but charred smoking wreckage, and a few rats and dogs scurrying about.

• • •

Dolores Park was a natural bowl scooped out of a steep hillside just south of the new Mission High School. It was a sea of refugees turned sooty from fallen ash. Everywhere Reilly looked he saw dazed faces, babies crying, families squatting around pathetic piles of salvaged belongings, and here and there, relief workers offering ladles of water, hard rolls, and soup. He hobbled up to a Salvation Army wagon for a drink and a roll dipped in a mysterious stew. He wolfed the meal like an animal. It only made him hungrier, but the lady said, "One to a customer. Come back later." He hobbled away.

His head and ankle hurt more now. The morphine was wearing off. He considered taking a pull from the vial he carried, but decided to wait.

"Patrick! Patrick Reilly!" It was his Irishtown neighbor, Mavis O'Leary, a big milk-skinned strawberry blond whose broad hips had birthed seven children. "Thank God you're safe. The girls have been sick with worry."

"My girls!" Reilly wobbled over to O'Leary and embraced her. "How—?"

"They're fine."

"And yours?"

"Fine. Everybody come through fine, thanks be to God. They're all a wee bit up the hill with Brendan. Megan saved your family Bible and photo album—oh, and your baseball mitt." O'Leary smiled, and for the first time in what felt like years, Reilly smiled as well.

Then O'Leary noticed his bandages. "Good Christ, Patrick, what happened to you?"

Reilly sighed. "Fell off a horse and got shot." He suddenly felt exhausted. He had an overwhelming urge to lie down and sleep.

"For the love of God, man, how?"

"Long story," he murmured. "Take me to the girls, Mavis. Then I've got to get to the Mint."

They picked their way around knots of refugees clinging to salvaged belongings. It was slow going. The hillside was steep and crowded. Here, a family huddled in fur coats. There, another shivered in bedclothes and tattered blankets. West of the Park, on the hill above them, the old farm houses and new Victorians looked reasonably intact. But to the east, the teeming tenements of the Inner Mission were all gone, reduced to smoking charcoal.

Then, a man caught Reilly's eye. Something about him reminded the Irishman of the teamster. Reilly stepped over a Chinese family cooking rice over an open fire to get a closer look. The man was crouched in the grass by a table improvised from an overturned half-barrel, playing poker. "See your dime and raise another nickel." Coins were tossed on the barrelhead. The man was not wearing an Army uniform and his side was bandaged. Perhaps he'd been mistaken. Then Reilly spied the crescent-shaped birthmark by his eye, the same one he'd seen when Bohman sighted down on him.

"Patrick!" O'Leary called, "Where are you off to? This way!"

Reilly ignored her. There was no doubt in his mind. The gambler was the teamster. He plunged toward the card game as fast as he could work his crutch, and hurled himself at the treacherous bastard. Cards went flying as Bohman went down under him.

"Murderer!" Reilly cried, pummeling Bohman. "This man's a murderer and a thief! Someone get the police!"

Reilly and Bohman rolled in the dirt as those in the immediate vicinity scrambled to get out of harm's way. Reilly landed a solid punch on Bohman's ear, then grabbed him by the throat. Bohman flailed, alternately pushing his crazed assailant away and pounding him with balled fists. Both men were injured, and neither was at full strength, but Bohman was tougher, more of a fighter. He gouged at Reilly's eyes until the Irishman let go of his throat, then punched him square in the nose. Reilly fell backward, a bright red stream gushing from his nostrils. Bohman pounced and the two men grappled, hitting and kicking each other in the dirt. Reilly was soon exhausted. Where were the damn police? Then Bohman kneed him sharply in the groin. For a moment, Reilly froze in breathless agony. That moment was all Bohman needed.

He reached into his coat, pulled out a knife, and plunged it to the hilt into Reilly's side.

Bohman staggered to his feet. "Bastard attacked me for no reason!" No one in the vicinity moved. They just stared. "Never saw him before in my life." Then brandishing his bloody knife lest anyone attempt to detain him, Bohman stumbled away, and in an instant was swallowed by the mob of refugees.

• • •

Patrick Reilly languished mostly delirious for three days, then succumbed to the knife wound. During lucid periods before he died, he told his daughters and the O'Learys about the 17 bags of misstrikes, the wagon party's flight, and the teamster's treachery. Word spread, and it didn't take long for reporters to find their way to Reilly's deathbed, a musty pallet in a canvas Army tent in the Mission High schoolyard. When Walther confirmed the tale, all four papers—the *Examiner, Chronicle, Call,* and *Bulletin*—ran front-page stories: FORTUNE IN MINT GOLD LOST NEAR CITY HALL.

The Mint and the Main Post Office were the only two buildings South of Market to survive the fire intact. The glass in some of the Mint's windows melted from the heat, and a few iron shutters buckled, but the building's granite walls held, and the hosing and bucket brigade kept the roof and windowsills from igniting. In the weeks after the earthquake, the Mint had the only potable water South of the Slot, and lines of returning refugees queued up with buckets and bottles.

The mob Walther feared never formed. The smoke, flames, and heat drove the miscreants off. No one attacked. The $200 million in the vault was saved. But all anyone cared about was the 6,491 Double Eagles that had disappeared. Of all the stories to emerge from the Great San Francisco Earthquake and Fire, the tale of the Lost Gold became the most celebrated.

For a city born in a mad rush for the yellow metal, the Lost Gold struck a nerve. The moment martial law was lifted, thousands of San Franciscans flocked to Stevenson Alley near Eighth to sift the wreckage. Fights broke out. The police moved in and cordoned off the area. Walther, his men, and a detachment of troops searched it systematically, using horse teams to haul away wreckage. They found nothing.

A police artist spoke with soldiers who knew Private Ellis Bohman and came up with a sketch that was circulated far and wide. The Army scoured the West for him and alerted police departments from Seattle to San Diego and east to St. Louis. Several men were arrested, but none turned out to be the teamster.

On the chance that Bohman might be apprehended while attempting to dispose of the gold, the Treasury Department alerted banks throughout the country to be on the lookout for anyone presenting 1906-S twenty-dollar gold pieces with an SS mint mark. But except for the two coins Reilly accidentally grabbed, none ever turned up. Years later, one of his daughters, hard up for cash, sold the two Double Eagles to a collector.

Ten years after the earthquake, in 1916, with the country preparing to enter World War I, the Treasury Department closed the books on the Lost Gold. In his final report, Chief Investigator Thomas Conrad noted bitterly that the weight of the evidence pointed to Bohman's escape with the gold, which he must have melted down and quietly sold off as bullion.

The earthquake and fire were disasters to be sure, but as far as San Francisco's civic fathers were concerned, they also represented a unique opportunity to eliminate its dens of depravity. The whoremasters, saloon keepers, and opium merchants were forbidden to return to Morton Street and the Barbary Coast. Street names were changed. Chinatown was rebuilt with pagodas. And crews of laborers pushed debris from the fire into the pits where the brothels, gambling halls, and opium dens once stood. With great fanfare, Mayor Schmitz announced that like a phoenix, a magnificent new San Francisco would rise from the ashes and rubble of the old.

Shortly after the fire, the Secretary of the Treasury awarded Herbert Walther and his men commendations for risking their lives to save the $200 million in the Mint vault. Then a year later, he quietly demanded Walther's resignation for losing the seventeen bags of misstrikes. Coupled with his grief over Reilly's death, the disgrace of being fired unhinged Walther. He became addled, not crazy exactly, but stranger than eccentric. He took to wandering from his home through Union Square to the Mint, asking anyone who'd listen if they'd seen his lost gold. The doormen at the St. Francis Hotel took pity on him. They went out of their way to treat him kindly and protect him from the pickpockets who frequented Union Square. Every day when Walther asked, "Have you seen …?" they replied crisply, "Not today, Mr. Walther. Come back tomorrow." After a few years, the newspapers picked up on this ritual and Walther became a San Francisco character, rather like Emperor Norton, the self-proclaimed ruler of California and Mexico, who championed the ridiculous notion of building a bridge to Oakland.

Walther developed tuberculosis in 1917 and passed away during the influenza epidemic of 1919, with his wife, Mei-Lin, at his side. Mei-Lin had used her talent for languages to open a school near Chinatown that taught English to Asian immigrants and Asian languages to Americans doing business in the Far East. After Walther's death, she sold the school and her stately home on Pine Street, and returned to her village in China, a dowager who lavished her unbelievable wealth on the astonished remnants of her family. Mei-Lin was killed in 1938 during a Japanese bombardment. She was fifty-seven.

When Walther died, his casket was carried by a contingent of doormen from the St. Francis. All the papers printed sympathetic obituaries. The *Call* declared: "It's a shame the Treasury Department turned its back on Walther's heroism in saving the Mint and all the gold in its vaults, and instead made him the scapegoat for the loss of a comparatively insignificant sum. The blame for the lost gold lay not with Herb Walther, but with the Army that failed to transport it as promised and countenanced having the murderous scoundrel, Ellis Bohman, in its ranks. Yes, almost $130 thousand in gold was lost. But our politicians steal equivalent sums—more—every day. That is why every true San Franciscan will always remember Herbert Walther not as the Mint Superintendent who lost the gold, and not as the peripatetic oddball of his later years who never ceased inquiring about it, but rather as the man who saved our beautiful Granite Lady from the flames and gave our fair city its most enduring mystery."

1

September-October 1989

Ed Rosenberg hated being put on hold almost as much as the people who did it to him hated talking to reporters. He looked at his watch. 9:18 a.m. He washed down his second cup of coffee, now almost cold, and considered how to make the most of the situation. Maybe write a book, he mused, *101 Creative Activities While On Hold*. Trouble was, he couldn't think of any. Cradling the receiver between his chin and shoulder, he considered balancing his checkbook, but rejected the idea as too depressing for so early Monday morning.

Across the cavernous newsroom of the *San Francisco Foghorn*, Ed spied the new features editor, Karen Kaitz. She had abandoned an upwardly mobile career at the first-rate *Miami Herald* to slum at the second-rate *Horn*. In addition to a flair for putting stories together, word in the men's room was that she was well put together herself. Ed craned his neck to follow her as she strode up the row of cubicles toward him. Perhaps one chapter of *101 Creative Activities While On Hold* could be: "Ogle Women." But that wouldn't work. He did that all the time.

Still on hold, Ed scanned the Sports section. The A's won, of course, 7-6 over Milwaukee, a baseball juggernaut rolling inexorably toward another pennant, another World Series. In the AL West, their magic number was down to 16. But the Giants—damn!—fell to Atlanta 6-5. Reuschel had them up 5-1 on a one-hitter. Mitchell smacked his 43rd. Then in the eighth, Downs and Bedrosian gave up five runs. But the Giants were still five games up on San Diego, with a magic number of 13 in the NL West. Please, God, Ed prayed, a latter-day Tevya in *Fiddler on the Roof*, is it too much to ask to give the Giants the pennant just this once? As you know, God, it's been twenty-seven years.

Ed scanned the box scores, and contemplated the two magic numbers. At 16, the mighty A's seemed a whole lot closer to the World Series than the often-hapless Giants did at 13. He closed his eyes: Please, God.

When he opened them, he was still on Hold. What's with this guy? Ed wondered. Doesn't he realize I'm calling from "The Voice of the West"?

The lovely new features editor had disappeared from view, which left Ed nothing better to eye while on Hold than his story. He hated this story. It was a sad, tedious slice of banality, a pathetic comment on the tensions rife in a changing city, a small story about small-minded people. When would he ever get another big story, one that actually mattered? Probably never, now that the assistant city editor who'd loved his work had bolted to the *Baltimore Sun*, leaving him under the oily thumb of Mr. Insufferable, Ron Ruffen, who seemed to delight in making Ed's life miserable. Ruffen had been a newspaperman since San Francisco had belonged to Mexico, and knew how to shape a story. But he and Ed rubbed each other the wrong way. Ruffen considered Ed a wiseass, a failed academic who'd taken a wrong turn into journalism. As punishment, Ruffen tortured him with piece-of-shit assignments—POS, in *Foghorn* vernacular—which brought out the wiseass in Ed.

So Ed bent the rules every now and then. What good reporter didn't? Look at Woodward and Bernstein, the heroes of Watergate. You're no Woodward and Bernstein, Ruffen snapped during their last set-to. Yeah, Ed replied without thinking, and you're no Ben Bradlee. Their editor. Ruffen took umbrage and placed Ed "on notice," one bureaucratic step away from "probation," which was just a stone's throw from termination. The union guy told Ed to cool it, that if push came to shove, all the higher-ups would line up behind Ruffen and he'd be history. But no one told Ruffen to stop dealing Ed one POS after another.

San Francisco was filled with great stories. AIDS had hit the Castro so hard that apartments were going begging and some heteros were moving back in. Traffic was worse than ever, but Muni was cutting bus service. San Francisco was fast becoming mainland America's first Asian city, but not a single Asian held elected office. The Giants were threatening to bolt to San Jose unless city taxpayers coughed up $150 million for a downtown stadium. And the Health Department saw no connection between the Navy's 50 years of dumping toxic waste all over Hunter's Point and the fact that the neighborhood had three times the cancer rate of the rest of the city. So what was Ed writing? He peered at his screen, and felt nauseous. If he were lucky, this yawner would end up as filler on the Obits page. Or maybe the other editors would realize that Ruffen had lost his marbles, and just kill it.

Either way, Ed's story was a classic POS: Bird Man's Neighbors Squawk Over "Screamer." It seemed that one Roy Muller, a retired firefighter way out on Forty-fifth Avenue had, some years earlier, begun collecting exotic birds and housing them in an aviary he built off the back of his Sunset district home. The parrots, macaws, cockatoos, and cockatiels didn't bother anyone, and they helped the old guy survive the loss of his wife, who'd contracted AIDS from a transfusion back in '82 before they figured out how to screen blood for the virus. The Bird Man, as he became affectionately known around the neighborhood, ran local errands with one of his extravagantly plumed pets on his shoulder and everyone, especially the kids, loved it—that is, until he obtained a rare Sumatra Screamer, a bird whose wail sounded like an opera star with a megaphone being burned at the stake. The bird screeched at all hours, which didn't bother the Bird Man—he was hard of hearing. But it infuriated his neighbors. They complained. He flipped them the bird. They called the police, the San Francisco Neighborhood Mediation Service, and the Bird Man's old buddies at the firehouse on Forty-third where he'd spent his career. But there was no end to the Screamer's caterwauling. Finally, a few of the neighbors took the Bird Man to court for causing a public nuisance. He was Old San Francisco: white and of German extraction, while his antagonists were New San Francisco: Chinese, Filipino, and Vietnamese immigrants. The Bird Man was quoted in the neighborhood newspaper making derogatory remarks about people from the other side of the International Dateline. This brought the city's Asian civil rights groups into the fray. The Bird Man vigorously denied having slurred anyone's ethnicity. He charged that, under pressure from the neighborhood, the local pet-store owner, a woman from Hong Kong, had tried to kill the Screamer by poisoning the special food the thing ate. One of the aggrieved neighbors, a Burmese nurse, worked at the American Heart Association with Ruffen's wife, which was how this POS got dumped on Ed.

Unfortunately, before he could bid the sorry tale good riddance, Ed had to get a quote reacting to the poisoning charge from the pet-store owner, Lilly Wong. But she refused comment, referring him to her attorney, who put Ed on Hold … eons ago. The schmuck didn't even have Hold Muzak, though, on second thought, Ed decided that was a blessing.

Reporting was a far cry from the historical research that, for eight delightful years, had engrossed Ed at Michigan and Berkeley. Delving into primary sources—diaries, memoirs, musty public records, sunken ships' manifests—there were always surprises, strange and wonderful discoveries that sent you deeper into the remote recesses of the enveloping past. Despite the much-ballyhooed mythology of investigative journalism, that was almost never the case in newspapering. Half the paper was little more than rewritten press releases and the other half contained stories so predictable, that a fool could make up the quotes and be right 97 percent of the time. Ah, Ed thought, the perfect diversion while on Hold.

He turned to his screen and set up for another round of Let's Make Up Some Quotes, the game that had saved him from psychotic breaks during previous POS assignments. What would this lawyer, Eric Chin, say about the poisoning accusation? Ed keyed the possibilities: Numero uno: "Ridiculous. Ms. Wong categorically denies having done any such thing." Number two: "Mr. Muller is trying to deflect attention from the serious problems he has caused by impugning the spotless reputation of a respected businesswoman." Or how about: "Mr. Muller's racist innuendo is an affront to the entire Asian-American community." And finally: "The Bird Man should have his head examined. I think you'd find a bird brain in there."

"Ed," Ruffen barked over the intercom, "when do I get Bird Man?"

"Soon as I get a reaction to the food-poisoning charge."

"What food-poisoning charge?"

"The food-poisoning charge that has become the latest wrinkle in—the story." He caught himself before saying, "this POS."

"Details?"

"The Bird Man says a Chinese pet shop owner tried to poison his Screamer. But I can't close it up until I get a reaction from the pet store owner's lawyer."

"I'm waiting."

"I'm on Hold."

Just then, the lawyer came on the line and delivered a crisp professional comment in the best interests of his client. Unfortunately, Ed was distracted and didn't quite catch it. Nearby several reporters were noisily wagering on the odds of a Bay Bridge World Series. And the new features editor chose that exact moment to sashay her perfumed assets right past his cube.

The lawyer rang off. Ed was left staring at his screen, uncertain what he said. Monday morning, 9:24 a.m. It was shaping up to be a very long day. He might call the lawyer back, but the effort didn't seem worth another century on Hold, not when he already had four perfectly serviceable quotes. He liked the "bird brain" quip best, but then thought the better of it, and went with the straight denial. That was what this POS deserved, a predictably boring quote. He slugged it "Bird Man," hit the SEND key, and sent it on its way to Ruffen and the next morning's Home edition, or with any luck, the trash.

Ed cranked himself out of his chair and headed to the coffee machine for java number three. He considered how much he could comfortably wager on the Giants making it to the World Series. A hundred bucks. He could go that much. But if he made the bet, he would be putting a *kinehoreh*, a Jewish jinx, on his team, and the Giants were certain to wash away like a sand castle at high tide. Ed did not want to be responsible for his team's demise, so he decided not to bet. He poured the coffee, and threw in some whitening powder. The brew tasted as bad as he felt.

Wandering back to his cube, Ed caught another glimpse of the new Features Editor. Maybe he could. … Then he saw the major rock shimmering on her finger. Sorry, sailor, another one taken.

How long since he'd gotten laid? Way too long … since Diane had left him for the A-frame with the big garden in Grass Valley. Lost in regrets about his ex, Ed didn't notice the tall rail-thin man leaning on the chest-high wall by the entrance to his cube.

"Hello, Ed," the man ventured. "Long time." He was about Ed's age, but his face was lined, not with the crow's feet that marked a certain maturity, but rather with deeply chiseled creases that bespoke a life that had not played out as expected.

Ed regarded his visitor, momentarily befuddled. "Chet?" he whispered tentatively. The man smiled. His small teeth were the giveaway. "Chet! Jesus H. Christ! It's really *you!* Rumor had it you were about to start. How long has it been, man? Eight years? Nine?"

"Ten."

"And, hey, congratulations on that Pulitzer—and under a pseudonym, no less."

"Not a pseudonym," Chet corrected him gently, "an assumed name. I was underground, remember? I got the job at the *Anchorage Pioneer* using my alter ego. It was weird at first. But it gave me the chance to make it on my own, not just because I'm a Gilchrist." Chet was, in fact, Chester Worthington Gilchrist IV, heir to the *San Francisco Foghorn* media empire: the *Horn,* a dozen other papers, five TV stations, twenty-odd radio stations, a book company, and enough property to become the fifty-first state.

"So, what are you, psychic?" Ed couldn't resist ribbing his old buddy. "You write a series about oil tanker crews boozing their nights away, and what happens a month later? A drunk captain runs the *Exxon Valdez* aground, spilling a zillion gallons of crude. You were a lock for the Prize. That wasn't reporting. It was prophecy."

"Hardly. Those tankers were a disaster waiting to happen. We just stumbled into the right story at the right time."

Same old Chet, Ed thought, modest to a fault, uncomfortable with success, and even less comfortable with his family's wealth and power. Chet had always been thin. Now he looked positively gaunt. Most of his hair was gone and the horseshoe ring that remained was gray verging on white. But the old mischievous gleam still shone in his eyes.

"What about—?" Ed couldn't bring himself to finish the question.

Chet smiled at his discomfort. "You mean: What about the charges pending against me? Heroin possession? Flight from prosecution? Felonious details like that?"

Ed nodded gravely. He never figured Chet for heroin and couldn't believe it when the story broke and his friend fled. The whole episode still made no sense to him. "Our story said the governor pardoned you. Is that for real?"

"Correct," Chet replied with a dismissive wave of the hand. "The governor has granted me a full pardon, effective last night. It seems I was the victim of a miscarriage of justice, that I've made good and contributed enough to society as a journalist to close the curtain on my unseemly past. Of course, I have to do a thousand hours of community service. And it didn't hurt that Daddy endorsed our esteemed Guv last election and showered enough money on his campaign to buy Panama. I just had an offer from Hollywood for a TV movie: The Prodigal Gilchrist, or some such nonsense."

"Hey, don't knock it," Ed advised. "Having your life turned into a TV movie has become the number-two American dream, after winning the Lotto, at least according to a sociologist I interviewed at Sonoma State."

"Spare me," Chet groaned. "Whatever happened to the dream of home ownership?"

"You've been gone a long time," Ed replied. "Real estate has gone so crazy, most people have a better shot at the Lotto." Then he remembered that housing hyper-inflation didn't matter to Chet. He was a Gilchrist. "So what about this TV movie?"

"I told the slimy little producer to take a hike. Televisionland will have to survive without my sordid tale of youthful indiscretion and filial impiety. I've embarrassed my father enough. I don't want to reopen old wounds. I just want to come back home and work on the paper."

A moment passed in awkward silence, then Ed said, "And eventually take it over, right?"

Chet's lips curled into a weak smile. "I owe it to my mother," he said softly. "She always said it was my destiny. I decided to stop fighting it."

Ed flashed on the painfully reserved Chet he'd met a dozen years earlier at Cal Berkeley on their first day as graduate history students. He seemed so burdened by who he was that during the introductions, he hung his head and uttered his last name in a whisper. This new Chet was a different person—confident, comfortable with himself. Ed was intrigued.

"At the *Pioneer*, to my utter astonishment, I fell in love with reporting. No one knew who I was. No one kowtowed. I was just another grunt, one of the guys, for the first time in my life. I loved it. When our team won the Pulitzer, it felt like time to make things right. Not to mention that I can't wait to see the Giants win the World Series."

"You wish."

"I *know.*" A true believer.

"So you called a hotshot lawyer?"

"Yes, and my father. You know what the old man said? The first words out of his mouth? Guess."

"I don't know: 'Thank God you're alive?' 'Good to hear from you?'"

"Hardly. 'It's time to collect on a few campaign promises.'"

Ed shook his head. "Your father is a real operator."

"That he is. But what about you, Ed? The last time I recall us spending time together, we were knocking back Dos Equis at the Bear's Lair and you were starting your dissertation. What was your topic? Something about fishing, wasn't it?"

"Whaling. The History of Whaling out of Sausalito."

"Right. You ever finish?"

"Oh yeah, about two years after you, uh … left the program. You're looking at a man with a Ph.D. in History from Cal Berkeley. You may kiss my ring." With a flourish, Ed held his hand out to his friend.

Chet turned the palm up. The pads of Ed's fingers carried the dark smudges of having read the morning's *Foghorn* hot off the press. "So, Mr. Cal Berkeley Ph.D., how'd you wind up an ink-stained wretch working in this dump?"

Ed laughed. "You know the story: Those who ignore history are condemned to repeat it. And those who take it seriously are condemned to unemployment. I wasn't cut out for academia. I taught for two years at Hayward State—liked the students but couldn't stand the politics and didn't have the energy to publish enough to grovel for tenure. So I quit, knocked around awhile, fell into a part-time gig at the *Grass Valley Ledger*, parlayed that into a reporter's job back here at the *Defender*, and after a few years, wound up here."

"You like it?"

"When I get decent assignments. I think I'll like it more now that you're back. You and Laura still together?"

"Super-glued. She stuck by me through everything. Didn't see her parents, her sister for ten years. Hell of a woman. What about you and … Diane, right?"

"Divorced. Last year. No kids, thank God. Di was always a country girl. She loved Grass Valley and hated following me back here when I got the *Defender* job. It wasn't a bitter divorce. She wanted me to move to Grass Valley with her, buy a place, have a garden, raise a family. But I've always been a city guy. One day, she just left. I saw it coming, but it hurt more than I expected. She's got a little business up there, Blackberry Creek Preserves: blackberry, blueberry, strawberry, some others. They're really great. I'll give you a few jars."

"You dating?"

"Not really. But Ms. Right is destined to appear any moment—at least, that's what my fortune cookie said last night."

Ruffen waddled up the row of cubicles. In a diaper, he would pass for a sumo wrestler: no neck, three chins, a beach ball with stubby arms and legs. Ruffen smoked—and just about quit the paper when the suits upstairs banned it in the building. He could often be found sucking beers after work at the M&M, the bar on Howard that catered to the *Foghorn* staff. And his typical lunch consisted of an Extra—a sub with two kinds of ham and three kinds of cheese from the Front Page deli on the ground floor of the *Foghorn* building. Meanwhile, his wife was the PR honcho for the Northern California affiliate of the American Heart Association. Go figure.

"Excuse me," Ruffen said to Ed's visitor, moving his great bulk into the space Chet occupied, forcing him to take a giant step backward. Ed started to introduce them, but Ruffen cut him off. "Ed," he intoned sarcastically, "your Bird Man piece was so sterling, I'm giving you another honey of a pet assignment—"

"Ron, please," Ed pleaded wearily.

"It seems there's a poodle in the Haight that plays a passable game of tic-tac-toe."

Behind Ruffen, Chet rolled his eyes.

"Come on, Ron, I haven't had a decent assignment in weeks!"

Just then, Elena Ruiz appeared, her dark Chicana eyebrows tweezed into high arches. Pursed lips showed she was not happy. "Jesus, Ron, can't you find anyone else to cover Gilchrist donating his coin collection to the California Museum? It's a total puff piece."

"The Gilchrist Coin Collection?" Ed jumped up and grabbed the press release from Elena's hand. "Ron, let me have this one. I *know* coins. I collected them as a kid. And I *know* this collection. It's famous. *Priceless*. It contains a 1906 SS Reilly Double Eagle, one of only two known to exist, the most valuable American coins ever minted. Let me give this story the play it deserves. Hey, 'Lena, you like poodles?" He handed her Ruffen's memo.

"A poodle that plays tic-tac-toe?" She squealed with delight. "This I've got to see."

"How about it, Ron?" Ed implored. "Switch us. We'll both do better pieces this way."

Ruffen looked from Ed to Elena and back again. "Oh, all right." His tone said: I'm too good to you turkeys. "Lena, I need this piece yesterday as a local-angle sidebar to a thing Science is doing on animal intelligence, so get going." When Ruffen spoke, he wheezed. The ten-yard walk from his office to Ed's cube had covered his forehead with a shiny film of sweat. If the Giants and A's weren't in hot pennant races, the Sports guys would be making book on the date he'd keel over. "And Ed, about the Old Man's gift: Play it straight and keep it short. Give us enough hoo-hah to do justice to any super-famous coins, but don't go overboard. I don't want the competition accusing us of giving the boss a blowjob just because he owns us body and soul, all right? Here's the file the PR clowns gave me."

Behind Ruffen, Chet's eyes danced.

"Ron," Ed tried again, "there's someone I'd like you to—"

But Ruffen continued to bark orders. "You've got an interview with Gilchrist in thirty minutes." He glanced at his watch. "No twenty-five, so get cracking. And an interview with the Museum guy—whatshisname?—at two. Then the hoo-hah at the Museum tonight at eight. One or two quick quotes from Gilchrist, then get out of town. And nothing about the Handgun Control Initiative, okay?" It was Gilchrist, Sr.'s current pet project.

"Right, chief," Ed said, mimicking Jimmy Olsen from the old *Superman* TV show.

Lost in thought, Ruffen didn't realize he was being mocked. "Gilchrist gives a priceless coin collection to the California Museum, but what kind of coin does he give the bums who made him rich?"

Chet bit his lip to keep from laughing.

"Ron!" Ed grabbed his sleeve and turned him around. "This is Chet Gilchrist."

Chet stepped forward and thrust out his hand. Ruffen shook it absently and looked his future boss up and down. "I heard you'd be coming on, working for Marty in Business."

"That's what they tell me."

"Well, as far as the editors are concerned, you're just another reporter. Don't expect any favors."

"I don't want any."

"Good." Ruffen turned and began waddling back to his lair. Then he stopped and looked over his shoulder at Chet. "Nice job on that Pulitzer. Hell of a series."

"It was a team effort."

Ruffen took another few steps, then turned back to face Chet. "What I said about your father, it was out of line."

"I've said much worse."

Ruffen gestured toward the suite of Editorial offices at the lobby end of the newsroom. "Have you met the gang?" By that he meant Gus Oberhoffer, the C.E., John Gagliano, the M.E., and Walter French, the X.E., newspaper-speak for city editor, managing editor, and executive editor. "I'll introduce you around."

Ruffen led Chet down the row of cubes. He called back to Ed: "Laura and I will be at the party tonight. See you there."

2

Ed had worked at the *Foghorn* for four years, but had never ascended to the paper's fifth floor, the rarefied realm of publisher Chester Worthington Gilchrist III. He'd heard about it, of course. The reporters called it "Gilville," and the few who'd visited said it made Versailles look like a Sixth Street welfare shelter.

They were right. The lobby reminded Ed of the fabled Redwood Room at the Clift Hotel, only more opulent—dark, floor-to-ceiling redwood paneling polished to a jewel-like luster, deep wall-to-wall, and on top of that, antique Persian and Chinese carpets, with groups of potted palms arranged just so, and soft indirect lighting except for tiny spots that illuminated a half-dozen framed *Foghorn* front pages: GOLDEN GATE BRIDGE OPENS: Thousands Walk Magnificent New Span. MOSCONE, MILK KILLED IN CITY HALL SHOOTINGS: Dan White Charged with Murder. N.Y. GIANTS COMING TO S.F.: Dodgers to L.A.

The receptionist buzzed Ed through a security door, and into a wide hall like the lobby: richly paneled, deeply carpeted, and decorated with more spotlit front pages: DOW FALLS 508: Worst Crash Since 1929. SNEAK ATTACK: Japanese Planes Sink Fleet at Pearl Harbor. VICTORY: Dazzling 49er's Win First Super Bowl.

A uniformed guard acknowledged Ed's arrival with a subtle nod and escorted him past various suits' offices to Gilchrist's private secretary, a middle-aged gay man impeccably dressed in a gray suit, lavender shirt, and matching tie, who presided regally over his domain. The secretary pressed a button: "Mr. Rosenberg to see you, sir." Ed heard a faint click from the direction of carved redwood burl double doors. The guard ushered him into the Sanctum Sanctorum.

Chester Worthington Gilchrist, III, known to his friends as Worth—as in "net"—was a tad shorter than his son, but still taller than Ed. Decades earlier at Stanford, he'd been a nationally ranked tennis player, and even in his late sixties still exuded tanned, sinewy vitality. He was exquisitely dressed in a charcoal suit Ed guessed came from Wilkes Bashford. Gilchrist rose from behind his huge desk crafted from a gold-flecked burgundy wood Ed didn't recognize and held out his hand. He looked the way Ed imagined President Kennedy might have if he'd lived and his hair had turned silver. Gilchrist looked more like an investment banker than a newspaperman. Considering all the media companies and property he owned through Gilcorp, he *was* more of a banker. He shook Ed's hand firmly and gestured to a leather chair Ed guessed cost more than the combined total of all of his home furnishings.

"I just saw your son in the newsroom," Ed ventured, the commoner reaching for an ice-breaker during his first audience with the King. "Chet and I were friends at Cal."

"Really." Gilchrist's tone was more polite than cordial.

"In the graduate History program. You must be very proud of his Pulitzer."

Gilchrist pursed his lips. "Yes. Let's hope his … *problems* are behind him."

The office was larger than Ed's Mission District cottage. It was decorated as exquisitely as everything else in Gilville. In addition to Gilchrist's kidney-shaped desk, crafted, Ed presumed, from some impossibly rare Amazonian wood, there was a large conference table, more spotlit front pages, and a leather sofa group surrounding a rustic flagstone fireplace. Behind Gilchrist, floor-to-ceiling windows looked across Mission Street to the Old Mint, decommissioned in the 1950's, then resurrected in the '60's as a museum of the Gold Rush and Comstock Lode, and the coinage struck because of them.

Ed felt a deep affection for the Old Mint. Compared with the new one out Market Street above the Safeway, it was small and seedy. But he didn't care. He grew up as a change-sifting coin collector in the suburbs of New York City. Coins bearing San Francisco's "S" mint mark rarely made it that far East. He saved every one he found. The summer after Ed completed eighth grade, his family took a cross-country motor trip and when they arrived in San Francisco, all he wanted to see was the Granite Lady and its coin collection. Forget Fisherman's Wharf, the

Golden Gate Bridge, and the cable cars, he told his parents. Just drop me off at the Old Mint and pick me up when it closes. His parents argued, but Ed was adamant. Eventually, they caved and spent the day showing the other kids the sights, wondering how much they should worry about their weird, coin-obsessed eldest. Ed reverentially climbed the granite stairs and entered numismatic heaven. The Old Mint's collection consisted of uncirculated or proof specimens of every coin that had ever been struck there—except, of course, for the 1906-SS Double Eagle, the most storied coin in U.S. history. There were only two Reilly Double Eagles known, one at the Smithsonian, the other in the private collection of Chester Worthington Gilchrist III. Now, Ed's memories of that trip were dim, except for Zion National Park and the day he spent at the Old Mint, in Stamp I and Stamp II, the enormous halls where the coins were struck.

Ed's parents put his bar mitzvah gift money away for his college education, but using ten years of old Blue Books, the wholesale price guide to U.S. coins, he pitched them on investing some of it in rounding out his collection of Lincoln cents. When it came time for college, he vowed, he would sell at a tidy profit. His parents were dubious, but eventually allowed him to acquire extra-fine specimens of the four rarest coins in the set: 1909-S, 1909-VDB (because the initials of the designer, Victor D. Brenner, appear prominently on the reverse), 1914-D, and 1922 plain (minted in Denver, but because of an error, without the "D"). For a while, the collection was his most prized possession.

Ed stopped collecting coins at sixteen when he began collecting girlfriends. But as he prepared to depart for Ann Arbor, he couldn't bring himself to sell. Fortunately, his parents never raised the issue. He still had his collection squirreled away in a dresser drawer. And he still religiously searched his change for pennies carrying "S" mint marks, increasingly rare even in San Francisco since the Mint closed. When Ed found an "S" coin, he deposited it in a mayonnaise jar on his mantel. Now the government was talking about closing the Old Mint Museum and moving its coin collection to the Smithsonian. But even if that happened, the combined government collections wouldn't equal the one Gilchrist was about to donate to the California Museum. His was the nation's largest, most complete collection of U.S. coins, from colonial times to the present.

"I have to tell you, sir," Ed explained, flipping open his reporter's notebook, "I pulled strings to get this assignment. I collected coins as a kid. And I've actually seen your collection, or at least the small fraction that you displayed a dozen years ago in Hillsborough."

"You have?" Gilchrist cocked his head. He hadn't expected to hear that the plebeian before him had visited the castle. "Do tell."

"I forget how the subject came up, but shortly after I met Chet, we discovered a shared interest in numismatics. He'd written a paper on the search for the lost 1906-SS Double Eagles—"

"His senior thesis at Stanford. It won the Truman Prize."

"Yes. Chet offered to take me to the house and show me the rarities you displayed in that little room off the library. I couldn't believe you had one of the five known 1943 copper pennies—"

Gilchrist smiled. "Actually, it's one of four known."

"—or one of the seven 1804 proof silver dollars, or one of the two known 1841-O Half Eagles. But my favorite was the Reilly."

Gilchrist's smile broadened. "Yes, it's always been my favorite, too. Sometimes I look over at the Old Mint and try to imagine what it was like there right after the earthquake—the chaos, the smoke, the heat from the fires, the pressure Herb Walther must have felt to protect the $200 million in his vault. He risked his life to save the building. God knows what he was thinking when he decided to run the double-S misstrikes up to the Presidio. In his thesis, Chet did a wonderful job tracing the search for Bohman and the Lost Gold. Have you read it?"

"Uh, no, but now that Chet's back, maybe he can dig it out for me." Ed flipped open his notebook. It was time to get down to business. "I know you're busy. I don't want to take too much of your time. ..."

Media people are the toughest interviews. They know how frequently quotes got mangled, how routinely stories get botched. But Gilchrist clearly enjoyed Ed's knowledge of coins. He leaned back in his *Starship Enterprise* captain's chair, relaxed and ready to expound.

"You've spent a lifetime building the Gilchrist Collection of U.S. Coins. Why are you giving it away? And why now?"

Gilchrist pressed his fingertips together, making a pyramid with his hands. "Because I love it, and I'd like others to experience the pleasure of seeing it, as you have, and you saw only a tiny fraction of it. As I've grown older—I'm almost seventy now—it's seemed increasingly silly to keep something so magnificent largely locked away in a vault. Chet saw that years before I did. From the time he was a boy, he always wanted the collection displayed in the Museum. But back then, it was a work in progress. It was incomplete, and I felt it wasn't ready to be displayed. By the time I filled most of the gaps, Chet was … gone. When he contacted me, and the governor pardoned him, and he returned to us, it felt like the right time to grant his wish, a way of honoring his homecoming, his new beginning. Beyond Chet's return, at my age you start to think about how little time you have left and what you'd like to do with it. California has given me so much. I'd like to give something back. Donating the collection is one realization of that desire. Another is my work as chair of the Handgun Control Initiative on the November ballot."

Oh, Christ, Ed thought, here comes gun control. Gilchrist was like every other Major Turd—convinced that the Earth revolved around him, that every cause he championed had God Almighty's stamp of approval. But downstairs, Ruffen thought differently. He didn't want Ed even mentioning the initiative. Ed let Gilchrist rattle on for a while about his "sacred duty to stop the carnage," then gently coaxed him back to the matter at hand.

"About the collection, how big is it exactly?"

"You know," Gilchrist chuckled, "I'm not even sure. Gregory has had a team of assistants cataloguing it these past few weeks."

"Gregory?"

"Gregory Murtinson, director of the California Museum. The specimens I displayed at the house—the ones Chet showed you—represent only one or two percent of the collection. For a good ten years, from the 1970s well into the '80s, I pre-emptively purchased every major collection that came on the market—"

"Pre-emptively?" Ed asked.

"Yes, before they were officially presented for sale, my agents would offer a price well above the appraised value. Lloyd Zemrick never even got close." Gilchrist's lips curled into a smug grin. "It annoyed the hell out of him."

"Zemrick?"

"Curator of the Smithsonian's coin collection. I could move much faster than he could and offer more money. In fact, when I announced the donation, he called and begged me to donate several key pieces to him."

"He begged you? As in *grovel?*"

Gilchrist's eyes narrowed. "Bad choice of words. Let's say he *asked* me, shall we?"

"Right, *asked.*" Ed scribbled furiously as Gilchrist reminisced about starting the collection when he was eleven by picking Indian Head pennies out of the change the *Foghorn's* street vendors brought back to the old building on Kearny Street. From there, he described how he created a syndicate of dealers around the country to acquire his many rarities, and concluded with the afternoon at Sotheby's in New York where he netted his Reilly, paying a then-record amount for a U.S. coin. "Everyone said I was crazy," he sniffed. "But with the way the investment market in rare coins has appreciated since then, that 'crazy' investment now looks quite shrewd."

"How valuable *is* the collection? I know pieces like the Reilly are 'priceless,' but even priceless treasures have a price."

"Frankly, I have no idea. I stopped keeping track after it was appraised at five million some years ago. But that was before I acquired some of the most valuable pieces, and before the market in rare coins took off."

"But, pardon me, sir," Ed feigned deference before plunging the knife. "Presumably, you'll deduct the donation as a charitable contribution ..."

Gilchrist eyed him as though he were a cockroach on a slice of cheesecake. "I really haven't given that a thought," he declared with an imperious wave of a hand. "You'd have to discuss it with my tax attorney."

"And who might that be?"

Gilchrist was about to answer when a chime sounded. "Excuse me. My high-priority line." He picked up a handset built into the arm of his chair. "Yes? I see. All right. Put him through." Ed rose to leave, but Gilchrist waved him back into his chair. "Some detail about the ceremony tonight. I'll only be a moment."

Ed noticed that Gilchrist's fingers showed no ink stains. The man didn't read his own newspaper. He probably had little gnomes read it for him and present daily summaries like the ones the CIA gives the President.

"*What?!*" Gilchrist spat. His chair snapped upright. His free hand grasped his forehead as if to keep it from exploding. "*When?! My God!* Hold on." He motioned for Ed to pick up the extension on his desk. It was Walter French, the *Foghorn's* executive editor. The new kid on the police beat just called in saying that California Museum director Gregory Murtinson had been found shot to death in his home in Seacliff. When he didn't show up at the Museum that morning, someone called. The maid found him in the study. There was no weapon at the scene, so it couldn't have been suicide. The police were running the usual tests on the slugs found in his chest, but from the look of the wounds, they guessed the weapon was a handgun.

Gilchrist, ashen-faced, dropped the receiver into its cradle. "*Goddamn* those handguns," he hissed in a shaky whisper.

"What about the ceremony tonight?" Ed asked softly. "Will it be canceled?"

"Yes," Gilchrist replied vacantly, staring across the room into the fireplace. Then, as if hypnotized, he snapped out of it. "I don't know. I suppose I'll have to find out …" He closed his eyes, fighting back tears.

Ed rose and thanked his publisher for the interview. He didn't have a moment to lose. He had to scurry back down to the newsroom and lay claim to this new wrinkle in the story before any of the cop-chasers jumped on it.

Gilchrist dismissed him with a curt nod. He swiveled his chair toward the window and gazed across the street at the Old Mint.

As Ed withdrew, he noticed that the blood had drained from Gilchrist's face. But he did not look grief-stricken. He looked … angry. Under his breath, but loud enough for Ed to hear, the Old Man said, "Just like that son of a bitch to upstage me at my own party." Then he shot Ed an acid look that said: Print that and you're fired.

3

The elevator doors parted and Ed found himself face-to-face with a Chinese kid only recently out of his teens. The young man had jet black hair hanging long over his ears like the early Beatles. He was dressed in jeans, a corduroy sport jacket, and a denim shirt with a skinny black-leather tie. In one hand, he carried a reporter's notebook. On his jacket lapel, mounted crookedly, he sported a *Foghorn* Visitor badge.

"Ed!" the kid exclaimed. "I stopped by your desk, but they said you were up here."

"Timmy?" Ed blinked. He grasped the young man's outstretched hand, then embraced him. "Timmy Huang? Jesus Christ! You grew up."

It had been five, maybe six years since he'd last laid eyes on Timmy, who couldn't have been more than seventeen at the time. They were sparring at the dojo under the watchful eyes of Timmy's uncle, Master Chen, the teenager wearing his brown belt, Ed his green. As Ed recalled, Timmy was a tad slow in defending against quick side kicks, but came back from a two-point deficit to win with a flurry of inside punches capped by a lightning-fast roundhouse kick that came dangerously close to decapitating him.

"It's 'Tim' now," the young man said, disengaging. "Great seeing you, Ed. Turns out we're on the same story."

"We are?"

Ed stepped into the elevator and they looked each other over. Tim was a few inches taller and maybe twenty pounds heavier, which suited him. He was still trim, and he moved with the catlike grace of those who are serious about martial arts.

"I'm a reporter for the *Defender*."

"The *Defender?*" Ed grinned. "Working for Jocko?" Jocko McKenzie, Ed's old boss, friend, and nemesis.

"You got it. I was in computer science at UCLA, and one of my room-mates worked at the paper. I started hanging around there, and now here I am, Tim Huang, journalist."

Ed dimly recalled young Timmy having worked on the high school paper at George Washington.

The elevator doors opened and Ed led Tim into the vast newsroom. They strode down a long aisle bordered on both sides by cubes emitting the mumbling of telephone interviews and the clicking of fingers on key-boards. At his cube, Ed motioned Tim into the only chair, a new high-back number that was supposed to prevent repetitive stress injuries at the keyboard. It didn't feel any different than the cheap POS it had re-placed. Tim spun a quick 360 and took in the view: several awards tacked to the gray carpet walls, the Anchor Steam beer stein where Ed kept his pens, several reference books and local directories, and the half-dozen jars of Blackberry Creek preserves Ed used as paperweights on the piles of paper that littered his desk, counter, and floor.

"Jocko still paying slave wages?"

"Yeah," Tim replied, "but I don't need much money. I pick up extra bucks teaching at the dojo three nights a week. I'm using the *Defender* for experience so I can move to a daily."

Ed had sung that same tune not too long before.

"So which story are you on exactly?" Ed inquired.

"The Gilchrist Coin Collection donation. Massa finally letting the darkies see it."

The image was vintage Jocko. McKenzie viewed the San Francisco newspaper scene as a plantation, with the reporters as slaves, and him-self an emancipated field hand struggling to scratch a living from a hardscrabble plot far removed from the lush bottom land the big boys controlled. Of course, the metaphor had its limits. *Foghorn* reporters had a union and made decent money, while Jocko had broken several union-ization drives and fired anyone who objected to the pittance he paid.

"You hear about Murtinson?" As Ed recounted the latest, Tim's eyes grew as large as the lenses of sparring goggles. "I've never covered a murder before."

"It probably *is* murder, but we can't call it 'murder' just yet," Ed cor-rected him. "Right now, it's still 'homicide.' Didn't they teach you anything at the UCLA paper?" Ed smiled as he ribbed his friend, but his message was clear: You're the Master on the mats, but this isn't the dojo.

Ed told Tim to amuse himself while he checked in with Ruffen. Ed was all set to argue that he—and not the police guys—should cover Murtinson's untimely demise as part of the Coin Collection story. But no argument was necessary. One cop chaser was on vacation. Another was out sick. And the third was covering a hostage situation in Embarcadero Three.

Back at his cube, Ed told Tim, "I'm running out to Murtinson's place in Seacliff. C'mon along. I'll give you a ride. We can catch up and cover the rollaway together."

"Rollaway?"

"When the paramedics roll the body out."

"Give me a minute to call in."

"Use my phone. But listen, Tim, for your own good, don't tell Jocko you know me."

4

"Jocko already knows," Tim explained as Ed maneuvered his beat-up ten-year-old Mustang through the midmorning traffic out Howard, then up Ninth.

The 'Stang had started out fire-engine red, but a decade of San Francisco sun, rain, and salty fog had faded it to an odious orange. A few years earlier, a tourist in a rented Lincoln had plowed into the car's right side, necessitating replacement of the passenger door. But Ed didn't have collision, so his mechanic neighbor scrounged a door from a junkyard near Candlestick. Only it was green. On Dolores Terrace, the dead-end alley where Ed lived, the neighbors took to calling the car "Behind the Green Door," after the porno film by the city's bad-boy filmmakers, the Mitchell Brothers.

Ed turned down the radio to merely loud as KFOG segued from Robert Cray into the Traveling Wilburys' "End of the Line."

"… It came out my first day there," Tim continued. "Jocko asked if I knew anyone on the paper. I said I knew a former reporter."

"Did he throw anything?" Ed zipped through Civic Center. A half-dozen men in the filthy coats of the homeless were curled up asleep on the plaza grass. Ed ran up Larkin past the hulking Main Library and into Little Saigon, where Vietnamese restaurants and markets were crowding out the previous wave of Chinese immigrants and the old-time poor, black and white, who had inhabited the area's cheap hotels since the 1950s.

Tim laughed. "No. But he said," Tim dropped his voice an octave. "'I fired that asshole, so don't believe a word he says about me.' Then he added, 'Actually, I'm worse.'"

"He said that?" Ed smiled and shook his head. "He *actually* said he was worse? Vintage Jocko. He's one of the few people in the world you can despise and love at the same time. He also happens to be a great newspaperman."

Ed headed out Geary and settled in for the cross-town trek to Seacliff, where some of San Francisco's priciest real estate perched on the rocky bluffs just west of the Golden Gate Bridge.

It was a glorious autumn day, sunny and clear, in the mid-sixties, with a pleasant breeze blowing in from the ocean, the kind of day Easterners love in January and hate in July, the kind San Franciscans call "normal." They passed Japantown and the surrounding urban renewal projects that had wrenched the heart out of the Fillmore, until the late 1950s, the city's main black neighborhood. The old jazz clubs and dance halls were long gone now, supplanted by more stately places like the Chinese consulate and the Miyako Hotel, where touring rock acts liked to stay because of the sunken tubs in the bathrooms.

"When I called in, Jocko told me to give you a message—"

"Let me guess: 'Tell him to fuck himself.'"

The subtle angles of Tim's face sharpened with surprise. "How did you know?"

"I know Jocko. He's never forgiven me for getting on with the *Horn*."

"But he fired you."

"Doesn't matter. Does he still bluster around the newsroom every Monday railing about the schlock in the Sunday *Horn?*"

"Yeah. Especially if you have a big piece in."

"Figures. Has anyone complained of writer's block?"

"I don't think so. Not since I've been there. Why?"

"Well, don't. We had a City Hall reporter for a while, Wendy Forray, quiet, cute, real sweet, and real smart when you got to know her. She's at the *Sacramento Bee* now. One time she had this assignment, and deadline was coming up, and for some reason, she couldn't get into it. She made the mistake of telling Jocko she had writer's block. I'll never forget it: His face turned beet red. His eyes bugged out. I thought he was going to have a stroke. He starts screaming: 'Carpenters don't get carpenter's block! Plumbers don't get plumber's block!' Now he's right in Wendy's face: 'And writers don't get writer's block!' He pounds a fist on her desk: 'Writers write. If you're not writing, you're not a writer. And if you're not a writer, you don't belong here!' Wendy burst into tears. She got up, walked out of the newsroom, and never came back. It was a shame, too, because she was a hell of a good reporter. She covers the governor for the *Bee*. The thing about Jocko is that he's always been his own worst enemy. He would have self-destructed long ago if it weren't for Melissa."

Melissa Rubin was listed on the *Defender's* masthead as Assistant to the Publisher, but in fact, she ran the paper. Jocko assigned the stories, wrote the editorials, and made sure that coverage always glorified the city's neighborhoods and vilified City Hall and the downtown corporations, especially PG&E. But Melissa did just about everything else. She was the mother hen, every reporter's surrogate Mom. She edited copy, dealt with personnel, dickered with advertisers and the printer, and occasionally restrained Jocko from slugging the politicians who trooped in around election time looking for endorsements. The typical *Defender* staffer lasted two years, but Melissa was pushing 15. Without her, the paper would have collapsed under the weight of its owner's insufferability, and everyone knew it, even Jocko. Melissa was the only person he allowed to edit him, the only one who could stand up to him in a shouting match and live.

"Yeah, Melissa's great. She sends you her best."

Ed threaded his way past a convoy of articulated Muni buses. They cruised past the Fillmore Auditorium, quiet as a tomb in midmorning. The marquee proclaimed, Tonight: Fine Young Cannibals. Ed liked the band, especially "Good Thing," and would have felt tempted, except for the Coin Collection party … and the fact that, ever since he'd turned thirty, he couldn't deal with weekday shows whose headliner came on at midnight.

"I don't get it," Tim mused. "Jocko fires you, but Melissa says you're one of his few real friends."

Ed chuckled. "I wouldn't go that far. But we get together for a few beers every month or so, go to some Giants games, and the occasional movie. We were at the Stick the other night when Clark hit that grand slam."

"That was a great game. You think they have a shot?"

"God knows. I've been holding my breath since June."

"Me too." Tim ran his fingers through his hair, then shook it out. "So, if you don't mind my asking, Ed, what happened? Why'd Jocko fire you?"

"It's a long story, man. …"

They fell silent as they passed the Kaiser Medical Center and shot through the tunnel. *Sex, Lies, and Videotape* was showing at the Bridge. A little farther out, the Coronet had *The Abyss*. West of Arguello, the businesses became more polyglot, with signage in Chinese, Japanese, Vietnamese, Thai, Korean, and Russian. On KFOG, Dave Morey announced Springsteen's "Born to Run."

Ed's firing was actually a short story. He just wasn't in the mood to rehash it with Tim. The reason was insubordination, specifically his refusal to participate in the paper's weekly taste tests, one of the *Defender's* most popular features. Every week, it was something else: burgers, chocolate cake, burritos, cappuccino, croissants, whatever. Readers nominated their favorites, then the staff sampled, discussed, and voted. The winners were awarded "Best Of San Francisco" certificates, which they displayed prominently. When Ed joined the paper, he dutifully showed up every Tuesday afternoon and for about a year enjoyed the taste tests. It was fun being in the know, conferring "Best Of" awards. But the process became tedious and then oppressive. He stopped caring about who made the best falafel or pesto pizza, and his colleagues' impassioned arguments for or against some contestant began sounding pathetic. He realized why Jocko was always so uncharacteristically quiet at the Tuesday ritual. Taste tests were one of many silly ingredients he had to stir into the mix to keep enough people reading his paper so enough advertisers would keep it afloat. Ed began ducking taste tests. Of course, his absences were noted by the boss, who believed that if he himself had to endure fatuous arguments about which bakery's cheesecake was creamiest, everyone should. For a few months, Jocko contented himself with sarcastic little digs. Then he cornered Ed and demanded to know why he'd become a consistent no-show.

"Watching my weight," Ed lied.

Jocko replied that weight control shouldn't be a problem without an income, then fired him just as Melissa was setting up a dozen steaming plates of Pad Thai for the weekly go-round.

Ed wasn't surprised. He knew his time at the *Defender* was up. He'd learned all he could there and understood that Jocko grew bored with reporters whose leads he could no longer improve.

Three days later, the *Foghorn's* night police reporter dropped dead of a heart attack—early fifties, but a heavy smoker and drinker. Ed knew a few reporters on the *Horn* and got the job.

Jocko didn't speak to Ed for a year. Then, out of the blue one Sunday afternoon, with the 49ers in the playoffs, Ed answered his doorbell to find a smiling Jocko holding a six-pack of Anchor Steam and Chinese in boxes. Ed wondered how long Tim would last in Jockoland. He also wondered if his former employer knew that Tim could easily break his neck with one well-placed side kick.

They crossed the green ribbon of esplanade that framed Park Presidio Blvd. The temperature dropped ten degrees, and the ocean breeze grew stiff and salty. On KFOG, the Stones pounded out "Gimme Shelter." "Rape, murder, it's just a shot away. ..." Fitting, Ed thought, for where we're headed. At the gilded minarets of the Russian Orthodox church on Twenty-sixth Avenue, Ed turned right and gunned it for Seacliff.

"So, you must have made black belt years ago," Ed ventured, trying not to sound too impressed.

"Yeah, toward the end of high school," Tim replied modestly. "Do you remember what Master Chen always said?"

"A black belt is a beginner."

Tim smiled. "You remember."

"How could I forget? You still call him Master Chen? Not uncle?"

"At family functions, he's Uncle. But in the dojo, he'll always be Master Chen. I see a lot more of him on the mats. Master Chen feels more comfortable."

"How is he?" Ed's voice softened, and carried wisps of longing and remorse.

"Good. Healthy. He's sixty-seven now. He's stopped teaching students below brown, but he still coaches the advanced group. And his kata is perfect. He took a first in the Senior Tournament in San Jose last month."

"I'm glad."

As they approached Seacliff, the boxy, three-flat, bay-windowed places, pressed together shoulder to shoulder, gave way to single-family homes, then large ones. Across Camino del Mar, past the stone pillars that announced SEACLIFF, they entered another world, one of enormous mansions surrounded by dramatically landscaped yards that recalled Tuscany.

On the radio, a growling Steven Matthew David was flogging his stereo store: "Matthew's! 6400 Mission Street, top of the hill, Daly City."

Ed drifted back to his years of studying karate with Master Chen. He recalled another of his teacher's sayings: "Karate is not about fighting. Karate is about kata." Katas were the elaborately choreographed combinations of blocks, punches, and kicks designed to develop strength, flexibility, speed, and harmony of body, mind, and spirit. They look easy, but in their own way, are more demanding than sparring. Practicing katas inspired great respect in Ed for ballet dancers and figure skaters.

"He misses you," Tim said tenderly. "That picture of you with your kata trophy is still on the bulletin board."

"I only took second."

"Yes, but you came within two points of beating Jimmy Zhu. Master Chen was very proud."

"Jimmy Zhu. Jesus. I haven't thought about him in years. He was incredible."

"You know what he does now? Coaches kung-fu movie stars in Hong Kong, choreographs the fight scenes. Did you see 'Fangs of the Serpent?'"

"Missed it."

"One of his."

Twenty-sixth snaked around to Seacliff Avenue. To the right and very close, the Golden Gate Bridge was framed against an azure sky and cobalt water dotted with whitecaps. Some sailboats frolicked in the breeze, and a huge Suzuki container ship chugged out to sea. Across the Golden Gate, the Marin Headlands rose out of the ocean, craggy cliffs softened by surf spray and haze. Ed turned left and they entered an enclave of palaces.

"I miss him, too," Ed admitted wistfully. "I think about him, wish him a long healthy life. Tell him for me, would you?"

"Tell him yourself," Tim replied, with an edge of bitterness.

"Maybe I will." But Ed knew he wouldn't. He felt guilty about it. Master Chen had always been good to him, more than a teacher, a mentor. But Ed's study of karate coincided with his years in graduate school. When he started teaching, it was hard to get to the dojo. Then he moved to Grass Valley. When he returned, he kept meaning to stop by, but never quite made it.

"Why didn't you go on after—what was it?—brown belt?" Tim asked.

"Green. I don't know. Too many changes in my life, I guess. And I realized I was there for the wrong reason."

"What reason?"

"To learn how to fight."

"Ah, yes," Tim reflected, "the most common mistake. Every time one of Jimmy's movies comes out, we get an influx of new students dying to learn flying spin kicks. Master Chen always tells them: 'Karate is not about fighting—'"

Ed completed his old teacher's saying: "'—Karate is about serenity.'"

They looked at each other and smiled. Tim said, "It's funny: When I was coming up through the ranks, I never understood what he meant by that. But now that I've had my black for six years, and I'm teaching, I'm beginning to get it."

Ed turned off Seacliff Avenue onto Seacliff Court, the classiest address in the neighborhood. Murtinson's place was the most palatial home on the cul-de-sac, a sprawling four-story Spanish-style hacienda with a tile roof and enough beveled glass glinting behind wrought iron grillwork to make Ed reach for his sunglasses. Two police cars were in the driveway. An ambulance was parked at the curb, flanked by TV vans with microwave dishes pointed at Sutro Tower. Ed pulled up at a rarity for San Francisco, a big open stretch of curb, and the two reporters sauntered up the brick walk just as the paramedics eased out the front door wheeling a gurney topped by a dull black bodybag. Ed pulled a reporter's notebook out of his inside jacket pocket and reached into a pants pocket for a Bic. "Maybe that's why I quit," he mused. "I'm incapable of serenity."

5

The perfect backdrop—that's what TV reporting is all about. As the paramedics rolled Murtinson's body down the bumpy brick walkway toward the ambulance, a petite Japanese-American woman wearing a navy blue suit stepped out from behind the Channel 5 van, swept a hand over expensively coifed obsidian hair, and positioned herself perfectly in her cameraman's foreground, with the Golden Gate Bridge rising majestically behind her. When Murtinson's remains rolled into the frame, the cameraman gave her the "go" sign. Kim Nakagawa launched into her live shot:

"One of the Bay Area's most prominent figures is dead today at seventy-three—Gregory Murtinson, murdered last night in his palatial San Francisco home in what police say appears to have been a burglary and art theft. Murtinson was the founder, and for forty-one years, director of the California Museum, a shining jewel among Bay Area cultural institutions and a famed international tourist attraction. Police say the burglar broke in around midnight through a first-floor window"—she gestured to her right—"and was in the process of stealing three renowned paintings, a Picasso, a Degas, and a Rembrandt, when Murtinson apparently confronted him. The intruder shot him three times in the chest, and escaped with the paintings, valued at more than $28 million. The gun appears to have been silenced because no one nearby heard any shots—including Murtinson's longtime housekeeper, Verna Washington, who was upstairs in her room at the time of the shooting. Washington found Murtinson's body in his study this morning. When she retired last night around ten thirty, Murtinson was excitedly making last-minute preparations for a ceremony marking one of his Museum's greatest acquisitions, the fabled Gilchrist Collection of American Coins, being donated by *San Francisco Foghorn* publisher Chester Worthington Gilchrist. The ceremony in the Museum rotunda was scheduled for tonight, and sources say it *will* go on as planned because—in the words of Assistant Director Myrna Hoskins—'Gregory would have wanted it that way.' At the home of the late Gregory Murtinson in San Francisco, this is Kim Nakagawa. Back to you, Scott."

Like most print journalists, Ed despised TV news for its smugness and superficiality. He thought even less of TV reporters. They were bubbleheads, more worried about how their hair looked than getting their facts straight, or, God forbid, displaying any insight. And compared with ink-stained wretches, they made a fortune. But Ed had to admit that Nakagawa was good. A young kid, mid-twenties, she'd arrived from some third-tier market a few months earlier and seemed to be thriving in the big time. Her stand-up was smooth and polished, and she seemed pretty sharp, which fueled Ed's resentment even more.

Ed motioned for Tim to accompany him into the house, but the *Defender* reporter couldn't take his eyes off the lovely Ms. Nakagawa. Ed had to grab the kid by the elbow to get his attention, and for a moment feared his friend might snap his wrist with a slashing downward block. Instead, Tim followed him into the house, taking the stairs three at a time.

Murtinson's mansion looked huge from the outside. From the inside, it appeared even larger. Off to the right, the entry to the hangar-size study was cordoned off with police tape, so the reporters milled around the foyer, which was big enough to accommodate the Carousel at the Zoo. Hanging on the dark wood of the wall at the base of a majestic staircase was a framed spread from *Architectural Digest*. Four pages on the house, with photos galore, including one of the foyer and sweeping stairs. The pull quote caught Ed's eye: "A residence fit for a king." An apt description. To San Francisco society, Murtinson was tantamount to royalty.

Ed stepped up to the yellow tape. A cop he vaguely recognized from his stint on the night police beat guarded the entry to make sure no dickhead reporters sullied the room before the lab guys finished dusting for prints. A chalk outline was drawn on the Persian carpet, a rug Ed guessed would set him back a year's salary. In the middle of the outline, at chest level, was a large dark discoloration. The far wall was filled with paintings illuminated by tiny spotlights like the ones up in Gilville. Three of the spots shone on empty frames.

A large window stood to the left of the purloined paintings. Under a clamshell clasp, one pane had been punched out. A tech was dusting the sill. A steer of a man in an ill-fitting gray suit conferred with him, then swept across the room and ducked under the tape. Ed knew Mr. Beef from his cop-chasing days, Detective Matt Harrigan, a methodical, dyspeptic, by-the-book officer, who didn't go in for grandstanding and hated the press. Reared in a family of Irish cops, thirty-odd years earlier he'd been a star halfback at Balboa High, then an All-American at San Jose State. He was drafted by the Redskins, played a season, then got waived. He returned home to claim his patrimony on the police force. He started as a beat cop in the Fillmore and wound up busting People's Temple leader, Jim Jones, for having a van full of firearms. Jones jumped bail, fled to Guyana, and eventually ordered eight hundred of his followers to drink poisoned Kool-Aid, shooting the ones who refused. In the aftermath, Harrigan was lionized as the one cop who saw through Jones, and with a little family pull, he parlayed his fifteen minutes into a promotion to detective.

Harrigan was six-foot-four, and an ox. The muscle was on its way to flab now, but when he approached the knot of reporters, he was a Goliath among Davids. Ed nodded to a few of his colleague-competitors, reporters from the *Examiner, Gazette, Tribune, Mercury-News, Times,* and the other *Times.*

"So what do you think," the guy from the *Oakland Trib* asked. "Murtinson heard the window break, came running, and the burglar iced him?"

"That's one possibility," Harrigan said, unwrapping a roll of Tums and popping two. It was a classic police non-answer. Ed knew what he was thinking: When are these clowns going to clear out so I can do my job?

"No one heard any shots?" This from Bruce Ahred, an ex-*Foghorn* hack who'd gone over to the *Merc.* Not the swiftest car in the garage. At the *Horn,* people called him Bruce Air Head.

"Correct. And the dog next door didn't bark."

"That's bizarre."

"No," Harrigan deadpanned, "that's a silencer."

A wire-service guy Ed knew from Press Club luncheons said, "You're sure the gun was silenced?" Wire guys usually just rewrote what they read in the local papers, and only crawled out of their holes for free meals or stories the top editors in New York cared about, usually touristy things:

the cable cars, the Golden Gate Bridge, and the killing of the founder of the California Museum.

Harrigan grimaced. "At the moment, I'm not *sure* of *anything*. But no one heard any shots. And the slugs the lab guys dug out of the bookcase looked like they'd been propelled through a noise-suppression attachment. When we have anything definite, I'll let you know."

"What about the alarm system?" the guy from the *L.A. Times* asked. "Why didn't it go off?"

"It was turned off," Harrigan replied.

"Why?"

"You have an alarm?" the detective asked. "You leave it on when you're home?"

"What about the maid?"

"What about her?"

"Can we talk to her?"

Harrigan sighed, and with uncharacteristic solicitude, said, "Look, Miss Washington is in no shape to talk to anyone right now. You have any idea what three .38 slugs do to a man's chest at close range? When she found Murtinson, he wasn't pretty."

"But we understand she told the uniforms that Murtinson expected Foxsen at nine, and that she went to her room before he arrived."

"That's correct."

"Just for the record," said a woman Ed didn't recognize, "you mean Lawrence Foxsen, the owner of Prima Gallery, right?"

"Correct."

"The art gallery on Union Square."

"Correct."

"You think Foxsen had anything to do with it?"

"No comment."

"Is he a suspect?"

"I wouldn't call him a suspect," Harrigan said carefully. "But we've been in contact with Mr. Foxsen through his attorney. We intend to question him. We also intend to question many of Murtinson's friends and business associates."

"Nothing missing except the paintings?" the old codger from the *Gazette* asked. The guy had been a cop chaser since the Gold Rush, and usually hit the Jim Beam before noon.

"Correct," Harrigan said, "nothing but the paintings. Murtinson's wallet was in his pocket and it contained a good deal of cash." The reporters scribbled in their notebooks. All except Ed. Harrigan hadn't revealed a damn thing. He'd just given predictable nonanswers to the predictable questions.

Ed drifted toward the hallway by the stairs that presumably led back to the kitchen, where the housekeeper, Verna Washington, might be. What was with Harrigan, anyway? The cops usually let reporters get a statement from the body-finder, even when the body was hamburger.

"Sorry," said a cop who looked like a black version of the Michelin Man. "Off limits."

Ed looked past him into the pantry, saw no one, and returned to the foyer in time to watch the lab tech finish up at the window, then pack up, duck under the tape, and head out. Ed followed, catching him on the front porch.

"Get any prints?"

"Lots. Now we have to see if they belong to anyone besides Murtinson and his maid."

"You dust the picture frames?"

"Of course." The tech shot him a look that said: Asshole.

Undaunted, Ed pressed on, trailing the tech as he walked down the stairs: "I didn't notice any glass on the rug. Did you?"

"No," the tech replied, striding toward a police van.

Ed trotted after him. "I didn't see any dirt or mud on the rug either. Did you?"

"Talk to Harrigan." The tech flung his case into the back of the van, and pulled out a ring of keys.

Ed drifted around to the side of the house. The broken window was seven, maybe eight feet off the ground. Below it, two cops were sifting through the dirt, picking up things and putting them in a plastic bag. As Ed approached, one looked up at him. "This area's off limits to the press. You want anything, talk to Harrigan." That same old song.

Ed returned to the foyer where the detective was distributing an appraiser's report on the paintings. The Degas landscape and the Picasso nude portrait of his mistress were certainly valuable, but in monetary terms, they were chump change compared with the Rembrandt, *Rabbi Comforting a Widow*.

"The guy left all those other paintings," the unfamiliar woman said. "Isn't that a Monet over there?" She pointed to shimmering water lilies next to the empty frame that had held the Rembrandt. You think this was a steal-to-order heist?"

"Possibly."

"I don't get it," the guy from the *Merc* ventured. "How many burglars carry guns with silencers?"

"Art thieves are a cut above your average smash-and-grab," the *Gazette's* lush intoned sagely.

"Why didn't he take the frames?" Tim asked.

"They're bolted to the wall," the *New York Times* reporter replied. "Big painting thefts, they always cut them out of the frames."

"Oh," Tim murmured sheepishly as he scribbled in his pad.

Ed kept an eye on the Michelin Man. The cop glanced away and Ed darted into the dining room, a sumptuous chamber dominated by a crystal chandelier hung over a table the size of a stretch limo. He headed for the door at the rear, which led into the pantry. Off to the right, he heard whimpering. He peeked into the hall. The cop's back was toward him. He slipped across and into the breakfast room where he found the housekeeper, Verna Washington. She was a large black woman with short processed hair and big gold-hoop earrings. She cried quietly, occasionally emitting a loud sob. She dabbed her eyes and blew her nose as another African-American woman made tea.

"Miss Washington?" Ed asked. The housekeeper looked up. Her eyes were red and puffy, her cheeks shining from tears. "I'm terribly sorry about what happened. I'm Ed Rosenberg from the *Foghorn*. It must have been awful for you ... finding him."

"I never seen nobody *shot* before," Washington moaned.

The other woman handed her a steaming cup. "Drink this, baby." Then she turned to Ed. "I'm Pat Lucas, from Verna's church. The pohleece already questioned her." Her tone said: Leave us alone.

Ed stood there, looked at his feet, shook his head slowly. "Such a terrible thing, especially for you." He waited for media magic to work on the maid. People are quick to say they hate the press, but it's a rare bird who doesn't relish talking to a reporter.

"He was always good to me," Washington sniffed. "Mr. Murtinson wasn't good to many. But he was always good to me."

"Amen," Lucas concurred. "Sent her to church every Sunday in a cab, and had her picked up, too. From here to Bayview and back, that's a forty-dollar cab ride—"

"Fifty," Washington corrected her.

"—but he paid it every week for years. How many years, baby?

"Twenty-eight."

"That's a long time, twenty-eight years," Ed observed softly. "What do you mean? He wasn't good to many?"

"Mr. Murtinson, he had a nasty streak. Went to all those society parties, but didn't have hardly no friends. Never went to church. Always hollering at people. I heard him yelling on the phone all the time. Never hollered at me, though. He was always good to me."

"I feel terrible about intruding at a time like this," Ed said with a glance at the protective Ms. Lucas, "but my boss, Mr. Gilchrist, knew Mr. Murtinson well, and—"

"I know he knew him. And let me tell you: Them two didn't trade much sugar. Old Worth Gilchrist. Mr. Murtinson always called him 'Worthless.' See, Mr. Gilchrist, he was jealous of young Chet's feelings for Mr. Murtinson."

"Young Chet?" Ed was suddenly intrigued. "You mean Chet Gilchrist?"

"That's right. Worthless' son, the one got hisself all messed up with drugs."

"What did Chet have to do with Murtinson?"

"His momma was one of Mr. Murtinson's very few friends. She'd visit, oh, two, three times a week when the boy was young and always brought him. When I started, Chet couldn't have been more than nine or ten. Mr. Murtinson doted on him. Chet called him 'Uncle,' even though they wasn't really kin. As the boy growed up, he and his momma spent lots of weekends here or at Mr. Murtinson's place up in Inverness. Sometimes seemed like Chet was over here more than he was home."

"So … when you found Mr. Murtinson, what did you do?"

"I called 911." Recalling the horrible moment, Washington started crying again, and Pat Lucas placed a gentle hand on her shoulder.

"How long did it take for the police to get here?"

"Not long. A few minutes is all."

"And while you were waiting, what did you do?"

"I run out the house. I didn't want to stay with no … *dead body*."

"Amen," Lucas intoned, rolling her eyes.

"You didn't … clean up any glass by the broken window?"

"No, suh, just got out of there—fast."

"So. Then the police arrived. Uniformed officers, right? Not the detective."

"That's right. Two of 'em. They called the detective."

"And what did they do?"

"Checked Mr. Murtinson. He was already stiff and cold." More tears, a sob, and shudder. More eye-dabbing and nose-blowing. "Then they asked me what I heard, when I went to bed, that sort of thing."

"Did you hear anything last night?"

"Nothing. Just watched Cosby and went to sleep."

"And the cops? They just hung around until Harrigan arrived?"

"Pretty much. Well, one of them ask if I had any rubber gloves, so I come back here to get a pair for him, and when I went back, the detective was there."

"Why rubber gloves?"

"To pick up the painting on the rug."

Ed drew a sharp breath. "There was a *painting*? On the *rug*?"

"That's right. I never liked it. A woman, you know, undressed, but not really a woman, and not really naked. Just shapes kind of look like a woman not wearing nothing."

The Picasso nude. Ed's heart raced.

"And what did the police do with that painting?"

"Rolled it up and took it out."

Movement by the kitchen door caught Ed's eye. It was the Michelin Man. "Hey!" He glared at Ed. "You're not supposed to be in here. Out."

"Oh, sorry officer," Ed waved good bye to the ladies. "I was just looking for a bathroom." He squeezed by the officer, and strode quickly down the hall back to the foyer.

"Yo. There you are." It was Tim. "Things are breaking up. Listen, I hope you don't mind if I catch a ride back with the Channel Five van."

"You mean with Kim Nakagawa?"

Tim blushed remarkably red for a Chinese-American.

"I don't mind at all." Ed smiled. "Good luck." But Tim was already out the door.

Ed waited for the last reporter to depart, then sidled up to Harrigan and asked for the sheet describing the stolen paintings. Back during his football days, Harrigan's hair had been thick and blonde. Now, it was thin and gray, heading toward white. "You know, Detective, this doesn't add up."

"What doesn't, Rosenbaum?" Harrigan popped another Tums.

"Rosen*berg*. This bullshit about a burglary."

"Oh?" Harrigan arched an eyebrow. "Since when are you a detective?"

"Since I walked in here with two eyes open and no hangover. The window is eight feet off the ground. To get to it, your burglar would need either a ladder or a boost. But there are no tracks in the dirt—no footprints, no ladder marks."

The corners of Harrigan's lips curled into a tight smirk.

"The only thing in the dirt was glass. I watched your guys pick it up before they chased me off. Your tech said there was no glass on the rug. And the maid just told me she didn't pick up any. No mud from the garden on the rug either. Ergo, that window was punched *out*, not *in*. There was no burglary. The bad guy came in through the front door, then punched out the window to make it look like B&E."

Harrigan raised his chin. His smirk showed a few teeth. "That's a possibility."

"Come on, Harrigan. Get real. I know about the Picasso."

Harrigan stopped breathing, then started again. "What about it?"

"The bad guy dropped it. You have it."

"So?"

"So that tends to discredit art theft as a motive, doesn't it? How many art thieves drop a zillion-dollar Picasso?"

In spite of himself, Harrigan's smirk evolved into a sheepish grin. A uniformed officer took the tape off the entrance to the study. The Michelin Man lumbered past on his way out. "So, Sherlock," Harrigan ventured, "what's your theory?"

Ed recognized the question as the opening gambit of a game cops and reporters sometimes play: Who Knows What? Who Confirms What? If Ed's theory agreed with Harrigan's, it meant the detective had misled the other reporters—or had allowed them to mislead themselves. Their stories would be wrong, their papers embarrassed, and some powerful publishers might call the chief about a certain son-of-a-bitch who hadn't played straight with the Fourth Estate. The department might give Harrigan a wedgie. So Ed had him over a barrel. But only so far. If Harrigan wouldn't confirm Ed's theory, if the detective refused to give him a big wet kiss of a quote, Ruffen would dismiss Ed's conclusions as mere speculation and insist he go with the official line, the burglary story.

"If we're in the same ballpark, will you confirm?"

"Maybe," the detective said, no longer smiling, wearing a poker face to play this hand.

"But—"

"No 'buts,' Rosenberg," Harrigan snapped. "I got me a seriously dead big shot here. I got the chief, the mayor, and for all I know, the fucking governor screaming for an arrest. That changes things. Now, tell me your theory, and if we're on the same wavelength, I'll confirm *some* of it—but then you and me have to come to Jesus about a few things."

They glared at each other a moment, then Ed blinked. "Deal."

Harrigan nodded, and with a subtle gesture, invited Ed to spin his web.

"Murtinson knew the bad guy," Ed explained, "let him in the front door. But the guy was after Murtinson, not the paintings, hence the silencer. The bad guy shoots Murtinson, then breaks the window and takes the paintings to make it look like a burglary. But this schmuck is a killer, not an art thief, and he drops the Picasso on the way out."

"All right," Harrigan allowed, choosing his words carefully, "I'll confirm that the forced entry was faked, that this looks more like an assassination than an art theft. But you've got to play ball with me on the Picasso. You've got to say *three* paintings were stolen."

"Why?"

"On the decent chance that it happened a little differently."

Harrigan clenched his jaw, pursed his lips. Ed saw he was sweating this one. Murtinson was not your average stiff. "I'm listening," Ed said.

"Most of the time, murder is a family affair. The victim gets done by someone he knows, usually a friend or loved one—"

"Hence my scenario," Ed tried to quell impatience, unsuccessfully.

"Thing is: Murtinson had no family, and from what I hear, his only real friend was Margaret Gilchrist, your boss' wife, who died years ago."

"Okay, so maybe it wasn't a bosom buddy, but Murtinson knew lots of people, had people over, like the art dealer, Foxsen—"

"Murtinson was a major client of Foxsen's. You think the art dealer would kill the goose that lays the golden egg?"

"For those paintings, he might."

"Then why would he drop the Picasso?"

"Maybe to deflect suspicions away from him."

Harrigan sighed. "Possibly, and believe me, I've got a guy running

Foxsen through the wringer. But it could have happened differently."

"How?"

"Murtinson was the crown prince of San Francisco society, the biggest snob west of New York. He rarely spoke to anyone whose blood wasn't as blue as his. So you can bet that whoever wanted him dead moved in the same circles, which suggests a heavy hitter is behind this. Now maybe our society type came over here and pulled the trigger. But rich fucks usually shy away from dirty work. So let's suppose he hires a flunky to do it—"

"And risk being blackmailed? Or turned in?" Ed was incredulous. "I don't think so."

"Think again. I've investigated a good hundred murders. Exactly two of them involved a silenced weapon. This one, and Needle Meadows."

Ed remembered the case from a few years earlier. Danny "The Needle" Meadows had been kingpin of the Bay Area heroin trade until a Vietnamese gang decided to muscle him out. A dozen street dealers and middle managers on both sides wound up dead, some mutilated. Then Meadows turned up hanging from a meat hook in a Hunter's Point warehouse, shot several times.

"Forget Hollywood, Rosenberg. Silencers are pretty rare in homicides. I'm guessing our shooter is a contract killer, a professional."

"So?"

"So our rich guy has been here. He knows Murtinson has a fortune in art, and tells the shooter to grab the three most valuable paintings, the ones in the gaudy gold frames. He also knows he can't sell them. They're too famous. But they make the job look like an art theft instead of a contract hit. After the shooter drops off the paintings and gets paid, our mastermind is one happy fuck. Murtinson is dead. And he's sitting on twenty-eight million worth of canvas. He likes that, likes having them all to himself. His dick grows two inches just thinking about it. But here's where things get interesting. The TV, the papers, everyone says three paintings were stolen, but our shooter only delivers *two*. I'm hoping our society type freaks and accuses the hit man of fucking him by palming the Picasso—"

"So they turn on each other—"

"Right." Harrigan smiled. "And one of them fucks up and gives me the break I need—if I can keep that blabber-mouth housekeeper quiet."

Ed pondered Harrigan's theory. A contract killing sounded far-fetched.

Who in the Opera crowd would even *know* a hit man, let alone think through a phony art theft? But the ultimate accuracy of Harrigan's hunch didn't matter. Harrigan wanted him to say three paintings, needed him to say three paintings, was practically *begging* him to play it his way. That put Ed in a strong bargaining position. How much of the moon could he reasonably ask for? All of it, he decided. He could always take less later. "All right," Ed said, "let's say my story says three paintings, and you break this thing—I want an exclusive on the capture of *both* the hit man and the society mastermind."

"Done."

Shit, Ed thought. That was too easy. The Chief must have a blowtorch up Harrigan's butt. "I'll have to run this by my editor ..."

Harrigan produced a business card, and scribbled on it. "My private line at the station and my home phone. Your editor has any problems with our deal, have him call me."

"I'm going to quote you saying it was an assassination, not a burglary-art theft."

"Be my guest."

Harrigan turned and walked out the door. Ed took one final look around the study to fix everything in his mind, then bounded for the 'Stang. The sun shone bright and hot, but a cool ocean breeze tickled his cheeks. Seagulls wheeled overhead. As he started the car, KFOG launched into Joe Jackson's "Sunday Papers:" "... If you wanna know about the Bishop and the actress, If you wanna know how to be a star, If you wanna know about the stains on the mattress, You can read it in the Sunday papers." Harrigan slid into his cruiser, scowled at Ed, and drove off. An Arco tanker inched under the Bridge on its way to the Richmond oil refinery.

Ed took one last look at Murtinson's place. He loved being a reporter.

6

All four honchos—Ruffen, City Editor Gus Oberhoffer, Managing Editor John Gagliano, and Executive Editor Walter French—rolled over faster than a snorer kicked in the ribs. They loved sitting on inside information, sharing secrets with the police, using the power of the media to lay a trap for the bad guys—even if it meant knowingly lying to a half-million readers.

Ed's fingers made like Fred Astaire around the keyboard. The story wrote itself, as all good stories do. He slugged it MURTINSON and hit the SEND key just as Chet Gilchrist materialized at his cubicle, his eyes red, his face contorted.

"I—I can't *believe* it," he whimpered, slumping against the wall of Ed's cubicle. "Gregory Murtinson was like a father to me. I grew up calling him Uncle Greg. He was there for me in ways my own father never was. When I was young, school plays, open houses, Little League, my father might show up every now and then, but Uncle Greg was always there. Always. He even came with Mother to visit me at summer camp—" His head dropped into his hands.

"I'm terribly sorry, Chet," Ed mumbled. The words sounded lame, but what else could he say? Ed held out a box of tissues.

Chet plucked a few, wiped his eyes, blew his nose, pulled himself together. "He was one of Mother's closest friends. She was on the Museum Board. She was the first society person to join back when everyone else thought the whole idea was crazy. She talked my grandfather into leasing Uncle Greg the Museum's first site, where Hastings Law School is now, before he built the building in Civic Center." Chet clamped his eyes shut and a tear rolled down his cheek. "KGO said it was a burglary, an art theft, the Rembrandt." The remark was more of a question than a statement.

"Whoever did it wanted it to look that way. But between us and the cops, the break-in was faked, and the shooter dropped the Picasso on the way out. The way it looks, someone Murtinson knew wanted him dead, killed him, and walked in through the front door to do it."

Chet looked horrified. "My God. *Who?*"

"Got me. But right now you wouldn't want to be Larry Foxsen. He had an appointment with Murtinson last night."

"Foxsen. Doesn't he own the—the—oh, hell, I can't remember the name, some art gallery—"

"Prima Gallery."

"That's it. You know, he helped my father assemble the Collection. Why would he—?"

Ed's phone cut off Chet. The voice, an older man, identified himself haughtily as Armand Hitchens of Foster, Hitchens, Smithson & Boyle in New York, Mr. Gilchrist's personal attorney. Three independent appraisers concurred that the coin collection was worth, conservatively, $16.5 million. He had recommended that Mr. Gilchrist take a charitable deduction in that amount. Ed thanked him and hung up.

"You know what's really weird," Ed said. "The ceremony is on. Everyone says Murtinson would have wanted it that way: black tie, champagne, chicken skewers with Thai peanut sauce, the whole nine yards."

"I know," Chet sighed. "It's disgusting. Father tried to get it postponed, but the handgun people insisted on going forward—more publicity for their precious initiative. And the board wants the collection asap to keep the turnstiles spinning. Mother must be turning over in her grave. And Father insists that Laura and I attend. Stiff upper lip and all."

"Then I'll see you there. I'm covering the festivities."

"Don't expect them to be too festive."

Ed's phone rang again. Gilchrist wanted to see him. Immediately.

This time, he didn't have to identify himself. The lobby secretary buzzed him right through and the private secretary didn't even make him break stride. "He's expecting you." The heavy redwood doors swung open and suddenly Ed was back in the buttery leather chair taking in his publisher's view of the Old Mint.

"Tell me everything you know," Gilchrist ordered. He looked shaken. His brow was deeply furrowed, his lips pursed, his eyes dull.

Ed ran it down, from the obviously faked burglary to the deal with Harrigan about the number of paintings stolen. Gilchrist listened intently, frowning, periodically massaged his temples.

"It was a handgun, wasn't it?" Gilchrist murmured contemptuously.

"Looks like it, probably a .38. The cops won't be sure until they get the ballistics report, but a handgun is a safe bet."

Gilchrist swiveled his chair and stared out the window toward the Granite Lady. A group of Hare Krishnas in orange robes were beating drums on the corner of Fifth and Mission, singing the only song they knew. No one paid any attention. In the distance, across Market Street, a huge crane hoisted steel for a new hotel. On Gilchrist's desk, Ed noticed a large framed portrait, Gilchrist, his second wife, and two young boys.

"He wasn't a charitable man." Gilchrist mumbled the words, and Ed wasn't sure if he'd been meant to hear them.

"Excuse me?"

The publisher spun back around to face him. "I asked him to donate to the Initiative, but Gregory was not a charitable man. He refused—in rather vulgar terms."

Ed pulled out his notebook. "Which vulgar terms exactly?"

But Gilchrist waved his palm, a king dismissing a footman. "That comment is off the record."

Ed shifted in his chair. The leather creaked softly. To the extent that journalism has any ethics, one was supposed to say "off the record" before the comment, not after. But the rules were different for the *Foghorn's* publisher, so Ed tried another tack: "Why off the record? The irony is incredible. He refuses to donate, then—"

"You may say that much, that he refused to donate, but don't mention his vulgarity. It's unseemly to speak ill of the dead. And don't say 'refused.' Say 'declined.' And don't quote me. Attribute it to Claire Solkind, the press agent for the Initiative."

In other words, lie. Ed sighed. Journalism is to truth what teaching is to education, what law is to justice.

Ed flipped his notebook closed. "All right, off the record and for background only, just about everyone I talk to says Murtinson was a mean, nasty, insufferable snob who'd happily pour gasoline on a kitten and light a match. You called him an SOB this morning. Got any idea who'd want to kill him? How about Lawrence Foxsen?"

Gilchrist stared into his hands for a long moment.

"I think I'm hearing a 'damning silence,'" Ed ventured.

"No," Gilchrist said firmly. Then he shrugged. "I don't know. You have to understand that Larry and I are well-acquainted. He brokered the acquisition of many pieces in the Coin Collection, and advised me on the purchase of the Reilly Double Eagle. But when something like *this* happens, it's difficult to be sure of anything. I don't know everything about Larry's and Gregory's relationship, but from what I gather, it was like all of Gregory's relationships—stormy. I can imagine Larry wanting to strangle him occasionally, but it's hard to imagine him killing him, though you never know ... Resentments build up, then something snaps. ..."

"How closely did they work together?"

"Oh, very. The California Museum wouldn't have half its pieces—or cachet in the art world—if it weren't for Larry. He has an international reputation, especially when it comes to brokering Old Masters. The Rembrandt in Gregory's study, the one that got stolen—as I recall, Larry acquired it for him. And Larry's success behind the scenes at the Museum helped make his reputation."

"That would argue *against* him being the killer," Ed said.

"True. But now that his reputation is secure, perhaps he thought ..." Gilchrist started off into space.

"Perhaps he thought it was time to avenge a thousand old slights."

"Possibly ... But, it's difficult to believe that Larry would—" His voice trailed off.

"Well, *someone* did."

Gilchrist sighed. "You have to understand: Gregory was a very bitter man. He was a friend of the family, and I loved him, but I can't say I ever really *liked* him. He took his fortune and built the greatest museum in the West, some would say one of the finest in the world. But he stepped on a lot of people to do it. Gregory had a sadistic streak. He seemed to enjoy hurting those around him. There are probably two dozen people ready to wring his neck over Club memberships alone."

"Excuse me?"

Gilchrist's eyes became deep pools of condescension. "The Golden State Club."

"You mean that country club down the Peninsula?"

"Woodside Estates. It's *the* club in the Bay Area. Old money. Very prestigious. Gregory has been president—" Gilchrist caught himself, closed his eyes briefly, then reopened them, and continued: "*was* president for … I don't know, maybe twenty years. He blackballed just about everyone who applied, even big donors to the Museum. I remember arguing with him about the nominations of several people I sponsored—billionaires, captains of industry, a Supreme Court Justice, men whose wives chair the Opera's Opening Gala. But Gregory wouldn't budge. 'No new money,' he always said, like they were riff-raff. God knows how many people might have considered shooting him for his vetoes."

"Was Lawrence Foxsen blackballed?"

"I believe so. It would be easy to find out. Just call Elizabeth Fehrin-Cott. She's in charge of memberships. No, wait. Votes are confidential. Tell you what: I'll call her and tell her to disclose the information to you." When the King decreed, his subjects obeyed.

Gilchrist looked at his watch, then at Ed. The meeting was over. Ed rose and took two steps toward the door, then turned back. It was time for the zinger. "You know, one thing strikes me as strange …"

Gilchrist shot him a sidelong glance.

"The only person I've interviewed with anything good to say about Murtinson is Chet. Seems they were very close."

The publisher eyed him the way a cat studies a bird before pouncing. "Sit down."

Ed returned to the chair. The leather was still warm.

"So Chet told you about his 'Uncle Greg'?"

"Yes." Ed was tempted to flaunt a detail, but experience taught him that when asking about sensitive subjects, it was better to keep quiet and wait for the source to become uncomfortable enough with the silence to open up.

"This is off the record."

"Of course."

Gilchrist inhaled, then exhaled sharply. "I mentioned earlier that Gregory was a bitter man. Many people have wondered why. He and Margaret, my late wife, grew up together, and he confided to her what he called his 'awful secret.'"

Gilchrist paused. Ed waited.

"You see," he said, gazing past Ed toward a framed front page from Bloody Thursday of the General Strike of 1934, "Gregory was gay."

"Gay?" Ed couldn't help smiling. "So what? This is the gay-est city on Earth."

"It is *now*, but when Gregory—when my generation—came of age, it was a very different place. He grew up not only completely in the closet, but also deeply ashamed of his … orientation. He consulted psychiatrists and tried all sorts of supposed cures. He even got married—to a Ross as I recall, a girl from the old mining family for whom the town of Ross is named. A big society wedding. She didn't know about him, but when she found out, she left him for some British earl. Their divorce was a major scandal. It took all of Margaret's charm to convince her father, who ran the *Foghorn* at the time, to hush up the rumors about Gregory. Why do you think he founded the California Museum? To rehabilitate himself in the eyes of San Francisco society after the debacle of his marriage and divorce."

"But that was years ago," Ed observed. "Today we've got half a million people turning out for the Gay Pride Parade, and one of the Sisters of Perpetual Indulgence running for Mayor. Didn't gay liberation open Murtinson's closet door?"

"On the contrary. Gregory resented the younger generation for their openness and considered most gay shenanigans an embarrassment. Meanwhile, he used his name and money and position to seduce socially prominent gay men. I understand he broke up several couples, and then, of course, with the conquest made and the damage done, he dropped them and moved on. If the police want to find his killer, I suggest they follow the condoms."

"What about Lawrence Foxsen? Is he gay? Did Murtinson steal a lover from him?"

"The answer to your first question is yes. As to your second, I wouldn't know."

The intercom buzzed. It was Walt French telling Gilchrist to turn on Channel 5 immediately. The Old Man clicked the remote on his desk and a television built into the wall behind Ed snapped to life. There was Kim Nakagawa back in front of Murtinson's house spilling the beans about the Picasso that got left behind. So much for Harrigan's little trap.

Ed ran downstairs and flung himself into his chair. He glanced at his watch. Just enough time to rewrite his story and tell the truth. His fingers raced around the keyboard. He included everything he had that Kim Nakagawa didn't: Harrigan's little deception in hopes of driving a wedge between the trigger man and the rich—quite possibly gay—mucky-muck who put him up to it. Then he deleted the gay business. That was speculation. It didn't come from Harrigan, but from Gilchrist, and the Old Man wanted it off the record. Not to mention that one had to be careful pointing fingers in a town as sensitive as San Francisco. But by casting Harrigan as the wily hunter patiently setting an elegant trap, Nakagawa became the off-road motorcyclist, thundering blindly through the wilderness, scaring off the big game. Without saying so, the piece clearly implied that she'd aided the murderer. Fuck her, Ed thought, as he hit the SEND key. No one steals my scoop without getting singed, especially not a young, gorgeous, overpaid, TV bitch.

But how did she find out about the Picasso ruse? Clearly, Murtinson's housekeeper told someone else, but who? Ed called an acquaintance who used to sell ads for the *Defender* before moving over to Channel 5. Turned out it was a classic case of big city as small town. Verna Washington's niece was the secretary to the station's news director. Figures.

Next Ed called the Golden State Club. Elizabeth Fehrin-Cott sounded elderly. She had a high breathy voice that made Ed think her collar was buttoned too tight. He stated his business, and said Mr. Gilchrist had asked him to call.

"What did you say your name was?"

"Rosenberg, Ed Rosenberg."

"Ah, yes, Mr. *Rosenberg*." Her voice dripped disdain. A Jew. Ed had to understand that membership votes were held in *strictest confidence*. But Worth had *assured her* that the information would be treated with the *utmost discretion* and might help catch the *beast* responsible for Gregory's *tragic* demise.

"Definitely," Ed interjected. "Utmost discretion Very important to the investigation. Crucial." He had a vision of a much younger Elizabeth, a debutante during the Big Band era, presented at the Cotillion, but never asked to dance.

"In that case, I'll make an exception." Ed heard a file cabinet drawer open and a shuffle of papers.

"Yes?"

"I have the *file* right here. Mr. Lawrence A. *Foxsen* was presented for membership *three times*—and *rejected* three times."

"Really." Ed tried to sound nonchalant. "And when was this? Recently?"

"Four years ago, two years ago, and last month."

"Do your records indicate who blackballed him?"

"We don't use *that term*, Mr. Rosenberg. But *naturally* my records chronicle both the *Aye* and *Nay* votes."

"And could you please tell me who voted Nay?" Ed imagined her family pushing her into the arms of some ne'er-do-well society swain, who married her for her money, robbed her blind, then skipped, leaving her with nothing to buoy her self-respect but a job babysitting the Golden State Club's office for her family's snooty friends.

"At *all three* presentations, there was *only one* Nay vote. Gregory Murtinson."

Bingo.

"Just one last question: Have you by chance been called by anyone from the San Francisco Police Department? A Detective Harrigan, perhaps?"

"No. No police. Just members *bemoaning* the *terrible tragedy*."

Ed dialed Harrigan, but hung up before it rang. The detective was certain to be smoking from the ears about Nakagawa's report, and every other journalist was automatically tainted. On the other hand, Harrigan was a methodical professional. He had to be interested in Murtinson's penchant for blackballing applicants to the Golden State Club, and the possible gay revenge motive. If that panned out ...

Ed dialed again. Of course, Harrigan wasn't at the cop house. He was at lunch. In a town with one restaurant for about every dozen residents, that meant he could be anywhere. But Ed guessed that after Nakagawa kicked him in the nuts, Harrigan would opt for comfort food. He dialed Mulligan's, an Irish pub police hang-out. The corn beef was dry, but the Guiness was cheap.

Come on, Harrigan, *be there,* Ed prayed. The bartender said he was. His brogue pegged him as a recent transplant from the Old Sod. He called, "Detective!" Ed imagined him waving the handset.

Harrigan hated having his lunch interrupted, especially by a reporter. He railed about Kim Nakagawa's ethics, her ethnicity, her gender, and the aroma of her genitals. Ed let him rant until he ran out of steam. "I have some information that might interest you."

"Thrill me," the detective sighed.

Ed recounted his conversation with Elizabeth Fehrin-Cott.

"Yesterday's news. Foxsen was just one of hundreds of high-and-mighties who got reamed up the ying yang by our boy. Everyone I talk to says Murtinson was a USDA Choice prick."

Ed played his trump card, Gilchrist's theory about it being a gay revenge killing. Harrigan made no reply. This was a good sign. He was thinking about it. Finally, he said, "I'll look into it. Thanks."

In the game of Cops and Reporters, "thanks" meant "I owe you one." There was no time like the present to collect.

"So what about Foxsen?" Ed asked. "What did he say about seeing Murtinson last night?"

"Why should I tell you now when I'm playing Meet the Press later this afternoon?"

Christ. A press conference. Ed hated them: Predigested news spoonfed to salivating reporters.

"Because," Ed said, wracking his cerebrum for an angle, "if you don't, I'll tell every reporter from San Jose to Sacramento where you eat lunch."

Harrigan laughed. "Fucking Rosenbaum. Always got a rabbit in the hat." Ed decided not to correct him on the last name. He had him laughing. The old charm was working.

"All right," Harrigan relented, "We played footsie with Foxsen's asshole lawyer most of the morning. Nada. Then we started in with Obstruction and Murder One, and he produced his solid citizen. Foxsen said he arrived around eight-thirty and left around nine."

"Why was he there?"

"Business, he said. Some shit about a coin collection."

"And after he left? Where'd he go?"

"To a meeting of rare book nuts at the Pacific Heights Library. They confirm he got there around nine-thirty and left after eleven."

"And the coroner said the time of death was around eleven."

"Give or take."

"Suppose the coroner's wrong?"

"That's possible, but I can't arrest a guy with a decent alibi on a 'suppose.' Unlike you guys, I need evidence that stands up in court."

Ed ignored the dig. He knew his time was running out. "So, what do you think? Gut feeling. Is it Foxsen?"

"I doubt it."

"Why?"

"Because of a little bomb he dropped during our conversation."

"What ?"

"No comment until we check it out."

The conversation was over. Ed gently reminded Harrigan that he'd

7

Prima Gallery occupied trophy real estate on the corner of Stockton and Maiden Lane across from Union Square. The gallery catered to the well-heeled locals who passed it on their way from Tiffany to Neiman-Marcus and to tourists staying at the St. Francis, Campton Place, the Hyatt Union Square, or any of the dozen four-star hotels within a five-block radius. Prima featured contemporary artists familiar to the *ArtNews* crowd, with prices starting at $20,000. But the gallery's hooded sweatshirt was just $59.95, and as Foxsen became well-known, the multitudes who couldn't afford the art he peddled snapped up the shirts. The real action at Prima took place not in the ground-floor gallery, but on the second floor, where Foxsen negotiated deals for museums and a select group of private collectors around the world.

Ed walked the half-dozen blocks from the *Foghorn* to Prima. He slung his sport jacket over his shoulder, it being mid-day, the three-hour window of warmth between the cool foggy morning, and the cold, blustery late afternoon. He stayed on the south side of Market to skirt the Powell Street cable car turnaround with its crush of street artists, musicians, mimes, beggars, and Bible-thumpers all working the tourists waiting to ride half-way to the stars. There was a line out the door at the Giants store as fans snapped up tickets for the rest of the season, now that the home team was looking serious about taking the NL West … please, God. Ed turned up Stockton and saw the TV satellite vans circled around Prima like a wagon train under Indian attack. Only in this case, it was the reporters doing the attacking. Ed sighed. Here we go: Wolfpack journalism out to corner Larry Foxsen. Ed dodged a bike messenger and a green-haired skateboarder, then joined the gang of reporters loitering around the gallery's front door.

Ed nodded to those he recognized, scribblers from the *Ex*, the *Merc*, the *Times*, and the wires, as a giant sequoia of a doorman/security guard insisted politely but firmly that the group stand back to allow patrons to pass. Ed counted six TV vans—parked in yellow and red zones, up on the sidewalk, and blocking a lane of Stockton. Whatever happened, the TV dweebs would have it first. If Foxsen were smart, he'd wait to release his statement until after 6 p.m. so it couldn't get on the air until 10 or 11, when the audience is small. But when you look out your window and see a lynch mob, the impulse is to spill asap just to make the damn TV vans go away.

Preening in the side mirror of the Channel 5 van was Our Lady of the Major Scoop, Kim Nakagawa. And standing dangerously close to her was Tim Huang. Tim noticed Ed and sauntered over.

"Foxsen's supposed to release a statement any minute," Tim explained breathlessly, "but his security guy has been saying that since we got here an hour ago."

"We?" Ed raised an eyebrow. "Who's we?"

Tim grabbed him by the elbow and steered him toward the Channel 5 van. "There's someone I'd like you to meet."

"Let me guess—Kim Nakagawa. I didn't know you two were such friends."

Tim blushed. "We're not—I mean we—met this morning at Murtinson's."

"She's a decent reporter," Ed had to admit. "Very ambitious from what I hear."

"She's also a green belt at Lou Jung's Tae Kwon Do on Balboa."

"Do tell. When you spar, good luck on the take-down."

Tim shot Ed a look, then made the introductions. Kim held out a dainty hand. Ed shook it. Her nails were perfect, painted bright red. She'd changed. Now she was wearing a pale blue knit suit over a navy blouse with a blue and white silk scarf. The effect was 90 percent business and 10 percent sexy, more business than most young TV gals. Kim had a naturally pretty face. She wore very little makeup, just a little eyeliner and rich red lipstick that matched her nails. "Well, Ed Rosenberg. Finally we meet. I've been reading your stuff for years in the *Horn* and the *Defender*."

"And I've been viewing yours these past few months. Quite a scoop this morning about the Picasso." Ed tried hard not to sound bitter.

"She had a Deep Throat," Tim explained admiringly. Kim smiled at him.

"Yes," Ed replied, fighting—and failing—to keep the sarcasm down, "her news director's secretary, as I understand." Kim frowned, taken aback. "Hey, no problem," Ed retorted brightly, working at coming off as something other than an ass. "You get your sources where you find them. But if I were you, Kim, I'd steer clear of Harrigan for the next forty years or so. Your report put him in a mood that makes the eruption of Mt. St. Helens look like a pimple popping."

"You're telling me. He screamed bloody murder at my G.M. Some nonsense about a trap. But what was I supposed to do? *Not* go with a great story that falls into my lap?"

Ed looked across Stockton to the winos passing a bottle on the grass of Union Square. That's what I did, he mused, recalling his deal with Harrigan and the negotiations with the *Foghorn* brass. Now he felt like a chump.

"I'd just give Harrigan a wide berth." An expression of pain spread across Kim's round face as Ed's words sank in. She was *persona non grata* with the detective in charge of the biggest story she'd landed since she hit town. Not an enviable position.

Tim noticed that his damsel was in distress. "The hell with Harrigan," he reassured her, cupping a hand tenderly under her elbow. "It'll blow over."

"If it's any consolation," Ed added, "Harrigan hates all reporters. Always has."

Just then, a stunningly beautiful blonde in cream-colored cashmere and major heels strode out of Prima Gallery and handed flyers to the assembled media. She introduced herself as Mr. Foxsen's public relations representative and said in no uncertain terms that the statement contained all the information Mr. Foxsen had to say. There would be no interviews, no Q&A.

Ed scanned the leaflet. Lawrence A. Foxsen was profoundly saddened by the loss of his old and dear friend, Gregory Murtinson. He deplored the murder, prayed for the quick capture of the animal responsible, and swore on his mother's grave that he had no involvement whatsoever in the heinous crime. Surprise, surprise. Ed thought: A six-block hike for this?

He flipped to page two, where Foxsen recounted that Murtinson invited him over to discuss expanding the famed Gilchrist Coin Collection, recently donated to the California Museum. And blah, blah, blah. He'd been the soul of cooperation with the police, voluntarily submitting to a polygraph test, which showed he was telling the truth, and a nitrate test for gunpowder residue on his hands, which came back negative.

Everyone began yelling questions at the PR flack. But she turned a very firm tail and ducked back inside the gallery, safely away from the clamor of her interrogators who were prevented from following by the guard.

Kim hustled across the street to set up in Union Square with Prima in the background.

"A nitrate test is bullshit," Ed said to Tim. "You wear latex gloves and your hands stay clean."

"What do you make of the polygraph?" Tim asked.

Ed shrugged. "Guys who hustle rich fucks into buying ridiculously overpriced art have to get pretty good at making lies sound like the truth." He enjoyed playing the veteran reporter around Tim.

"Why don't you like Kim?" Tim demanded, half-disappointed, half-incensed.

Ed's impulse was to deny any antipathy, but one look at Tim's furrowed brow persuaded him he wouldn't buy it. "Is it that obvious?"

"Yes."

Ed sighed. "Number one: She's TV. Which leads to number two: She's overpaid. Number three: She's too damn good-looking. Number four: She scooped me on the Picasso. I had that story—"

"How?"

"Right out of the housekeeper's mouth while Harrigan was feeding the rest of you BS. And number five: She has heartbreaker written all over her."

"Meaning what, exactly?" Ed noticed that Tim had assumed a readiness stance. Tim could feed him his teeth in a millisecond with one explosive punch.

"Meaning, *old friend,* that I'm concerned about you. I don't want to see you hurt."

Tim glanced from Ed to Kim doing her stand-up across the street. "I'm not a kid anymore. I can take care of myself." With that, he pivoted, dodged the traffic on Stockton, and headed for Kim. Ed noticed that his movements lacked their usual grace.

8

Pack journalism always gave Ed a headache, and this one was aggravated by the fact that Tim appeared to be cruising for a romantic bruising. Back at the paper, he tossed down two aspirin with a swig of coffee, burning his tongue. He reacted with an epithet unsuitable for a family newspaper, then punched up the Foghorn's electronic Archive. The Archive was one of the features Ruffen and the other bigwigs had insisted be built into the clunky, ridiculously temperamental Editorial computer system the paper had installed a few years earlier when the *Horn* finally jettisoned typewriters. At the touch of a few keys, you could retrieve anything the paper had run for the last decade by subject, by-line, date, proper names, or other keywords—at least in theory. In practice, the Archive was about as reliable as the paper's horoscopes. Computer guys were forever tinkering with it, usually with little success.

Ed typed two names—Gregory Murtinson and Lawrence Foxsen—along with the AND function to limit the search to pieces that mentioned them both. Then he waited, sipping coffee and praying to the mischievous gremlins inside the system that his screen would not mock him with the all-too-familiar Unable to Proceed. It didn't. Instead, a long list of entries popped up, mostly from the Society column: Murtinson and Foxsen at the Opera Gala this year, last year, the year before. Foxsen landing major acquisitions for the California Museum. Murtinson and Foxsen at the Black and White Ball, at the Getty's Christmas party, at the Mayor's Salute-to-the-Arts Extravaganza. And on and on. Ed pulled up the stories. Nothing juicy, just lists of local notables including our two boys. And no photos, just text. It occurred to Ed that if his hunch panned out, he was more likely to hit paydirt in photos.

Ed downed the last of his coffee and headed for the elevator. He pressed B2, the sub-basement, the eerie netherworld that housed the *Foghorn* Morgue. Since the computer Archive went in, few reporters ventured down to the land of yellowed clippings and microfilm anymore, but Ed loved the Morgue. It appealed to the historian in him. Quiet and peaceful, it exuded the sensual fragrance of forgotten information waiting to be unearthed and imbued with meaning.

The elevator door opened and Ed heard classical music. He bellied up to the counter. It was covered with potted plants, which flourished under the fluorescent lights and the loving care of Claire DeLange, officially the *Foghorn* librarian but affectionately known as Mistress of the Morgue. Claire was an odd woman. Ever since automatic archiving had arrived, she had little to do. But she never seemed bored, and always appeared cheerful—probably because her job was union-protected. Claire had to be pushing 60, but she always wore low-cut tops that showed a good deal of cleavage. She was single and a major flirt. Over the years, she'd attracted a good deal of attention from horny *Horn*-men, but she'd never, to the best of anyone's knowledge, dated anyone on the paper. She brought a different man to the Christmas party every year, always introduced him as her "fiancé," but never married any of them. Claire was watering a tall dracaena that just about hit the ceiling. "And what can a lonely girl do for a handsome reporter today, Ed?" She stashed the watering can under the counter, turned down her radio, and leaned over the counter, providing Ed with a good look into the Grand Canyon.

"I'm not sure, Claire. But I've got a hunch and it won't leave me alone."

"Try me. As you can see," she gestured behind her down endless rows of moldering clip files, "I'm not busy."

"It's about the murder of Gregory Murtinson."

"Yes, terrible. It's all over the radio."

"Well, there's a chance, a slim chance, but a chance that the motive was revenge for stealing a lover, a gay lover."

"Really? Any candidates for the one who got jilted?"

"Just one so far—Lawrence Foxsen, the art gallery guy."

Claire let out a high-pitched whistle. "Seamy, isn't it?"

"So, here's the deal: I pulled up five years worth of stories that mention Murtinson and Foxsen, and came up with nothing. I'm wondering if there are any photos of the two of them at society functions—"

"With the boy toy who came between them."

"Exactly."

Claire shook her head. "You're looking for a needle in a haystack."

"I know."

"I'll give it a go, see what I can dig up in the microfilm."

Ed thanked her and left. As the elevator door closed, Claire smiled, waved, and turned up the music.

Back in the newsroom, Ed strode past his cube into the Business section to the cube occupied by Lionel Atkins, the black, gray-bearded, discreetly gay reporter who covered San Francisco's largest industry, tourism. Atkins was around 55, a quiet hard-working man, with a stocky build and round belly. He resembled those statues of the laughing Buddha. Atkins was wearing what reporters called the press-conference uniform: gray slacks, blue shirt, sport jacket, and forgettable tie. Only Atkins' tie wasn't forgettable. It was an arty mosaic of playing cards. Ed dimly recalled that he competed in bridge tournaments.

"Lionel, excuse me. I've got a problem. I hope you can help me."

Atkins swiveled around from his screen to face him. "Yes?" He had a rich baritone that belonged on the radio, Ed thought, not in this hell-hole.

Ed hesitated. He didn't know Atkins well. "I'm wondering how familiar you are with the local gay press."

"Familiar enough." Atkins raised an eyebrow as if to ask: Thinking of running a personal?

"I'm covering the murder of Gregory Murtinson. It's possible he was killed for muscling in on the wrong man's lover. I'm wondering if any of the gay papers cover things like society gossip—who's sleeping with who."

Atkins leaned back, kicked his feet up on his desk, and crossed them at the ankles. He was wearing gleaming white Nikes. *"Out and About.* It fawns all over the galleries and museums, and the rich gays involved in them. I think I have this week's here … somewhere." His feet returned to the floor. He rummaged around his desk, then in his trash can, where he found a modest tabloid. He handed it to Ed, who thumbed through it.

"It's half obits."

"No kidding. AIDS has raised the obit to an art form. The arts community has been particularly hard hit."

"Yeah, I've read our coverage … Do you know anyone over there?"

"Gary Hanover is the features editor. We work out at the same gym. Nice guy. But you're barking up the wrong tree."

"Excuse me?"

"I seriously doubt that Murtinson was killed over a gay love triangle."

"Why?"

"Because jealousy murders are a hetero thing—men fighting over the possession of women. Gay relationships are about pleasure, not ownership. There's less jealousy, more acceptance of moving on."

"But what about the slave auctions at the leather bars? Aren't they about ownership?"

"Hardly. That's theater." The word rolled off his tongue in three distinct syllables: the-ah-ter.

"You may be right. But at this point, lover's revenge is my best angle."

The *Out and About* office was located in the heart of the Castro at Market and Noe in a converted flat above a crafts store celebrated or vilified, depending on one's point of view, for its name, Hand Jobs. Ed climbed the stairs and found the receptionist, a skinny boy in a tight lavender T-shirt, maybe twenty, quietly weeping at his desk. An older man emerged from an office that had been the parlor before the flat was converted, and tapped him lightly on the shoulder: "Why don't you take five in the C.R." The receptionist hurried away, clutching a tissue to his nose. Ed caught a whiff of his cologne. The older man wore faded black jeans and a maroon turtleneck. He looked gravely at Ed, who introduced himself, mentioned Lionel Atkins, and asked for Gary Hanover.

"That's me," the man said. He was shorter than Ed, with a round face that recalled Winston Churchill and small wire-rimmed glasses, the kind John Lennon wore on a few Beatles album covers.

"What's the 'C.R.'?" Ed asked.

Hanover sighed. "Until about '83, it was the Conference Room. Then, with so many people dying, it became the Crying Room. It has photographs of staff members we've lost to the Plague. We're up to seventeen now—make that eighteen, with Brent—Brent Early, our restaurant critic. Fortunately, his was an easy passing. He entered a coma over the weekend and died yesterday. David just cleaned out his desk, and became … emotional."

Ed offered condolences, then stated his business.

Hanover stepped down the long hall and beckoned Ed to follow him through the kitchen and into the pantry behind it that served as the *Out and About* archive. "I've interviewed Murtinson and Foxsen a few times over the years, but I don't know them personally. And I know nothing of their love lives. From his reputation, I'm surprised Murtinson even had one. But we might have a few pictures." He swept a hand around the stacks of old issues. "Have at it," Hanover said, then disappeared.

It was a small room that exuded the musty aroma of ink and old newsprint. It overlooked the back patio of Hunx, a popular Castro bar that was beginning to fill up with the afternoon crowd, all men.

Ed pulled out the last year's worth of weekly issues, 50 in all, and heaved the heavy load onto the kitchen table. He helped himself to a cup of coffee, was impressed by the half-and-half in the refrigerator, then sat down and delved. The task was only half as tedious as he imagined, because he could skip the half of each issue devoted to obits.

Ninety minutes later, Hunx's patio was packed and the music, a post-disco dance mix, pounded like a pile-driver. Ed was glad he didn't live next door. He found a half-dozen photographs of Murtinson and Foxsen. Most were shots of each one individually, usually holding champagne glasses at various parties. But two showed them together—and in the company of a third man, a square-jawed Aryan blond identified in captions as Kurt Willem, a jewelry designer and owner of Gems, a boutique on upper Polk Street. In one photograph, taken several months earlier, Foxsen's arm encircled Willem's waist, and Willem's draped intimately around Foxsen's shoulder. Willem's fingers were adorned with gaudy rings, no doubt some of his creations. Both men smiled broadly. Murtinson stood off a ways next to Foxsen looking rather stiff and dour. In the other photo, taken just a few months earlier, the threesome appeared again, this time with Willem between Murtinson and Foxsen, their arms around each other's waists. Murtinson and Willem were smiling, but Foxsen looked rather glum … or did he? It was hard to tell. Had Foxsen and Willem had a thing? Had Murtinson come between them? Possibly, but two grainy photos were not enough for a story. Ed ripped the pages and headed back downtown, convinced he'd wasted his time.

Back in his cube, he had a message from the Morgue. Ed found Claire engrossed in filing her nails. "I may have something for you," she said, reaching into a manila folder and producing a printout from microfilm. It was a photograph from the *Foghorn's* Society page taken at the opening of a California Museum show devoted to Impressionist seascapes. According to the story, Foxsen helped Murtinson create the show by borrowing 30 stellar paintings from museums and private collections around the world. The party had taken place a few weeks earlier. The photograph was your typical Society shot—Murtinson and Foxsen side by side both holding champagne glasses. Murtinson was smiling broadly. Foxsen was frowning and looked put out, which struck Ed as odd since he'd played such a central role in assembling the show.

But Ed knew that even people who are delighted can be caught by the camera frowning, scowling, or worse. The supermarket tabloids published celebrity shots like that every week. The photo was a dead end. Claire saw it in his face. "Sorry," she shrugged. "I tried."

Ed thanked her profusely for her efforts.

"You want the picture? Or should I trash it?"

Disgusted with the afternoon's wild-goose chase, Ed was about to tell her to throw it away when the historian in him bubbled up. No document, however trivial it appeared, was insignificant. "I'll take it. Thanks."

Claire slid it across the counter. That's when Ed saw the detail he'd initially missed. There was an arm around Murtinson's shoulder, but its owner had been cropped out. Only the hand remained. It snaked cozily around Murtinson's neck, and was festooned with several large rings. Willem's hand. Maybe that explained Murtinson's grin and Foxsen's scowl.

And Murtinson's death.

● ● ●

"I'm sorry to bother you, sir." Ed was back up in Gilville in the buttery leather chair facing his silver-haired publisher.

"No bother at all if it helps find Gregory's killer. What have you got?"

Ed recounted Foxsen's predictable statement deploring the murder and his vehement denial of any involvement. He also reminded Gilchrist of his suggestion to "follow the condoms," then showed him the three photographs charting what looked like Willem's transformation from Foxsen's boy toy into Murtinson's.

Gilchrist frowned. "Not exactly what I'd call a smoking gun."

"I agree. But the photographs suggest a fit with your theory. Foxsen wouldn't appear this morning. A PR flack handed out his statement. As far as I know, except for his interview with the police, he's been barricaded in his office all day and won't take any calls. You mentioned that you'd done business with him, that he'd helped you buy the Reilly. I was wondering if you'd—"

"—do your legwork for you." Gilchrist smiled, amused.

Ed sighed, and spread his palms. "I'm out of options."

"I understand. And I must say I'm impressed. I said, 'Follow the condoms' off-handedly. You ran with it, and came up with something … intriguing. I intend to commend you to your editor. Of course, I'll call Larry." He reached for his telephone console and pressed a single button. "His private line, reserved for his best clients."

On the second ring, a voice came on the speakerphone, "Foxsen."

"Larry. Worth Gilchrist. I gather you haven't had a good day."

"Now there's an understatement." Foxsen emitted a feeble chuckle. "The police were *all over* me this morning, and I had more reporters out front than you have on your payroll. No offense, Worth, but I *hate* reporters. They're—" he fished for the right word—"*vermin*."

"This may surprise you," Gilchrist said soothingly, "but I know how you feel. When Chet had his … troubles, I, too, felt besieged."

"I remember." Suddenly, Foxsen's tone changed. The shift was subtle, but discernible. Ed couldn't quite put his finger on it, but the words "I remember" held a hint of something. … Foreboding?

"Listen, Larry," Gilchrist said brightly, "the reason I called was to ask if you plan to attend the ceremony this evening."

"That depends." Again the odd tone.

"May I ask on what?"

"On what Detective Harrigan tells the vermin at his 5:15 press conference."

Ed glanced at his watch. Thirty minutes.

"Well, I, for one, hope you attend. In my remarks, I'm going to thank you for helping me assemble the collection, especially the Reilly. I'm also going to say that I've known you for more than twenty years and I'm certain you had nothing whatever to do with Gregory's death."

"Thank you, Worth. We go a long way back, you and I … which is how I know that this isn't just a social call. You want me to talk to a reporter, don't you?"

Gilchrist laughed. "I've always said you're shrewd."

"Look, Worth" … That ominous tone again. "There are things you don't know …"

"That's precisely why I called. My reporter, Edward Rosenberg, is here on the speakerphone—"

"No, I mean there are things you may not *want* to know."

"Nonsense, Larry. I want to know everything that helps bring

Gregory's killer to justice." Gilchrist nodded to Ed, who leaned toward the telephone console.

"Mr. Foxsen, Ed Rosenberg here. Thank you for speaking with me. I'll try to keep it brief."

"Good."

"What were you doing at Murtinson's last night?"

"Discussing how to round out the Gilchrist Coin Collection."

"But I thought it was the greatest."

"Oh, it is. It's unsurpassed. Personally, I didn't think it needed up-grading. But that's the kind of person Gregory is—*was*. He didn't want to give Worth or me the satisfaction of accepting it as we assembled it. He always had to find fault, and then fix it."

Gilchrist frowned and nodded.

"So what did he want you to do?"

"He asked me to locate museum-quality specimens of some fairly common pieces: Indian-head cents, Buffalo nickels, Mercury dimes, that sort of thing."

"And did you?"

"More or less. A collector in New Hampshire had most of what Gregory wanted, but he wanted more money than Gregory had authorized me to spend. I went out to Seacliff to show him the grading reports and urge him to go a little higher."

"Why higher?"

"Because in the long run, it's cheaper to buy substantial collections, even if they contain pieces you don't need, than it is to go fishing for a few pieces here and there. Just ask Worth. That's how we assembled his collection."

"What did Murtinson say?"

"He authorized me to up our bid by up to 20 percent."

"But why go all the way out to Seacliff? Couldn't you have spoken by phone? Faxed him the reports?"

Foxsen laughed. "You don't—*didn't*—know Gregory. When he whistled, he wanted his dogs to heel."

"Who do you think killed him?"

"I haven't the foggiest. But I assume you've discovered that he never won any popularity contests."

"Possibly someone he blackballed from membership at the Golden State Club?"

"Possibly. Who knows?"

"Isn't it true that you were rejected three times, most recently a few months—"

"What are you saying? That I'd kill one of my most important clients to get into a club I never wanted to join in the first place? Ridiculous."

"You 'never wanted to join in the first place'?"

"That's right. Other clients kept sponsoring me. Is Worth still on the line? He sponsored me once."

"That's right," Gilchrist chimed in. "I'd forgotten. I did."

"I knew Gregory would veto me. I was concerned that my repeated nominations—I think there were three or four—would irritate him to the point where he might take his business to some of my competitors. The world of museum-quality art acquisitions is a small one. I didn't want to antagonize Gregory."

"Does the name Kurt Willem mean anything to you?"

"Yes, he's a jewelry designer. A good one."

Ed took a deep breath. "I have reason to believe that you were lovers, and that he left you for Murtinson."

"*What*!?" His voice took the elevator up three floors. "Kurt leave *me* for *Gregory*? Please." He pronounced the word the gay way, in two syllables: puh-lease. "I threw that skinny bitch out of bed and he wound up in Gregory's for a night or two. He's cute, and his jewelry is lovely, but neither of us wanted him. Ask him yourself. You want his number?"

"I have it." If Foxsen wasn't telling the truth, he was a damn good liar. "Is that all?" he demanded impatiently.

"Just one more question. Earlier, you said you'd attend the ceremony tonight if Harrigan says something at his press conference. What?"

There was silence on the line for a long moment, then Foxsen replied, "That I'm not a suspect."

Ed detected the odd tone again. Years of interviewing told him Foxsen knew more than he was letting on. "Anything else?"

"Go and find out."

"He'll be there," Gilchrist interjected, "but I won't. If you know any more, Larry, I'd appreciate hearing it."

"Worth," Foxsen's tone was now plaintive. "I'd rather not."

Ed recalled Harrigan's lunch-time comment that he was checking out "a bomb Foxsen dropped." He put that together with the art dealer's ominous tone, and didn't like the result.

"Whatever it is, Larry," Gilchrist coaxed, "the cat will be out of the bag in twenty-five minutes. Tell me. You know how close Gregory was to Margaret and Chet."

Foxsen sighed. "I left around nine. As I pulled away, someone else pulled up."

"Who?" Ed and Gilchrist said in unison.

"Chet."

Gilchrist inhaled sharply. "You don't say."

"I'm sorry, Worth."

"No need to apologize. I'm sure Chet has a perfectly reasonable explanation."

"I'm sure." Foxsen sounded dubious.

Gilchrist said good bye, clicked off the speakerphone, and spun his chair around to face the Old Mint, his back to Ed.

"I can't believe it," Ed said. "I spoke to Chet this morning. He was very shaken by the—" he couldn't bring himself to say *murder*. "—by what happened. He didn't say a thing about being at Murtinson's last night."

Gilchrist whirled around and hit a button on the intercom. "Business," the voice said. It was Marty Liu, the Business editor.

"Gilchrist here. Where's Chet?"

"Last I heard, with the police. They called around lunch time and asked him to stop by. Said they had a few questions about his relationship with Murtinson."

"Thank you."

"You don't think he—?" Ed ventured.

"Of course not," Gilchrist snapped. "But God knows what the media will think." Chet had a history, and it wouldn't take much dredging to cover him with mud.

Ed stood up. "Is there anything I can do?"

Gilchrist's eyes burned into Ed's. "Your job."

As Ed left the office, he heard Gilchrist order his secretary to contact his attorney and PR people immediately.

9

The room at the Hall of Justice was packed. Ed counted nine radio microphones clipped to the battered podium, seven photographers and six TV cameras, plus reporters from every paper from Monterey to Sacramento, along with the *L.A. Times,* the wires, *Time, Newsweek,* and *U.S. News,* and stringers from the *New York Times, Washington Post, People*—even the *National Enquirer.*

Ed nodded to a few fellow toilers in type and threaded his way to the far side where Tim was flipping through his notes, getting his details straight in case he lucked out and got to ask a question. But before Ed could catch his eye, he noticed Kim and her crew bull their way in the other door, the way TV people do, as if they owned the place. Kim scanned the multitude, spied Tim, and pushed straight through the crowd toward him. By the time he looked up, she was standing beside him. They smiled greetings that were more than collegial. How much more Ed couldn't tell. They'd met just that morning, but they were both young and attractive, and there weren't that many Asians in the media. Something seemed to be happening. Ed wondered if he'd made an ass of himself warning Tim about her. Probably. But as he sidled up to them, Tim greeted him cordially and didn't seem irritated. Kim smiled at him, then conferred with her producer while freshening her makeup peering into a mirrored compact.

Harrigan called the conference for 5:15, knowing the TV crews would send live feeds to the various five o'clock news broadcasts, then replay them at six, ten, and eleven. Kim's job was an intro that was already in the can and a wrap-up afterward. But during the spectacle, she would, no doubt, hang back and let the print and radio guys duke it out to ask the questions. Print and radio are hot media that love a brawl. TV is cool. TV reporters learn quickly never to get excited and absolutely never to *look* excited. On TV news, overeagerness comes across as unprofessional. Better to appear above the fray—with perfect makeup.

Harrigan stepped to the podium looking weary. His posture sagged. His suit needed pressing. He donned reading glasses, extracted some notes from his jacket pocket, flattened them before him, and adjusted the mike. A hush fell over the crowd. "Ladies and gentlemen." He cleared his throat. The photographers started shooting, their clicking punctuating his words. "This afternoon I would like to announce some developments in the continuing investigation into the murder of Gregory Murtinson."

Ed braced himself. When Harrigan revealed that a visitor had arrived at Murtinson's just as Lawrence Foxsen was pulling away, everyone held their breath. Mention of the name Chester Worthington Gilchrist IV triggered gasps so loud it was as though the air had been sucked from the room. The TV cameras zoomed in on Harrigan. The photogs twirled lenses for close-ups. The radio guys strained to shove their mikes closer. And everyone began yelling at once:

"What was he doing there?"

"Did he kill Murtinson?"

"Is he under arrest?"

And on and on.

Harrigan held up a hand and waited. For a guy who despised the press, he was quite skilled at working a roomful of reporters. At times like this, his years of media attention as a football star came in handy. Harrigan kept his hand up, staring down the jackals before him. He set his jaw, frowned, and looked down at his notes. His body language made it clear that he would not say another word until the room quieted down. Eventually, it did.

Harrigan ran down the details: After Mr. Foxsen placed Mr. Gilchrist at the scene, the police asked him to come in for an informal interview, which Mr. Gilchrist did voluntarily and without legal counsel. He said he'd stopped by Murtinson's to pay his respects because Murtinson was a long-time family friend. Mr. Gilchrist has known Murtinson all his life and called him Uncle Greg. The two chatted briefly, and then, according to Mr. Gilchrist, he left around ten to meet his wife and a realtor at a building in Pacific Heights to see a condominium that was for sale. The realtor, Matthew Helmut, confirmed this, saying that he and Mr. Gilchrist and his wife, Laura, met the building manager, Renata Sanchez, at approximately 10:15. The manager corroborated their meeting time. Meanwhile, the coroner has established TOD—time of death—sometime between 10 p.m. and 1 a.m. Because Mr. Gilchrist was at Murtinson's home so close to the time of death, the police asked him to come in for formal questioning in the company of an attorney. The attorney, Joseph DeRoy, of DeRoy, Lewin, and Wong, advised Mr. Gilchrist not to answer any more questions and not to submit to a polygraph. He did, however, allow his client to take a nitrate test for gunpowder residue. It came back negative. The police have not arrested Mr. Gilchrist and do not consider him a suspect at this time, but have asked him to remain available for further questioning should it become necessary.

Harrigan looked up. For a moment, the room was silent. Then the yelling began.

"Why don't you consider him a suspect?"

"Do you *have* any suspects?"

"Why wouldn't he take a polygraph?"

"Isn't that suspect?"

Those not screaming questions were engaging in what members of the press call "analysis," but which was, in fact, jumping to conclusions:

"I smell a fix."

"The long arm of old man Gilchrist."

"The guy's a junkie, for Chrissake."

"Someone got to the realtor."

"This stinks to high heaven."

Ed suddenly felt hot and restless. Next to him, Tim was gesticulating wildly, trying to get Harrigan's attention, shouting: "Why'd he refuse the polygraph?" Next to him, Kim was scribbling on a pad, working up her wrap-up. Everyone else seemed to be jumping, waving, and shouting. Ed felt dizzy. The Old Man had been right. Without any real evidence, the Fourth Estate was pulling out the hammers and nails to crucify Chet.

Harrigan answered the questions as best he could. Mr. Gilchrist is not a suspect at this time because he has no motive we are aware of, and because three people confirm his whereabouts elsewhere at the estimated TOD. No, the department has not come under any pressure from Mr. Gilchrist's father, or from the chief, the mayor, or anyone else. Mr. Gilchrist did not explain his refusal to take the polygraph, but he is within his rights to refuse.

More shouting, more gesticulating. Ed had seen this sort of thing before. One minute, he was hanging with friendly wisecracking journalists who love a good joke: What's the difference between a reporter and a pizza? A pizza can feed a family. The next minute, the clown masks came off, revealing the black hoods of executioners. Ed had made the switch himself on several occasions. He gazed at people he knew around the room and didn't recognize them. They weren't journalists anymore. They were a lynch mob.

"What about motive?!" Ed was startled by the shrillness of his own voice. When he finished shouting the question, his throat felt raw.

Harrigan adjusted his glasses. "As far as we can determine, Mr. Gilchrist has no motive to kill Gregory Murtinson."

Ed scanned the room. Few pens moved. Motive-shmotive. The reporters' minds were already made up. Chet was with Murtinson close to the TOD. His wife would say anything to protect him. The realtor and condo guy could be bought off. And there was the heroin business, the feeling that junkies were capable of anything, and that ex-junkies—if he *was* an ex—weren't much different. Harrigan's dissembling didn't matter. A negative nitrate test didn't matter. Nothing mattered. The room felt uncomfortably close. Ed's skin turned clammy. All the reporters would file stories pointing the fat finger of accusation at Chet—Chet the drug addict, Chet the spoiled rich kid, Chet the long-time fugitive. This time around, no one would mention his Pulitzer, or the fact that he'd spoken to the police voluntarily, and hadn't run. When dawn broke, it would be String-Up-Chet-Gilchrist Day.

The press conference was over. Harrigan pocketed his glasses and notes and stepped down from the podium. Microphones clicked off. Lens caps snapped on. Notebooks flipped shut. Everyone began surging toward the exits.

Just then a petite black woman jumped up to the podium. Her hair fell around her shoulders in radiant bronze ringlets framing a comely cafe-au-lait face. Deftly, she turned on the PA system and leaned into the mike: "Ladies and gentlemen!" she boomed in a surprisingly big voice for such a compact frame. "My name is Julie Pearl, acting director of Public Affairs at the *Foghorn*. I'd like to present four people you need to hear right now." She gestured toward the back of the room, where two men and two women began working their way forward. "Chet Gilchrist, Laura Gilchrist, realtor Matthew Helmut, and building manager Renata Sanchez."

For a moment, the mob of reporters stopped dead, as if caught in the flash of a strobe light. The photographers were the first to break the spell. Several jumped up on chairs to shoot the procession as the four of them worked their way through the crowd. Next, the TV guys swung their cameras around to catch the parade. Radio mikes switched back on. Reporters' pads opened to clean pages. "Mr. Gilchrist would like to make a brief statement. Then the group will take questions."

The black woman stepped down and Chet bounded up to the podium. He appeared so suddenly, the room was stunned into silence. No one shouted questions. Chet stood tall. He surveyed the throng, and smiled. He looks relaxed, Ed thought, the smile looks genuine, even boyish. Innocent. Chet leaned into the microphone: "I hate to keep you from the Giants game. It's top of the second, and our guys are up one-nothing."

Dead silence. Nixon could have gotten more laughs during the last days of Watergate.

"Seriously," Chet pressed on, "I'm a reporter myself, so I know what at least some of you are thinking: Chet Gilchrist killed Gregory Murtinson. But I'm here to tell you that's ridiculous. Gregory Murtinson was like a father to me—" He choked up, wiped his eyes with his hand, fought to regain composure. "I would sooner kill myself than do anything to hurt the man I called Uncle Greg my whole life. He invited Laura and me for dinner last night, but things have been so crazy since we returned to San Francisco—since we returned *home*—that we couldn't make it. Instead I said I'd stop by later in the evening. I almost begged off, because finding an apartment has turned out to be more difficult than we anticipated. Prices here are outrageous." That elicited grudging chuckles. "But I wanted to see my Uncle Greg, shake his hand, hug him, hold him close." Another choke-up, longer this time, another struggle to speak. "I would do anything, *anything* to find his murderer."

"What about the polygraph?" someone down front shouted.

"If you've covered the police as I have, I'm sure you know that polygraphs are notoriously unreliable when people are fatigued or sleep deprived or under emotional stress. I've had a hell of a last few days: having the past forgiven, flying down from Alaska, hardly sleeping, starting a new job, and then …" He wiped his eyes, "… *this*. It just didn't seem like a good time to take a polygraph. My attorney advised me not to, so I didn't. But I'll gladly take the test in a few days when I'm rested and past the initial shock of Uncle Greg's … passing. Nitrate tests are not subject to emotional ups and downs. I took that test and my hands were clean."

"You were at Murtinson's very close to the time of death." Ed would recognize that whiny voice anywhere. It was the gal from the *Contra Costa Times*.

"As I understand, the coroner's estimate ranges from ten to one. Three hours is a long time when it takes only moments to shoot someone. There was plenty of time for the killer after I left." Chet actually appeared *comfortable* up there, loose, sympathetic.

"You could have sent a hired killer to Murtinson's." A wire guy.

"Anyone could have. Even *you*."

That got some laughs. Ed looked around the room. The lynch mob had loosened the noose. They almost believed him.

"Your family is very powerful," someone called. "How do we know you were actually at that condo by 10:10?"

"I *resent* your implication!" It was the realtor, Matthew Helmut, Chet's alibi. He jumped up to the podium and glared into the sea of upturned faces. "My integrity is *not* for sale." Long-necked and supercilious, with his nose and chin in the air, he reminded Ed of Eustace Tilly, the haughty emblem of the *New Yorker*. All he needed was the monocle and top hat. Helmut recounted his movements the previous evening in clipped prose, the appointment to meet Chet and Laura in front of the condo building at nine forty-five, Laura's arrival at ten, and Chet's about ten minutes later.

Ed didn't like the realtor, but he believed him. Unfortunately, snobs gall reporters. The guy was a schmuck, and the commission he stood to collect from the kind of apartment the heir to the *Foghorn* fortune would buy was enough to bend many people's memories a crucial half-hour or so. Out of the corner of his eye, Ed caught Tim shaking his head and whispering to Kim, "Bullshit." He gazed around the room. No one believed Helmut. That put Chet back on the gallows.

Then it was the condo manager's turn, Renata Sanchez. The PR gal gestured for her to step forward to make her statement, but she stood frozen against the wall. Sanchez was clearly no public speaker, especially in front of a hostile mob bristling with cameras, microphones, and imprecations. Sanchez was a plump, copper-skinned woman of about 45 who wore a white linen dress adorned with colorful woven trim in the

Central American style, the kind of outfit you see on labels of refried beans. The black woman gestured again for her to step forward. No dice. Finally, Ms. PR stepped off the riser, took Sanchez's hand and gently pulled her up to the podium, whispering encouragement in her ear. Sanchez looked down at the microphone, incapable of making eye contact with the room: "Last night, I—I was watching TV. My show came on at ten."

"What show?" someone called. It wasn't a request for information. It was heckling.

"*Star Trek.*"

Another reporter immediately retorted, "*Star Trek's* on at *nine* on *Wednesdays.*" Gotcha. The room had almost been swayed by Chet's heart-felt statement and tears, but then Helmut blew it, and now this bimbo had *Star Trek* on at the wrong time on the wrong night.

But the attack seemed to inject some steel into Sanchez's spine. "*New episodes* are on at nine on Wednesdays," she rejoined, "but *reruns* come on *every night* at *ten.*"

"She's right!" someone yelled from the back of the room. Sanchez smiled, vindicated. Could this woman lie? Ed didn't think so.

"Which episode?" the guy from the *Bee* shouted from in front of Ed.

Sanchez did not hesitate: "The one where Dr. Crusher falls in love with the Trill ambassador who has the worm-creature living in his belly."

"She's right!" one of the radio guys called out. "I saw it." A miracle: The assembled multitude was ready to believe her.

"I watch *Star Trek* every night," Sanchez continued, now looking up, more comfortable. "Mr. Helmut said he was bringing some people by at nine forty-five, so I set my VCR to tape it. But they didn't show up, so I sat down and began watching. About ten minutes into the show, they rang my bell. I hit the Record button so I could watch the rest after they left. Check my tape if you want."

The room believed her. The lynch mob loosened the noose.

Chet stepped back up to the podium. "Any more questions?"

"Any idea who killed Murtinson?" the man from the *L.A. Times* asked.

Chet hung his head and shook it sadly. "I can't imagine."

"He had a nasty reputation …" The *New York Times*.

"So does the mayor, the governor, *my father*, but no one's shooting them." That drew a hearty laugh.

"What's next for you?"

"Detective Harrigan has asked me to remain available and I told him

I would. I just *got here*, just started at the *Horn*. Laura and I are planning to attend the event at the California Museum tonight. My father is donating the Gilchrist Coin Collection. I'd urged him to do it for years, and I'm glad that I'm here to see it … even if—" He closed his eyes, then re-opened them. A tear tricked down his cheek, and he wiped it away. "—Uncle Greg isn't."

Everyone packed up for the second time. Ed looked around at his colleagues. Chet wasn't off the hook, but no one was sharpening knives to fillet him.

Ed turned to Tim. "Okay, here's the deal: I'll give you a juicy angle on this story if you do some legwork and tell me what you find."

Tim's eyes widened. "What angle?" Kim leaned in to hear.

"If Chet didn't do it, that leaves Foxsen. Suppose I were to tell you that Foxsen and Murtinson were vying for the affections of the same pretty boy, and that Murtinson won." He ran down the story of Kurt Willem, jewelry designer to the glitterati. "Foxsen's a lover scorned. That gives him something Chet doesn't have—a motive, a big, seamy, sexual motive."

Tim and Kim had the same reaction. Their jaws both dropped. "How'd you dig this up?"

Ed waved off the question. "Now here's what I need—what *we* need: A better fix on the TOD. If Murtinson got it around ten, Chet's on the hot seat. But if the time of death was, say, eleven or later, then Foxsen could have gone to his cockamamie meeting, and returned to Murtinson's and bang-bang."

"Or sent a hit man do it after Chet left."

"Right."

"I'm on it," Tim said with resolve.

"Good. When you find out, leave me a message at the *Horn*."

The knot of reporters around Chet and company was dispersing as Ed approached. The PR woman ushered her four charges out the door. Ed fell in beside Chet, who greeted him warmly.

Ed did not reciprocate. Instead, he hissed, "You stood in my cube this morning and didn't say a goddamn thing about being at Murtinson's last night. What was *that* about?"

Chet had a good four inches on Ed. He gazed down at his interrogator as an indulgent parent looks at a naughty child, then stepped aside, revealing the woman on his arm. "Ed Rosenberg, my wife, Laura. Ed was in the History program at Cal. Now he's an ace reporter at the *Horn*."

Laura Gilchrist extended a hand, and smiled. Did she hear what Ed just said to her husband? Her smile was on the cool side, but seemed genuine. It crinkled the corners of her sky-blue eyes. "You probably don't remember me," she said. "We met at a few History Department functions way back when."

Ed took a deep breath as he shook her hand. It, too, was cool. "Of course I remember you, Laura. It's good to see you again. I hope Chet realizes how lucky he is to have a wife who put up with his little sojourn in the Klondike."

Laura chuckled. Ed remembered her as a handsome woman with angular, patrician features that might have looked severe except for the openness and warmth of her manner. She was still attractive, but a decade on the run had taken its toll. Crowsfeet radiated from the corners of her eyes, and frown lines framed her mouth. Blondes rarely age well.

"I know I'm a lucky man," Chet chimed in, slipping an arm around his wife's thin waist. "I never would have survived without Laura."

"Weren't you in medical school?"

"Excellent memory, Ed. UCSF. I was in my third year when we…" She left the sentence unfinished.

They descended the stairs, skirted the metal detectors at the security station in the lobby, and emerged on Bryant Street. The late-afternoon sun was dipping into the cloud bank piled up against Twin Peaks. Around them, trees swayed in a chill wind. Trash blew around their ankles.

"Think you might go back? Get the M.D.?"

Laura gazed down Bryant to the construction cranes looming over the South of Market. "I don't know. All this has happened so suddenly. I'd like to get settled, then see."

A black Lincoln limousine pulled up, and Sanchez, Helmut, and Laura piled in. Chet turned to Ed: "I'm sorry about this morning. I was in shock. Still am. I was afraid I'd be seen as a suspect—which I was. Still am."

"That's why you should have said something. Maybe I could have helped. We're friends, aren't we?"

Chet looked Ed in the eye, took his measure. "We're *old* friends, Ed. I don't know *what* we are now. I'd like to be friends, really I would, but living underground has changed me. I'm not as good at friendship as I used to be." Then he smiled and touched Ed's arm. "But I'll try, okay? I didn't kill him. Tell me you believe me."

"I believe you. But God knows what the rest of them think."

"Reporters," Chet said wearily. "In a few days, I'll pass the polygraph. The cops'll catch the killer. This'll blow over."

"I hope you're right."

Chet placed a hand on Ed's shoulder. "You still going tonight?"

"I'm working it. And I'm psyched to see the Reilly."

"Then I'll see you there." Chet slid into the limo. The door closed with the solid thud of money, and the car disappeared into rush-hour traffic.

Ed turned and found himself face-to-face with the PR woman. Up close, her ringlet hair and milk-chocolate skin looked even more alluring. It had been so long since he'd … "That was quite a coup you pulled off in there, a PR tour de force. The whole room was lined up to burn Chet at the stake. Then you showed up and five minutes later, the Inquisition was blowing out its matches."

Julie Pearl looked up at him and blushed. "Why, thank you. It wasn't much really. Standard operating PR. In a volatile situation, you put your people out there, answer everyone's questions, show the world they have nothing to hide."

"You're too modest. Lots of PR people would have battened down the hatches. Stonewalled. Did you say you're the *acting* PR director? Where's the real one?"

"On maternity leave. We don't know when she'll be coming back. Or if."

"Well, if she doesn't, I'd say you're a lock for the job. By the way, I'm Ed Rosenberg, *Foghorn* cityside." He held out a hand. Julie took it.

"I know. I read your stuff. I like it."

"You do?" Ed was always surprised when people noticed his byline. "Well, thank you." Reporters pin their names on their work, but to the vast majority of readers, they remain utterly anonymous.

"Didn't you do that piece about the pool tournament where the Vietnamese kid blew everyone away?"

Ed smiled. "Yeah, Nine-Ball Tran. Really nice kid, and a helluva pool player."

"How'd you come up with it?"

"I play where he plays." He gestured up Bryant. "I've followed him over the years."

"I used to play every now and then with my father."

"Used to?"

"He died a few years ago."

"I'm sorry." Ed suddenly realized he wanted to learn more about her.

Like most journalists, Ed instinctively looked down on PR people, who were universally known as "flacks." But the emotion behind the condescension incorporated considerable self-loathing because every reporter also knew that a great deal of what the world calls "news" comes directly from press releases PR people write and media events they organize. If flacks were whores, so were the reporters who depended on them. But Julie was no flack, not after what she'd just pulled off. She was a magician.

"I've got to get back to the paper, rewrite my Murtinson lead for the fourth time today."

"I'm going there, too. Gotta tie up some loose ends, then get over to the Museum for the party."

"I'm walking," Ed said. "You have a car?"

"You kidding?" Julie replied. "You can walk it in less time than it takes to find parking."

Ed laughed. "Spoken like a true San Franciscan." He gestured grandly down Bryant toward Fifth. "Shall we?"

Julie smiled. "Let's."

10

Naturally, there was no legal parking anywhere around Civic Center, so Ed pulled up at a fire hydrant on Golden Gate at Gough. The afternoon wind had died down, which took some of the bite out of the evening. But it was still chilly and he felt underdressed in his assistant-professor outfit, wool slacks, an oxford shirt that had seen better days, a knit tie, and a blue blazer. He pulled the jacket tight around him and walked briskly toward Van Ness.

Tim's message had been waiting for him at the paper. Murtinson died sometime between ten p.m. and one a.m. Coroners always give themselves a three-hour window. The coroner wouldn't narrow it down any more.

That meant Chet was still a prime suspect. Ed felt vaguely ill. Who was Chet, anyway? A guy who happened to be in the wrong place at close to the wrong time? Or a killer? Ed's heart said the former. But his head was undecided.

Ed turned down Van Ness into Culture Gulch. Before him loomed the holy quintet: City Hall, the War Memorial Building, the Opera House, Davies Symphony Hall, and the California Museum. When Murtinson had the Museum building erected in 1962, he instructed the architect: Make it the grandest. And it was, the Palace of Versailles by way of the Fairmont Hotel.

In front of the Museum, TV crews were already setting up to shoot the evening-gown crowd soon to descend for the Big Donation. Money coming to mingle among rare coins. On the lawn, a technician was firing up two enormous searchlights. San Francisco was one of only a few cities in the country—New Orleans, Las Vegas—where nothing could post-pone a party, not even the host's murder.

Ed took the stairs two at a time, flashed his press card to a uniformed guard, mentioned the name "Vandenburn," and was directed through the Rotunda to the elevator just past the stone staircase that swept up to the Gold Rush Collection. On the fourth floor, he stepped into the Museum's administrative suite. It was surprisingly small and grubby, a dingy warren of cramped offices. It was after hours, but the place was abuzz with party preparations. Matronly docents in black skirts and white tops were darting this way and that under the direction of the Museum's administrative staff. Ed mentioned his appointment to a gray-haired woman with a dowager's hump and was pointed down a hall to an open door.

"Denise Vandenburn?"

"Ed Rosenberg? Come in. Sit down. Want some coffee? You'll have to forgive me. I'm not very prepared for this interview, between the insanity around this party—and Gregory ..." Her voice trailed off.

"I understand completely. I'm very sorry about your loss, the Museum's loss. Thank you for seeing me. I won't take much of your time."

Vandenburn was a thick woman with a man's short haircut and no makeup. She wore a mannish gray pinstriped suit cut to de-emphasize feminine curves. But hammered copper earrings, and a friendly manner softened her butch look. She cleared a stack of trade journals off a chair for Ed, who caught two titles: *Modern Museum* and *Exhibit Display*. "Maybe it's better that we're having the party. It's kept my mind off Gregory."

"As the assistant director, you must have worked closely with him."

She looked through her grimy window across Civic Center Plaza to the Main Library. "Close enough."

"What do you do, exactly?"

"I manage the Museum's day-to-day operations: plant, maintenance, security, warehousing, pretty much everything except personnel and curating—we have two other assistant directors for that—and what Gregory does—*did:* acquisitions, fund-raising, dealing with the Board."

"Sounds like you have a big job."

Her smile said: You don't know the half of it. Then her voice kicked in: "At most museums this size—the Metropolitan, the Smithsonian—I'd be an associate director, not an assistant, but Gregory would never give me, or the other two assistants, the title."

"Pardon me, but everyone I talk to says he was insufferable."

Vandenburn sighed and laced her fingers in her lap. "Gregory was difficult, but geniuses often are."

"Genius?"

"He built this Museum single-handedly from nothing into a world-class institution. He was obsessed, but it was a magnificent obsession."

"How did you two get along?"

Another sigh. "Quite well. Gregory was a bully. He enjoyed pushing people around. But scratch a bully and you find a scared little boy. You can't be bullied unless you *let yourself* be bullied. I never let him bully me, so we got along fine."

"How did you stop him?"

"When he acted like a jerk, I told him so, and I didn't hesitate to do it in public."

"You weren't concerned about getting fired?"

"Of course I was. I like this job. But I could make more money managing an office building downtown. There's a huge demand for good facilities managers and I've made a point of keeping in touch with the right people. Gregory could fire me, but he couldn't threaten me."

Ed flashed on Ruffen, the bully he had to deal with. He tried not to feel cowed, but sometimes … He admired Vandenburn's pluck.

"But," she continued, "I don't want to create the impression that our relationship was combative. We got along fine. I actually liked him. He saw abilities in me that I never imagined I had and encouraged me to develop them."

"Like what?"

"I started here as a janitor twelve years ago. You'd figure a man as busy—and snobby—as Gregory would never notice the janitors, but he noticed me and promoted me, first to Maintenance Manager, then to more responsibilities, and four years ago, to this." She swept a hand around the room. "Beneath Gregory's gruff shell was a good man … a surprisingly good man." She squeezed her eyes shut, fighting tears, then grabbed a tissue and blew her nose loudly, as a man would. "I'm sorry. It's been quite a day."

"No need to apologize. I assume you know Lawrence Foxsen, the—"

"Of course. Not well. He dealt mostly with Gregory and the curators. But he was over here a lot. We have a nodding acquaintance."

"What kind of relationship did he and Murtinson have?"

"The kind Gregory had with most people. Larry allowed himself to be bullied and Gregory was happy to oblige."

"What about recently? I understand that Foxsen lost a lover to Murtinson, Kurt Willem, the jewelry designer."

"I wouldn't know. Gregory and I travel—*traveled*—in very different social circles."

"Now that Murtinson is … gone, do you think the Museum will do more business with Foxsen? Or less? Or about the same amount?"

"Oh, more, I imagine. Much more."

"Why?"

"Because whoever the Board hires as the new director can't possibly have the kind of family and social connections Gregory had. So we'll get fewer bequests and donations and become more dependent on brokers like Larry."

More motive.

11

The Rotunda was so full of women in sequin-spangled gowns that the polished granite walls shimmered as though a mirrored disco ball hung from the ceiling. Most of the men wore tuxedos. In his shabby assistant-professor outfit, Ed was sorely underdressed, but didn't care. He'd been in similar situations at other silly functions. He was just a reporter doing his job, no more, no less. If the Old Man wanted him decked out like this crowd, he could pony up some bucks.

Everyone was packed together pretty tight. The smiles were broad, the booze flowed, air kisses abounded, and the noise largely drowned out the string quartet laboring in a corner. The Handgun Control Initiative would make a bundle on the affair, and with the media frenzy over Murtinson getting it with a handgun, the Initiative was bound to gain in the polls.

Ed jumped up on a stone bench and surveyed the crowd. Five hundred, maybe more. Looking down into the assemblage, he noticed the Mayor chatting with one of California's U.S. Senators and some other upper crusters he vaguely recognized from the *Foghorn's* Society page. A little farther off, the princely conductor of the San Francisco Symphony was enjoying an apparently very funny joke with the grande dame of the city's literary scene, a romance novelist who'd grown rich beyond belief churning out bodice rippers, and then, some years earlier, had turned serious, and released a string of critically acclaimed novels, at which point she became respectable in the eyes of the literati. By the bar, Ed spied Old Man Gilchrist with Irene, the anorexic socialite he'd married after Chet's mother passed away. Gilchrist was deep in conversation with Ian Cavanaugh, the Sebolt Distinguished Professor of California History at Berkeley and author of the definitive *Gold Rush Coins of California*.

Cavanaugh had aged, Ed realized sadly. He leaned on a cane. His diabetes must be getting worse. In a previous life, Cavanaugh had been Ed's graduate advisor and dissertation committee chair. Standing next to him was a tall thin man with graying hair and delicate features, none other than Lawrence Foxsen, who'd decided to attend after all.

Peppered around the Rotunda, in spotlighted kiosks flanked by discreetly armed guards, were some choice pieces from the Gilchrist Collection. The gown-and-tux crowd ooohed and aaahed, impressed by the pricelessness of the coins. But Ed knew he was one of only perhaps a half-dozen people in the room who had any real appreciation for the rarity, lore, and beauty of such gems as the 1804 proof silver dollar, or the uncirculated 1943 copper penny, or the 1887 five-dollar gold piece. The vast majority of the assembled guests were numismatically nowhere—except that every one of them knew the story behind the twenty-dollar gold piece in the center of the Rotunda. Surrounded by four guards, it stood on a pedestal encased in a thick clear plastic cube with sides ground into lenses so that the coin appeared to be the size of a dinner plate. It was, of course, one of the two known Reilly Double Eagles.

Ed jumped down and slowly wormed his way toward the Reilly. Actually, he felt pulled by the force of its bloody history and by the memory of his adolescent obsession with coin collecting. The reporter in him tried to remain blasé. Sure, it's storied and priceless, but bottom line, it's just a coin. However, the reporter was silenced by the ghost of the boy who'd spent so many summer days sifting through $50 bags of 5,000 pennies from Long Island Bank and Trust looking for minor rarities until his eyes burned—and occasionally finding some.

The Reilly was in a class by itself, the equivalent of a Gutenberg Bible, or a First Folio Shakespeare. Magnified as it was, the Liberty profile on the obverse shone like a movie-star in close-up, and the thirteen stars around the border sparkled more brilliantly than anything in the heavens. Elbowing his way around the cube, Ed felt himself become mesmerized by the tragically flawed reverse, the blurred eagle and shield, and the "SS" double-die mint mark. Where were the other 6,489 misstrikes? Whatever became of the villain of the piece, Ellis Bohman? Did he escape and melt down the gold, as the Treasury Department eventually concluded? Or were the coins still stashed somewhere waiting to be discovered? The lost gold had fired the imaginations of generations of Americans, yet the mystery endured.

"So there you are! I've been looking all over for you." Ed turned and found himself pressed so close to Julie Pearl that he was enveloped in her perfume. Cinnamon? She offered him a flute of champagne.

"I'd love to," he demurred, "but not while I'm working."

"No? Too bad. You should try PR," she laughed, tossing bronze ringlets over her shoulder. "Drinking on the job is required. And I'm doing my best." She took a sip.

Ed had work to do. If he spent time looking at anything, it should be the Reilly and the other coins in the kiosks. But he couldn't take his eyes off Julie. Her smile and white teeth rivaled any toothpaste commercial. Her delicate cheekbones were a work of art, and her sculpted shoulders, revealed by her gown, danced erotically as she moved. Her gown fit so perfectly, it looked like it had been made expressly for her. Its shimmering black fabric—silk?—looked as though it had been painted on her. Its silver-bordered top was cut low enough to reveal the alluring swell of her breasts, and silver piping meandered around the rest of it like a finger caressing a lover during afterglow. Ed felt even more shabby in his wrinkled tie and corduroy jacket.

"You look fabulous," he sputtered. "That dress is incredible."

"You really think so?" she replied, blushing and executing a curtsey as best she could while holding two champagne glasses in the mob gathered around the Reilly. "Glad you like it. I made it myself."

"You *made* it?" Ed was incredulous. Diane could barely sew a button. "Clearly, a woman of many talents."

Julie flashed him another celestial grin gone slightly cockeyed from the champagne. Then something snapped and suddenly she was all business. "You might be interested to know that the champagne was donated by Gilchrist Vineyards."

"Gilchrist has a vineyard?"

"Two actually, one in Napa, the other in Sonoma. You might want to mention that Gilchrist Vineyards donated all the champagne tonight to keep costs down so that the Initiative could net more."

"Uh, yeah, sure." He tried not to let her see his grimace. For a moment he thought she actually liked him. But no: She just cozied up to hustle him. PR people. There was no way Gilchrist Fucking Vineyards would get a mention.

Julie frowned, embarrassed. "Oh, Ed, I'm sorry. I didn't mean to pitch you on the vineyard angle. Forget it. I don't care. I just wanted to ... *talk* to you, and that was the first thing that spilled out of my mouth. Stupid of me." Their eyes met. Hers were the mile-deep brown of African-Americans, with a hint of something else Ed couldn't discern. Yearning? Maybe.

"Julie!" It was Gilchrist with his stick-figure wife in tow. They were pushing through the crowd.

"Uh-oh." She placed her hand lightly on his arm, leaned in close, and confided, "Duty calls. And here I am, half looped." Ed luxuriated in her fragrance, definitely cinnamon … with a hint of cocoa.

"Julie!" Gilchrist was within striking distance now. The crowd parted. "I thought you set up the CBS interview for afterward, but the producer wants to do it now. He won't leave me alone!"

"It's after. Don't worry. I'll handle it." She shot Gilchrist a sympathetic look, then turned back to Ed and rolled her big eyes. Then she was gone, swallowed by the crowd, leaving only the aroma of cinnamon.

Ed extricated himself from the crush around the Reilly and ran into a waiter, who held out a tray. "Duck breast on toast with goat cheese and caviar."

Ed took one. It was beyond delicious. He lunged for another, and gobbled it down. He couldn't remember the last time he'd had duck or caviar, let alone both in the same bite. Campbell's didn't put either one in soup.

"Ed!" A long arm waved at him. A break in the crowd revealed Chet and Laura. Chet was wearing a tuxedo just a tad short in the wrist. Laura was in an electric blue gown with a body-hugging spaghetti-strap bodice and a billowing skirt.

"I haven't worn a tux since I can't remember when," Chet confessed as he sidled up next to Ed. "I think they're illegal in Alaska—unless they're flannel." He laughed then turned serious. "Tell me you're not still pissed at me." Chet wrapped one arm around his wife's waist, and the other around Ed's shoulder. His expression said: Let's be friends.

I could use a friend, Ed thought, trying not to fasten on the fact that one day, this friend would morph into his boss, his obscenely rich boss. "No, I'm not pissed. I never really was. Sorry about my tone at the Hall. I was stressed out. You were in shock. It's been a really long day."

"No argument there," Chet retorted. "I was just telling Laura: I aspire to a boring life—nice, quiet, and boring. Boring is looking very good to me."

"How are you doing? Really?"

Chet closed his eyes momentarily, pursed his lips, and shook his head. "Like you said: I'm in shock. Nothing feels real. I'm floating somewhere between Anchorage and San Francisco. Coming back, I was so looking forward to spending time with Uncle Greg, and now ... I don't know. ... There were times today I couldn't even visualize his face. Then at other times, someone mentioned his name and I dissolved in tears."

"I'm sorry. It's awful what happened."

"Yeah," Chet sighed, then soldiered on. "My father and I had words about tonight. I thought it should have been postponed. He said he wanted to, but the Initiative people insisted on going ahead ... because of the way—" He closed his eyes to hold back tears. "Because it was a handgun."

"As a student of the impressionable electorate, I'd have to say they're right."

"True. But it still stinks."

"I agree." Ed was about to ask if Chet had checked out the Reilly when he exclaimed, "Oh my God, there's Bob Lurie. I've got to talk to him. Would you excuse me a sec, Ed?" Lurie owned the Giants. Chet disappeared into the crowd and Ed found himself hip-to-hip with Laura Gilchrist.

Her eyes followed her husband. She smiled weakly and shook her head. "Everyone says it was the Pulitzer and the pardon that brought us back," she said. "But if you really want to know, it was the Giants. He thinks they're going all the way."

"They just might," Ed replied. "Their magic number is down to thirteen. Their pitching is hot. And Clark and Mitchell keep knocking them out of the park."

"You a fan too?"

"This year—when they're winning."

"You know, it's funny," Laura mused, "Chet didn't miss much about San Francisco. I missed the city more. But he *really* missed the Giants, going to games, reading all about them in the *Horn* ..."

Laura's blonde hair was piled high on top of her head. Ed was generally not partial to blondes. He preferred Diane's coloring, a Mediterranean look, brown hair and olive skin ... or maybe something darker. But Laura appeared effortlessly attractive, the way rich women do. Of course, the jewelry helped. She wore sparkling diamond earrings that dangled halfway down to her shoulders and a matching double-strand diamond choker strung tight around the base of her long neck.

"And what did you miss?"

"Pardon?"

"What did you miss about San Francisco?"

She sighed and gazed off across the Rotunda. "Oh, I don't know, little things mostly: running my dog on Marina Green, browsing the poetry at City Lights, the chocolate fudge cake at Just Desserts, seeing the sunset behind the Golden Gate Bridge ... Oh, and the barbecued chicken burrito at La Cumbre—with whole beans, not refried."

Ed laughed. "La Cumbre! I go there all the time! It's just a few blocks from where I live."

"Before I met Chet, I lived at nineteenth and Valencia."

"I'm on Dolores Terrace."

She looked quizzical. "Where?"

"A little one-block cul-de-sac off Dolores by seventeenth. You could pass it a million times and not notice it, which is what everyone there loves about it."

"I used to go to La Cumbre two or three times a week," Laura sighed. "There isn't a decent burrito to be had in the entire state of Alaska. All they have is salmon, salmon, and more salmon."

"Hey, I love salmon." At the mere mention of the fish, Ed began to salivate.

"I did, too—until we moved up there. Now, I swear: If I never have another piece as long as I live, it'll be too soon."

She smiled, then looked away. An awkward moment passed.

"Look, Laura," Ed said, "I hope you don't think I'm a total jerk for leaning on Chet after the press conference this afternoon."

"No, I don't think you're a *total* jerk. Maybe 80 percent." Then she smiled. All was forgiven. "It's been a rough day for all of us. I understand you were all over the city chasing Gregory's story."

"Yeah. Quite a day." How did she know where he'd been? Old Man Gilchrist? Ed recalled the few times he'd socialized with Chet and Laura at Berkeley. He liked her. She never seemed cowed by Chet's family or money. She was always her own person.

"How are you holding up—with all the changes?"

She grimaced. "Not great, but I'll survive."

"Maybe the three of us could go to La Cumbre some night."

"I'd like that ..."

"I sense a 'but' about to rear its head."

"No, no 'but.' It's just that …"

"What?"

"Doing something like that, something carefree and fun, something *normal* still feels out of reach. Chet's had no peace. *We've* had no peace. Ten years of jumping every time the phone rang or a stranger knocked. Then, we're not back two days before he's a murder suspect! But instead of dealing with that, duty dictates that we spend our time fishing formal wear out of storage and getting it altered so we can attend a party that should have been postponed for months. Our lives are a cross between *Twilight Zone* and Salvador Dali." Her lower lip trembled. She clamped her eyes shut, fighting tears.

"You're right," Ed said gently. "Life's a bitch. But things will calm down. The dust will settle. You're home."

Laura dabbed her eyes with a tissue, inhaled deeply, and forced a smile. "I'm sorry. I shouldn't have … *let go* like that. My lack of breeding is showing. There are people starving in Eritrea. AIDS is ravaging the city. What am I complaining about?"

"Laura! Laura Summers! Is that you?" A voice called merrily from nearby. Ed vaguely remembered that Summers was her maiden name.

They turned and a stocky handsome man stood before them with a taller curvaceous woman on his arm. The man had a swarthy complexion and thick, wavy, black hair swept straight back. His tuxedo was burgundy. A statement? Or just bad taste? He reminded Ed of the guy who did the Cut-Rate Diamonds commercials on late-night cable. His companion was a strikingly beautiful, milk-skinned, young blonde, who looked Scandinavian. Her dress was semi-sheer, tight, and cut low. It revealed a lace bra that barely contained what it contained. The man held out his arms as if to embrace Laura. "Welcome home, kid. It's great to see you again."

But Laura shrank away from him, as a toddler might from a witch on Halloween. "Hello, Ted," she deadpanned.

Hearing the name, Ed placed him: Theodore Calderone, editor and publisher of *Full Disclosure*, San Francisco's answer to *Penthouse*, a slick monthly that combined gutsy investigative reporting with pricey toys for wealthy boys wrapped around extravagant photo spreads of naked women who displayed a fondness for bananas, champagne bottles, and garden hoses. Calderone was the enfant terrible of San Francisco publishing. He'd launched his magazine right out of Stanford when he didn't have two nickels to rub together, and in 10 years, had built it into a million-circulation money machine with major buzz from coast to coast.

Spurned by Laura, Calderone cozied up to his companion. "This is Charity Swenson, our upcoming Miss February. Laura's an old friend from Stanford, honey. Helped launch the magazine way back when. Big changes since then, huh? Would you believe I'm a major contributor to the Museum now?"

Laura made no reply. She just stared at Calderone. In her expression, Ed read disgust, and something else—hatred?

Undeterred, Calderone turned to Ed and held out his hand. "Ted Calderone, *Full Disclosure*."

They shook. "Ed Rosenberg, the *Foghorn*."

"Oh, yeah, I've read your stuff."

"And I've read your magazine."

"With one hand or two?" Calderone chortled at his joke and elbowed Charity Swenson, who giggled obligingly along with him. "Seriously, the articles are just as important to me as the photography. You know we've won three National Magazine Awards? I'm always looking for good writers with compelling stories to tell. You got one, call me."

"I'll keep it in mind. Thanks."

Ed glanced at Laura. Her face flushed red. She looked like a soup pot about to boil over. Then she did. She slapped Calderone hard across the face. "Asshole!"

Calderone stood there stunned, eyes wide with disbelief.

Laura wound up for another blow. Ed moved to grab her arm, but Chet got there first and pinned it against her side. "What the hell's going on?"

"Your bitch of a wife just slugged me, that's what." Calderone rubbed his cheek. "Fucking assault and battery. I should call my lawyer." His expression said: Woman or no, if we weren't here, I'd rip your lungs out.

"Since when have you ever obeyed the law?" Chet was spitting mad. He towered over Calderone and used his height the way tall men do, as a weapon.

Calderone stood his ground, puffed up his chest, a Napoleon. "Well, fuck you, Mr. Rich Kid."

"You tried that, but it didn't work. I'm back."

"Tried what? The fuck are you talking about?" Calderone looked genuinely perplexed.

"You know very well—"

"Bullshit." Calderone grabbed his date's elbow and maneuvered her away. "C'mon, Charry. Some people should get their prescriptions adjusted." A moment later they were swallowed by the crowd, but not before Calderone pointed a finger at Chet and spat, "And fuck your Pulitzer, too. Did Daddy buy it for you?"

The insult hung in the air as Chet and Laura turned to one another and embraced with the ferocity of two mud-covered survivors of a flash flood. Ed was thunderstruck. What was *that* about?

But before he could ask, the PA clicked on and some toady with the Handgun Initiative introduced the Mayor. Time to get to work. Ed fished out his notebook and pushed through the mob to a spot near the small stage. He hated covering speeches. You yawned your way through them to pick up one or two utterly predictable quotes. Oratory was a lost art. Most Americans simply changed the channel. But reporters inhabited a special circle of Hell that obligated them to listen and take notes and pretend that what they heard actually meant something. The Mayor, predictably, delivered a fawning eulogy of Murtinson—"the keystone of this city's cultural vitality"—pausing occasionally to dab his eyes with a hankie. Then he thanked Gilchrist for his "glittering donation," making special mention of the Reilly, "a civic monument as important as the Golden Gate Bridge," and wound up with a thunderous endorsement of the Handgun Control Initiative, which was greeted with equally thunderous applause.

Next came the Senator, who was the initiative's honorary chair. She followed in the Mayor's footsteps: a eulogy of Murtinson, acknowledgment of Gilchrist's gift, and a ringing endorsement of the initiative.

Then it was Gilchrist's turn. He spoke straight from a hypocritical heart, eulogizing Murtinson warmly as a lifelong friend, which Ed knew was bunk. He reiterated his morning comment about "giving something back," without mentioning the millions he stood to realize from the tax deduction he was taking on the Collection. And he concluded with another rousing endorsement of the initiative, urging its passage as a memorial to all handgun victims, especially Murtinson, without mentioning that his own son still had a few things to explain.

None of them gave Ed much to work with. He labored to extract two decent quotes per speaker. It was a struggle.

Afterward, there was more fashionable milling around to the strains of the string quartet. Ed drifted back to the Reilly, and imagined Bohman whipping the horses as he drove the wagon laden with SS misstrikes somewhere … but where?

"All I know about coins is how to spend them," said a familiar voice beside him. Julie. "Is it true you used to collect them?"

She looked even more radiant than she had earlier.

"Where'd you pick up that little tidbit?"

"Worth. Mr. Gilchrist."

His ice-breaker that morning. In front of Julie, Ed felt embarrassed about his old hobby. "At the risk of appearing to be a dweeb, yes, when I was thirteen and fourteen, I was a collector. Got into it going through the change from my paper route."

"You had a paper route?"

"*Newsday*—"

Julie's eyes widened. "You're from Long Island? I grew up in Westchester—Yonkers, but friends of the family lived in Long Beach. I spent a lot of time there."

"I'm from Malverne. As I recall, our basketball team used to cream theirs," Ed said mischievously.

"I wouldn't know," Julie retorted, elbowing him. "Franny and I mostly talked about boys."

"An endlessly fascinating subject, and one I know just a little about. Why don't we discuss it over lunch tomorrow?" Ed heard the words before realizing he'd said them. They just flew out, the way they do when you're writing a good story.

Julie glowed. "I'd love to." Then she frowned. "Oh, damn. Tomorrow I have a meeting until 1:00, then the Burlingame Women's Club at 2:30. How would you feel about a quickie at the Front Page, say, 1:15?"

Ed smiled. "Quickies can be fun."

Julie blushed. "I didn't mean—."

"Too bad."

A smile and a toss of ringlets. "1:15?"

"I'll be there." Her smile was a baited hook, and Ed was a hungry trout. "I'd love to chat some more, but I have to phone this in." He waved his notebook in the air. "Story of the century." He yawned extravagantly.

Julie tried to appear disapproving. This is my event. Give me good ink. But she couldn't pull it off. She laughed and said, "See you tomorrow."

By the time Ed returned to the Rotunda, the party was breaking up. All at once, he felt exhausted. From the moment Chet showed up at his cube that morning, he'd been running a marathon. Now all he wanted was to go home, play some music. Maybe Steely Dan, or Aretha, or Bruce, maybe finish up with some Keith Jarrett and an inch of cognac—while contemplating the lovely Ms. Pearl. There was something about her, something deep and provocative. She moved him the way Diane once did. He took in the Reilly one last time, then headed for the door.

Just then, Chet grabbed his arm, his eyes wide as soup bowls. "Ed! The most amazing thing! Could you do me a big favor and take Laura home?"

"Uh …" Ed slowly resurfaced from fantasies of undressing a certain new acquaintance.

"Laura. Would you take her home for me? I'd really appreciate it. Something has come up."

"This late?" Ed's tone was whinier than he intended. "It's midnight."

"I know, and this whole thing may be crazy, but it's a story, quite possibly a *big* story."

"So? Spill."

"Tomorrow, okay? I promise. Right now I've got to go. Thanks for taking Laura."

Chet turned and jogged to the far side of the Rotunda toward a man standing near a Conestoga wagon from the Donner party. Ed didn't recognize him: straw-colored hair, boyish face, mid-thirties, in a suit instead of a tux, and wearing Birkenstock sandals, of all things, instead of shoes. Very San Francisco. But something about him looked wrong. Chet and Mr. Birkenstocks were engrossed in conversation as they hurried toward the door. Before he realized what he was doing, Ed found himself walking after them, then trotting, and finally running. By the time he reached the door they were down the stairs, enveloped in chilly mist. Ed drew up short, suddenly nonplused about chasing after Chet for no discernible reason. In the distance, he heard their voices. They sounded excited. Their words were indistinct above gusts of wind and the traffic on Van Ness. But Ed thought he heard the words "cost sold," or maybe "tossed cold." Then it hit him: Lost Gold.

Someone touched his shoulder, startling him. Laura. "You weren't going to leave without me, were you?"

"Of course not. I was just about to find you. Who's the guy Chet ran off with?"

"No idea." She sounded annoyed. "Elliott Something. Warrell? *Wardell*. Worth—Chet's father—introduced them just now."

"Chet mentioned getting a line on a story."

Laura's lips curled into a frown. "Yes, the only one he's ever really cared about, the Lost Gold. Any cockroach crawls out of the woodwork claiming to know something and Chet's a greyhound, off and running."

So he heard right.

"I hope it's not a huge imposition taking me home. You must be exhausted."

"No imposition at all, if you don't mind a funky Mustang ankle deep in crap."

"Not at all."

Laura wasn't dressed adequately for San Francisco after dark, so they hurried through the foggy mist to his car. "I forgot how bone-chilling it gets here."

Ed pulled into light traffic. KFOG was playing B.B. King's "The Thrill Is Gone." "So what does this Wardell know about the Lost Gold?"

"Who knows? It's probably just another wild-goose chase." The long-suffering wife. "But it can't be too earth-shaking. Chet said he'd be home in an hour."

Ed headed up Franklin, cut over to Steiner, and followed Laura's directions past Alta Plaza Park and into Pacific Heights, land of huge homes and bigger bank accounts. The radio played the Stones' "Brown Sugar." Ed flashed on Julie, then swerved to avoid a skateboarder. The dipshit was out in the street dressed entirely in black, almost invisible in the night. "Maybe it's none of my business, but what's with you guys and Ted Calderone?"

"Ancient history," Laura sighed. It didn't take a seasoned reporter to realize she didn't want to talk about it, which, of course, egged Ed on.

"Didn't look that way. More like Arabs and Israelis."

"Look, Ed, I appreciate your driving me home, but I'm just too tired to go into all that now. Maybe some other time, okay?"

"Fine. Sorry I brought it up."

They drove in silence for a while. KFOG launched into a lost classic Ed loved, "Driver's Seat." Who did it? Some one-hit wonder with a funny name … Out of the depths of pot-ravaged neurons, it came back to him: Sniff and the Tears. *Yes.*

He tried conversation again: "Chet and his father seem to be getting along. As I recall, they didn't used to …"

Laura snorted. "That's an understatement. They were completely es-tranged. Worth disinherited Chet after he jumped bail. But now he's back in the bosom of the family."

"I wasn't all that close to Chet at Cal, but I never figured him for hard drugs. Pot, sure. But not heroin."

"Ancient history." She didn't want to talk about it.

"He told me he's been clean for years."

"Yes," Laura replied vacantly. "Here we are."

She pointed to a dramatic three-story wood and glass building with cantilevered balconies jutting out at odd angles. It looked incongruous tucked between two stately Victorians dripping gingerbread.

"Nice digs," Ed ventured. Way more than nice. On what he made, he probably couldn't afford to rent the mailbox.

"It's okay. We won't be here long. Just until we buy something."

"Good thing you're looking. Gave Chet an alibi for last night."

"Yes. That condo was twice as expensive as I thought it should be."

"Welcome home."

"Alaska was expensive, but I can't believe what housing costs here."

"Me either." Of course, price was just an inconvenience to Chet and Laura. They were rich. On what Ed made, he'd never be able to buy any-thing in the city. Fortunately, his cottage in the Mission was comfortable and rent-controlled, and his landlord wasn't a total putz.

Laura thanked him for the ride, then leaned over and delivered a cool peck on his cheek. Ed waited as she gathered her gown and climbed the half dozen steps to the iron grill.

Up and down the block, luxury vehicles claimed every curbside place: BMWs, Mercedes, Jaguars, a Maserati. But directly across the street, Ed noticed a white van, old and beat-up, with curtained windows, the kind hippies used to live in, and more recently, the homeless. Odd for this neighborhood, Ed thought.

Laura inserted her key, but the gate wouldn't budge. She tried again. No luck. She turned, looking frustrated and exhausted.

Ed rolled down the passenger window. "Problem?"

"I can't work the key."

It being so late, there was no parking anywhere. Ed slid into a bus zone. The lock was sticky, but after a few tries, it yielded. "There you go. Good night."

He was halfway down the steps when Laura called to him. "How about a nightcap? I know it's late, but I don't feel comfortable being here alone yet."

They took the elevator to the top floor and stepped into an apartment that cried for photo play in the paper's Home Section—high ceilings, big rooms, all glass on the north side, providing a post-card view from the Golden Gate past Alcatraz and Angel Island all the way to Berkeley. Laura apologized for the rental furniture, which she called "tacky." Ed aspired to such furnishings.

"Beer, wine, juice, water?"

"Got any bubbly water?"

"Calistoga."

"Perfect."

"Lemon? Lime?"

"Either. Thanks."

They sat quietly at opposite ends of the sofa and contemplated the view. The lights of Sausalito, Belvedere, and Tiburon shone beneath a sky full of stars twinkling through the mist.

"So, what's on your agenda, Laura? Beside house-hunting."

She sighed. "I leave for Anchorage first thing in the morning to pack up our house. Not much there we really want, just the stuff with sentimental value: books, photographs, that sort of thing. Then, who knows? We've been talking about a family. It feels weird to have normal choices again."

Ed finished his drink and stood up. At the door, Laura noticed something that escaped them on the way in. The phone machine was blinking—one message. She pressed the button: "Hi, it's me." Chet, but he didn't sound himself. Perhaps it was the machine, Ed thought, but his voice sounded strained. Scared? "Change of plans. I'll meet you up in Anchorage, help you pack. Remember to feed the fish. Love you."

Laura looked ashen.

"What's the matter?" Ed asked.

She slumped against the wall. "'Feed the fish' is code."

"For what?"

"Trouble."

12

The Front Page Deli occupied most of the *Foghorn's* ground-floor front-age on Mission Street. The food was decent and cheap, and all the sandwiches had newspaper names: Headline, Business Section, Sports Section, Crossword, even an Obituary, a bacon cheeseburger with melted brie served on butter-drenched garlic bread. The FP, as the reporters called it, was open 24 hours a day to accommodate the crazy schedules of printers, truckers, and night-shift reporters and editors. Management opened it to deflect union demands for a cafeteria that offered more than vending machines. *Foghorn* employees and guests got a deep discount and the South of Market got a minor landmark that, over the years, had become a hangout for the wee-hours crowd: cops, cab drivers, musicians, Flower Mart folks, and the occasional hooker. The place was loud and raucous. The floor was perennially grimy. And the Arab family that ran it had never been to charm school. But day or night, the FP offered some of the best people-watching in the city, and if you worked at the *Horn*, you couldn't beat it for convenience and price. Some bachelors on the paper took all their meals there.

Ed and Julie had to elbow their way in for lunch. All the tables were taken, so they settled for a couple of high-rise bar stools at the counter in back under an autographed photo of Tony Bennett, who made it a point to stop by whenever he was in town to sing his trademark song at the Fairmont. Julie ordered a Headline—turkey and Swiss on whole wheat, with a diet Coke. Ed chose a Sports Section—roast beef, cheddar, and guacamole on a French roll, with iced tea.

The noise level was even higher than usual. The Giants were playing the Braves on the large TV suspended from the ceiling in a corner. Bottom of the sixth, 2-2. Garrelts was going for his seventh win in a row, his thirteenth in sixteen starts. Every time the Giants got a hit or executed a smart defensive play, the place erupted in cheers.

Ordinarily, Ed would have been annoyed by the noise, but like everyone else, he had developed Giants fever, not to mention that the hullabaloo meant that he and Julie had to lean close to hear each other. "So," he said, "after graduating from Vassar and a stint with Craig and Brawley PR in New York, how did you wind up in San Francisco?"

Julie's expression bounced from surprise to almost irritation, then to almost flattered, and wound up somewhere between amusement and consternation. Her eyes sparkled. "How'd you know I went to Vassar and worked for C&B?"

"We reporters have our ways."

"No, really." She meant it.

Ed affected a sheepish grin. "A friend in Personnel."

She arched an eyebrow. "Do you investigate everyone you have lunch with?"

"Only the ones I like."

"And the ones you don't?"

"I don't have lunch with them."

Julie laughed. Ed listened carefully. Her laugh sounded real, as though she truly appreciated his sense of humor. He did not detect the studied chortle of women who train themselves to titter at men's jokes.

"When I was working at C&B, my boyfriend got a job at Apple—he's a programmer—so we came out here. The agency had a San Francisco office. They let me transfer."

"Boyfriend?" Ed frowned, held his breath.

"We broke up about six months later."

He exhaled. "I'm sorry." Then he smiled. "No, I'm not."

She smiled back. "I wound up working on some projects with the PR people at the *Foghorn,* and eventually I moved over. That was four years ago. Anything else you'd like to know?"

Their food arrived and Ed handed the woman his *Foghorn* staff card and a few bucks.

"Uh, yes, as a matter of fact. But it's not the kind of investigation I'd pursue in a delicatessen."

Another shared smile. Ed was suddenly overwhelmed by desire, the first time he'd felt it in ages. Every square inch of Julie aroused him. One of her ears peeked out from under her hair. An elegant teardrop lobe. He imagined nibbling on it.

"What about you?" Julie inquired. "You in a relationship?" She held her breath.

"Divorced."

She exhaled. "I'm sorry. No, I'm not." Their eyes met. Neither of them looked away.

"No kids," Ed continued. "My ex, Diane, and I are still friends. We talk. She lives in Grass Valley. Has a little line of canned preserves: blueberry, blackberry, strawberry. Real good. I'll give you a few jars. She wanted the country life, fresh air, and a big garden. I wanted the city, though, frankly, sometimes I forget why. It might have worked if we'd wanted the same surroundings. But we didn't, so it didn't. Now my most intimate relationships are with two cats."

"What kind?"

"A long-hair gray and a short-hair calico."

"Really? What are their names?"

"Rhythm and Blues."

"Cute. I have a dog but I like cats."

They munched their sandwiches. The Giants retired the Braves with a double-play. Two tables away, the Editorial Page editor got so excited, he knocked over his Coke.

"Now, about your dress last night: You said you made it?"

"With these very fingers." She held them up, and wiggled them. "I make most of my clothes. I made this outfit." She struck an exaggerated model's pose: head turned, hand on her ear, elbow out, leg extended.

Her blouse was a pale yellow floral print with a V neck and big floppy collar. Her skirt was made from the same material, and deeply pleated. Over them, she wore a long loose vest, a shade of umber that complemented her skin. As an ensemble, the outfit looked comfortable, elegant enough for a serious career woman, but casual enough to suggest that she didn't take her career too too seriously.

"It's lovely," Ed said. "Looks like it could have come from a fancy store."

"My family didn't have much money. Sewing became an affordable way for me to dress well. Once I got the hang of it, I could sew nicer, better-fitting outfits than I could buy."

A practical gal. Ed imagined the skirt, top, and vest strewn around his bed.

"Who taught you to sew so well?"

"My grandfather was a tailor. Saul Stavisky."

Ed just about choked on the bite he was chewing. "Your grandfather's *Jewish*?"

"Was. He passed away when I was in college," Julie said matter-of-factly. "Why are you so surprised? I'm light-skinned. The hair is in-between." She ran a hand through her ringlets. "Any black person would know I had white in me."

"I'm not surprised about the white. Just the Jewish."

"Well, *Mr. Rosenberg,* my Mom's parents had a tailor shop in Yonkers. Mom was never much good at sewing, but I had a knack for it, which helped my grandparents deal with the fact that their daughter ran off with a black jazz musician."

"Jazz musician?"

"Sax. Ever hear of Charles Mingus?"

"Of course."

"Daddy played with him."

Ed's eyes widened. "I'm impressed."

"Don't be. He and my Mom split up when I was four. I didn't see him much after that. He died a few years ago. Cirrhosis."

"I'm sorry. And your mom?"

"Getting older, but still going strong. Does social work in White Plains. What about your family?"

Instead of answering, Ed held up an index finger and reached for his hip. His pager was vibrating. He excused himself apologetically and grabbed one of the five house phones the *Foghorn* maintained in the Front Page to ruin reporters' lunches. Typically, a page at this time of day meant that Ruffen wanted to hassle him about some silly detail in a piece he'd filed. But his story about the party was long gone, and he didn't have anything else in the hopper.

It wasn't Ruffen. It was the *Foghorn's* main operator. "Ed Rosenberg? Please hold for a patch-through from Laura Gilchrist."

She was calling from Anchorage—and sobbing. She didn't know what to do. She didn't know who else to call. She was at a neighbor's house. She arrived to find police crawling all over her place. There was a dead man on the floor in her living room.

Ed's stomach knotted up. He recalled Chet's message on the phone machine: See you in Anchorage. Could Chet have arrived before Laura did? That seemed unlikely. She told him she was flying up first thing.

"Who?"

Laura was whimpering, then erupted in sobs.

"Who is he, Laura? Talk to me. Do you know who the dead man is?"

But Laura couldn't answer. She was crying and moaning. It's Chet, Ed decided. It has to be. His heart sank.

A sharp banging sound smacked Ed's ear, as though the handset on the other end had been dropped on a hard floor.

"Hello?" It was another woman's voice. The neighbor. "The dead man isn't Chet."

Ed exhaled sharply. "How do you know? Did you see him?"

"No, the cops put him in a bag and took him away. But he didn't have any ID, so they showed me Polaroids, asked me if I knew him."

"And—?"

"He was husky with a full head of dark hair. Dave—I mean Chet—he used Dave, you know, before … he's thin and balding."

Laura pulled herself together enough to get back on the line.

"You have any idea who the dead guy is?"

"No."

"Where's Chet?"

"I don't know. I haven't seen him since last night, since he went off with that man … Wardell. Oh, Ed, I'm so frightened. They keep *asking* me about Chet." Choking sounds. Then sobs.

"Who? The police?"

"Yes."

"What do they want to know?"

"Where he is. When I last saw him. If he owns a gun."

"Did you tell them Chet said he'd meet you up there today?"

"No! But they act like he's *involved* in this. Oh, God …" More crying.

"Have you been inside your house? Is there anything that points to Chet?"

"No, they won't let me in." More crying, harder now.

"Laura, you want me to come up? Say the word and I'm on my way."

Nose-blowing. "Thank you," she whimpered weakly, "but I'll be okay."

Like hell. "Suppose I come up anyway?"

"Oh, would you?" It was a plea.

"Absolutely. Be there tonight."

"You're sure it's not too much trouble …?" Another nose-blow, with low moaning.

"Of course I'm sure. Chet's a friend. You're a friend. He may be in trouble. It's a *mitzvah*."

"A what?"

"Yiddish for a good deed."

Ed hung up and returned to Julie, who was engrossed in the ball game. It was tied, 7-all, in the top of the tenth. "I hate to make our quickie even quicker, but—" He explained the situation. Julie's eyes widened.

"Of course you should go," she said as they hurried through the door that led into the *Foghorn*.

"I have a bad feeling about this. Laura says she never told the cops Chet was flying up to meet her, but they seem to think he's involved anyway. They asked her if he owns a gun."

"What does that mean?"

"That they found something in the house that incriminates him."

"What?"

"Got me, but it's high on my list of things to find out."

The elevator was full, so they ran up the stairs to the second floor, Ed's floor. Julie worked on four. They faced each other on the landing. It smelled of fresh paint. "You know," she said wistfully, "we've only had half a lunch date, and already you're leaving me for another woman."

"Best half a lunch date I ever had. How about a whole dinner date when I get back?"

"I'd like that."

"I'll call you."

"Have a good trip."

"It won't be."

"But it's the right thing to do. What my family called a *mitzvah*."

Ed smiled. "Yes." He squeezed her hand and stepped into the newsroom, where the *Fog*hands were bouncing off the walls. Butler singled, bringing Weaver home. The Giants won it 8-7. Their magic number was down to twelve.

13

Assistant City Editor Ron Ruffen looked disgusted. Ed couldn't tell if the cause was his presence or the news he'd just delivered. "Jesus. Chet's back, what, two days, and already he's playing footsie with two dead bodies?" Ruffen ran his fingers through what remained of his hair. A Pizza Hut box and a crescent of crust littered his desk. A small glop of tomato sauce conspicuously marred his tie, but given his boss' mood, Ed decided not to mention it. "And *no*, you *can't* go to Anchorage. You're already covering one murder here. That's enough. Anchorage is too far away. Too expensive. Besides, you're not objective. You're Chet's old buddy."

"Just because there's a dead man in his living room doesn't mean he did it."

"But you just said he was on his way up there."

Ed didn't mention Chet's promise to the SFPD to stay put in San Francisco. "He'd have to be out of his mind to kill someone in his own living room when he's already under suspicion for a murder here."

"So maybe he's out of his mind. He was a drug addict—"

"I'll pay my own way."

"We'll pick it up from the wires."

"I won't stay a moment longer than I have to."

"Nixo."

"Ron—"

"Don't 'Ron' me. You're trying my patience, Rosenberg." Ruffen's face contorted into a jowly frown that reminded Ed of someone. Someone detestable. J. Edgar Hoover.

Now Ed was in a bind. He'd promised Laura he'd come up. "If we don't jump on this, if we use the wires, we'll be the laughingstock of journalism. Everyone will say we punked out because we didn't want to embarrass Gilchrist—which will embarrass him even more."

Ruffen glared at him. His expression said: You're an ass, but you have a point.

Ed pressed on. "The corpse is still warm. Chet's disappeared. And the only person who can shed any light on this just asked me to come up."

"*Asked you?*"

"Yes, when I spoke to her just now. I've known Laura Gilchrist since Chet and I were in grad school together. She won't talk to the wires. She and I both saw Chet leave the Museum last night with a guy named Wardell. Laura said she didn't know him, but maybe she does. I was with her when she got Chet's message saying he'd meet her in Anchorage—"

"*With* her? What—standing over her phone machine?"

"When Chet left with the mystery man, he asked me to drive her home. She invited me in for a drink—"

"Oh, great. Real objective." Ruffen's frown was as exaggerated as a circus clown's. His mind was made up. Ed wasn't going.

That left Ed only one alternative. "I have vacation and comp time coming. If you don't send me, I'll go up there on my own, investigate the shit out of this, and then *not file.*"

Ruffen's left eye began twitching, another bad sign. "You ever hear of 'persistent, incorrigible insubordination'?" Under the terms of the Newspaper Guild contract, it was legitimate grounds for termination. "I've had it up to *here* with you, Ed." He snapped a hand to his forehead as if saluting.

"So fire me. Last night, Ted Calderone offered me a ton of money to cover the Murtinson story for *Full Disclosure.*" That was a lie. Calderone had done no such thing. But under the circumstances, it played well.

Ruffen looked down and noticed the stain on his tie. He undid it, threw it in a desk drawer, and extracted a clean one. Slowly, he hoisted his bulk out of his chair and stepped toward the window, his back to Ed. Deliberately, he knotted the new tie. Across Mission, on the windowsills of the Old Mint, pigeons were jostling for position. North of Market, the crane was lifting more steel for the new hotel. The wind had picked up. Puffy clouds tumbled across a dazzling blue sky. Seagulls soared on the breeze. Ruffen turned to face Ed.

"Nick Helios." His tone combined exasperation and resignation.

"Who?"

"Nick's the city editor of the *Anchorage Pioneer*. He drinks Jack Daniels. Buy him a few and he'll tell you everything he knows."

Yes. "Thanks, Ron. I really appreciate this. You won't regret it."

"I *already* regret it."

In his mind, Ed was at the airport, striding down the jetway.

"This story is getting bigger," Ruffen continued. "While you're up there, I'm going to have Hubig dig a little deeper into Murtinson's money, and put Miller on Chet and Laura." It was standard operating procedure. As stories expanded, so did the number of reporters assigned to cover them. But Ruffen's tone carried a veiled threat. He seemed to be saying: Rub me the wrong way, and I'll hand your precious story to other worker bees. Then the veil came off. "And Ed, a word of advice: You're a good reporter. But read your contract. We've got the makings of persistent, incorrigible insubordination here. And if I play that card, the union can't do shit for you. Think about it."

14

Anchorage surprised Ed. He expected a rough-hewn frontier town, but found himself in San Jose, only ringed by better mountains, their peaks capped by icefields. The weather was raw and damp with winter approaching, but oddly, not much colder than San Francisco two thousand miles to the south. The sky, huge and vaguely sinister, roiled with fast-moving clouds. A stiff wind whipped the slate gray water of Cook Inlet into whitecaps. Downtown was small and seedy, its handful of high-rise buildings oddly squat. Most of the city was suburban, little boxes on little lots extending off to the foothills of the Chugach Range. The better neighborhoods were on canals. Everyone there seemed to have two Jeeps in the driveway and a float plane tied to a pier out back.

Ed checked into The Thunderbird, a dingy motel with an exhausted 1950s ambience. It was a single-story, flat-roofed, cinderblock affair in a neighborhood bordering downtown that looked like it had been trying to turn things around since the motel's namesake Ford had two seats and porthole windows. The clerk wore a sweatshirt that proclaimed: The Best Thing About Anchorage: It's Close to Alaska.

Chet and Laura rented a two-bedroom cottage in need of a paint job in a tedious neighborhood south of downtown that had never been fashionable. Their small front porch listed to one side and several of its floor boards looked rotted. No water, no planes, no new Grand Cherokees. Just battered pickups, and behind every third house, a rusting junker up on blocks or a discarded washing machine or refrigerator.

Ed pressed the doorbell. No answer. He pressed again, harder, then knocked. Nothing. He ambled around back, and saw Laura slouched over her kitchen table, staring vacantly at the telephone and past it out the window to the mountains. Her face was deeply lined and puffy. Her eyes were bordered in red. Her hair was a mess.

Ed knocked on the back door. She looked, but did not get up. He tried the knob. Open. He let himself in, and gave Laura a platonic embrace. She neither resisted nor responded. But the contact seemed to draw her out of her reverie. She said, "Thanks for coming."

"How are you holding up?"

She closed her eyes. Her lower lip trembled. Then her eyes reopened. "We did everything *together*. It's not like him to …" She cupped her face in her hands, drew her fingers down her cheeks.

Ed placed a hand gently on her shoulder. "Hang in there. Things'll work out." He didn't quite believe it, but it felt like the right thing to say.

Laura tried to smile, but couldn't. She just stared at the phone.

"Mind if I look around?" Ed asked.

Laura gestured: Go ahead. There was a chalk outline on the living room rug with a dark stain in the chest area. Ed shuddered. He'd seen too many of those lately. The place had been tossed—or maybe the dead man put up a fight. Then the room had been picked over by the police. Laura and the neighbor he'd spoken to had tried to straighten up, but without much success.

Ed returned to the kitchen, made a pot of tea, and found some Saltines and peanut butter in the pantry.

"Did you see the … body?"

She shook her head. "No, he … it was gone by the time I got here."

"So the police didn't ask you to identify the guy?"

"They showed me Polaroids."

"And?"

She closed her eyes, as if trying to erase the memory, then shuddered. "There was so much blood."

"Did you recognize him?"

She hesitated. "No."

"But the police suspect Chet was involved?" He spread peanut butter on a cracker and offered it to Laura. She shook her head. He ate it.

"They don't suspect," she said flatly. "They're *convinced* he did it."

"Did you ask why?"

"The lady detective just said, 'We have information.'"

"She didn't provide details?"

Laura shook her head. Her hair was a string mop that had swabbed too many dirty floors. "But it *can't* be Chet. I *know* it."

Ed took a sip of tea. "How?"

"There was mail in the box. Chet has a thing about mail. He always brings it in. *Always*. If he'd been here, he would have brought it in."

Unless, perhaps, he was holding someone at gun point and shooting him, Ed thought. "Did you mention that to the police?"

"Yes, but I don't think they believed me."

Ed wasn't surprised. The cops he knew would dismiss a wife's observation about uncollected mail as LWB, loyal wife bullshit. "Did you mention his phone message last night?"

"Of course not!" Ever protective.

"So they had their own information that he came up here."

She nodded, and took a sip of tea. Her hand trembled and some spilled. "But he couldn't have gotten here before I did. I took the first plane."

Ed debated whether to reply, and decided to go for it. "He could have chartered one. He's rich."

Her eyes became razors slicing him into tiny pieces. "You think he did it, don't you?"

"Laura—"

"Don't you?!"

Ed sighed. "I don't know what to think. He tells the cops he'll stay in San Francisco, then his message says he's coming up here. Next thing I know there's a corpse in your living room. I want to believe he had nothing to do with it, but—"

"Get out." She pointed at the door. "I thought you were a friend, but you're not. You're one of *them.*"

"Laura, please—"

"No. Get out. Now!"

15

The Coal Tender was a long, narrow, windowless bar frequented by the staff of the *Anchorage Pioneer*. Its walls were decorated haphazardly with old railroad paraphernalia, rusty testament to the city's origins as a staging area for construction of the Alaska Railroad during the early twentieth century. The place smelled of beer, popcorn, greasy hot dogs, and cigarette smoke.

There was a TV over the bar, video only, no sound. Scores flashed on the screen: The Padres beat the Giants 5-3, and the A's fell to the Red Sox 7-2. Ed ran the numbers in his head as he followed Nick Helios into the gloom. The losses stalled the Giants' magic number at 10, the A's at 13.

Helios led Ed to a small booth in the back. Its vinyl looked like it had arrived back when Anchorage was no more than a collection of tents. Two lumberjacks with full beards were shooting pool nearby on a half-size table. Nothing larger would fit the room. Both shot poorly with open bridges. They were either drunk, or chumps, or both.

Helios was tall and bony, with thin dark hair, and thick glasses perched on a parrot-beak nose, a middle-aged Ichabod Crane. The sleeves of his rumpled shirt were rolled up to mid-forearm. His collar was open, his tie knotted but loose. He ordered Jack Daniels. Ed was more into beer, but following Ruffen's advice to drink along, he told the haggard Inuit waitress, "Two."

"So, what's it like writing for Ronnie?" Helios inquired, breaking the ice, which in Alaska can get pretty thick.

Ed couldn't imagine anyone calling Ruffen "Ronnie," not even the man's mother. "It's … interesting," he evaded, reluctant to speak freely to one of Ruffen's friends.

The drinks arrived. Helios saluted Ed with his and took a big swallow. "Don't bullshit a bullshitter. How bad is he?"

"We get along okay," Ed lied, "but Ron has his moments."

"By which I infer that he's often an ass."

Ed shrugged. "Something like that."

"He still a blimp?"

Ed meant to say "the Goodyear," but what came out was "the Hindenberg."

Helios nodded knowingly, took another swig, and settled in. The vinyl creaked. Across the room, one of the pool players broke the pack with a loud crack. "Ronnie's had some hard knocks. You may not believe this, but twenty-five years ago, when we were both young bucks at the *Philadelphia Inquirer,* Ronnie was as thin as I am. He was also a hell of a good reporter, a real bulldog. Never sat still. Went after stories like Willie Mays after a long fly ball. He had a hunger, wanted a Pulitzer real bad."

Ed cocked his head in disbelief.

Helios continued: "He also had a real looker of a wife ... what was her name? Cindy. Not just pretty, real sweet, too. Ronnie was crazy about her, and she seemed to be just as gone on him. Well, 'long about '67 or '68, she left him, no warning, nothing. A month later, she moved in with the Business editor."

"God."

"Ronnie was never the same after that. Gained a ton of weight, quit the paper, basically went to hell. I tried to stay in touch, but he disappeared. 'Maybe five years later, I ran into him at an editors conference. He was in New Orleans at the *Times Picayune.* Still huge, still looked lost, and he had this vicious sarcasm that was hard to take. But, hey, he was an old friend, and he'd landed on his feet. I was glad of that. You know his wife, Suzanne?"

"Not really. I see her at the paper's Christmas party."

Helios waved for another Jack. Ed held up two fingers.

"Suzy's a good woman, the kind who goes for the bird with the broken wing, which I guess is what Ronnie needs. We have dinner when the wife and I go down to Frisco, every couple of years. Where'd they take us last time? A place near the paper ... figured in one of Dashiell Hammett's books."

"John's Grill?"

"That's it. Nice place."

"Ron's a good editor, knows news." Ed wanted a generous assessment to filter back to the *Horn*. "But I know what you mean about the sarcasm."

Their second round arrived. Helios raised his glass: "To Ron Ruffen!" Their glassed clinked. Helios took a big gulp, Ed a tiny sip.

"So," Helios said, "the wires picked up your piece about that bigshot's murder. I liked it. You didn't pull any punches about Dave—I mean Chet—being under a cloud of suspicion, despite his alibi. I tell you, my hat is off to his father. His son steps deep into shit, but he doesn't keep his paper from doing the story right. How much of it was you? How much was Ronnie?"

"The word came down to play it by the book, so I did—and Ron made sure I did."

Helios sighed. "Now *this.*" He shook his head, scratched an ear.

"When Chet was working for you, did you ever suspect he wasn't who he said he was?"

"Not for a minute. I'm a little embarrassed to admit it, but that's the truth. He came to us on an internship from U of A. Older than most J-school kids, but, hey, this is Alaska. No one asks questions. He did good work—very good work—and we hired him. Simple as that."

"What was he like?"

"Damn good reporter. Busted ass, never fucked off—or up. Didn't party. I don't think I ever saw him take a drink. Bunch of us come over here on Fridays after work, but he never did. Quiet. Intense. Kind of a drudge, really. But a helluva softball player. When his group won the Pulitzer, I thought, yes, goddamit, nose-to-the-grindstone can pay off. Then he blows everyone's mind by announcing who he really is. I couldn't believe it. I mean, I could wrap my mind around him being a Gilchrist. But I couldn't believe he came to Alaska on the run from drug charges. He's the last guy I'd ever pick for a heroin addict. I asked him about it. He just said it was in the past. Now it looks like the stiff in the living room was his dealer."

"What?!" Ed gagged on his drink and had to grab for a napkin.

"Yeah," Helios rolled his eyes dolefully. He produced a few sheets of folded paper, unfolded them, and handed them to Ed. "Copy of the police report, and a print-out of the story we're running tomorrow."

Ed took the papers, but the light in the Coal Tender was too low for reading. Fortunately, just as Ruffen had predicted, two drinks had loosened Helios' tongue. "The dead man had traces of white powder in his coat pocket. The preliminary police report says it's heroin. And his wounds were unusual. Up here, most people shoot each other with shotguns. But this guy got it with a .38."

Ed bit his lip. His mind raced ahead of Helios with a horrible guess. *Please, no.*

"The slugs were weird, too. The cops are still running them, but their best guess is that the gun had a silencer."

Oh my God.

"Just like your murder in San Fran. I tell you, I wouldn't want to be Chet Gilchrist right about now."

Ed looked down at the table, old wood with a million initials carved into it. His drinks sat between his hands, the first finally finished, the second still full. He downed half of it in a gulp.

"The cops figure it was a drug deal gone bad. Chet got pissed, shot the guy, took the heroin, and split."

Ed shook his head. "That's not the Chet I know."

"Tell me about it," Helios said. "You think you know a guy, then it turns out you don't know him at all."

"What about the body, any ID?"

"The cops may know by now, but we didn't have anything by press time."

Ed dropped some bills on the table. "I wouldn't want to be Chet now either." Or his father. Or his wife.

16

The lady detective was named Sally Mazer. She was overdressed by Alaska standards in a business suit, a navy jacket, pleated skirt, and a white blouse with a bow tied primly at the hollow of her neck. Her silky hair looked like it had once been blonde, but the years had turned it a dull beige. She motioned Ed to the only chair in her small office. A grimy window overlooked the railyard and canneries on Ship Creek where it empties into the Knik Arm of Cook Inlet. On her battered gray desk was a sign: Native Alaskan. In a corner were a few family photos. In one, taken years earlier, she was posed with a handsome man and two young boys, all grinning, proudly showing off hooked fish. Another showed them all on horseback in snowcapped mountains, the boys a little older. Then there was a shot of her husband waving from the cockpit of a small plane. Then a pair of portraits in a hinged frame, one son in a Navy uniform, the other dressed as a Marine. The Marine's photo was bordered in black ribbon, with a small crucifix hanging from a chain.

"The prelim shows that the slugs passed through a noise-suppression device," Mazer said, her words measured, her tone professional. "We don't see many of them up here. The white powder was heroin, pretty pure, too. We rarely see that quality up here. And no needle marks on the deceased. Usually, guys who deal heroin also shoot it. But this one didn't."

"Any ID?"

She pulled a paper from her file. "Just came in. Juan Cabral, a small-time hood from the Lower 48. Did time for heroin trafficking in California. Folsom and San Quentin. A scumbag."

Cabral. The name rang a distant bell, but Ed couldn't place it.

"Chet's wife—Mrs. Gilchrist—got the distinct impression that you had information linking her husband to the shooting."

"Correct."

"Can you share it? If it's sensitive, just say the word, and I won't print it. Laura—Mrs. Gilchrist—is going crazy and really wants to know."

"We got a 911 call. Guy says he's jogging by the house, sees shadows on the curtains, a tall thin guy pointing what looks like a gun at a short guy, no gunshot sound, then the short guy keels over."

"So no one ID'ed Chet."

"No, but he's tall and thin."

"So's Kareem Abdul-Jabbar."

Mazer grimaced, no fan of sarcasm. "There were no signs of forced entry. Whoever pulled the trigger had a key and let himself in. Afterward, he drove off in the Gilchrists' car. There were fresh tracks in the driveway. If you were me, who would you suspect?"

"How do you know Chet was even up here? I was with him yesterday in San Francisco." He stayed mum about the message on the phone machine.

"We checked. Charter company flew him up early this morning."

Ed couldn't meet her gaze. Instead, he looked past her out the window. It was getting dark. The sky was filled with low gray clouds. A jet was gaining altitude, its wing lights blinking. A hawk circled nearby over something unseen, then flapped its wings and flew out of view.

"Who called 911?"

"Didn't say. The caller, a male, used a pay phone at the gas station down the street from the Gilchrist home. He was gone by the time our unit got there. The attendant had no recollection of the guy."

"Is there a warrant out for Chet's arrest?"

"We're working on it."

"You mind if I make copies of your reports?"

Mazer shrugged. "Suit yourself." She pulled a few pieces of paper out of the file. "Copier's down the hall. I have to enter my code."

Ed followed her to the cramped copy room, which doubled as the coffee bar. Without looking at Ed, she said, "I've been a cop 26 years, detective, 14. I got a strong hunch that this is the same weapon that killed your guy in San Francisco."

I hope to God you're wrong, Ed prayed. But I'm afraid you're right.

17

Ed knocked on Laura's front door. It was dark and there was no porch light. He was about to go around to the kitchen when the neighbor opened it and motioned him in. Laura was right where he left her, at the kitchen table, staring at the phone, willing it to ring.

"He hasn't called?" Ed asked, though it came out as more of a statement than a question. He crossed the room and took Laura's hand in his.

She shook her head and started to whimper. He cupped her head in his hands. She nuzzled into his belly like a baby looking for the breast, and wrapped her arms around his waist. Her crying grew louder and more grief-stricken. Her body shook. Ed gently massaged her neck and shoulders. She'd forgotten about throwing him out earlier. After a while, she pulled back and looked up at him red-eyed.

"I've gotten your shirt wet." She reached for tissues, dabbed her eyes.

"It'll dry."

She blew her nose noisily. "Not very ladylike, am I?" She tried to smile, but didn't quite make it. "Irene would be scandalized." Her mother-in-law, Chet's socialite stepmother.

"Irene's a million miles away. Forget about her. Want some tea?"

Laura nodded, and Ed set about the familiar ritual.

"Something terrible must have happened," she lamented. "He always calls. *Always.*"

Ed poured the tea and pulled a coffee yogurt out of the fridge. Laura took a sip of the hot drink, but shook her head at the food. "I'm not hungry."

Ed looked at her disapprovingly. Their eyes met and Laura looked away. "Starving yourself doesn't do any good."

"He's right," the neighbor chimed in. She stood in the kitchen door-way, a chubby Inuit woman in a shapeless housedress. "You've got to eat. I'll be home if you need me." She let herself out, crossed a patch of weed-covered yard to her place, and disappeared into her kitchen.

Laura sighed and took a bite of cracker, chewing it with a force of will. Ed spread peanut butter on another and offered it to her. She shook her head.

A ringing sound punctured the silence, startling them. The phone. Laura lunged for it. "Chet! Chet, darling! Is it *you?!*"

Her face, momentarily animated, quickly sagged as though she were a figure in a wax museum and someone turned the heat up too high. It wasn't Chet. She slumped over and let the handset drop. Her head fell into her hands as her disappointment found expression in tears.

Ed picked the phone up off the floor. "Hello? ... No, a family friend. Who is this? ... And the reason for your call? ... Reaction? Yes, she has a reaction. She is 100 percent certain that her husband is incapable of vio-lent crime ... No, and don't call back!" He slammed the receiver down. "Fucking reporter." Laura looked up at him, her eyes big and red and wet. "They issued a warrant for Chet's arrest. Murder."

Laura ran through some more tissues. Then she jumped up and ran into the bedroom, a woman possessed. "I've got to pack! Be ready for his call!"

Ed followed her, perplexed. "What are you doing?"

She threw clothes helter skelter into an old suitcase. "We'll run. We'll disappear again. We're good at it. He sacrificed everything for me. I won't abandon him!"

Ed grabbed her by the arms and held them. "Laura! Get a grip. You're not going anywhere. And if Chet shows up, he better *not* run. Running just makes him look guilty. He's got to answer these charges."

"Who's going to believe us?"

"Well, me, for one. At least I'm *trying* to. But you're not making it very easy. Now please, sit down. Chet's hip deep in alligators, and if I'm going to help—and I want to—we need to talk, okay?"

Laura nodded and calmed down. Ed relieved her of the clothes she was about to stuff into the suitcase and placed them on the bed, then led her back to the kitchen, where they both took seats. Low clouds obscured the mountains. Ed drew the curtains. He told Laura about the anony-mous 911 call, the heroin, the silenced .38, the absence of forced entry, and the killer's departure in their car.

Laura took it all in, then stared off into space.

"The cops are betting that the same gun killed both Gregory Murtinson and the guy here, Juan Cabral."

Laura's jaw dropped. "Cabral? Did you say Juan Cabral?"

"You know him?"

"I don't know if it's the same person, but a Juan Cabral used to be the Gilchrists' chauffeur."

When Detective Mazer mentioned the name, Ed thought he recognized it, but he couldn't place it. Now it all came flooding back. Shortly before Chet's first heroin arrest, Cabral had been fired. Subsequently, he was arrested for selling heroin and wound up in and out of jail. After Chet's second bust, his father appeared at a press conference and accused the ex-chauffeur of turning his son into an addict. He said if he ever caught up with him, he'd kill him. The remark triggered media pandemonium. The *Foghorn* PR people spent several days in full-court-press spin control: The publisher of the *San Francisco Foghorn* would *never* consider taking the law into his own hands. Beside himself with anguish over his son's drug problem, he *misspoke* … But the damage had been done. The media had a field day. Then Cabral got a long stretch in prison and Chet disappeared.

"You ever see Cabral after he lost the chauffeur job?" Ed asked.

"No."

"Did he ever come up here before?"

"No."

"Well, you know what the police are going to say—that Cabral was Chet's original supplier, and after he got out of prison he continued supplying him. They had a meet set up here. Something went wrong and Chet grabbed the heroin and shot him."

Laura pressed her palms together in front of her and bowed her head so that her forehead touched her fingertips as though praying. Then she raised her head and looked searchingly at Ed. "Chet *never used heroin!* You've *got to* believe me."

Ed had to consciously suppress a smirk. "Laura," he said as gently as possible, "whether or not I believe you is beside the point. Chet was arrested for possession twice. Convicted once. Fled the second charge. Junkies usually deny using. It's a classic MO."

"But he never had any needle marks!"

As Ed recalled, that was true. Chet's lawyer had hammered away on that point when he was awaiting trial before he went underground. "True, but there are other ways: You can smoke it. Or snort it. Or use those needleless injection things."

He expected another explosion, another eviction, but Laura was spent. The fight had seeped out of her. She gazed past him with glazed eyes, bent her head, and rubbed her temples. Her hair fell over her face, a veil. "I have a headache," she announced. "I want to lie down."

"Let me help you." Ed took her elbow and guided her into the bedroom. He pulled the half-packed suitcase off the bed and sat her down. "Ruffen's leaning on me to get back. But if you need me to stay, I will."

"That's okay. My sister's coming up from San Diego. I haven't seen her since … Chet and I … left. She's going to help me pack up the house."

"Then what?"

She kicked off her shoes and lay fully clothed on her side curled up in a fetal position. It was an effort for her to reply. "Then I guess back to San Francisco." She looked lost. "I have nowhere else to go."

"Then I'll see you there. I'm still thinking the three of us should hit La Cumbre." He tried to sound hopeful, but didn't quite make it. He reached down and squeezed her hand. She gazed up at him, returned the pressure.

Then she started, and sat up. "It's *gone!*"

"What is?"

She reached for the night table. It contained a telephone and a small framed black-and-white portrait of a young woman in a wedding gown. "Chet's book!"

"What book?"

"His Stanford thesis. On the Lost Gold of San Francisco. When we came up here, he brought only two personal items—this picture of his mother and his book. He kept it right here under her portrait."

Ed rummaged around the table, checking the floor and under the bed. "What's it look like?"

"Like a book. A hardback with an orange cover. He had it custom bound by the same people who bound a copy for display in the Truman Room when he won the prize."

"Well, I don't see it. Maybe he took it to San Francisco."

"No, he just took a garment bag. If he'd taken it, he would have taken Margaret's picture. He always kept them together."

"Maybe the police took it."

"But why?"

"Got me. Want me to call them?"

"Would you? That book has great sentimental value to him … to us."

"Soon as possible. Promise."

"Thank you, Ed … for everything." She lay back down and curled up again.

"You sure you'll be okay here by yourself till your sister arrives? I could stay, bunk on the sofa."

"I'll be all right. Sue and Wes are next door, and Rosemary's coming tomorrow."

"Then I'll see you back in the city."

Laura didn't reply. She was asleep. Ed found a quilt in the hall closet and placed it over her. He locked the doors, turned off the lights, and stepped into the cold Alaska night. The cloud cover was down to treetop level, and reminded him of San Francisco fog swirling among the palms on Dolores Street.

18

Jerry Krasnow wore wire-rim glasses and had a strong jaw, thinning kinky black hair, and a scraggly beard that was starting to show streaks of gray. He gazed intently at the brightly colored balls arrayed around the green felt.

"Four ball, long."

He bent over the table, lined up his shot, stroked his stick smartly, and sent the cue ball into the four at just the right angle to dispatch it across the table into the far corner pocket. He smiled.

"Nice shot," Ed allowed. Rap music blared from the PA. Ed hated rap and avoided it, but this one he recognized in spite of himself—the new hit by the Bay Area's own MC Hammer.

Jerry hit the cue below center, giving it backspin. Leaning against the wall a polite distance from the table, Ed saw immediately what his old friend hoped to accomplish—setting up either the twelve in the side or the six at the other end. But the cue ball drew back farther than Jerry hoped, making both shots more difficult than he'd planned. Jerry tossed a grimace in Ed's direction, as if to say: Damn, this could have been easy, but now it's a bitch. Ed shrugged and gestured toward the table, where a half-dozen balls were still in play: Your shot.

Jerry made a show of sizing up the twelve and six, but Ed knew he'd take the twelve. It was a no-brainer. Both shots were of equal difficulty, but the six would leave him high and dry at one end of the table with all the balls at the other. The twelve kept him closer to the action, with better position for subsequent shots.

With a loving tap, Jerry sank the twelve, then ran three more before hitting the thirteen a little too hard. It rattled in a corner pocket, but refused to drop, just sat there a millimeter from the precipice. Jerry shook his head, disgusted with himself. "When am I ever going to learn to keep those soft?"

Ed chalked up, and ran the remaining balls, finishing with a long, straight, corner-to-corner shot that proved he did more than just fool around at the game.

"Sweet," Jerry said.

Jerry racked up, and Ed broke, playing safe. He tapped the corner of the pack, kicking the seven out to the rail, but leaving the other fourteen balls in a tight triangle. With the seven on one side of the pack, and the cue ball on the other, Jerry had nothing, so he also played safe.

In bars, most people played the drunk's game, eight ball. In pool halls, it was nine ball, the fast-paced game invented for televised pool tournaments. But Ed and Jerry played the classic game, slow, stately straight pool: any ball, call your shots.

They played in the Games Room of the Inner Mission Youth Center, where Jerry worked. The room held an assortment of tables: three pool, three bumper pool, three foosball, and two ping-pong, plus an array of arcade video games that didn't require coins. The IMYC was a drop-in facility where kids could go after school and on weekends, get help with their homework, and in addition to the games, draw, paint, work with clay, or play basketball, whiffleball, volleyball, or computer games. It was located on Valencia near Seventeenth, a few blocks from Ed's place. It closed at eight p.m. A few nights a month, Ed stopped by after hours to shoot pool with his old friend.

Compared with the other pool halls Ed frequented—Palace Billiards out Geary, and The Great Entertainer South of Market—IMYC's tables were poorly maintained, always in need of new felt, and sometimes in need of leveling. But Jerry was his oldest friend, the price was right, it was close to home, and when you missed a heartbreaker, you could always blame it on the table being off true.

Ed and Jerry had been classmates back on Long Island from kindergarten through junior high. Then, Jerry got religion and transferred to a yeshiva in Brooklyn. Soon after, his family moved, and the two boys lost touch. Jerry went to rabbinical school and wound up at a small congregation in Daly City. The experience convinced him he did not want a pulpit. It involved too many egos, too many arguments, too much politics, in short, as he quipped to Ed, "too many Jews." Jerry had two loves, Jewish history and working with kids, so he opted for two part-time jobs, teaching history afternoons at Brandeis Hillel Day School near SF State, and working at IMYC after school and into the evening. Shortly after Ed joined the *Defender*, Jerry noticed his byline, and they reunited.

"Two-nine combo," Jerry announced. Combination shots are harder than they look, but the two was close to a corner pocket, allowing a good deal of leeway for the nine. The two dropped.

"Eleven." He nodded to the corner pocket at the other end of the table. He sank it, putting enough follow on the cue ball to bring it around and set up the three.

"Nice," Ed said, "but tell the truth: Did you have that figured?"

Jerry answered with a rabbinical proverb: "Pray like everything depends on God. Act like everything depends on you."

Ed answered Jerry's run of six balls with six of his own. That left three. Jerry ran three, but had nowhere to go with the final ball. "Bank, long."

It was a desperation call, an impossible shot. Ed chalked up, confident Jerry would miss. But it rolled the length of the table, bounced off the rail, and rolled all the way back—straight into the pocket. Jerry pumped his stick in the air in triumph.

Ed racked up. "This job has worked wonders for your game, Jer. I'm envious. Paid good money to shoot pool."

"I wish. More like: Paid next to nothing to grovel before funders who have better things to do with their shekels."

The IMYC had been having a tough time with grants, and everyone on staff had been impressed into the fund-raising effort.

"So how's it going?"

"Lots of pats on the back, a few small things, and one big challenge grant. If we raise $500,000, some foundation will match it."

"That sounds promising."

"Yeah, but we're nowhere near raising the half mil. Arturo is working his butt off, but so far, it doesn't look good." Arturo Velasquez was the IMYC executive director. "Everyone applauds what we do, and wants a place for Mission kids to get off the street. They just don't want to pay for it."

Over the past few months, Jerry's assessments of the Center's prospects had grown increasingly pessimistic. He sank a few quick shots.

"But enough of my *tsuras*"—Yiddish for problems—"how are your two murders?"

"A nightmare. Chet's nuts are in a vise. The ballistics matched. The same gun killed both of them. There are two murder warrants out for him now, one here, one there. The cops are licking their chops, convinced he's guilty. The other papers practically have him convicted. And have you listened to any talk radio lately?" Jerry shook his head. "Bobo Burns said Chet should get the gas chamber the other day, and most callers agreed."

"But in your piece this morning, you seemed to bend over backwards on Chet's behalf. Did Gilchrist lean on you?"

"Absolutely not. The Old Man's been incommunicado since the ballistics report. He may be an arrogant, super-rich old fuck, but I feel for the guy. Chet's put him through the wringer. As for bending over backward, someone's got to point out that the case against Chet is completely circumstantial. There are no witnesses. He had no motive to kill Murtinson. The charter company says he caught a plane to Anchorage, but their people couldn't pick him out of a photo line-up. And I find it odd that no one in his neighborhood up there laid eyes on him. No one heard a fight at the house. The neighbor, Sue, was home the whole time. She didn't hear a thing."

"But she's their friend, right? For all you know, Gilchrist could have slipped her some bucks to say that."

Ed sighed. "That's possible, but I don't think so. I interviewed her before Gilchrist even heard that Cabral was dead. And believe me, Laura was in no shape to bribe anyone."

"So where does that leave you, big guy?"

"Up you-know-where without a you-know-what. Until Chet shows, we've all got our thumbs up our butts."

"You know who intrigues me in all this—that guy who pulled Chet out of the party."

"Wardell?"

"You said he was talking about the Lost Gold, then Chet's book disappears."

"Yeah, and the Anchorage cops swear they didn't take it."

"So who did?"

"The cops say Chet must have grabbed it after he shot Cabral, which almost makes sense, but not quite. Laura says he always kept the book with a picture of his mother. If he took the book, Laura swears he would have taken the picture. But it was still there on the night table. I saw it."

"Which brings me back to Wardell. You said he was talking about the Lost Gold. He was the last person to see Chet, right?"

"Yeah, but Wardell has evaporated."

Jerry leaned over the fourteen, a short rail shot into the corner, eminently makable, except that the seven sat not much more than a ball's diameter off the rail right on top of the pocket. There were two ways to go. He could thread the needle, send the fourteen past the seven without touching it. Or he could kiss the seven, have the fourteen graze it. Kiss shots were trickier. "Fourteen. No kiss." He tapped the striped ball. It rolled straight down the rail, but at the last moment popped off and grazed the seven before dropping. No point. Ed fished the ball out and placed it on the spot. "Did you see that?" Jerry was disgusted. "How did it come unglued?" Pool talk for a ball that comes off the rail. "Damn table!"

Ed chalked up and missed an easy shot. His mind wasn't on the game.

19

"Wardell may hold the key. I assume you have an invitation list from the party. Is he on it?"

Ed stood over Julie's desk on the fourth floor. She had an office with a window, a door, and two chairs for visitors, a palace compared with his spartan cube down in the bowels of the newsroom. Showed you where the *Horn* placed its priorities.

"Let's see." She hit some keys, then some more. Ed drifted around to her side so he could view the screen over her shoulder. He could feel the warmth radiating from her and inhale her scent. Cinnamon with a hint of cocoa. She was wearing navy slacks and a navy vest, both with robin's-egg-blue trim, and a top of the same light blue with navy trim. "Nice outfit. Did you make it?"

"As a matter of fact, I did." She shot him a quick smile. "Got the fabric on sale at Mendel's in the Haight."

"I like frugal women."

"And I like generous men." She smiled and their eyes met for a moment. Hers were deep shimmering pools. Then Julie turned back to her screen. "Wardell. Wardell. That's his last name, right?"

"Presumably."

"No Wardell on the list. I'm searching it as a first name. Nothing. Sorry. Have you checked with the Initiative and the Museum? They sent invitations to their own lists."

"Not yet, but I will."

She swiveled in her chair, looked up at him. "You know, you could have phoned me. You didn't have to come up here."

He touched her shoulder. "I wanted to see you."

Julie blushed. "And do you like what you see?"

"Very much." He bent down and kissed her lightly on the cheek. It felt natural, right. Then she turned and their lips met and their arms found each other's backs and Ed pulled Julie up. Their lips parted and they kissed deeply.

"We still on for dinner tomorrow night?" Ed asked, breathless.

"Unless some other woman drags you off to Alaska again."

Tomorrow suddenly felt too distant. "How about moving it up to tonight?"

"I'd love to, but I have an event. The big Handgun dinner at the Fairmont. Gilchrist is speaking, and I have to be there. If he puts his foot in his mouth, I'm on spin control."

"Lucky you. Okay, tomorrow then. I'll pick you up at 7:30."

"Pull into the driveway. Parking's impossible."

They kissed again, but less passionately, suddenly aware that they were at work.

Ed returned to his cube, which looked smaller than usual, and called Denise Vandenburn at the Museum. No Wardell on their invitation list, either. Next he tried the Handgun Control office. Ditto. Then he checked the San Francisco phone book. Nothing. New listings. Nada. The Registrar of Voters. Three Wardells, two in their seventies, one, twenty-two. No go. He repeated this exercise for Alameda, Contra Costa, Marin, San Mateo, and Santa Clara counties with the same results. Then he called the *Horn's* police reporter and asked him to finagle a quick check through the Department of Motor Vehicles. Twenty minutes later, he got the word: One hundred ninety-seven Wardells in California. Did he want their information? Ed considered a messenger, but couldn't stand the thought of waiting around for the delivery. Instead, he sprinted down to the press room on Bryant Street. About half the Wardells were women, and most of the men were too old or young. Of the forty possibles, there were eight worth following up. Ed prevailed on the cop reporter to call in another favor, and get computer-generated copies of their photos. None bore any resemblance to Mr. Birkenstocks.

● ● ●

"Walt wants you at the meeting." It was Ruffen calling Ed into the daily Budget meeting. Walt was Walter French, the *Foghorn's* executive editor. Ed took a seat at the big conference table, the only reporter in a room full of department heads. The few times he'd attended Budget meetings, they reminded him of his orals at Cal. Today was no different, except that he had fewer answers.

"So Ed, what have you got?" French asked.

"Two murders. Same gun. Suspect on the run." Ed flipped through his summary notes. "The Anchorage cops found no prints in the house except Chet's, Laura's, Cabral's, and the neighbor's."

"Chet's toast." It was Marty Liu, the business editor.

"But he had no motive to kill Murtinson," Ed retorted. "Foxsen did."

"Whoever shot Murtinson, or had him shot, could have sent the shooter to Anchorage." Here was Ruffen sticking up for Chet, running interference for Ed. Had he softened for some reason? Had he spoken to Helios? Or had Ed's perceptions of the man changed now that he knew a bit more about him?

"But Foxsen has no motive for Cabral, does he?" Now the foreign editor was weighing in. He started out decades earlier as a cop chaser in St. Louis and still thought he owned the crime beat. "Who has a motive to kill both of them?"

All eyes turned to Ed. "No one … unless someone was trying to set Chet up."

"Sounds fetched from pretty far." This was Karen Kaitz, the new features editor. She was good, but she was showing herself to be cut from the Ruffen mold, a hardass—even if hers was an eyeful.

Ed sighed. "Maybe. Probably. I don't know."

"What do the cops say?" John Gagliano, the M.E., tapped his pen absently on the table. He was getting bored.

"They're convinced Chet did both of them. Between Chet's disappearance and his history of buying heroin from Cabral, they don't seem to care that he has no motive for Murtinson."

"I spoke to the Old Man." French cast his eyes upward, indicating Gilville three stories above them. "He thinks it's Chet."

Ed squirmed in his chair. "I know it looks bad with Chet running and all, but when I knew him at Cal … he just wasn't the heroin type."

"What type is that exactly?" Marty Liu was also getting impatient.

"And Laura swears on a stack of Bibles that he was as clean as the inside of an operating room." This elicited snorts of derision: Loyal wife bullshit.

"What about the mystery man you've been chasing?" Ruffen asked.

"Wardell, the guy Chet left the party with. Thirtyish. An oddball: business suit with Birkenstocks. I overheard them talking about the Lost Gold, which is a big interest of Chet's. But Wardell doesn't exist. I've tracked him though every database imaginable. There's no record of him anywhere in California."

"You sure you got his name right?"

Ed turned up his palms. "I'm *pretty* sure ..."

"What do you think, Ron?" French was a popular X.E. because he always made a show of involving the department heads in his decisions.

"I think Ed's done a hell of a job chasing this thing down. But all we've got at the moment is dead-ends. I think Ed should keep in touch with the cops, but otherwise wrap it up with a more-questions-than-answers piece, then move it to the back burner. Until something new breaks, we're beating a dead horse."

"My thoughts exactly," French said.

Ed gritted his teeth, debated opening his mouth. It was no debate. He couldn't help himself. "May I just say one last thing? I think Mr. Gilchrist would want the investigation to proceed. People like Wardell don't just vanish without a trace."

"Chet has." The Sports Editor.

"What do you want to do, consult a psychic?" Marty Liu was an irritating little schmuck.

"All the evidence against Chet, every bit of it, is circumstantial."

"Good point." French said. "Stress that in your wrap-up. And keep your ear to the ground. If anything breaks, I want to know."

• • •

Ed slugged the story NOT THE END and hit the SEND key. He sensed movement behind him and looked up to find Ruffen leaning against the opening into his cube.

"You knew how the meeting would go." Ruffen's tone was philosophical, almost tender.

"Yeah." He didn't like it, but he knew.

"An old buddy in deep doo-doo. A pile of unanswered questions. This story is a bitch, and you've been running yourself ragged chasing it. So take the rest of the day off. Go watch the Giants, then have a filet mignon dinner on me. Take a date." He held out two tickets. "The Handgun Control dinner at the Fairmont. Gilchrist is speaking. File after. No need to go more than three hundred words. Two quotes ought to do it."

Ed couldn't believe his good fortune. He could have dinner with Julie after all, even if they'd both be working. Still, they'd be together.

Back home on Dolores Terrace, Ed popped the cap off an Anchor Steam, spread some cream cheese on a poppy-seed bagel, and watched the Dodgers hand it to the home team. The Giants went down 2-1 in the first and couldn't climb out of the hole. Then, in the seventh, a miracle, two runs. The Giants went up 3-2.

Ed drained his beer and thought about spending the evening with Julie. Then he remembered that he had an extra ticket to the dinner. He called the Handgun Initiative office, then the assignment desk at Channel 5, and finally *The Defender*.

"Tim Huang," a familiar voice chirped, just as Brett Butler doubled to win the game 4-2. The Giants' magic number was now 5.

"Hey, bro," Ed said, a little tipsy from the mid-afternoon beer and the Giants' victory. "How's the big romance?"

"Hey, Ed, those pieces from Alaska were good."

"Thanks, but the news was shit."

"What can you do? You don't make the news. You just report it."

"Yeah. So, Tim, you been seeing the lovely Ms. Nakagawa?"

Tim hesitated, as though discussing it might jinx things. "Uh ... yeah."

"But not tonight, right? She's going to the Handgun dinner and *The Defender* wasn't invited."

"You're certainly well-informed ..."

"Officially, only dailies and electronics were invited, but I bet Jocko was spitting nails about being snubbed."

"He wasn't too bad. I'd say spitting thumbtacks. But where's all this going?"

"The question, my man, is where are *you* going? And the answer is— to the Handgun dinner. I have an extra ticket. I thought perhaps you and Kim might like to double-date with me—and Julie."

"Julie? Who's Julie?"

"Julie Pearl, does PR for the *Horn*. Remember the press conference at the Hall?"

"The cute black woman? Ed, you dog!"

Ed barked like a spaniel, but what came out sounded more like the howl of a wolf.

20

Ed knotted his best tie in front of the bathroom mirror and was ironing his dressiest slacks when the phone rang.

"Please hold for Mr. Calderone," a sultry woman's voice crooned. For a moment, Ed thought it must be a wrong number. Then he realized: Ted Calderone, *Full Disclosure*. Why would Calderone call him?

"Another day, another corpse, huh?"

"Something like that."

"Interesting reports from up in Iglooland. Too bad you didn't know a few crucial details."

"Which details?"

"Just some information that recently came my way. Very intriguing information about Juan Cabral and the Gilchrist family."

"Shoot."

Calderone snorted. "Poor choice of words there, friend. And not over the phone. I'll be up at South Tahoe this weekend. I have a place in Heavenly Vista." He rattled off the address and phone number. "My information is worth the trip."

Then Calderone hung up.

Julie lived in a second-floor apartment behind a large ginkgo tree on Elgin Park, a narrow block-long street between Market and Duboce below the new Mint and up against a spur of elevated freeway. In the 1880s, a builder from the Scottish city of Elgin erected stately Victorians along it, but after the earthquake and fire destroyed them, workers' tenements were hastily thrown up and the street descended into seediness, which was cemented by the coming of the freeway. Now, with gentrification marching down Market from the Castro, the old buildings were getting renovated and Elgin Park was looking up.

Ed's knock was greeted by growls and loud barking. "Ella!" Julie's voice admonished. "Down, girl!" When she opened the door, Ed saw a menacing German shepherd. "Don't worry," Julie reassured him, "she's all bark."

"Ella?"

"Fitzgerald."

"Great singer."

"The best."

Julie looked stunning in a low-cut, figure-hugging, black cocktail dress with lavender spaghetti straps, lavender trim, a black-and-lavender scarf, and amethyst earrings with a matching necklace that looked incandescent against her umber skin.

"Yes," she answered before he could ask the question. "I made the dress—after I got the scarf, earrings, and necklace as a gift."

"Nice gift," Ed observed, squiring her to his newly washed and vacuumed Mustang.

"If you can't be rich," she replied, "have rich friends."

"Anyone I might know?"

"I never kiss and tell."

"What never?" he sang in a poor imitation of Gilbert and Sullivan.

"Well, hardly ever." She rejoined in song. They both laughed.

The Fairmont's immense Grand Ballroom was packed with upwards of a thousand well-heeled supporters of the Handgun Control Initiative. Ed, Julie, Tim, and Kim were seated off to one side of the dais in the media ghetto. Kim was growing on Ed. She was charming and intelligent, and seemed sincerely infatuated with Tim. The four of them enjoyed each other, as well as the filet and Merlot, which went down a lot easier than the questions the press hurled at Gilchrist at the end of his speech.

"Did your son commit these murders?"

"Has he contacted you?"

"Do you think he used a handgun to embarrass you?"

"There's a rumor that you helped him flee the country. Did you?"

"Do you think he deserves the death penalty?"

Ed squirmed in his chair. Even by his own brass-knuckles standards of fairness, these hacks were being vicious. It was obvious why. Gilchrist was the billionaire owner of the largest paper north of L.A. and west of

Chicago. He was, therefore, fair game under the journalistic rubric of Screw the Rich. He was also a major player in the initiative, therefore a public figure, which meant that these turkeys could print just about anything without risking a libel suit. Every reporter in attendance, except Ed, had been instructed to disembowel him, including Kim, whose editor told her to "castrate" him. She assured Julie she wouldn't. "Just a little circumcision," she said.

Gilchrist stood ramrod straight, his hands grasping the lectern, and answered every question. He was brief, but respectful. He never raised his voice or lost his temper, a study in patrician poise.

When Kim left to do her stand-up, Julie leaned close to Ed. "I hate reporters. Present company excepted."

"Me too," Ed replied. "Gilchrist is either very brave or out of his mind to let himself in for this shit. But he handled himself very well. Do I detect the guiding hand of Ms. Pearl in his performance?"

She smiled. "He and I had a little conversation this afternoon."

"Do tell."

"I just told him to take his lumps, answer every question without getting mad, and then walk off holding his head high."

"You're not going to be acting PR director much longer."

An icy wind gusted atop Nob Hill when Ed and Julie left the Fairmont. The California Street cable car clanged as it passed them smelling of fresh lacquer and cold steel. Their breath formed clouds, and they huddled close together on the way to Ed's car, parked at a hydrant two blocks down the hill by an all-night laundromat. He unlocked the passenger door, then turned and kissed Julie. She kissed him back, deeply. "Let's go to my place," she whispered urgently into his ear.

"Let's."

• • •

"Why don't you put on some music?" Julie pointed him to the music corner of her living room. Like everyone else, she was changing over from vinyl to CDs. She had an old stereo for the former and an oversized boom box for the latter.

"Got anything your father played on?" Ed called.

"Uh … it's buried in there," she called from her bedroom. "I'll pull something out later. In the meantime, put on whatever you like."

Her records looked worn, so Ed thumbed through the CDs, mostly R&B and some cool jazz. He selected *Wake Up Everybody* by Harold Melvin and the Blue Notes.

Ella was curled up docilely on a pile of garage-sale throw pillows in a corner of the living-dining room. There was a rickety futon sofa, two stuffed chairs that had seen better days, and a glass coffee table with a chipped top piled high with recent issues of *The New Yorker*, *Ebony*, and *Vogue*. The apartment reminded Ed of others he'd visited, the homes of single women who seemed to be more camped out than moved in, as if waiting for some man to give them a reason to nest.

Julie appeared wearing a silk kimono with an embroidered dragon. Her profile suggested she was not wearing a bra. In her hands, she carried a small enamel box. She sat down on the sofa, beckoned Ed to sit next to her, and then opened it with a flourish. It contained a hand-rolled cigarette, a small mirror, a razor blade, a tiny spoon, and a vial of white powder.

"Pot and coke," she murmured, nuzzling close to Ed, "are great for sex, don't you think?"

Ed would have left it at pot. Coke was not his drug. Never had been. The high was no better than a double espresso, but it wired him horribly, made him irritable, and left him with sore jaw muscles from clenching his teeth. Under the circumstances, however, he was not about to argue.

They had a few hits and did a few lines. Then Ed untied the sash on Julie's kimono. It was all she was wearing.

• • •

Afterward, they lay in her bed and joked about Coit Tower's resemblance to part of the male anatomy. Sleep was out of the question. They were too thrilled with each other, and too coked up. Julie had a craving for orange juice and got up to get some. She did not pull the kimono back on, just walked out of the room gloriously naked.

Ed's mind raced. Images collided with one another: The kimono slipping off Julie's shoulders. Chet's appearance at his cubicle. Murtinson being wheeled out. The curve of Julie's hips. The opulence of the fifth floor. Tim looking moon-eyed at Kim. Julie's tongue circling his nipples. The Reilly Double Eagle big as a frisbee. Laura at her kitchen table in Anchorage. Julie's ringlets bobbing up and down over his belly. Nick

Helios recounting Ruffen's saga. Jerry's end-to-end bank shot. Calderone saying, "My information is worth the trip." Julie's smile. Julie's fingers. Her laugh. Her shoulders, breasts, thighs, and orgasm. Julie.

She reappeared, bearing two glasses of OJ. She slipped under the covers beside Ed, enveloping him in erotic warmth. He kissed her cheek.

"I'm way too wired to sleep," he said.

"Me, too." She kneaded his inner thigh.

"Let's drive up to Tahoe for the weekend."

She looked him in the eye. "Are you serious? Now? This late?"

"I'd like to see a source up there. Shouldn't take long. The rest of the weekend, we could have a lot of fun."

"You are serious."

"I could use some time away. Couldn't you?"

She took a sip of juice, considered the idea. Ed cupped a hand over her breast. "How about it? A romantic hotel, a hot tub, a little hiking, romantic dinners, and then—"

"Okay!" She beamed. Ed realized she felt flattered to be asked. "Know what? I may even be able to get us a place."

"How?"

"We—the PR department—lease a house up there, where the honchos entertain big wigs. I'll call in the morning. If no one is using it, I don't see why we couldn't. If not, we can always find a motel or stay at a casino."

"Where's the house?"

"South Lake. Heavenly Vista."

"You're *magic.* That's where my source is." Ed pulled her close and inhaled deeply. He had never known a warmth so nurturing, a fragrance so intoxicating.

21

Julie couldn't call her dog-sitter in the middle of the night, so they took Ella with them. She slept most of the way, doggie-snoring on the back seat.

Ed brought a box of cassettes, and experienced pure pleasure at Julie's enthusiasm over them. They took turns selecting tapes. She opened up with *The Atlantic History of R&B*. Then Ed picked *Solomon Burke's Greatest Hits*. Julie played *Ray Charles in Concert*. Then Ed went with Santana's first. They sang duets and shared wistful stories about the events they associated with various tunes.

Traffic on 80 was light to Sacramento. Highway 50 was empty east of Placerville. The sun came up as they crested Echo Summit. On the way down into Tahoe Basin, the lake sparkled, a blue diamond in sunrise light.

They ate a ridiculously huge breakfast at Harrah's $2.99 buffet, and put fifty bucks on the Giants to win the World Series. Then Julie made her call. The house was vacant, all theirs. They stopped by the management office, picked up the key, and headed up the hill.

The house turned out to be a four-bedroom, five-bath, modified A-frame built on a promontory overlooking the Lake. It had a cathedral living room with an enormous deck that looked south to Heavenly Valley, and a giant hot tub on a back deck that looked north into the deep green of the national forest. From the front deck, the lakeshore and casinos of Stateline were a picture postcard far below them. Off to the right, the mountain was criss-crossed by ski runs, minus the snow. In the distance, the Sierra ascended into clouds.

"So, Gilcorp owns this?" Ed inhaled the sharp aroma of a million pine trees.

"No, the department leases it. We rotate every few years: Incline Village, Mt. Shasta, Las Vegas. Got to give the big advertisers and celebrities some variety to keep them happy."

"Celebrities?"

"Movie stars, sports figures, politicians. Gilchrist has always moved in celebrity circles."

"And I imagine that when a big advertiser rubs shoulders with some movie star over cocktails on the deck, the ad account gets renewed."

Julie laughed. "You have a future in PR."

"And what does a PR person do when the publisher entertains up here?"

"I have a little fun and deal with lots of logistics. Endless logistics. As complicated as a wedding. To organize the last retreat, I was on the phone for weeks. You wouldn't believe how difficult some celebrities' people can be."

"Maybe I'll stick to reporting."

She squeezed his hand. "Come on, I want to show you something."

She led him into the master bedroom and motioned for him to join her on the big bed. It faced double French doors that opened into a fern-filled greenhouse on a private deck. A bed, a great view, and Julie. My luck has definitely changed, Ed mused. He was just getting comfortable when Julie pressed a button on the headboard, and the bed lurched into motion.

Ed started. "Wha?"

"You're not going to believe this."

The bed rumbled slowly toward the French doors, which swung wide open. Before Julie could unbutton Ed's shirt, the bed came to a halt in the center of the greenhouse, surrounded by leafy ferns, multi-colored crotons, and several tall figs and dieffenbachias. Julie pressed another button. Something rumbled overhead. A large panel of glass roof retracted and suddenly they were gazing up at a cornflower-blue sky.

"Ever do it under open sky?" Julie coaxed Ed's shirt over his shoulders.

"My closest was on hard ground in a tent that smelled of insect repellent."

Julie pulled her top over her head, unhooked her bra, and tossed it aside. She bounced on the mattress. "Nothing hard about this." Her breasts danced. Then she snaked a hand between Ed's legs. "Now, here's something getting hard." They laughed.

Ed pulled her down on top of him, drew crazy patterns on her back with the pads of his fingers. "I get the feeling you've done this before …"

She pulled away suddenly, regarding him dubiously. "That's not a problem, is it? We've both had relationships. But right now, I'm not thinking of anyone but you. I'm here with *you,* Ed. Are you here with *me?*"

Ed looked into her eyes and saw reproach mixed with insecurity and longing. She was a doe in the forest, lithe but skittish. Her bronze ringlets fell over one eye and he hooked them behind her ear. "Yes, totally here with you. Every molecule. Right here."

He pulled her back down on top of him and kissed her, then ran his fingers through her hair and nibbled on an ear lobe. She wriggled out of her slacks, then undid Ed's and pulled them off.

"You are the sexiest woman on Earth."

Julie smiled, then nestled herself back down on him. Her mouth found his. They were both hungry. "You're not just saying that to seduce me, are you?"

Ed caressed the small of her back. "Yes."

More laughter and rolling around.

The sun's warmth added to their heat. Huge pines towered over them, swaying approvingly in the morning breeze. Two butterflies, lighted on the edge of the retracted roof, then fluttered away. Ed drew Julie close. It wasn't just a line. She *was* the sexiest woman on Earth.

22

Julie took Ella for a hike along the lakeshore through Tahoe Keys, while Ed drove the winding roads that snaked across Heavenly Vista to the secluded canyon where Calderone's place was perched in deep forest at the edge of a granite cliff that turned into a waterfall in spring as the snow melted.

Calderone's retreat made the *Foghorn* chalet look like an RV. At the end of a high stone wall that extended some fifty yards, Ed pulled up at an imposing iron gate, and identified himself to a video camera. The gate swung open and Ed drove up a set of switchbacks to a back-country palace the art director at *Sunset* would die to photograph. A muscleman sans neck with very close-cropped hair and a chest as broad as the Giants' scoreboard opened the front door and escorted him through a living room that evoked the lobby of the Ahwahnee Lodge: enormous river rock fireplace, potted trees, deep carpets over wide boards of polished wood, and wicker with deep cushions. Crossing a dining room that could seat thirty, passing a three-room kitchen suite and an office almost as large as Gilchrist's at the paper, Ed finally entered a steamy room with a large bubbling hot tub. The air was heavy with warm mist and the smell of chlorine.

Calderone was crouched down by the tub. Dressed in faded jeans and a blue and gray cotton sweater, his dark hair swept straight back and glistening in the mist. He held a fancy camera. In the tub was Ms. Voluptuous from the Museum party. Chastity? No, definitely not. Charity, Miss February. She was naked. The water bubbled around her mammoth breasts.

"Ah, Rosenberg. Glad you could make it." Calderone's damp hand shook Ed's firmly. "Take a break, okay, honey?"

He held out a hand to Miss February, who surprised Ed by blushing as she stepped out of the tub. Calderone grabbed a terrycloth robe and held it out for her. Her pubic hair was trimmed into the shape of a heart. Calderone saw him notice.

"Miss February. Valentine's Day."

Charity wrapped the robe around her, tied the sash, and padded off. Calderone and Ed trekked back through the house, down a hall, and into the pantry.

"Care for a drink? You name it, I got it."

Ed was still feeling the after-effects of polydrug abuse, and asked for herb tea. Calderone nodded at a Hispanic woman in a white uniform and moments later, she handed him a cup of hot yellow liquid. Chamomile. Calderone requested a bloody Mary.

Calderone's study had a wall of windows with a view of forest and high peaks, a wall of bookshelves filled with hardbacks and knick-knacks, a wall containing a large collection of rifles under the stuffed head of a four-point buck, and a wall displaying dozens of framed covers of *Full Disclosure*.

No, Ed realized, not framed covers, entire issues encased in hard plastic sleeves. The early covers carried screaming headlines of major exposés, along with shots of a boob or two, nipples discreetly covered. But over the years, the headlines shrank and the covers became increasingly devoted to nubile young women's breasts … and points south. Monster tits and manicured pubes now dominated every cover. Miss February would fit right in.

Calderone noticed him scanning the magazine wall. "In some ways, the most interesting issue is the one the public never saw, the prototype." He used a cherrypicker to reach up and pluck it from its sleeve, then dropped it into Ed's hands.

Ed flipped pages. Compared with recent *Full Disclosures*, the protoype was quite thin with an ugly typeface, amateurish art direction, and next to no advertising. But it had launched the publishing empire that built this place. Who was Ed to disparage humble beginnings? "An interesting historical document," the former historian allowed.

"You missed the most interesting part."

Ed arched an eyebrow quizzically.

"Take a look at the cover model."

In the prototype, she was confined to a box in the upper left corner.

Most of the cover was devoted to a headline: "How Banks Steal Your Money—And Charge You For It." The model was a generically pretty blonde in her early twenties, naked but demure, the kind of arty portrait that graces perfume ads in the *New York Times Magazine*. She was seated on a rug with her arms folded across her breasts, obscuring them, her legs cleverly positioned to hint at what resided between them while revealing nothing. "Okay," Ed said. "What about her?"

"Now take a look at the TOC." Magazine talk for table of contents.

Ed flipped in a few pages. There she was again, a little larger, shot at an angle from behind, her head turned to smile at the camera, her long straw locks hiding one boob and her firm butt positioned to show nothing beyond what the skin-cream ads in the women's magazines reveal. "Okay."

"Now flip to the centerfold."

That was easy. Unlike more recent issues that were perfect bound to accommodate a fatter magazine and type on the spine, the prototype was saddle-stitched and flopped open to the staples. Three photos comprised the center spread: the model in a bikini walking along Ocean Beach with Cliff House in the background; then a shot of her knee deep in the surf, bare-breasted, holding her top over her head, a flag in the breeze; and finally, a shot of her lounging on the sand naked playing gynecology patient. What game was Calderone playing, Ed wondered. Girlie books always have center spreads with naked babes. He felt himself becoming impatient. "So?"

"So take a closer look."

"At what?"

"The centerfold's a different girl."

So she was. The beach bunny had hair a shade darker than the other gal and more curves in her figure.

"What happened? Your cover girl decide not to go all the way?"

"Not exactly. Take another look at her."

Ed hesitated. His patience was wearing thin. So what if Calderone was a media mogul. Ed didn't like having his chain yanked.

"Come on," Calderone coaxed, "the cover girl is part of your story."

"What?" Ed flipped back to the prototype cover. Compared with more recent covers that had been shot by some of the country's best photographers, the perfume-ad blonde was disappointing. Kind of skinny, shot by an amateur. "I don't—"

Calderone chuckled. "Take a closer look. At her face. At the head-line."

The face was pretty with a college girl's naive innocence. The head-line read: Summers Is Hot. A typo? Then, with a start, Ed recognized Laura Gilchrist. Summers was her maiden name. He gazed at the photo. Laura was much younger then. But there she was, in the buff. Ed's jaw dropped to the bottom of Tahoe. He looked at Calderone.

"Laura had a life before Junior," Calderone explained. "Back at Stanford, she and I were a major item, hot and heavy for quite a while. Even talked marriage. Then His Highness stole her away from me, the prick, and threat-ened to sue me up the ying-yang if I circulated the prototype with guess who showing her nips and vertical smile. Had to reshoot the centerfold with a new model. Held up printing. I lost an investor. Damn near killed the magazine. And you know what? I had a bombproof release from Laura. I could have plastered her pussy on billboards if I wanted. But I was young and stupid. When the *Foghorn's* lawyers threatened to turn me into a so-prano, I caved. Fortunately, just when I maxed out my credit cards, an-other investor opened his checkbook, and the rest is history."

"Is that why Laura slapped you at the party? Photos of her nude?"

"That and the fact that because of an inadvertent clerical error at the magazine, I accidentally didn't turn over all the negatives. She and Jun-ior were in the process of suing me for them when somebody's drug problem sent them to parts unknown."

"Clerical error?"

"Totally."

"How'd they find out you still had any negatives?"

"My original art director was a dickhead. I fired him. He got pissed and told them. But we're talking almost fifteen years ago. They never showed up in court, so their suit got tossed. I had no idea she still carried such a grudge."

"They could reinstate their suit."

Calderone shrugged. "Wouldn't do any good. The negatives got lost years ago when the magazine moved to North Beach."

"Lost?"

"Pissed me off royally. I was toying with the idea of running those pictures in my memoirs." Then he laughed.

Ed didn't. Instead, he stared at the cover shot of Laura. He found it difficult to take his eyes off her. She didn't have the … assets of current

Full Disclosure models, but she looked fresh and innocent, alluring. "Who was the investor you lost?"

"A silent partner. Very silent."

"And the replacement?"

"Even quieter, but very happy with the way the business developed."

"I'm not surprised." Ed wondered if the rumors were true, that mob money financed Calderone. "So, here I am. You said you had information that you didn't want to discuss over the phone. Laura's photos?"

"Partly, and other things. You have any idea what I pay writers for big investigative features?"

Calderone had a reputation for paying more than top dollar. "Not really."

"How about $25K?" That was more than top dollar. Way more. Calderone gestured for Ed to sit in a wicker throne chair, and sat himself down in its mate. Bright mountain light streamed in through high windows, triggering in Ed a recollection of old photographs—shafts of sunlight slanting across New York's Grand Central Station.

Calderone leaned forward in his chair. "Chet fucked me royally way back when. But it's hard to hold a grudge when I wake up in the morning in this place with Charity purring next to me. Fact is, I like the way you've been covering the Second Going of Christ. Good research. Solid writing … within the limits of newspaper style. I want you to cut loose, write the inside story for my readers. I'm talking 3 million circulation, with lots of pass-along." That was six times the *Foghorn's* readership. And though they denied it, many important people in the New York media community never missed an issue. A writer could do worse.

"So, you give me a tip, and I write the story for you. Is that it?"

"I'd put it a little differently: I provide you with explosive information that turns this story into a blockbuster. I pay you enough to dump that dipshit job of yours. And I give you the right to keep all the money from the bestselling book you write off the story you do for me."

"Generous offer … but I'm not about to quit my job."

"So keep your dumb job. I don't care. Just do the piece. When you see how much fun it is playing in the big leagues, *then* you'll quit."

Twenty-five thousand was a major chunk of change for a magazine feature. Ed decided he had nothing against come-fuck-me photos in the service of investigative reporting. But why was Calderone so eager? What wasn't he saying?

"I'll have to run this by my editor."

"Go ahead. Other *Foghorn* reporters have written for me. No one had a stroke."

If he turned Calderone down, Ed would never learn his real agenda. It was something he wanted to know. "All right … if it flies at the *Horn*, you've got yourself a deal. But it all depends on your information—if it's really as explosive as you say. If it isn't, I have no story, so you have no story, and I've wasted a trip." No I haven't, Ed thought, reflecting on the low whirr of the greenhouse roof retracting.

"Fair enough." Calderone leaned back in his chair, the raconteur: "Ten, maybe 11 years ago, just as the magazine was taking off, your dead guy number two, Juan Cabral, contacts me saying he knows some nasty shit about the Gilchrists that he's willing to spill for a price. Naturally, I'm interested. We set up a meet, but he never shows. Next thing I know, he gets popped for heroin. His lawyer won't let me near him. He gets put away. I write him off. End of story.

"Then, a few months ago, right before Chet became the Prodigal Son, out of the blue I get another call from Cabral. He's out of prison. He still has his information, and am I still interested? I tell him to fuck off. If he's so eager to deal, why did his lawyer stonewall me way back when? Why didn't he contact me when he was in prison? Cabral swears he has no idea his lawyer stiffed me. And he didn't contact me because he can't read much English beyond traffic signs, and his writing is worse. He's persistent, and sounds scared. Makes me curious. So I tell him to stop by my office. Again, he doesn't show. Next thing I know, he's a beef taco on Junior's floor. Now, what does that sound like?"

"If I can believe you—"

"Believe me."

"It sounds like blackmail. Cabral figured he could squeeze more out of Chet than he could get from you."

"Bingo. I'm guessing Cabral pulled the gun, but was tanked up on horse so Chet got it away from him and shot him."

"How do you explain the fact that the same gun killed Murtinson?"

"I can't be sure, but Murtinson was a close friend of the Gilchrists, very tight with the first Mrs. G. Maybe Cabral's info had something to do with her. Maybe Cabral was trying to put the squeeze on Murtinson too, and when the old coot got testy, bang bang."

Ed's mind raced. Cabral might be the bad guy, *not Chet*. And if that were true, then … "Maybe Chet wasn't buying heroin from Cabral. Maybe the guy's stash was his own private supply."

"Possibly. One thing I've liked about your stories has been the be-tween-the-lines skepticism about Chet's heroin use. I mean, I think the guy's a spoiled prick, but I never believed he was a junkie. The guy I knew at Stanford had a quick wit and an acid tongue. I've known a few upper-class junkies. They're not your pathetic street types, but it's clear they're using. They lose their edge. Chet never did."

"Okay, so Chet refuses to pay off Cabral. They fight. Chet wrestles Cabral's gun from him, and shoots him with it. So, why does Chet run?"

"It's your story. You tell me."

Ed considered the question while scanning the room, from the wall of rifles to the wall of magazines. "I could imagine two reasons: One, Chet's already under suspicion for killing Murtinson. And two, if he hangs around and claims a blackmail attempt, suddenly every reporter on Earth is looking to rattle bones in his family's closet—focusing on his mother, whose memory he reveres."

Calderone nodded. "And let's not forget reason number three: The guy's a coward. He has a problem he can't buy his way out of, he runs."

"But there's a big problem with this scenario: Cabral and Murtinson are both dead, and Chet's gone, so there's no way to confirm your black-mail hunch, or, if it's true, find out what Cabral had on Chet's mother."

"That's why I'm offering you the big bucks. To find out."

Miss February floated into the room, barefoot, still in the white robe, which was tied just loosely enough to be provocative. "Teddy, honey, how long you gonna be? When can we go to Caesar's?"

"You feeling lucky, baby?"

She smiled, reached inside the robe, and scratched herself under a boob.

"We're just about through here. Why don't you get dressed? Then we'll go. I'm feeling lucky, too."

• • •

Ed recalled Calderone's final words later that evening on the chalet's back deck, while sitting naked on the edge of the hot tub, taking in the view—mist rising from the bubbling water, Julie in the buff playing with tub toys, and behind her, the inky darkness of the forest at night.

"Would you pour me some Chardonnay?" she asked.

"My pleasure." Ed leaned back and poured two glasses.

He held one out to her. She dived into the bubbling cauldron and came up between his legs. She perched her elbows on his thighs. He offered her a wine glass. "*L'chaim,*" he said. The traditional Jewish toast: To life.

Their glasses touched, and chimed. Crystal.

"*L'chaim* back at you," Julie replied, with a proper guttural *ch.*

She took a sip, licked her lips, then leaned forward and licked something else.

"You are the most fantastic woman on Earth."

Julie didn't answer. She was busy.

23

Ed was awakened by chirping birds and the aroma of fresh coffee wafting his way from somewhere beyond the French doors. The birds sounded wonderful. The coffee smelled wonderful. The whole world was wonderful. He stretched luxuriously, considered rolling out of bed to find Julie, then decided to stay and take in the cottonball clouds tumbling over dancing treetops in the impossibly blue sky above their magical bed on the magical deck.

Julie appeared wearing his shirt and nothing else, carrying a tray with a pot of coffee, two cups, and a stack of English muffins dripping butter. Ed felt starved, but not for breakfast. He snaked an arm around her waist, and coaxed her toward him, kissing her neck. He directed her hand between his thighs.

"Pretty early to be so … excited," she said, stroking him gently.

"You excite me."

"We have to drop the key off by noon."

"That's eons from now." He ran a hand up under her shirt, cupped a warm breast.

"Maybe we should postpone breakfast," Julie ventured.

"You read my mind." He drew her close, nibbled her shoulder.

She snuggled close. A hawk soared in circles above them riding the thermals, but neither of them noticed.

• • •

Highway 50 was empty. Tahoe is a summer-winter destination. Spring and fall are off-seasons, especially that autumn, with the Giants and A's selling out every game.

Ed gunned the 'Stang up the switchbacks to Echo Summit, then cruised down the long western slope of the Sierra. They played Stevie Wonder's *Innervisions*. The windows were down. They bathed in R&B and a pine-scented breeze. Ella paced the back seat, barking at the occasional chipmunk racing along the side of the highway.

"So," Julie ventured, "in the bright light of a new day, do you have a story?"

"No," Ed replied firmly. "All I have is tantalizing speculation, not enough to hang a story on, especially considering the source."

"Calderone isn't credible?"

"On trends in lingerie, sure. But Ruffen and the higher-ups hate him. He's brash. He's unapologetically sleazy. And he's a howling success: Not a formula for popularity in the newsroom."

"So, was it worth it seeing him?"

He threw her a sidelong glance, reached over, and squeezed her thigh. "Are you kidding? Seeing him got me a fabulous weekend with the greatest woman on Earth." Julie grinned and blushed. She enjoyed his compliments. "And as far as the story is concerned, Calderone's tidbit opens the door to the possibility that Cabral's the killer. He might have had something on Chet's mother, who, as I recall, drank pretty heavily."

"Any ideas?"

"None yet. But Cabral was their chauffeur. What does a chauffeur see? Hanky panky in the back of the limo?"

"All the limos I've been in had blackout glass between the driver and the passengers. The driver can only see in back if the passengers let him."

Ed glanced at her. "And just how many limos have you been in?"

"Oh, a few—you know, corporate events."

The tape ended and Julie replaced it with a Motown collection. The road was all theirs. They wound through alternating expanses of forest and granite mountainsides following the South Fork of the American River down from the pass. The river was low as always in autumn with the snow melt gone. They rolled past Twin Bridges and Strawberry.

A few miles shy of Kyburz, the windshield suddenly became a spider web. Ed pumped the brakes and eased over to the shoulder thinking a rock had hit it. But then Ella howled, and Julie screamed, and there was something warm and red and sticky all over him. Blood. Someone was *shooting* at them.

Ed skidded to a stop in a graveled turnout. He heard faint popping sounds behind and above them. Julie's left arm looked like hamburger. She was bent forward, her head against the dash, screaming, clutching her wound. Blood dripped though her fingers.

Ed released her seat belt, ran around to her door, and pulled her from the car. A bullet's impact kicked up a spray of dust near his foot. Then another. Closer.

Ed half-carried half-dragged her down a rocky ravine toward the river below. She was howling, sobbing, and covered with blood. Remembering some first-aid, Ed set her down on the moist river bank and pulled off his shirt. He began tying it around her arm. Then something whizzed by his ear, and he decided the bandage would have to wait. Stumbling down the mossy rock of the river bank, he pulled her into the underbrush. He slipped, and they slid down. They wound up at the water's edge with a large boulder between them and their assailant. Ed was ankle deep in the cold stream. Julie was splayed out on the muddy bank, clutching her arm, moaning incoherently, her face contorted in pain.

Ed propped her up as best he could. He tied his shirt around her shredded arm, pulled it tight, and pressed a hand against it.

"Hey! Son! You all right?!" a voice called from downstream.

Ed spun around, losing his balance. He slipped deeper into the water, banging his knee on a rock.

"She hurt?" the voice hailed.

Across the river maybe fifteen yards away an elderly couple was fishing. They waved, set their gear down, and picked their way upstream toward them. The man was stout, with a hint of belly. He had a weatherbeaten face, and an old naval cap covering what appeared to be a bald head. He wore old jeans, and a T-shirt displaying a photograph of an antique car. A Model T? The woman was short and plump, with long gray hair wound into a knot on top of her head. She wore a faded yellow jumper over a white top. A visor shaded her face.

"She's been shot!" Ed yelled. "Shot!"

"I hear you!" The man called. Then to his wife, "Syl, go get one of our lounge chairs."

The woman turned up the bank toward a cottage in a clearing above. The man picked his way across the stream on stepping stones. Reaching them, he crouched down and took a look at Julie. "Hold her."

Ed scrambled behind Julie and cradled her in his arms. She was whimpering, semi-conscious, shot and banged up from the slide down the riverbank. Her entire left side was covered with blood. The bandage Ed tied was already crimson.

"I hate to move her," the man deliberated, "but we've got to get her out of the mud and up to the house."

The woman returned carrying a folded aluminum chaise lounge and a blanket. The man met her in the middle of the stream and took the chair.

"I called 911," she said, "and put some water up to boil."

The man nodded and turned back to Ed and Julie. He unfolded the chair into a makeshift stretcher and set it beside her. "Okay. Help me get her on this. I don't think her neck's broken, but hold onto it. Easy now. Okay, one, two, three!"

Ed scrambled for a foothold and grabbed Julie under the arms, bracing her head and neck against his chest. The man grasped her legs under the knees. They slipped and splashed. Ed suddenly became aware how cold the river was. Then Julie was supine on the nylon webbing. The woman threw the blanket over her.

"Now comes the hard part," the man said. "Getting her across."

"I'll help at this end," the woman said, moving into position next to Ed. She leaned down toward Julie. "It's okay, honey. You're going to be all right. Ambulance is on the way."

They lifted her and slowly stepped from stone to stone across the stream. It took forever. Ed's arms ached. His head ached. His legs, back, and hips all hurt. But at least the shooting had stopped. "Try not to move," the man told Julie. Some of the stepping stones wobbled, but no one fell. They hoisted Julie up the opposite bank, then maneuvered her into the metal-roofed cottage.

"Forget the bed," the woman said. "Just set her down in the kitchen."

They swung the chaise's U-shaped legs into place. Ed watched in a daze as the woman went to work on Julie's arm. With a scissors, she cut off his impromptu bandage and what was left of her sleeve. "Lord," she sighed. Julie's triceps was shredded. Blood dripped to the floor. "But I think it missed the bone." The woman washed the wound quickly with soap and hot water, then pulled some rags from a closet and tied a neat bandage. "That ought to hold till they get here."

Ed felt a hand on his shoulder. "You okay, son? Up for a look-see?" The man held a shotgun.

Ed looked at the man, then at Julie.

"Sylvia's got things in hand here. I'm going up to the highway. You want to come? Or stay?"

Ed's mind cleared. "I'll come." He knelt by Julie. "Hang on, babe. I love you. I'll be right back."

The two men scrambled back down the river bank.

"What happened?" the man asked, cradling the shotgun at his side.

"We were driving down, and then someone started shooting."

They picked their way across the stream and hustled up the other side. Ed guessed the man was in his early seventies. He was amazingly agile. Ed struggled to keep up with him.

Atop the bank, level with the highway, the man crouched behind a thick shrub and motioned for Ed to do the same.

"Don't hear nothing." The only sounds were the breeze, the water below them, and the whoosh of the occasional vehicle on 50.

The man placed his cap over the end of the gun barrel, and waved it out beyond the shrub, baiting the shooter. Nothing.

They stepped into the sun about twenty yards above the Mustang. A late model Ford with a Hertz bumper sticker stood beside it. A man was bent over Ed's car, looking inside it, a big, no neck guy with a shaved head … or—Ed squinted in the sunlight—maybe close-cropped hair.

"Hey!" The old man called out, swinging his shotgun to his shoulder.

Mr. No Neck looked up, dived into his rental car, and pulled onto the highway with a major spray of gravel. In an instant, he was gone.

"You get his license?" the man asked Ed.

"No. You?"

"No. Too far away."

They ambled down to the Mustang. The back window was shot out. Only a few jagged bits remained in the frame. Ella lay stiff on the back seat covered in blood and broken glass. Her head jutted out at an odd angle. Her tongue hung out of her mouth.

"Looks like your dog got it in the neck," the man said. "At least it was quick."

Part of the windshield littered the hood. Much of the rest had collapsed onto the front seats, now dyed with Julie's blood. Here and there, the 'Stang's body was pockmarked with small holes.

"Got your keys?"

Ed swept broken glass off the driver's seat and worked the ignition. It started, purred.

"Well, at least that's something," the man said. "By the way, I'm Bill. Bill Kay."

"Ed Rosenberg. Thank you. For everything."

"Just being neighborly."

Back at the Kay's cabin, Ed sat next to Julie sponging her face with a damp cloth. She was feverish, out of it, moaning softly. Now and then, her head thrashed back and forth.

"I gave her some pain pills," Sylvia explained, "left over from when I threw my back out last Christmas."

Ed nodded. "Thank you."

"Looks like you're headed back to Tahoe," Bill said. "That's the closest hospital. I know a guy there, does auto glass. Fix your car up."

• • •

Ed followed the ambulance to South Tahoe Community Hospital. Without a windshield, the incoming breeze burned his eyes and the impact of bugs stung his cheeks. His chest felt tight and he had to wipe tears from his eyes. *Julie and Ella took bullets meant for me.*

What could he say to her? Gee, sorry for getting you shot. Too bad about your dog. My mistake.

Would she even want to see him? Talk to him? Or would she shun all contact? Banish him from her life forever? Ed hoped for the best, but knew he deserved the worst, knew he was as good as dumped. You're a nice guy, Ed, but I have a problem with men who get me shot. …

Rather than stewing in a cauldron of despair, Ed pondered who was behind the shooting. It had to be Calderone. The son of a bitch lured me up here so I'd be a sitting duck for his thug on the way down.

But it couldn't be Calderone. He had no reason to go after me. Hell, he just recruited me as a writer, gave me the tip about Cabral. Calderone didn't get where he was by taking out his own reporters.

Still, who could it be but Calderone? The arrogant fuck has an armory on his wall. No one else knew I was coming up.

But it couldn't be Calderone. He may be a sleaze, but he's not stupid. You want to shoot someone, you do it in the city, make it look like a robbery or a drive-by. You don't do it in the mountains the day after your target visits you.

24

After a session with the Highway Patrol, Ed paced the Emergency waiting room making deals with God. *If she's all right, I'll fast on Yom Kippur. I'll go to services. I'll—*

"Mr. Rosenberg?"

The woman addressing him was a zaftig Earth mother in a white coat with long tawny hair and kind eyes that hinted at secret sorrow. Her badge said Lisa Mann, M.D. Ed held his breath, unable to reply.

Dr. Mann smiled. "Ms. Pearl is going to be fine. She was lucky. The bullet missed the bone. She lost a fair amount of muscle and blood, but nothing that rest, time, and some physical therapy won't heal. She's resting comfortably."

Ed sighed from the depths of his soul. *Thank you, God. Thank you.* Then he made Dr. Mann repeat everything just to be sure he'd heard right.

"When can I see her?"

"Later. She's sedated and sleeping. You look like you could use some rest yourself. I can't offer you a bed, but there are sofas in the lobby. I could leave a note at the nurse's station to have you paged when she wakes up."

Suddenly, Ed's limbs felt leaden, his eyelids droopy. "Thanks. I'm fine—now that she is. But I could use a cup of coffee … or three."

Dr. Mann directed him to the cafeteria. "By the way, have you spoken to that reporter?"

"What reporter?"

"Probably from the *Tahoe Citizen*. We don't get many shootings up here that aren't domestic disputes. You're news."

Oh great, Ed thought, wondering if he should duck out a side door to avoid the small-town yahoo. But no, whoever it was would just camp out by Julie's door and pounce on her once she came to. By talking now, he could spare her that.

The reporter turned out to be a mini-convention of print, radio, and TV people from the Sacramento-Tahoe-Reno corridor. They buzzed around him like flies on spilled Coke.

"What happened?"

"Who are you?"

"Who's the victim?"

"She your wife?"

"How'd you escape?"

"What were you doing up here?"

"Who called 911?"

"Any idea who did it?"

"Any idea why?"

It was not a pleasant experience. Where was Julie when he needed a PR pro? Now Ed knew why politicians, celebrities, and cops called such encounters "gang bangs." It was a violation, journalistic rape. Ed answered the who-what-where-and-when as briefly as possible, and said he had no idea about the why. He did not mention Calderone or the *Foghorn's* chalet. Just two friends up for a weekend of blackjack and hiking with the dog, the late dog. They pressed him on the why. These things don't just happen. He shrugged. Maybe not, but that's all he knew. They didn't like that and circled in closer. Then Ed realized what they wanted—a sardonic quote to tie the ribbon on this mystery-shooting-in-the-mountains story. "Maybe whoever it was thought my Mustang needed better ventilation." They bought it and dispersed.

Ed burned his tongue on a lousy cup of coffee, then figured he better check in with Ruffen. It being Sunday, his editor was no doubt at home, organizing the Bud and potato chips for the Giants game. He dialed Ruffen's number.

"What the hell happened to you? The desk just called with a wire report saying you and some girl got shot. You okay?" Ed felt touched. Ruffen sounded like he actually cared.

Ed recounted the story for what felt like the umpteenth time. He was okay. Julie got winged. The doctor expected a full recovery. Then he filled in what the wires didn't have, that he'd driven up to interview a source on the Murtinson-Chet-Cabral story.

Ruffen's tone executed a quick U turn. "I thought you wrapped that up." Once again, Ed was the problem child with the attitude problem.

"I did. You saw the piece. But at the meeting, Walt said I should keep an ear to the ground for new leads. This one was too good to pass up. It's possible that Cabral had some dirt on Chet's mother, that he tried to blackmail Murtinson, her dear friend, who wouldn't pay, so he killed him. Then he tried to blackmail Chet, who wrestled the gun away and killed him. Ron, maybe *Cabral's* the bad guy."

"Yeah, and maybe I'm the Virgin Mary. Where'd you get this? And why'd you have to go all the way to Tahoe to get it?"

"The source wouldn't talk over the phone. He was up here."

"And who might this reticent soul be?"

Ed took a deep breath before saying, "Ted Calderone."

"That sleaze bag? I wouldn't believe a word he said on sodium pentothal."

"Ron, he knew Chet at Stanford. Knew Laura, too. Knew her well."

"Don't 'Ron' me. So did a thousand other kids. You're trying my patience, Ed."

"Hey, it was the weekend. Free time, remember? I can't drive up to Tahoe?"

"Drive anywhere you want. But when I see my reporters' names in print, I want them as bylines, not headlines."

"Like it's my fault some asshole shot at us?"

"The desk said the chippie works at the paper."

"Julie Pearl, acting PR director."

"Pearl … yeah. I've seen her in the elevator. Cute. And how long has this been going on?"

"Ron, I don't see how that's any of your—"

"It wouldn't be, except that you're breaking a rule I learned the hard way many years ago: Don't get your meat where you get your bread."

"What can I say? It was chemistry."

"So's dynamite. You think Calderone could be behind this?"

Ed ran down both sides of the ledger, why it had to be him, and why it couldn't.

"Either way, it's speculation. Your story can't mention Calderone."

"What story?"

"The human-interest feature you're going to file fifteen minutes ago: My Bang-Bang Weekend in Tahoe. I want the blow-by-blow."

"Give me a break, Ron. I've got to take care of Julie."

"And pick up a story about one of our own reporters from the *wires*? Not on your life. Call the desk and start dictating. And I'm going to put someone on the Cabral angle, see if the Archive has anything that might tie him to Chet's mother. Oh, Christ! You know what I'm looking at right now?"

"No. What?"

"You—on the TV news. 'Better ventilation'? You can do better than that, Ed. Get cracking. When I read your piece, I want to cry."

• • •

Dictating finished, Ed poked his head into Julie's room. She was still sleeping. He plopped down exhausted into the chair by her bed. A bag of clear fluid hung from a pole beside her and a tube ran into her arm. She had other lines running in and out of her as well. Her sepia skin looked yellow, almost translucent. Her bronze hair lay lifeless and matted. She moved her head from side to side, moaning softly. Ed kissed her forehead, held her hand, and whispered in her ear: "I'm right here with you. I won't leave you. You're going to be all right."

With an effort, Julie pried her eyes open. They were glazed, red-rimmed, and teary. Ed couldn't be sure she could see him. Her lips parted as if trying to speak, but all that came out was a low groan.

Ed leaned over her, kissed her forehead and cheek, and repeated: "I'm right here. I won't leave you. You're going to be all right." Then he added: "I love you."

He squeezed her hand. She smiled weakly and squeezed back.

The day passed. Julie drifted in and out of drugged sleep. Ed napped fitfully beside her, startled awake by horrible dreams of war and fox-holes and machine-gun fire that left him covered in blood-soaked dirt and gore.

A nurse came by to dope up Julie for the night. She brought two pillows and a blanket for Ed. He turned a few chairs into a makeshift bed, but was too wired to sleep. He spent a while watching Julie's covers rise and fall, then turned on the TV.

He watched a *Rockford Files* episode he'd seen a few times, then the news came on: Hurricane Hugo was flattening Charleston, South Carolina. Kaiser was boosting rates 19 percent because of the cost of AIDS care. Montana threw five TD's as the Niners beat the Eagles 38-28. The A's topped the Twins 9-3. Their magic number was down to 2. And the Giants—*yes!*—crushed the Astros 10-2, on a three-run homer by Robbie Thompson. Their magic number was also 2.

Ed turned off the TV, tried to sleep, but couldn't. He turned the tube back on and suffered through a made-for-TV movie about a girl who was a high-school track star until a car wreck left her paraplegic. Like most TV movies, it earned an A for emotional manipulation and a C- for everything else. Ed began to nod around the time the girl joined a wheel-chair basketball team. Then suddenly he jumped up and stared at the screen wide-eyed. Could it be? No. Wait. *Yes.* The wheelchair basketball coach was the mystery man from the Museum party. Wardell.

25

When Dr. Mann said Julie could go home, she handed her a prescription for Tylenol with codeine. One of the nurses eased her arm into a sling. Ed helped her into a wheelchair, rolled her to the Mustang, and helped her in. The car had a new windshield and back window—and several residual holes in the sheet metal. Julie knew about Ella, but when she saw the brown stain on the back seat, she cried.

Ed fell all over himself apologizing for everything, telling Julie he wouldn't blame her if she never wanted to see him again. She smiled weakly and whispered that she didn't blame him: "We can't be sure it has anything to do with your story."

Ed's heart swelled. What a wonderful woman. Of course, they couldn't be sure. But what other explanation was there? He'd checked the local paper's morgue. There hadn't been a highway shooting like theirs around Tahoe for as long as anyone could remember. Ed felt like a prize chump. I finally meet someone special, and what happens?

It was spooky driving down 50 again. Just past the place where it happened, they turned on Silver Creek Road, and pulled up at the Kays' cabin. The carport held a newish Toyota and a restored antique car with a crank starter, thin tires, and wood-spoke wheels. Bill's hobby. They presented the Kays with a bouquet of flowers, a fancy tackle box, two bottles of wine, and a lavish picnic lunch: cold cuts, salads, apple pie and ice cream.

Bill and Sylvia had been retired for ten years. Before that, Bill had owned a string of Texaco stations around Sacramento and Syl had been the office manager for a veterinarian. Bill built the cabin over a few summers when the kids were young. They'd been coming up for thirty-six years now. These days, they spent three seasons at the cabin, and in winter, shuttled between their daughter's family in Santa Barbara and their son's in Irvine.

Julie wanted to see everything. She was shaky on her feet at first, but got better. Bill and Sylvia led them down to the river and pointed out where they'd slid down the opposite bank, and her passage across the stepping stones to the cabin.

On the way out, Ed showed her where he'd ditched the car before dragging her down the stream bank. Shattered glass still littered the gravel.

They drove down to Sacramento mostly in silence, listening to a variety tape Jerry had made for Ed's last birthday, heavy on the Grateful Dead. Julie dozed. As they approached the Bay Area, she became increasingly agitated.

Here it comes, Ed thought, the big kiss-off. I don't blame you, but I need space. Goodbye.

But no. Something else was going on. "I don't want to go back." She sounded like a frightened child.

"What are you talking about?" Ed felt perplexed. She *wasn't* breaking up with him?

"I don't want to go back to San Francisco," she reiterated more emphatically.

"Why not? You need to rest. What better place than home?"

"I don't want to go back to the city. Can't we go somewhere else?" she pleaded. "Somewhere far away? I'm well enough to travel. Let's go to the Caribbean. Barbados. My father's people come from there. I've always wanted to see it. Hot sun. Beautiful beaches. What do you say?" Was it the codeine? Or the wringer she'd been through? Or both? Ed couldn't tell.

"Uh ... I thought you'd want to sleep in your own bed. Is it Ella? You don't want to be home without her?"

"That ... and everything. I need a change, a fresh start."

So this was her way of lowering the boom. "You're talking about us, aren't you? Ending it."

"If I was, would I be asking you to come with me?" Her deep brown eyes were imploring. She wasn't ending it. But she was serious about leaving town.

"What about our jobs?"

"What about them?"

"They pay the rent."

"So, you're not coming?"

"Are you *going*?" Diane had left him. Now Julie was threatening to do the same. She said she wasn't breaking up, but how was this any different?

Ed played for time. "The doctor said you need rest. Listen, the AIDS concert is next weekend—Santana, John Lee Hooker, and Chris Isaak in the Park. You should be up and around by then. Want to go?"

Julie didn't answer. She'd dozed off again.

Back on Elgin Park, Ed helped her up the stairs and into bed, then set about rearranging her apartment for one-arm living. After that, he ran out for barbecued chicken from Big Nate's and a spinach salad from Hamburger Mary's. He cut up her food, helped her eat, cleaned up, and assisted as she undressed, washed up, got into pajamas, and took her pain pills. "So you won't come away?" Her tone was plaintive.

"Are you going?" Ed didn't know what to think. Was she breaking up with him or not?

"I need to get away."

"You're in no shape to travel."

"A fresh start."

She *was* breaking up with him. He deserved it. You get your girlfriend shot, she leaves you. That's what happens. He fought to keep from choking up as he said, "I understand."

"But I don't want to go without you." So, she *wasn't* breaking it off? Ed felt more confused than a J-school student trying to comprehend the difference between "that" and "which."

He took a deep breath, held her hand, caressed it, "Julie, you've had a big shock. You're taking drugs that make it hard to think straight. The doctor said you should rest. When you're all better, in a few weeks, I'd love to take you to Barbados. Or anywhere. When you're all better, okay?"

She made no reply. The codeine was kicking in.

Ed kissed her forehead tenderly. "You want me to stay over? Make sure you're okay?"

"Would you?" Her voice sounded far away.

"Just say the word."

She considered it, then declined. "No. I'll be okay."

"You sure? It's no trouble."

"No. ..." She was sliding into the warm water of sleep.

"All right. I'll call in the morning."

"Okay."

"Call me if you need anything. Any time. Okay?"

She sighed. He tucked the quilt under her chin and kissed her full lips. They felt cool, distant. But she hadn't broken up with him. That was a relief.

• • •

Ed pressed a few keys and the screen said: WELCOME TO THE FOG-HORN ARCHIVE. He typed "Calderone" into the search field, specified that it was a last name, and hit Return. The file contained dozens of entries. Ed scrolled through the list: Calderone defending various exposés in *Full Disclosure.* Calderone denouncing libel suits over various exposés. His appearances at Opera Galas, the Symphony's Black and White Ball, and Ballet fund-raisers. Big donations to various charities. A flap over a battered women's shelter declining a big donation because its board considered him a pornographer. 7-Eleven banning the magazine from its racks. A major controversy over his election to the Ballet board. An arrest for slugging an anti-porn crusader outside the Washington Square Bar and Grill. All charges dropped. And on and on.

Ed focused on the libel suits. *Full Disclosure* had been sued nine times. In every case, Calderone had gone to the mats wrapped in the First Amendment, claiming truth as a complete defense. He'd won eight times. The only time he ever lost, the U.S. Supreme Court refused to review a State Supreme Court ruling ordering him to pay damages to the subject of a profile titled: "The Nastiest Man in America," which dealt with none other than Gregory Murtinson. The title was the nicest thing the article said about him.

Calderone had a motive.

• • •

The next morning, Julie's line was busy. All morning. Ed took a long lunch. He hopped Muni down to First and Howard, entered San Francisco Gun Works, and purchased a double-action .38 revolver. From there, he walked down First to Brannan and climbed the stairs to Home on the Range, the city's only public firing range, according to a recent piece in the *Horn*. An instructor ran him through the basic safety spiel, then gave him a set of EarSaver headphones and pointed him toward the range.

Ed checked in with the range master, who assigned him a lane. The guy looked vaguely familiar, an off-duty cop he'd met during his stint on the police beat. In the other lanes, a dozen men and two women were shooting at targets pinned to a sandbag wall twenty-five feet away. Some fired at NRA competition targets, others at male silhouettes with circular targets in the chest area. Ed requested a silhouette, loaded and fired. He ejected the spent casings, waited for the range assistant to replace everyone's targets, and fired again and again.

"Where'd you get that eye?" the range master said after reviewing a sheaf of Ed's targets. Most of his shots had hit in the general vicinity of the bull's eye. Every shot would have stopped a bad guy. Most would have stopped him for good.

"Must be from shooting pool," Ed replied. "Develops eye-hand coordination."

The range master scanned Ed's face as only a cop can. "Say, don't I know you?"

"I used to do some police reporting for the *Foghorn*."

The range master's eyebrows moved closer together. "No. Wait a minute. Aren't you the guy got shot at near Tahoe? I saw you on TV."

Ed silently cursed all video technology.

The range master looked at Ed's targets, then at his .38, unloaded now. "Any particular reason you're here today?"

"I'm taking up target shooting as a hobby."

"Most target shooters use rifles."

"I prefer this." He hefted the .38.

"Really. I thought the *Foghorn* was all for the Handgun Initiative."

"The publisher is."

"But you're not?"

"As I recall the chief of police is for it, too. Doesn't mean you are."

The range master shook his head in disgust. "The chief's an ass. Whoa. You didn't hear that. I get in trouble when I talk to reporters."

"So do I." Ed set about cleaning and oiling his weapon the way the guy at Gun Works had showed him.

26

Back at the paper, Ed called Julie every few minutes, but kept getting busy signals. He called the operator, had the line checked. It was working, just busy. Ed considered running over there, then decided Julie might consider it an intrusion. He didn't want to seem pushy, especially when he feared she might still give him the heave-ho. If she wanted to take her phone off the hook, or spend the day talking things out with everyone she knew, that was her business. He decided to stop by after work, with take-out Vietnamese from Tu Lan.

Her line stayed busy all afternoon. At four o'clock, Ed could stand it no longer. He called the operator again. "My sister's line has been busy all day and we have a family emergency. Can you please break in?"

The operator connected him with a supervisor, who was not keen on the idea. After some bureaucratic back and forth, Ed mentioned where he worked and observed that there might be a story in the phone company's refusal to respond to family emergencies, and by the way, I didn't catch your name. The woman relented, placed him on Hold, and said she'd connect him as soon as she'd contacted Ms. Pearl.

A moment later, the tele-functionary came back on the line. "I'm sorry. I can't break in. I'm reading the phone off the hook."

"Are you sure?"

"I'm telling you what my equipment tells me."

Probably nothing to worry about, Ed thought. Then again, maybe something was wrong.

Ed left work early. Fighting a rising sense of dread, he drove out Mission and up Duboce to Elgin Park. He found a Starving Students moving van in front of Julie's building. Two short, buffed welterweights who looked Central American were carrying boxes out of an apartment. Julie's.

"What are you doing? Where's Julie!"

They ignored him, just kept packing boxes into the truck like the mindless brooms in The Sorcerer's Apprentice. Ed stepped directly in front of one of them. "Where's Julie?" he demanded.

The mover shrugged. *"No ingles."*

Ed tried the other guy. *"No ingles."*

Ed conjured up what little Spanish he knew: *"La señorita ... aqui ... donde la señorita?"* Where is the woman who lives here?

Another shrug. *"No aqui."* Not here. He already knew that.

Ed pounded on the door across the hall. It was opened by a woman in her mid-twenties wearing a San Francisco State sweatshirt. She was holding a bag of microwave popcorn, just popped and exuding the aroma of warm butter. Ed smelled something else as well. Pot. He explained who he was and asked about Julie.

"Oh, she left." the woman said, spaced. "Are you Fred?"

"Ed."

"She said you might stop by."

"Where is she? Where'd she go?"

She gobbled a handful of popcorn and held the bag out to Ed, who shook his head.

"Didn't say." Or maybe asked you not to tell.

"Left to see a doctor? Or left town?"

"Town. Had a suitcase."

"The Caribbean?"

She shrugged.

"Barbados?"

"Maybe."

"The moving van?"

"Storage. Said she'd be gone a while and didn't want to keep paying rent."

"She leave a phone number? A forwarding address? *Anything?"*

"No. Just stopped by to say good-bye."

"Did she say *anything* else?"

"Just that she had to get away for a while."

Ed looked at his watch. It wasn't quite five. The people he needed were probably still at the paper. Julie's door was open, the two movers coming and going with boxes, chairs, the TV. Ed stepped into Julie's stripped kitchen and tried the phone. Still working. He dialed the *Foghorn's* PR department.

"Ms. Bearl resign dis morning." A young-sounding woman informed him. She pronounced her "p's" as "b's," and her "th's" as "d's." Filipina, foreign-born.

"Resigned? Not a vacation? Not a leave of absence? She actually *resigned?*"

"That's what dey tole me."

"Who told you?"

"My suberbisor."

"Let me talk to—"

"She gone por de day."

"Did Julie leave a phone number? A forwarding address?"

"Not wid me."

"You know, she wasn't well. She got shot a few days ago—"

"I know, boor ding. We send her plowers."

"Does *anyone* there know *anything* about where she went?"

"I'm de only one here, and it's pibe o'clock. I'm going home."

Next he called Personnel. An older woman who sounded white answered.

"Is Todd Dannish there?" The buddy who'd snooped in Julie's file for him before their lunch date.

"Mr. Dannish has left for the day."

Ed asked about Julie.

"Ms. Pearl resigned this morning."

"Not a vacation? Not a leave?"

"Correct. She resigned."

"Did she leave a phone number? A forwarding address for her final paycheck? Anything?" Ed realized he was yelling into the phone. His throat felt raw, his stomach knotted.

"I'm not at liberty to—"

"Somewhere in Barbados?"

"—divulge that information."

"But you don't understa*nd!"* He pleaded. "I *work* at the *paper*. Julie and I are … *friends*. I'm *worried* about her. She got *shot*—"

"I'm aware of Ms. Pearl's situation, but Personnel files are confidential—"

"Can't you make an exception? I was *with her* when she got shot. I *need to talk to her*."

"I'm sorry."

"I have her *medication!*" he lied. "She *needs* it."

"If her physician calls—"

"Oh, fuck that, lady! I *need* to get ahold of Julie *now!*"

"I don't stand for such language." She hung up. Ed redialed, but got the recording saying the office was closed, call back Monday through Friday during regular business hours.

Ed stumbled down the stairs in a daze. His throat was aflame. His chest felt tight, his legs rubbery. Why hadn't the shooter just killed him on 50? Then he wouldn't have to live with knowing he'd scared off the best thing to happen to him in years.

The movers were finishing up, stuffing the final few boxes into the back of the truck. One popped open. Some of Julie's records. The one on top was Marvin Gaye's *What's Going On?* Ed gazed at it. What was?

He drove home on autopilot, unaware of the fog hanging like cotton candy over Twin Peaks, or the breeze swaying the palms on Dolores, or the kids doing skateboard tricks by Mission High, or the exquisite quiet of Dolores Terrace. He unlocked his front door, pushed it open, and stepped over the day's stack of mail. On top was an envelope without a stamp or an address. All it said was: Ed.

He ripped it open and pulled out a picture notecard. The photo was a tropical beach scene: white sand, blue water, deep green mountains in the distance. Inside, in a small spidery hand, it said: "There's so much to explain, but not now. Someday, I hope, if you let me. You're a very special person, Ed. I rarely fall for anyone, but I was falling for you. I've done things I shouldn't have. That's why I was punished. That's why I have to leave. If you can, please forgive me."

The card was unsigned.

The next morning, Ed called his friend in Personnel. Julie's file had been removed, standard operating procedure when an employee resigns.

Ed leaned on Ruffen to lean on Gagliano to lean on the Director of Personnel to ferret it out. Right before lunch, the word came back: Ms. Pearl left no forwarding address. She instructed the paper to hold her final check for pick-up. She didn't say when.

Ed called the post office. No forwarding address. He tried the phone company and PG&E. Bills paid through the disconnect, no forwarding address.

He tried the airlines. There were flights to Barbados from Miami, Houston, JFK, and O'Hare. But none of the carriers would check recent passenger lists, not even for the family emergency Ed mentioned.

He tried contacting Julie's mother in Yonkers. There were twenty-four Pearls and six Staviskys listed. He collected the numbers and laboriously began working his way though the list. None knew a Julie Pearl in San Francisco. No message he left was returned.

Jimmy Buffett's, "Margaritaville," bubbled up in his head. That night at home, he played it over and over while drinking too much cognac: "Some people claim there's a woman to blame. But I know it's my own damn fault."

27

No one could believe it. The Giants and A's both clinched the West on the same day. The mighty A's shut out the Rangers 5-zip, for their second title in a row. Meanwhile, San Francisco *lost* to the hated Dodgers—but the Reds beat second-place San Diego, which meant the Padres couldn't catch SF. So typical for the Giants, Ed mused as he drove to Pacific Heights, to win by losing.

Adding to his good fortune, Ed found legal parking right across the street from Chet and Laura's apartment. After work. When everyone was home. When there shouldn't be a curbside spot for miles. It made him nervous. He looked twice to make sure he wasn't blocking a driveway. He felt more comfortable at hydrants.

Ed crossed the street, and was about to reach for the buzzer when a screech behind him made him turn around. A car with Domino's Pizza painted on its side had pulled up next to the 'Stang. The guy jumped out with a big flat box, but instead of running up the walk to the apartment building, he knocked on the back door of a beat-up white van parked behind Ed. The door opened, and whoever was inside—Ed couldn't see a face—took the pizza. The Domino's car drove off. Ed stared at the van. Hadn't there been a white van parked in about the same spot the night he drove Laura home from the museum? Pacific Heights was not a neighborhood where the cops would tolerate anyone living in a van. That left just one possibility—surveillance.

Ed walked back to his car, opened the door, and reached in as though he'd forgotten something. Meanwhile, he jotted down the van's license number and peered through the windshield. The back was curtained off, as if someone were living inside—or working surveillance equipment.

Why would anyone in this neighborhood hire a private investigator? Probably to see if the trophy wife was getting any on the side.

Laura was trying hard to look alive. She wore a brightly colored print blouse and stretchy beige stirrup leggings, with bare feet accented by toenail polish. Her hair was done up attractively and held with a wacky Minnie Mouse comb. But the gaiety of her outfit couldn't hide her sunken cheeks, her lips fixed in a frown, or the fact that the bags beneath her eyes would not fit under the seat in front of her or in any overhead bin. Ed embraced her as tenderly as was decent for a more-than-acquaintance-less-than-friend. She did not return the hug, just led him into the living room. Her stooped carriage reminded him of the drugged patients he'd seen in the Disruptives ward of that psychiatric hospital he'd profiled. "He hasn't called, has he?"

They settled into opposite corners of the sofa that looked out the picture window past Alcatraz and Angel Island as the lights of Marin came on in the gathering dusk.

Laura shook her head, curled her feet up under her. In the dying light, she looked gaunt. Her skin was cellophane over angular cheekbones.

"I'm sorry." Ed tried to sound comforting. "You must be beside yourself." He knew how it felt to have someone you cared about suddenly disappear. But Laura and Chet had been together for eons.

Laura gazed out the window. Suddenly, a moan erupted from her throat. Her face fell into her hands, and her emaciated body shook with sobs. Ed scooted to her side, stroked her arm. "Sometimes no news is good news."

But he thought something different: Life's a real bitch. There's a good chance that your husband is a murderer, a double murderer, and that this time he's on the run without you.

Laura leaned into Ed, taking comfort in his proximity. She pulled herself together, wiped her eyes with a tissue, blew her nose. "You ever pray, Ed?"

He flashed on the polished linoleum of the hospital corridor where he'd paced for hours making deals with God before he learned that Julie would be all right. What had he promised to do? He couldn't remember. "Not often. But sometimes. Like now, for the Giants." It was the wrong thing to say, but Laura didn't seem to notice.

"My family was never religious. But I've been praying my heart out that Chet's all right. That he calls. That he didn't—"

She unfolded her legs, got up, disappeared into the kitchen, made some noise, and returned with a tray containing two Perriers with lime wedges over ice and a basket of Wheat Thins.

"How've you been sleeping?" Ed asked.

"Horribly … but better with the pills my doctor gave me."

"You eating?"

She shot him a look that said he wasn't the first person to express concern on this subject. Her answer was curt and emphatic: "Enough."

"Laura," Ed said as soothingly as he could, "you know I want to help Chet, don't you?"

"Yes." She cocked her head, sensing something difficult coming. She turned toward him, dry-eyed, but apprehensive.

"I'm very sorry about this. Really I am. But to help Chet, to get to the bottom of … *all this*, I have to ask you some more questions. Obnoxious reporter questions. And you have to be *completely honest* with me."

Her chin thrust out. "I *have been.*"

"Really?"

"Of course. I wouldn't lie to anyone—especially you."

"Bull*shit.*" The word came out angrier than he intended. "You knew Cabral was in touch with Chet. He was in Anchorage for at least a week before you and Chet came back here. He visited you several times. I think you recognized him when the police showed you the photos. You lied to them and you've been lying to me. If I'm going to help you—and Chet— you have to come clean with me, Laura. *Completely*. Starting *now.*"

Laura's face reddened as though she'd been slapped. She slowly cranked herself off the sofa and drifted to the picture window, her back to her interrogator. She'd married money, but didn't come from it, which showed in her carriage. She had neither the straight back nor the dropped shoulders of the finishing-school set. Under pressure, her head sank and her shoulders rounded. "How did you find out?"

"Wasn't too hard. You persuaded that one neighbor to back up your little charade, but you neglected to get the rest of your neighbors on board. When Cabral's mug shot appeared in the *Pioneer,* two of them told the cops they'd seen him at your place. And the manager of the motel where Chet put him up came forward as well, said he'd seen Chet with Cabral there."

Laura slumped a little more and stared out the window. The night was clear. The Golden Gate Bridge was bejeweled in a necklace of dazzling lights. A huge oil tanker, red lights blinking, inched its way toward the Richmond refinery. "I messed up, didn't I?"

"Big time. Jesus, Laura, didn't you learn anything from Watergate? The crime is bad enough, but the cover-up is worse. Now the police are *convinced* that Chet killed Cabral over a drug deal gone bad."

"And that's *my fault*? I was trying to *protect* him. You have *no idea* what it's like to live on the run, thinking every cop is going to recognize you, arrest you. You have *no idea*." She rubbed her eyes, fighting tears.

Ed rose and took her elbow, guided her back to the sofa. "I'm not saying your … *dissembling* … screwed Chet with the cops. They would have come to the same conclusion anyway. What happened in Anchorage is water under the bridge. But I need you to level with me from here on. No more games. Okay?"

She nodded, chastened.

"So, you recognized Cabral from the police photos."

"Yes."

"And he'd been up in Anchorage a while, right?"

"Yes."

"Why?"

"Chet sent him money to come up."

"Why?"

Laura folded her arms across her chest and stared out the big window. Her voice was little more than a murmur: "When Chet's group won the Pulitzer, he was dying to tell someone, but we had an ironclad rule: No contact with anyone from our past. It was hard, but necessary. I had no contact with my family, none. My father died, and I didn't attend his funeral. All I could do was send a letter through Chet's lawyer. I felt terrible about that. Still do. Well, Chet broke our rule. He called Rosa—Rosa Melendez, the Gilchrist's old cook. She'd been like a mother to him. His own mother had … problems: booze, pills, you name it. Rosa was the nurturer in his life. So he called her. Of course, she was thrilled to hear from him. But he learned that she was very sick. Emphysema. She had a hard time breathing, talking. So, Chet sent her some money. And he wanted to be there for her in case of an emergency, so he broke another ironclad rule: He gave her our number."

"Your phone number? I can't believe—"

"No, our answering service, in Oakland."

"You had a service?"

"It was how Chet stayed in touch with his lawyer. If anything happened in the case, the lawyer would call the service, which was under a phony name. Chet checked it weekly."

"And how did you react when you found out he'd called Rosa?"

"How do you think? I got very upset. I mean, we'd been talking about returning to San Francisco. The lawyer was making discreet inquiries into the kind of jail time Chet might have to do. But we hadn't made a decision, and until we did, our deal was that we would stick to our rules. Then Chet called Rosa, and suddenly I felt exposed and vulnerable. But he was so excited about the Pulitzer—winning it completely on his own, with no help from his father—that he wasn't thinking straight."

"So, how did Cabral fit into this?"

"Cabral was Rosa's cousin. She gave him our number. Maybe two weeks after Chet talked to Rosa, he left a message. Chet spoke to him, sent him money to come up to Anchorage, put him up at the motel."

"How did you react to that?"

"I was furious. But Chet didn't seem to care. He'd basically decided to return to San Francisco, and didn't think our rules were necessary anymore."

"Did Chet give Cabral money?"

"Some."

"How much?"

"I don't know."

"A hundred? A thousand? Ten thousand?"

"I don't know. Chet handled our money. But I'm guessing it was around a thousand. Cabral had just gotten out of prison and had no clothes, nothing. Chet wanted to help him get back on his feet."

"Did Chet buy heroin from him?"

Laura's eyes blazed. "*No!* Chet *never used* heroin. *Never!* Why don't you *believe* me?"

"Laura, he was arrested twice for possession of major weight. Cabral went to prison for selling—"

"I know, I know. But I *swear* I *never* saw Chet fool around with any white powder. And Chet *swore* to me that he was clean. Swore to me *many times.*"

"Okay. So Chet gave Cabral money, and not for drugs. Could it have been more than a thousand?"

"Maybe. I don't know. Like I said, Chet managed our money. Why?'

"Because I have reason to believe that Cabral may have been black-mailing Chet."

Laura's face contorted. *"What?* Impossible."

"What makes you so sure?"

"Juan wasn't devious enough to blackmail anyone. When he showed up at our place, he wasn't just down and out. He was out of it, talking nonsense."

"What kind of nonsense?"

"You know, paranoid fantasies about people being out to get him. Chet was just trying to help him out. Who said anything about blackmail?"

"Ted Calderone."

Laura blanched.

"There are a lot of pieces missing, but Cabral contacted Calderone shortly before he went up to Alaska and said he knew about some dirty laundry in the Gilchrist closet, said he'd hand the information over—for a price. Then Cabral disappears and the next thing Calderone hears, he's dead on your living room floor. Calderone thinks Cabral figured he could get more money out of Chet."

Laura's jaw dropped. "I—this—I don't know what to say."

"Did things seem friendly between Chet and Cabral? Or tense? Did it seem to you that Cabral was making demands or threats? Did Chet act like he was being pressured?"

She thought about it. "No. Chet was just helping an old friend get back on his feet."

Ed took a slow deep breath. If Laura's observations were correct, if Cabral wasn't blackmailing Chet, then there was only one plausible explanation: He was dealing him heroin.

"All right," Ed continued, "change of subject. The night I drove you back from the Museum, you said the business with you and Chet and Calderone was 'ancient history.' As a former historian, I'm fascinated by that history, especially after your little dust-up at the party."

Laura pursed her lips, and glared at him. "That has nothing to do with any of this."

Ed glared back. "The hell it doesn't. Your husband is the chief suspect in two very ugly murders. In a naive effort to help an old friend, yours truly went up to Tahoe to see Calderone and wound up on the wrong end of target practice, with someone I care about getting shot. You want me to stay on this? No fucking way unless I get your *complete cooperation.*"

"I'm sorry about what happened to you and …"

"Julie." The sound of her name brought a stab of hurt and guilt.

"But I don't see how—"

"Don't you? Are you blind?" Ed stood up. "Goodbye, Laura. Have a nice life. I know my way out." He grabbed his jacket and headed for the door, not looking back.

"No, Ed. Wait," she pleaded.

He turned, took her measure. "What?"

Their eyes met and held, then Laura broke the contact. "All right. I'll tell you."

Ed returned to the sofa. The Bay was rimmed with lights. The only view Ed had from his living room was the garage across his narrow street, and it needed a paint job.

"At Stanford, we all worked together on the *Cardinal*: Ted, Chet, and me. We were friends."

"But you and Ted were more than friends. You were lovers."

"Yes. Ted was very charming back then, very attentive. He was exciting. And he was ambitious, which I admired. He was very serious about starting an art magazine."

"Art? You mean like painting?"

"Yes. His idea was to send famous photographers and writers to cover museum shows all over the world. *Architectural Digest* meets *Travel and Leisure.*"

"When was this?"

"Sophomore year, into junior year."

"Then what?"

"He couldn't get it off the ground. He started drinking and taking speed. He turned into a monster. That was when Chet and I got close. I broke up with Ted and got together with Chet."

"Just like that? Calderone doesn't strike me as the kind of guy to get dumped easily."

"He wasn't. He went crazy. He attacked Chet at the paper. Threw a typewriter at him. Hit him in the head. Gave him a concussion. It was horrible. Ted got kicked off the paper and almost thrown out of school. After graduation, I didn't see him again—until the party."

"Is that all?"

"Yes."

"You *sure* about that?" It came out nasty.

Laura drew back. "I *don't* like your tone—"

"Well, that's just too damn bad—because when I was up in Tahoe, Calderone showed me the prototype of *Full Disclosure.* Very interesting photos in there. Seems the cover girl didn't make it to the centerfold."

Laura hung her head and ran her fingers through her hair as though trying to pull it out. She exhaled a long sigh. "Stupid of me, wasn't it? Stupidest thing I ever did."

"How'd it happen?"

Laura folded her arms across her chest. "After the art magazine, Ted began developing *Full Disclosure.* I hated the idea of naked women, but he said there was no other way to finance investigative reporting, to bring in investors and advertisers. He had no money for photographers or models—"

"So he asked his girlfriend to pitch in and pose for him."

"It wasn't supposed to be for publication. Just practice. Ted could be very persuasive. And I wanted his magazine to succeed—"

"So you had a few drinks and took off your shirt, and it wasn't so bad, so you had a few more and took off the rest."

"Yes."

"And then he used them in the prototype."

"No. He only included them after I left him for Chet, after Chet filed assault charges over the typewriter incident. It was Ted's way of getting even."

"And that's when Chet had the Gilchrist lawyer lean on Calderone."

"Yes. Ted wanted the assault charge dropped. Chet wanted to spare me—and his family—the embarrassment of having Ted play up our romance in *Full Disclosure:* Heir to Publishing Fortune Has Nude Model Girlfriend. His father would have flipped."

"So Chet dropped the assault charge, and Ted pulled the photos that were really racy, and gave you the negatives."

"Or so we thought. We found out a few years later that he kept some of the negatives. For spite."

"He said that was an accident."

Laura exhaled sharply. "Like hell it was."

"So when Chet was at Berkeley, you sued for the rest of the negatives. But then you disappeared, so you never got them."

"Right." The word was wrapped in bitterness and disgust.

"If it's any consolation, Calderone says the negatives got lost when the magazine moved to its current office."

"Really."

"He also said Chet tried to kill *Full Disclosure,* and nearly succeeded."

"Yes."

"What was that about?"

"Ted had a big investor. Chet found out who he was and convinced him to withdraw."

"How?"

"By saying that Overland wouldn't carry the magazine."

"Overland? The big magazine distributor?"

"Biggest west of the Mississippi."

"How could Chet speak for Overland?"

"His father owns it."

Ed shook his head, thinking: I might have known. "So how did the magazine ever come out?"

"Ted got a new investor."

"Did he ever find out about Chet's shenanigans?"

"Yes, but not for a couple of years. We were at Cal."

"How do you know he found out?"

"He called. Screamed at Chet."

"And that was when Calderone's ex-art director contacted you about the negatives you never received."

"Yes."

"And you sued."

"Yes."

"So Calderone was furious that Chet tried to kill his magazine, and he was pissed that you were suing him for the missing negatives."

"He kept calling, leaving threatening messages on our phone machine, saying he was going to publish the photos of me before the courts forced him to return them."

"But he never did."

"Right."

"Why not?"

"I don't know. Maybe he was scared of getting dropped by Overland. Maybe my photos weren't up to the magazine's standards. By then

Ted was using only top photographers and models. By comparison, his pictures of me weren't much."

Ed jumped up and paced back and forth in front of the picture window. "And maybe Calderone decided to get his pound of flesh another way."

"Very good, Ed. Chet said you were smart."

"Maybe Calderone set Chet up for his drug busts."

"We always thought so."

"You should have told me."

Laura shrugged. "Chet—*we* were trying to put it behind us."

Ed watched a small plane fly over Alcatraz and disappear into the haze obscuring Tiburon. "It makes sense. Why should Calderone risk having Overland drop his magazine when he could arrange sweeter revenge? Calderone sets up Chet—Cabral, too, for all we know—and gets rid of you for ten years. That's what you meant the night of the party when you said Chet sacrificed everything for you, isn't it?"

"Yes."

"Why didn't Chet say anything at the time?"

"What could he say? We had no evidence. Just suspicions."

"Murtinson won a huge libel verdict against Calderone. There's another grudge. When did Cabral get fired?"

"The year? I don't recall."

"No, before or after Chet's first drug bust?"

"Uh, around the same time—no, right before. I remember Worth crabbing about having to drive himself to the arraignment."

"It fits. Suppose Ted knew that Cabral got fired and offered him good money to do a little dirty work that would stick it to his former employer. Suppose Cabral was the one who actually planted the heroin on Chet. Cabral didn't go to prison until after Chet's second bust, right? He could have planted the drugs on Chet *both* times."

Ed paced more quickly, rubbing his hands together vigorously enough to start a fire. "Okay. So if Calderone had Cabral plant heroin on Chet, then afterwards, Calderone would want to get rid of his errand boy. So what happens? Cabral goes to prison for trafficking. Very tidy. But then, unfortunately for Ted, Cabral gets out. Maybe Cabral thinks Calderone owes him. Maybe Calderone is his blackmail target, not Chet. Calderone had grudges against Murtinson and Chet. If he could arrange to have Murtinson and Cabral killed and make it look like Chet did them both, he settles three scores all at once and winds up home free."

"I don't know," Laura mused. "Ted can be reprehensible, but I have a hard time believing he's a murderer."

"Harder than believing your husband is?"

Laura looked away.

"If this is the way it happened," Ed continued, "it might explain why Calderone wanted me to believe that Cabral was blackmailing Chet."

"Why?"

"He was nervous that I'd link Cabral to him myself. His story deflects suspicion. And his line about Cabral blackmailing Chet makes it look like Chet's the killer."

Ed kept pacing back and forth in front of the sofa. Laura watched him intently. Then Ed stopped, stuffed his hands in his pockets, and stood there dejected. "I don't know. I *really* want it to add up, but it just doesn't. If Calderone's the one, then where does Wardell fit in? And who shot at me? And where's Chet?"

He stared out the big window. Wisps of fog blew past Alcatraz. Searchlights cut the sky, promoting something down by Pier 39. Below them on Lombard, four police cars, cherries whirling, were blocking an intersection for no apparent reason. There was no fire. No demonstration. Nothing. The cops' presence made no sense. A vision of Julie's smile floated before his eyes, then evaporated. Nothing made sense.

28

Chester Worthington Gilchrist III was perched regally on his leather throne. He motioned his four subjects to sit before him. Executive Editor Walter French and City Editor Gus Oberhoffer took the two middle chairs. Assistant City Editor Ron Ruffen and Ed flanked them. It was a brilliant autumn morning, not a cloud in an azure sky. At the corner, by the Old Mint, a Muni crew was working on a broken bus. Two cops waved traffic around it.

"Gentlemen," Gilchrist said with an expectant smile, "A delegation this size must mean good news."

The four of them exchanged glances. Finally, French spoke: "Some possible good news, some definite bad."

"The bad first." Gilchrist leaned forward slightly, his jaw set.

The X.E. turned to Ed. "It's your story."

Ed would rather have been anywhere else. The group visit had been French's idea. He drew a breath, forced his eyes to meet Gilchrist's. "The D.A. is going to indict Chet for Murtinson's murder. Tomorrow."

Gilchrist frowned, massaged the bridge of his nose as though he had to physically push the news into his cerebrum. "Go on."

"It's a classic case of the bird in the hand, even if the bird has flown, or maybe because of it. The case against Chet for Cabral's death is pretty strong, and since the same gun was used in both shootings, San Francisco's Finest have decided to ignore Chet's alibi and lack of motive for Murtinson."

"But the broker and building manager corroborated—" Gilchrist held up his hands as if to say: What gives?

"Yes. They did. But the coroner's estimate of time of death is broad enough to place Chet in Seacliff. And his disappearance after Cabral's death looks bad."

Gilchrist's frown deepened. He looked down into his lap. "It looks terrible. It looks like he did it."

Then French spoke up. "But there's good news, too. Ed?"

"It *might* be good news," Ed began diffidently. "It also might be a dead end. It's all very speculative at this point—"

"Let's have it." Gilchrist tented his fingers before him, a mark of impatience.

"It's possible that Chet was set up."

Gilchrist drew a sharp breath. "Set up? By whom?"

"Ted Calderone."

Gilchrist exhaled and laced his fingers tightly. "I'm listening."

Ed recounted what he'd already told his editors. Gilchrist wolfed every word like a starving man at his first meal. At the end of Ed's recitation, he looked heavenward as if thanking God for this ray of hope. "My son might be *innocent!*"

"Maybe," Oberhoffer interjected. "Of course, we can't print any of it. We have no substantiation. It would be libelous. And knowing Calderone, he'd sue before the ink was dry."

"Definitely," Gilchrist agreed.

"But we thought you should know."

Gilchrist leaned back in his chair and clasped his hands behind his head, elbows out like wings. "I'd forgotten about the bad blood between Ted Calderone and my son over Laura. I can believe Calderone would nurse a grudge all these years. He's that kind of person. Vengeful. Despicable. But I also know you got part of it wrong."

"Which part?" Ruffen asked, though it came out more like a demand.

"I have it on excellent authority that Chet did, in fact, use heroin."

"Excuse me, sir," Ed ventured, "but Laura swears on a stack of Bibles that he never did, that it was all part of the set-up."

The three editors glanced nervously at Ed. One did not contradict one's publisher, especially this one. But Gilchrist seemed unfazed.

"Laura is a darling girl," he said with a fatherly sigh, "and her loyalty to my son has gone far beyond the call of duty. But where her husband is concerned, she views the world through rose-colored glasses. Chet was a user. He confessed to me himself after his first arrest, and then again after the second, when he begged me to get him into rehab.

But that minor error in no way alters your analysis. In fact, it fits. Chet being an addict just makes Calderone's set-up easier." Gilchrist smiled a rainbow. "Anything that raises hope of Chet's innocence is terrific news. Excellent work, gentlemen. Ed, I assume you're following this up."

"Definitely. Speaking of which, I was hoping you could tell me who Wardell is."

"Ed!" Ruffen spat. That line was not in the script.

Gilchrist turned to Ed, "Who?"

"Wardell, the mystery man Chet left the Museum with. You introduced them at the party."

All three editors squirmed, thinking the same thought: Rosenberg is a loose cannon.

"Did I?"

"Laura says you did."

"Wardell … Wardell." Gilchrist thought it over. "I honestly don't recall. There were so many people that evening … and it was so strange … with Gregory and all. …"

"Gay guy, but not swishy. Slight build, dressed in a suit, but instead of shoes, Birkenstock sandals."

"Wait a minute. It's coming back to me. Yes. I'd never met him before. Ian Cavanaugh—you know Ian, don't you? Professor of California History at Cal? Ian introduced us and asked if I knew where Chet was. As I recall, this Warden, uh, Wardell fellow was interested in the Lost Gold. You say Chet and this man left the party together?"

"That's right. And that was the last anyone saw of him."

Gilchrist ran his fingers through his silver hair, straining to conjure anything else about the strange little man in Birkenstocks. He sighed and shook his head. "I'm sorry," he murmured, a note of helplessness in his voice. "I wish I could remember more. But I don't think I exchanged two words with him. I saw Chet in the crowd, pointed the man toward him, and that was that."

"The weird thing," Ed said, "is that his name isn't Wardell."

Ruffen glared at him. French and Oberhoffer both looked miffed. This was new information. Ed had broken a cardinal rule of newspapering. He'd kept his editors in the dark. Even for a loose cannon, this was over the top.

"He's an *actor*," Ed continued. "His stage name is Scott Gardener. His real name is Albert Skolinsky." He pulled an eight-by-10 out of a folder and held it up.

"Well, I'll be damned," Gilchrist said. "That's him. But why would an actor—?"

"No idea," Ed said, "but I intend to find out."

29

Theater Artaud occupied part of an enormous old brick building off Seventeenth in the industrial no-man's land between the Mission and Potrero Hill. The area was criss-crossed by railroad tracks and peppered with warehouses, machine shops, furniture makers, and some old Victorians that had seen better days. Recently, computer-related businesses had moved in. From the 1890s until Prohibition, the building housed a brewery. Then for several decades, PG&E used it as a warehouse. In the early 1970s, artists carved it into lofts, leaving one end for the theater, which presented offbeat productions, and survived, barely, on benefit dances and grants from the city's Hotel Tax.

Ed parked the 'Stang on some abandoned railroad tracks next to a sign that said: No Parking. Chemical Hazard. The only chemical in sight was alcohol, a few broken bottles of cheap booze strewn around the pavement. The fog hung thick and soupy over Twin Peaks, but the sky over the Mission was clear, deep blue, and almost warm in the breezy twilight.

Ed had brought Jerry along to try to get his friend's mind off the imminent demise of the Inner Mission Youth Center. The grants just weren't happening. The center was running out of money.

Unfortunately for Jerry, the play was not a cheery affair. It was an AIDS allegory, a macabre musical called *Tokens* about the bubonic plague decimating medieval London. The "tokens" were the sores that signaled the infection—and the beginning of the end, which took a few days. The story was told from the perspective of a group of corpse carters, human draft animals who pulled two-wheeled carts through the streets exhorting the living to "bring out your dead," which formed the refrain to one of the play's major vocal numbers. Scott Gardener, a.k.a. Wardell, a.k.a. Mr. Birkenstocks, was a corpse carter, one of the few to survive the plague. He spent the play handling corpses, and though they were straw-stuffed dummies, they came to life as the dead in a world where everyone was dying. At the final curtain, Gardener and a handful of dazed survivors stood arm in arm ringed by corpses stacked waist high, and in song, vowed to tell the world what they'd witnessed to preserve the memory of the departed.

After the bows, one of the actors stepped forward and made a fund-raising pitch for the AIDS quilt.

"Next time you want to cheer me up," Jerry said as the lights came on, "don't." Then he smiled. "Very moving."

As the audience filed out, Ed and Jerry stayed put. "Time to chase my actor," Ed said, leading Jerry down an aisle and through a door marked "Crew Only." Backstage, people were scurrying every which way: actors, their friends, stage crew, tech guys. A knot of actors, their makeup garish up so close, ceremoniously erased the number, 58, from a chalk board and wrote 59. The length of their run, and still counting.

Gardener stood tired but smiling on the far side of the number crowd, his arm draped around a woman whose character had belted a song condemning God for bringing the plague. Ed pushed through the crowd toward him, with Jerry tagging along behind.

"Scott! Scott Gardener!" Ed called.

The actor turned. Just then, a barrel-chested man with a shaved head, wearing a long coat and sunglasses, stepped out of the shadows and jammed something into Gardener's ribs. Ed saw a flash of fire, then heard a hideous explosion. Suddenly, he was a child again watching Jack Ruby shoot Lee Harvey Oswald in the basement of Dallas Police Headquarters.

At the sound of the gunshot, everyone jumped, except Gardener, who crumpled to the floor. The shooter turned. His eyes found Ed's. He fired again. On Ed's immediate right, a sandy-haired man was thrown back on his heels and went down hard, blood spurting from his chest.

The crowd panicked. Many screamed. Some stood paralyzed. Others slammed into one another, desperate to escape. But in the close confines backstage, it was hard to move. Ed and Jerry were pressed up against a corpse cart. Before them, a space opened. Two men lay very still on the concrete, surrounded by two red pools that grew larger then merged into one.

Ed looked around. The shooter was gone. He closed his eyes, conjured up the man's face. It was not Calderone's valet. Was it the man he saw nosing around his bullet-riddled car at the turnout on 50? He couldn't be sure.

30

"That second bullet was meant for me." Ed leaned heavily on a pool cue. He needed a shave and his clothes looked like he'd slept in them, because he had. "The lighting guy died because of me."

"You don't know that," Jerry replied. "Until they catch the shooter, no one knows."

Ed rolled his eyes: "He scanned the room. Found me. And fired."

"Hey, I was there, too, remember? Standing right next to you. It didn't look to me like he was aiming at you. It looked like a wild shot, a sad, terrible, awful shot—*wild*."

"He saw me. He was gunning for me. I know it."

"How?"

"Call it reporter's intuition."

"You're jumpy because of what happened on 50."

"I have every right to be."

"Absolutely. But that doesn't mean the two shootings are connected."

"No? Then, explain it to me, Jer. I live my whole life and never come close to gunfire. Then all of a sudden, I'm much too close *twice* in *10 days*. You call that a *coincidence*?"

"I don't know what to call it. All I know is that whipping yourself doesn't accomplish anything."

"First Julie. Now this." Ed hung his head.

"I understand that you feel responsible and I understand why. But what are you going to do, Ed? Drown in self-pity? Head for the Golden Gate Bridge? What happened at Theater Artaud wasn't your fault. No one blames you—except one person."

Ed stared vacantly across the Games Room of the Inner Mission Youth

Center. It was after hours, quiet, just a few staff getting ready to go home. Ed's eyes lighted on the anti-cigarette bulletin board some of the kids had put together: Smokers Suck. He turned back to the table and sighted down on the nine, aiming for the corner, an easy shot. But his stroke was jerky and it rattled out. "He had a wife, two little girls."

"Yes. It's very sad. Tragic. Horrible. But shit happens. You grieve, then you either move on or it destroys you." So far, Jerry thought, Ed was opting for the latter.

"Is this my rabbi telling me it's God's will?"

"No. This is a friend telling you that you don't have all the answers here, so maybe you shouldn't act like you do."

It was two nights after the double shooting. In the aftermath, Ed, Jerry, and everyone else backstage trooped in shock down to Bryant Street and gave statements to the police. Afterward, Ed dodged the reporters and walked to the paper on autopilot, where he filed a story he had no memory of writing. Then he went home, plopped down in his rocking chair, and stared at his fireplace for two days. KFOG's resident philosopher, Scoop Nisker, said, "If you don't like the news, go out and make some of your own." Ed wanted to, but couldn't move, had no idea if he'd ever move again.

The other dead man was the lighting designer, highly regarded in Bay Area theater circles, according to his obit. Thirty-three. Lived in the Excelsior. Wife taught middle-school math. Two young daughters. When Ed read about them, he cried. They would grow up fatherless because of him.

Why did he accost Gardener immediately after the play? Why didn't he wait until the crowd thinned out? Why didn't he see the shooter approach? Why didn't he fling himself at the son of a bitch? Why?

He considered driving out to the dead man's home, but what could he say? Whoops, sorry I got your husband/father killed. He considered stopping by the funeral home. Nice casket. He looks so natural, considering that his lungs got sprayed against the wall. He considered sending a condolence card, but couldn't imagine what he'd say. He was a writer at a total loss for words.

So he just sat in his chair staring at the charcoal remnants of logs burned ages ago, not eating, sleeping fitfully, not answering the phone, not even when Ruffen bellowed through his phone machine, "I know you're there, Ed. Pick up, goddammit."

Eventually Jerry showed up and threatened to break a window to get in if Ed didn't open the door. Jerry heated a can of chicken soup, forced Ed to choke it down, and then dragged him over to the Center.

Jerry ran a few balls, then missed on purpose, using follow to bring the cue off the rail so Ed would have an easy time of the two. "Your shot."

Ed missed, then missed on his next turn, and for several turns after that.

"Not your night," Jerry observed.

"Not my decade," Ed replied. He'd spent years busting his butt for a Ph.D. that turned out to be worthless. He'd married a perfectly lovely woman and botched it royally. He'd opted for journalism but never quite fit in, never settled into a groove. He'd fallen for Julie only to have her become the innocent bystander and decide that standing by Ed was a one-way ticket to an early grave. And now two little girls were minus a father—because he was so absorbed in a story that he'd become blind to everything around him.

Who *was* the shooter? He was bald like the man he and Bill Kay had glimpsed poking around his car on 50. But this guy wore sunglasses and his big collar was turned up, so Ed didn't get a good look at his face.

Jerry kept racking up and running strings of eight to ten balls to Ed's one or two, when he made any. Ed got annoyed. "This table sucks. The rails are dead. When was the last time it was leveled? 1960?"

Most of the Youth Center staff left. Jerry said he'd lock up. They kept playing, kept rehashing things. Hours passed. Around midnight, Jerry's boss, Arturo, shuffled in and silently handed him a single piece of paper. Jerry read it and looked at Arturo. The two men embraced, holding each other longer than heteros usually do. Then Arturo slouched out.

"What's up?" Ed asked, suddenly aware that he wasn't the only person on Earth with problems.

Jerry waved the piece of paper. "My thirty-day notice. A month from today, we close and I'm out of a job."

31

Ruffen called Ed into the conference room. Ed found him eating an enormous Crossword from the Front Page, a sandwich other delis would call a Reuben. Bits of rye bread coated with mustard were littered around a square of white paper next to a can of Diet Coke.

"You wanted to see me?" Ed had shaved, bathed, and changed his clothes. To all outward appearances, he was back among the living. Only he didn't feel that way. He'd just read the *Foghorn's* account of the lighting designer's funeral, by a reporter who could make the Sphinx weep, which is what Ed had done.

"Sit down." Where Ruffen was concerned, invitations to be seated did not bode well.

"What's up?" Ed tried to sound nonchalant.

"I'm pulling you off the story."

"*What*?!" Ed jumped to his feet. "You can't do that! Someone's trying to kill me! I've got to find out who!" He leaned on the table, glaring down at Ruffen, who used Ed's outburst to take another bite.

"Not on my time you don't. Let's leave it to the cops. It's their job. They'll find the bad guy."

"Oh sure, like they found the Zodiac Killer and Murtinson's killer—"

"Ed, we're not negotiating here. Your editor is telling you that you're off the story. O-F-F."

"But Ron—!"

"Don't 'but Ron' me. Do I have to draw you a picture? You're not objective. You're running around like a paranoid lunatic—"

"Because someone's trying to *kill me!*"

"My point exactly."

"Come on, Ron, that's not paranoia. That's two eyes open. You think it's a *coincidence* that the minute I find Gardener someone pops him, then shoots a guy standing right next to me?"

"Oh, and speaking of Gardener, the cops are furious that you never got around to telling them about him *like we agreed you would.* You know how that makes us look? Walt's had calls from the Chief, the Mayor's Office. Jesus, Ed, what's gotten into you?"

"I—I'm sorry about the cop thing. I was running to catch the play. That detail got away from me."

"The lion gets away from the circus and you call it a 'detail.' I don't think so. Meanwhile, the story you filed was shit. The AP had a better piece, and their guy wasn't even there."

"Hey, I came *this close* to getting killed! I had the lighting guy's blood on my fucking clothes! I was shaken up! Give me a break!"

"That's exactly what I'm giving you."

"Huh?"

"It's called vacation, Edward. You've been shot at twice in the last two weeks. You're a basket case. You're going to take some time off, starting now. I checked: You've got three weeks coming. Take it. Go to Europe or South America. Take the new girlfriend. Have fun. Maybe do a piece for the Travel Section."

"No way I'm leaving."

"Like I said, we're not negotiating here. Either you take a long vacation right now—or you're fired."

"Seriously?"

"Scout's honor. And don't tell me I can't because I can."

Ed glared across the table. So, it had come to this. He remembered Jocko canning him for the same reason—insubordination. He was younger then, less invested in his life. He remembered thinking: So what, I can get another newspaper job, or a teaching job, or tend bar, or work in a pool hall. He didn't care. But he was older now. If he got fired from the *Horn,* what decent newspaper would pick him up? And what else could he do?

"Okay," Ed said softly. "I'll take the vacation."

"Good," a smiling Ruffen said, swallowing the last bit of his sandwich. "Any idea where?"

Ed thought of all the places he'd never been: London, Paris, Rome, Rio, Jerusalem … Barbados. He imagined strolling along a white sand beach, snorkel, mask, and fins in hand, magically bumping into Julie, picking up where they'd left off as though nothing had happened. Then something tightened in his chest and he knew where he had to go: "To find out who the fuck's been trying to kill me!"

"Ed!" Ruffen hoisted his great bulk out of the chair.

"Hey, I'm on vacation, right? It's a free country." Ed skipped out of the conference room.

Ruffen called after him, "You're fired, asshole!" Then he shouted a few names, ordered them to assemble in the conference room. They were the reporters who'd been covering the other angles of the story, the story that was now theirs.

32

Ed met his old graduate advisor, Ian Cavanaugh, at a Thai place near the Berkeley campus. Ed hated seeing what diabetes was doing to him. He was more obese than ever. He had trouble walking. He leaned on his cane for dear life. And the short stroll from his office had winded him. Worse, the first thing he ordered was a beer.

"You okay, Ed? From what I read in the *Foghorn*, you came within inches of getting shot the other night."

"Yeah. I'm okay. Shaken up, but it beats the alternative."

"Horrible thing about those two men. I thought you wrote a good piece."

"Thanks."

"They know who did it?"

"Not yet."

The waitress had delicate Asian features and long black hair held in a knot atop her head by what looked like silver knitting needles. Ed ordered barbecued chicken and green tea. Cavanaugh ordered half the menu and another beer.

"So, Ian, tell me," Ed inquired tenderly. "How are you doing?"

"Going to hell," came the tart reply, one part irritation and three parts resignation. "Diabetes is a bitch. My doctor yells at me. My wife yells at me. My daughter yells at me. Last spring, I had a scare with my eyes. But laser surgery fixed me up, thank God. My eyes are all I really care about. Reading … and watching the playoffs."

Ed smiled. Ian had always been a rabid Giants fan. Memorabilia was strung around his office at Cal. "You see the game yesterday?" The Giants had trounced the Cubs 11 to 3 on two homers by Will Clark, one, a grand slam. They led the National League Championship Series 1 to 0.

"Great game," Cavanaugh sighed. "I wish they all could be like that."

"In your dreams."

"I know. The Cubs are actually good, for once."

They caught up and gossiped about the department a while, then the food arrived and Ed got down to business. "About the shooting the other night, a photo of the actor ran with my story. Did you notice it?"

"I suppose I did, but I don't recall."

Ed produced a manila envelope and pulled out agency photos of Wardell-Gardener-Skolinsky. "You recognize him?"

"No. Should I?"

"Think back to the party at the Museum. He was there in a dark suit and Birkenstocks."

"Sorry. I drank a little too much champagne that night."

"He spoke to you, said he knew something about the Lost Gold."

Something clicked. "Ah, yes. Larry Foxsen introduced us. They were looking for Chet. But why would an actor—?"

"I don't know. I was hoping you might."

"Sorry. No idea."

Ed sighed. "You said *they* were looking for Chet? Just the actor? Or the actor and Foxsen?"

Cavanaugh took a big gulp of beer. "Both of them. At least that's how it seemed to me. Larry seemed quite excited."

"How excited?"

"You know, eager to introduce the fellow to Chet. Larry's usually pretty reserved. Comes from years of standing beside rich people trying to decide if they should drop 50 thou for a few bucks worth of paint. But that night, he was animated. I was surprised since he'd been questioned in Murtinson's death that morning. I was surprised he attended at all."

The waitress appeared. Cavanaugh held up his empty beer bottle, signaling for another.

"So what did Foxsen say about the Lost Gold?" Ed pressed.

"Just that your actor had some intriguing information, and did I know where Chet was? I hadn't seen him."

"So you pointed them toward Old Man Gilchrist."

"Correct."

"And that was the end of it?"

"Yes."

They ate and chatted about other things: Cavanaugh's latest paper on the last silver dollars struck at the Carson City Mint, his ex's absurd demands, his daughter's resentment of his new wife. Ed thought about his own ex. What would Diane say when she learned he'd been fired—again? Probably nothing. She'd just give him That Look of hers, which came through even over the phone.

"By the way, Ian, did you ever see Chet's Stanford thesis on the Lost Gold? The effort to track down Ellis Bohman?"

"No, not that I recall. I only read the monograph he did for the *Journal of California History*. But that was a long time ago."

"Yeah," Ed said almost to himself, "ancient history."

The check arrived. Ed reached for it, but Cavanaugh clamped a fleshy paw over his hand. "On me."

"But, Ian, *I* invited *you*. It's an interview."

"No, it's a reunion. Scumbags have been shooting at an old student of mine and I'm glad to see him alive. Not to mention that I ate a lot more than you did."

"Ian."

"Indulge a sick old man."

Cavanaugh was still in his sixties, but looked considerably older. As he labored up out of his seat, Ed wondered when he'd open the *Horn* and see the obit. Suddenly, he was filled with regret for not having stayed in closer touch. Cavanaugh was the only member of the department's senior faculty who hadn't given him grief about writing for *The Daily Cal*, the only one who'd encouraged his interest in journalism. Everyone else treated him as a traitor to Academia.

"Thanks for lunch, Ian. Next time, it's on me."

"Oh, good," he chuckled, "Chez Panisse, if I can climb up the damn stairs."

"You're on."

They shook hands and Cavanaugh lumbered slowly back to campus with the help of his cane. Ed uttered a little prayer that his eyes would hold up. Then it was time to visit The Farm.

33

"The Farm" was the local nickname for Stanford. Ed pointed the 'Stang down the Nimitz. Just past downtown Oakland, the freeway was jammed with baseball traffic. The A's were hosting the Blue Jays in game two of the American League Championship Series after beating them handily the previous night on homers by McGwire and Henderson.

Traffic inched forward, brake lights as far as Ed could see. On his left, a Volvo wagon with a father and a gang of preteen boys rolled into view. They all sported crisp new A's caps. The kids were also cutting school. Ed recalled the time in ninth grade, maybe tenth, when he and some buddies all cut school to attend Opening Day at Shea Stadium. They bought bleacher seats, eluded the guards, and wound up nervous but triumphant in a lower box a dozen rows up from first base.

KFOG played "Sultans of Swing." At Hegenberger, the stadium crowd exited and things lightened up. Ed cruised across the Dumbarton Bridge, parked by Stanford Stadium, and hoofed it toward the center of campus. It looked like it had been designed by *Sunset* magazine, whose offices were nearby.

The Truman Prize Room was not listed on the campus map near Visitors Parking. Ed asked a half-dozen students playing frisbee on a thick carpet of lawn ringed by huge cypress trees. They'd never heard of it. He figured it was one of those obscure nooks universities create when a major endowment obligates them to live up to the terms of some big poobah's bequest. It probably occupied a crummy hole in the bowels of some library.

Ed crossed the Oval and Main Quad and headed for the libraries. A security guard directed him to the Meyer Library. A guard there sent him up to the top floor. The Truman Room occupied surprisingly choice real estate, a corner with a view of the Clock Tower, the Old Union, Lake Lagunita, and in the distance, the deep green of the coastal hills past Highway 280. The plaque was small, but it was brass and recently polished: The H. Wesley Truman Room. Truman Prize-Winning Manuscripts. Made Possible by a Bequest from Lilly and Paul Truman, 1938.

The room was larger and better lighted than Ed expected. Just inside the door was a framed nineteenth-century photograph of an imperious looking H. Wesley and a brief bio explaining that he'd been one of the first students at Stanford, and that he'd gone on to make a fortune in Southern California oil and real estate. Another plaque described Lilly and Paul Truman's notion of honoring their mutton-chopped forebear by endowing a generous prize for the best undergraduate senior thesis each year, then collecting them for posterity in the Truman Room.

"May I help you?" asked a dark-haired wisp of a young woman with big glasses seated at a small antique desk by a bank of windows. She had more ear rings than Ed could count.

Ed flashed his *Foghorn* ID as though he were still employed there, and asked how he might find a copy of a particular Prize-winning thesis. "Unfortunately, I don't know the exact title or year, but it was sometime in the mid-1970s. It deals with the Lost Gold of San Francisco. It's by Chester W. Gilchrist IV."

The girl looked at him quizzically. "That's funny. Very few people ever come in here. Even fewer ask to see a specific manuscript. But you're the second person to ask for that one this week."

Ed's mouth went dry. "Who else?"

"Some man," she said with a shrug. She obviously didn't pay much attention to what went on in the Room she babysat.

"Was he big, bald, thick-necked, and barrel-chested?"

"No, tall and thin."

"How old?"

"I don't know. Sixties maybe. What's this all about?"

Ed didn't want to go into details, because he wasn't sure of them. "The author of the manuscript I'm interested in is wanted for two murders, and I have a hunch his thesis might contain information about them."

Her eyes widened. "Oh, you mean *that* Gilchrist? The son of the newspaper owner."

"You got it."

"I've read the stories in the paper."

"This other man. Can you tell me any more about him?"

"Not really. I didn't pay much attention. I've been engrossed in *Anna Karenina*. Ever read it? Fantastic."

"Look, this is important. Try to remember. *Please*. He was white, right?"

"Yes."

"If he wasn't bald, he had hair. How much? What color?"

"I don't remember. Kind of gray, maybe."

"Mustache? Beard? Any distinguishing features?"

"Not that I recall."

"Did he give you a name?"

"No. He just asked to see the manuscript. He sat over there—" She shot her chin toward a heavy wooden table surrounded by matching chairs. "—and read it. After a while, he got up and left."

Ed frowned. "Did he take the manuscript?"

"Oh no," she insisted. "Nothing is allowed to leave the room. I told him. I tell everyone. He left it on the table. I reshelved it." She stepped over to a wall of bookshelves, crouched down, and pulled out a hardcover volume bound in orange, just like the one Laura described in Anchorage.

Ed took the book over to the table where his predecessor had sat, pulled out his pad and pen, and opened it. He scanned the first page, the second, the third. Then he flipped through the rest. Every page was blank.

The girl was appalled. "I—I can't believe it. What happened?"

"The other guy switched books on you," Ed explained. "The real one for this one. Did he have a briefcase? Or a big coat, maybe?"

"I don't recall. I think he had a trench coat."

"There you go. He came in with this phony under the coat, and walked out with the real one."

The door swung open, and two uniformed security guards entered, one Hispanic, the other black. "Who rang?"

"I did," the young woman said. She explained the theft.

One of the guards turned to Ed and asked for his ID.

"For Christ's sake. If I had anything to do with it, do you think I would have reported it to Ms.—"

"Crayden. Suzanne Crayden."

"Just a formality, sir. We have to file a report."

They eyeballed Ed's *Foghorn* ID, but fortunately didn't call the paper.

Then they asked him what was going on. Ed answered truthfully: "I'm not sure." Then he ran down what he knew: Chet was an expert on the Lost Gold. He was also wanted for two recent murders. He was last seen with a man who had new—and unknown—information about the Lost Gold. Chet's copy of his thesis was missing. Ed had a hunch it might point to the murderer. He came down to see the Truman Room's copy, and found it gone with a fake substituted for it. The End. The guards seemed satisfied.

"Is there anyone else who might have a copy of Chet's manuscript?" Ed asked Suzanne Crayden. "How do students enter the competition? Do they need a faculty sponsor or something?"

"Yes." She opened a long file box and flipped through three-by-fives. "Professor Ernest Velnock sponsored Chester Gilchrist."

"Thanks. Mind if I use your phone?"

She gestured: Go ahead.

The history-department secretary said Professor Velnock had left for UCLA eleven years earlier. The secretary at UCLA said he'd gone to the University of Arizona three years earlier. The secretary there said he was spending the year at Oxford. Ed gave up.

He trudged back to his car, disgusted. The trip had been an eerie waste. A waste because he didn't get a look at Chet's manuscript. Eerie because whoever was behind all this showed a real talent for anticipating his every move.

The afternoon traffic was heavy but moving on northbound 101. KFOG played "The Heart of Rock and Roll" by Huey Lewis. Then the DJ announced that Bette Davis had died at eighty-one—and played Kim Carnes' one big hit, "Bette Davis Eyes."

A Subaru wagon paced Ed on the left. He glanced over, saw a bald head, and stopped breathing. He braked hard, and cut sharply to the right. A horn blared behind him. The Subaru continued on its way unperturbed. Ed forced himself to breathe and slowly caught up with it. The driver was an elderly man with a rounded back. Ruffen was right. The stress was getting to him.

Back on Dolores Terrace, Ed pulled into his garage, and surveyed his little cul-de-sac. Serene as always. He slipped his key into the front-door deadbolt and turned it, but encountered no resistance. Which meant the door was unlocked. Ed tensed. Even at his spaciest, he *never* forgot to lock the door. He turned the knob and pushed. The door didn't want to open. Something was pressing against it from the inside. He leaned harder, and heard his two cats. They did not sound happy. The door opened a crack and Ed saw that his rocking chair—actually, the chair minus one arm—was upended and leaning against the door. He reached in, pushed the chair out of the way, and held his breath.

The place had been burglarized, more accurately, ransacked, torn apart methodically and sadistically. His sofa cushions were sliced open, their stuffing strewn all over the floor. His TV lay on its side, smashed. His phone machine was eviscerated, his stereo ripped apart. The contents of his bookcases were strewn in heaps on the floor. Some of the books had handfuls of pages ripped out and littered around like oversized confetti. Silvery objects like extra-large sequins caught his eye. His growing collection of CDs—cut into pieces. Next to them lay the black shards of what had been his vinyl record collection. And all around were long strands of thin brown ribbon—tape ripped from his cassettes.

Hyperventilating, fighting tears of rage, Ed stepped over his upended coffee table and into his kitchen. The refrigerator door was open. So were all the cupboard doors. Food dripped from the walls and covered the floor along with pieces of shattered dishes. The whole mess was covered with blue-black globs of some viscous gel. Diane's preserves.

He heard a sound upstairs, and froze. He inched his way up the staircase, and saw that one of the cats had knocked what was left of his bedroom boom box to the floor. His dresser was emptied, and everything in his closet was covered with preserves. He doubted he'd be able to get the stains out.

Ed tried to breathe, tried to feel his navel, tried to center himself as Master Chen had instructed years ago. But it was no use. He panicked. He bounded downstairs for the door. He had no notion where to go or what to do. All he wanted was to get out of there—fast.

Insistent ringing brought him back from the brink. The phone. Why hadn't it been yanked from the wall, he wondered, as he fished for it beneath the wreckage of a chair.

His automatic "Hello" caught in his throat and wouldn't budge.

"Ed? Is that you?" He knew the voice, but it took a moment to place it: Ian Cavanaugh.

"Yes. Ian?"

"The strangest thing," the professor wheezed. "I called the *Foghorn*, but they said you don't work there anymore—"

34

Ed parked at Sutter-Stockton garage, then walked the two blocks to Prima Gallery. Three stretch limos were lined up at the Hyatt, their uniformed drivers lounging on them, smoking. A Rolls stood at the door of Campton Place. Slipping into the passenger side was a woman with hair like Julie's. At the thought of her, Ed felt the familiar stab of guilt and self-loathing … then the beginnings of a strange new emotion, irritation. She said she didn't blame him. She said she wasn't breaking up. So why did she leave like that? Why did she cut him off at the knees?

The reek of urine wafted across Stockton from Union Square. The city kept promising to do something about the Square, but never did. On the corner of Stockton and Maiden Lane, Prima Gallery offered a refreshing contrast Ed didn't recall from his previous visit, when the place was ringed by TV vans and a phalanx of reporters. It was resplendent. Its glass facade gleamed, accented by polished brass fittings. At the entrance stood the same doorman who'd been there before. His impeccably tailored suit could not hide the hard body of a weight-trained bone-breaker whose job involved keeping the riff-raff out. This time Ed passed the riff-raff test. The man nodded discreetly as he opened the big glass door. Ed stepped into an airy room with a polished oak floor that extended to exposed brick walls. Spotlights illuminated the work on display—this month, large flamboyantly colorful oils by an up-and-coming Chicano painter who did impressionistic renderings of tropical birds.

The business desk was a chest-high counter done in oak that matched the floor. Several people were scurrying around behind it. Ed caught the eye of a young woman in a gray suit that didn't quite fit her. Probably an Art History major doing an internship.

Ed flashed his *Foghorn* ID. "Is Mr. Foxsen available?"

"He's in," she replied with a weak smile, "but busy."

Ed smiled back at her. "I'm busy, too. I need to see him. It'll only take a moment."

The student looked flustered. "I'm sorry—"

"Tell him," Ed said just a little louder, but still smiling, "that it has to do with the Lost Gold of San Francisco and a couple of recent murders in which he might be involved. Now, I can talk to him here. Or I can tell the police what I know and they can ask him to stop by Bryant Street. Which do you think he'd prefer?"

An older woman behind the counter heard this and shooed the young-ster away. Her face was etched with frown lines. "No need to raise your voice," she admonished. "Mr. Foxsen *always* cooperates with the press. What did you say your name was? I'll see if he can fit you in."

She picked up a phone, spoke in hushed tones, then hung up. "The door at the top of the stairs. Knock."

Ed ascended an industrial metal staircase with concrete treads. The adjacent brick wall was criss-crossed by steel girders in an "X" pattern, indicating a seismic retrofit, and adorned with two dozen plaques attest-ing to Lawrence Foxsen's many inestimable contributions to San Francisco's cultural vitality. Ed knocked on the door.

"What?" The voice sounded impatient.

Ed entered a cozy office furnished in chrome, glass, and brocade. Two windows looked across Union Square to the St. Francis. Between them hung framed posters of shows the gallery had presented in its early days back when Warhol and Diebenkorn first hit big. In a corner stood a coat tree. On it hung a beige trench coat.

Foxsen was in his early sixties, clean shaven, with small eyes set close together, and salt-and-pepper hair, mostly salt, swept straight back, ac-centing a high forehead. He wore a charcoal gray turtleneck and had the look of a guy you might see leaning over a string bass at Yoshi's.

Foxsen glanced up over half-glasses from several book-sized com-puter print-outs that lay open on his desk. "Are you the same reporter who grilled me when Worth called?" For a gay guy, his manner was de-cidedly straight and brusque.

"The very same."

Foxsen sighed. "It figures. Only an ass like you would barge in here making wild accusations."

"I didn't barge," Ed retorted, trying to be pleasant. "I knocked. I'm just trying to save you a trip to Bryant Street and some more face time with Detective Harrigan."

"You're too kind," Foxsen sneered. "Now what's this about?"

"Let me be clear: I haven't accused you of anything. I just said the police might see it that way—if we can't straighten things out before I go down there and tell them what I know."

"Which is?" Foxsen leaned way back in his chair and crossed his feet at the ankles atop one of the print-outs. He seemed relaxed, irritated by the interruption and innuendo, but not defensive.

"Does the name Wardell mean anything to you?"

Foxsen frowned and shook his head. "No. Should it?"

"At the party, you introduced a man by that name to Ian Cavanaugh. You know Ian, don't you?"

"We're acquainted."

"Do you recall introducing Wardell to Cavanaugh?"

"As I'm sure you recall, that was a *difficult* day." Foxsen gazed out the window. Pigeons rocked back and forth on the sill like old Jews in prayer. "A client of mine was murdered. The police questioned me as though I were a suspect. And then a particularly obnoxious reporter did the same thing. I drank too much champagne at the party and frankly, remember very little of it."

"Wardell was about my age and height, gay, wearing a suit but with Birkenstock sandals."

"Sorry, I'm not a foot fetishist. I don't recall any sandals. Look, I must have spoken to a hundred people that night."

"Wardell was very interested in the Lost Gold. At least, that's what you told Cavanaugh. He was looking for Chet Gilchrist. I saw the two of them leave the party together. No one has seen Chet since. But a few days ago, the actor who played Wardell got shot to death at—"

Foxsen bounced back to a sitting position. "He was an *actor?*"

"So you remember him."

"Is he the one who got killed at that theater in the Mission?"

"Yes."

Foxsen sighed. "I rarely read your newspaper. When I do, I often wish I hadn't. Your art critic is either blind or stupid or both." He reached for a mug sporting the Prima Gallery logo, and took a pull of whatever was in it.

"Someone," Ed explained, "I don't know who, hired an actor named Scott Gardener to play Wardell at the party."

"Well I'll be damned."

"What do you know about him?"

"Less than you, apparently. He called me that afternoon, said he had information about the Lost Gold. Wanted to know who might be interested in mounting a search for a percentage."

"And you said Chet."

"Hell no, I told him to get lost. You have any idea how many crackpots have come down the pike over the years blathering about the Lost Gold?"

"But you were with him at the party."

"Not *with* him. He *found me* there. I don't know how. He went on and on about some—" Foxsen's fingers made quote marks in the air— "'family secret' related to the Lost Gold. He was very insistent, said he *had* to speak to an expert, and if not me, then who?"

"And you said Chet."

"Yes. To get rid of him. I was the one who orchestrated Worth's purchase of the Reilly. I knew Chet was fascinated by the Lost Gold. Worth must have told me fifty times that he'd won some prize in college for a project having to do with it."

"The Truman Prize at Stanford."

"If you say so. But I couldn't find Chet, so I introduced your actor to Cavanaugh to get him out of my hair. And that was the end of it. Now, if you'll excuse me ..."

Ed didn't budge. "Cavanaugh said you seemed very excited about Wardell's information about the Gold, that you were *both* looking for Chet."

"Wrong. As I recall, Ian was drunk. The only thing I was excited about was unloading that little fag. I wanted to *avoid* Chet. If you recall, I was the one who told the police about his visit to Seacliff the night of the murder. I didn't think he'd want to have anything to do with me. Now I really have to get back to—"

Ed took a step closer. "Have you been down to Stanford lately?"

Foxsen's patience was wearing thin. "No. Why?"

Ed looked from his beady eyes to the trenchcoat and back again. "You fit the description of the man who stole Chet's manuscript on the Lost Gold from a library there sometime within the last week."

"So now you're calling me a thief? I should have you thrown out of here—."

"If you do, you won't find out why whoever hired the actor chose the name Wardell."

Foxsen eyes blazed, but his hands didn't move. If he had a call button under his desk, he wasn't reaching for it. He leaned back in his chair. "Okay. I'll bite. Just make it brief—and then leave."

"Chet's manuscript tracked down all the rumors about Ellis Bohman, the guy who—"

"I know who he is."

"The rumor Chet found most persuasive had him fleeing to Seattle, where he shortened his name to Bohn, then on to Alaska. An Ellis Bohn married a widow named Sarah Wardell in Anchorage in 1912. She had a young son, Lincoln Wardell, who would have been our Wardell's grandfather."

"Except that our Wardell was an actor."

"Right. But Chet didn't know that. I'm assuming he thought the actor really was related to Lincoln Wardell."

"So?"

"So I'm betting the actor was used to lure Chet out of the party for some reason."

"If you say so. All I did was hand him off to Cavanaugh."

"Did you bring Wardell to the party?"

"No. I already told you: He buttonholed me and wouldn't let go."

"He wasn't on any guest list. He had to come in with someone who was."

"Wasn't me."

"Did you put Wardell up to luring Chet out of the party?"

Foxsen's face contorted with rage. "I've had it with you, Rosenberg. Get out. *Now.*" His hand reached under the desk.

"Well, did you!? Why did you invent this charade to get Chet out of the party? *Where is Chet*!?"

The door behind Ed opened and in stepped the doorman, but without his suit jacket. His shoulders could have been transplanted from a water buffalo. His pecs and biceps bulged through his shirt. He sized up Ed the way a rattlesnake eyes a mouse.

Foxsen waved a hand. "Get rid of him."

The doorman took a step toward Ed, who retreated a step and dropped into the karate readiness stance: knees bent, weight distributed evenly between the legs, elbows bent, hands up and open like daggers. He forced himself to breathe, focused his consciousness on his navel, and trained his gaze on the doorman's hips. Every movement originates from the hips. That's what Master Chen always said. To see how an opponent will attack, always watch the hips.

The doorman hesitated.

"You're looking at a fourth-degree black belt," Ed lied.

The doorman glared at Ed, then looked at Foxsen.

"If we mix it up," Ed said to Foxsen, "you'll lose your pit bull and your lovely office will get trashed. If you call him off, I'll leave quietly."

Foxsen said nothing. The doorman took another step toward Ed, who held his ground and stared intently at his opponent. Like all buffed weight-lifters, the doorman was top heavy. His arms, shoulders, and chest were too big for his hips and legs. That meant two things. He would move slowly. And his knees would be particularly vulnerable. One well-placed side kick to a knee and their little altercation would be over. Ed hadn't sparred in years and wasn't sure he could hit the knee. But he focused on it, leaned back slightly to free his front leg for the kick, and uttered a low martial arts growl: "Ee-awww."

"Enough," Foxsen said. "Let him go."

The doorman backed off, but remained between Ed and the door.

"Tell him to back away from the door." No funny business on the way out.

Foxsen nodded and the doorman moved away. He was not happy about his instructions. A big vein strained against the skin of his neck and his hands balled tightly into white-knuckled fists.

Ed stepped out and forced himself not to turn back or run down the stairs. When he was halfway down, he turned and called back through Foxsen's open door. "Harrigan's going to hear about this."

Foxsen hissed, "As if I care."

35

When Ed pulled up in front of Julie's, Elgin Park was quiet except for the low rumble from the freeway overpass. New curtains adorned what had been her windows and her mailbox sported a new name. Ed wasn't surprised. With the vacancy rate running less than one percent, San Francisco apartments never stayed empty more than a millisecond, especially within walking distance of the Castro.

In a neat pile below the bank of aluminum mail boxes, Ed found what he was looking for—Julie's mail. She'd left no forwarding address, so it would just pile up until someone threw it away or sent it to her, or until her name got cold and she was purged from direct-mail lists. Junk, junk, and more junk. Nothing that might hint at where she'd gone, or why.

He trudged up the stairs and knocked on the neighbor's door, hoping that the passage of time might have softened her to the entreaties of a lover scorned. But no one was home.

Had they been lovers? Physically, yes, briefly. But in place of the emotional closeness he'd felt just a short time earlier, now there was a void. His life was a mess. No job. No girlfriend. His home disemboweled.

• • •

Ed's waterproof shower radio survived the ransacking. He set it on the mantel and tuned into the A's, hoping the game would take his mind off the sad tedium of cleaning up while waiting for the insurance adjuster. Oakland was just one win away from the World Series.

Knuckles rapped on the door. The insurance guy turned out to be a tall chunky blond woman, maybe 30, with a heavy Russian accent.

"Mr. Rosenberg?" Only it came out *Meester Rawsinbearg.*

She introduced herself as Yana Sverdlosk. She climbed the four steps and daintily stepped over the pile of diced sofa cushions. A strong odor of cigarettes followed her in. "Somebody doesn't like you," she said. "Or maybe they don't like Twin Peaks Casualty."

Ed handed her a sheet of yellow paper containing his inventory of the destruction, then showed her around. All of his upholstered furniture had been gutted. Much of the rest lay in pieces. Half of his vinyl records had been broken or gouged with some kind of knife. Most of his cassettes had been smashed, the tape strung around the living room like party decorations. And every one of his CDs had been cut into pieces with some giant tin snips. Diane's preserves had stained every surface in the kitchen, and upstairs, more preserves had been poured over most of his wardrobe, staining everything beyond reclamation.

Yana Sverdlosk glanced into a cabinet that contained what was left of Ed's supply of preserves, a dozen jars. "Why do you have this?"

"An old friend makes it. I buy a few jars whenever I'm at Safeway. To help her business."

The phone rang. Ed excused himself as Yana filled out the forms.

It was the Newspaper Guild rep from the *Horn*, one of the sports writers. "Bad news, Ed. Ruffen has all the paperwork in order. Reprimands. Warnings. The Improvement Contract. We'll go to bat for you, of course, but we'll lose. You'll lose. I'm sorry, guy. Truly sorry."

Ed almost smiled: The historian was history. He felt dazed, as though he'd fallen and hit his head.

That's when Yana appeared. "Here." She handed Ed a document. "I've estimated your loss and subtracted the deductible. She pointed to a figure that was almost twice what Ed guessed his things were worth. "They'll cut your check in seven business days." *Beezneez dayis.*

She held the claim form up for him to sign, gave him a copy, stepped over one lolling cat and the remains of his CD player, and was gone.

The extra money would certainly come in handy.

Ed stuffed the pieces of his former possessions into large trash bags. By the time he finished, his back and heart both ached. He felt hollow inside. Numb.

The cats rubbed against his legs. Ed crouched and caressed them. Rhythm purred, then Blues joined in. You guys are all I have left. You … and a children's game played by men. The A's won it, 4-3 on a triple by

Rickey Henderson, who was named the series MVP. Oakland was in the World Series for the second year in a row.

The phone rang. Ed took a few deep breaths. What now?

"Please hold for Mr. Calderone," a model of secretarial efficiency announced.

"I hear you're unemployed," Calderone chirped, amused.

"Yeah." Bravado kicked in. "The only guy who ever got fired for taking his vacation."

"Let's have lunch. Sam's Grill. Tomorrow at one. I'll be in a booth." He hung up before Ed could respond.

36

The New York financial markets close at 1:00 Pacific time, so the West Coast investment crowd starts drinking early. Sam's was packed, as usual, with Montgomery Street financial types standing three deep at the bar. They were especially rowdy because the TV suspended above the glass shelves of single-malt scotch bottles had the Giants game. The home team led the Cubs three games to one, a single win away from their first World Series in 27 years.

The waiters, all elderly men in tuxedos, sliced though the boisterous throng holding huge trays impossibly high. Ed elbowed his way to the host's kiosk and mentioned his lunch date's name. The old man responded with a thin-lipped smile, and escorted him down the long hall of curtained booths that had made Sam's a deal maker's watering hole for well over a century. He pulled a heavy curtain aside and motioned Ed in.

Calderone looked even more like a pimp than usual in a white linen suit, pink shirt, and loud tie inspired by peacock feathers. Next to him sat one of the most unusually stunning women Ed had ever seen. She seemed to be a combination of Mexican and Chinese, with nutmeg skin, almond eyes, and shiny mahogany hair. She wore a clingy low-cut knit dress that revealed the generous proportions Calderone liked in centerfolds. She had a huge mouth stretched into a big smile that showed off fluorescent teeth. She rested one arm on the table. Her other hand was in Calderone's lap, moving rhythmically. Calderone leaned back against the wall of the booth, looking relaxed and content.

"Ed," he said warmly, "sit down. This is Mirani, Miss March. From Bali. I love Indonesian women, don't you? Mirani, Ed Rosenberg, reporter—I should say *ex*-reporter—for the *Foghorn*."

Ed didn't take the bait. He just slid into the booth and nodded at the young woman, who appeared to be about 25. She had the smoothest skin he'd ever seen, not even a hint of a wrinkle. And the biggest eyes, deep brown. Like Julie's.

"You like swordfish?" Calderone asked playing host. "Best swordfish in the world right here."

A stooped waiter with a shock of unruly white hair poked his head through the curtain and took their drink orders. Calderone requested Anchor Porter, Mirani, a glass of Chardonnay, Ed, iced tea.

The drinks arrived and the waiter took their orders. Calderone requested the swordfish. So did Mirani. Ed ordered the salmon. Calderone noticed, and Ed was glad he did.

Calderone asked how the ax had fallen. Ed told the sordid tale as briefly as possible.

"Tough break," Calderone said. "but I can't say I'm unhappy about it. Fuck the *Horn*. Now you can write the story *exclusively* for me."

Ed squeezed a wedge of lemon, stirred his tea, and took a sip. "Just one problem, Ted. There is no story."

"Not yet."

"Just a bunch of leads that haven't led anywhere."

"They will."

"I wish I shared your confidence."

The food arrived. Mirani withdrew her hand from Calderone's lap. He kissed it. She giggled and set about eating her lunch, a task made challenging by mile-long maroon fingernails.

"My money's on you, Rosenberg. And I'll guarantee you a cover byline."

"If I bring it in—and that's a big if—what makes you think I'd want it in *Full Disclosure*?"

Calderone looked at him quizzically. "And why not? National exposure. The Big Time. Not to mention that we have a deal. I gave you the skinny on Cabral. And correct me if I'm wrong, but you're still paying rent, and PG&E, and the phone bill—but without an income."

"I'll get by." Ed had enough money for four months, maybe five or six with the insurance money if the 'Stang didn't break down and he stuck to scrambled eggs, canned soup, and the occasional burrito.

Calderone shrugged. "All right: Our deal was $25K. I'll go 30. I feel sorry for a guy who's out of work."

It was a very generous offer, much more than any other magazine would offer for a story still in total disarray. Ed needed the money, but hoped it didn't show. He met Calderone's steady gaze, then glanced at Mirani, then back at his host. He wondered how much he could say in front of the girl.

Calderone read his mind. "Don't mind her. Talk to me."

Ed stroked the bridge of his nose. "I'm not sure you want to hear this."

"Hear what? Why not? Talk to me."

Ed stirred his tea, took his time sucking down a few sips.

"Have you followed up on Cabral?"

"As a matter of fact, I have."

"And?"

"And, well, your information was … worthless."

Mirani stopped eating and looked at Calderone, who said nothing. Instead, he scooped a bite of garlic mashed potatoes onto his fork and made a show of savoring it.

"And," Ed continued, "depending on how you read the tea leaves, some people might suspect that you're mixed up in all of this."

Mirani's eyes widened, but Calderone just laughed. "Me? Involved? Jesus Christ. It's a while till bedtime, Ed, but tell me a fairy tale."

Ed drew a breath. "I can't prove any of this, and I'm not sure I even believe it. But there are those who do—"

Calderone wolfed a big bite of swordfish and took a gulp of beer. "Enough preliminaries already. Talk to me."

Ed put down his silverware. His palms felt moist. "Okay. Suppose—just suppose you never forgave Chet for stealing Laura. Suppose you decide to get even. Suppose you use Cabral to set him up for those heroin busts, hoping he does time, and that Laura comes crawling back to you. But before Chet goes to prison, he splits and Laura runs with him, so you never get your revenge or your girl. Fast forward: Chet comes back. Suppose you see a second chance for revenge. Suppose you enlist Cabral as your messenger in a little blackmail scheme. Either Chet pays big bucks or you leak those old crotch shots of Laura. But then, suppose you realize that setting Chet up for the murder of Gregory Murtinson is even sweeter. Murtinson gave you the one haircut of your career with that libel suit he won. And he'd roll over in his grave if Chet, the apple of his eye, wound up taking the fall for shooting him."

Mirani's eyes were saucers, but Calderone just kept eating, unperturbed. Then he leaned back, his lips curling into a tight smile.

"You know, Ed," he said amiably, "now I understand why you can't hold a job. You *really are* a prize asshole. But I've got to hand it to you: You've got major *cojones*. I buy lunch and offer you the biggest break in your shitty little career, and you accuse me of—what?—drugs, blackmail, and murder?"

"Like I said, *I'm* not the one accusing you," Ed backpedaled. "I'm just relating what certain people around town have implied."

"Certain people like Laura Gilchrist? Like Big Daddy Chester Fucking *Foghorn* Gilchrist?"

Their eyes met, and neither looked away. After a long moment, Ed said, "Now I get to say what you said: Talk to me."

"And I get to say what you said: You're not going to like it."

"Touché."

"All right." Calderone wadded his napkin and slapped it down on the table. "Sure, Junior stole Laura, and yeah, I was pissed—"

"You threw a typewriter at him. Gave him a concussion."

"He deserved it, the spoiled little turd. But it wasn't losing Laura that really fried my eggs. I mean, we had some fun, but you've seen the pictures: She was nothing special, and women have never been a problem for me." He elbowed Mirani's breast. "I was pissed because Junior had everything and I had nothing, except a prototype of *Full Disclosure*—and then he came along and screwed me with my key investor and threatened to kill my newsstand deal because Daddy owned the distributor."

"Overland."

"Right. But that was what? Fifteen years ago? I don't hold a grudge. Why should I? My magazine coins money. For company, I've got the world's most beautiful women. I live in Pacific Heights. I fly a private jet to my places in Tahoe and the Upper East Side. You were at the Museum. You saw me try to make nice to them. You saw them treat me like shit. Who's holding the grudge? She's a junkie's hag and he's a murderer."

"Unless someone set him up."

"Oh, please. The same gun did both Murtinson and Cabral, who bought it in Junior's living room. Your own stories said the cops are convinced Chet's the killer."

"Unless someone set him up."

"Like who?"

"You tell me."

Suddenly, Calderone's temper flared. "So, I'm guilty until proven innocent? Okay, asshole, add this up: If I used Cabral to blackmail Junior, why would I go to the trouble to tell you that Cabral tried to hustle me?"

"Because you were afraid I'd find out anyway, and you wanted to deflect my suspicions."

"Get real," Calderone sneered. "If I wanted to blackmail Chet, why do it now? I certainly don't need the money. And the dipshit's just a reporter at Daddy's rag. Why not wait until he inherits Gilcorp and Laura's a big society matron who wouldn't want the Opera crowd trading pictures of her pussy?"

Ed had no answer.

"One more thing: You know, the cops questioned me about your little problem on Highway 50. I'll tell you what I told them: If I wanted you dead, I wouldn't fuck it up."

Calderone's eyes bored into Ed's. Ed looked down at his plate. A long moment passed.

"So," Calderone asked, "how's the salmon?"

"Delicious. How's the swordfish?"

"Best anywhere."

They each took a bite and sipped their drinks in awkward silence.

"I've got to hand it to you, Ed, you've got balls. I like that. Question is: Do you have the brains to know that what the Gilchrists are feeding you is nonsense?"

"I never said I believed it."

"Oh, I'm *so relieved.*" He poked Mirani. "Aren't you relieved, honey? Ed says I'm in the clear." The girl smiled and batted her huge lashes.

"Just one more thing—"

"What? More Perry Mason?"

"Who'd you bring to the Museum party?"

"I don't believe you."

"You want a good reporter. This is how a good reporter works."

Their eyes met, and this time Calderone looked away.

"Did you bring a guy named Wardell?"

"No. Just the girl you saw me with."

"No one else? No entourage?"

"Who's this Moredell?"

"Wardell. A gay guy in Birkenstocks."

"No."

"He pulled Chet out of the party and that's the last anyone saw of him."

"Didn't bring him. Who said I did? Laura?"

Ed made no reply. He was fishing without a hook.

Calderone finished his beer. He leaned into Mirani and kissed her cheek. She finished her swordfish. Her hand snaked back down into Ted's lap, which brightened his demeanor. "You know, Ed, you're lucky you caught me in such a good mood."

"Or what?"

Calderone's face hardened. "Or you'd need dental work." Ed recalled the bodyguard up in Tahoe. He'd pushed too hard. Calderone was perfectly capable of crushing him like a bug. Of crushing anyone.

"I didn't mean to offend you."

That got a big laugh. Calderone rocked back and forth unable to control himself. Mirani tittered in her corner, and eventually Ed chuckled a little, too. Finally, Calderone calmed down, his joviality restored. "Christ, Ed, that's the best laugh I've had in weeks. You accuse me of blackmail and murder, but you don't mean to offend! Have you considered trying out for the Comedy Competition? You could give Robin Williams a run for his money."

Calderone scooped his final fork of garlic mashed. "So now that we've got the crap cleared away, are you ready to write this piece for me?"

"Like I said, there's no story."

"But there will be. And when you bring it in, I want it."

"As my grandmother used to say: 'If we live and be well, we'll see.'"

"I could get another writer. ..."

"Yes, you could. But we both know you wouldn't get the story you want because no one knows this story like I do, which is why I still have my teeth, right?"

Calderone chuckled. "You know, Ed, I should have you negotiate my print bill. I bet you could Jew them down a good 20 percent."

The slur stabbed Ed in the gut, but he worked to keep a poker face. Never let them see you sweat. "Thanks for lunch, Ted." He scooted out of the booth.

Out front, the barflies were going berserk. The score was tied 2-2, with two away in the bottom of the eighth. The Giants had bases loaded. Will Clark singled to left to put the Giants up by a run. In the 'Stang, Ed tuned into the game. In the top of the ninth, Bedrosian retired the Cubs in order. The announcer screamed himself hoarse. The Cubs were on their way to summer vacation, while the Giants were headed for the first-ever Bay Bridge World Series.

37

The *Defender* was located on South Park, a magic little oval-shaped by-way South of Market off Second that surrounded a vest-pocket park. Back in the 1870s, the street preceded Nob Hill as San Francisco's classiest address. Then the area between South Park and the Bay became Butchertown, the slaughterhouse district, and the area next to it Leathertown, where the hides of slaughtered cattle were tanned. The stench drove the rich out. South Park's mansions became brothels, and when the whores moved to the Tenderloin, the big homes were razed to make way for factories and warehouses. Around 1960, light industry began leaving the area. By the mid-1970s, half of South Park's buildings stood vacant and the park had become a homeless campground strewn with used syringes.

That was fine with Jocko McKenzie, who believed that newspapering required seedy surroundings. He bought a derelict auto body shop for a song and made a point of leaving two stacks of each new issue by the *Defender's* door for the street people to use as blankets and pillows.

Then, in the office boom of the 1980s, high-rise development pushed down Second Street. Architects, software companies, computer magazines, and clothing designers moved in. The park was renovated. The winos and addicts got chased out. The Palestinian grocery became a French bistro. Jocko railed editorially against what he called "Manhattanization" downtown and gentrification everywhere else, but he was no fool. The *Defender's* building was suddenly worth a fortune. He took out a second and bought himself a Victorian in Noe Valley.

Ed pulled into his old secret parking spot, the driveway of a defunct telephone answering service, only to find that the building had been taken over by an accounting firm and was now off limits. He circled the Park, grew frustrated, and finally dumped the 'Stang in a loading zone that had served a sausage company until a video-game developer moved in.

Jocko was on the phone, yelling as usual at some bureaucrat about the city's refusal to change Columbus Day to Indigenous People's Day. He motioned for Ed to sit down. But that was impossible because Jocko's office looked as though it had been visited by the same decorator who had just finished at Ed's place. Jocko threatened to organize a picket line in front of the official's home. "I know where you live!" he bellowed. Then he hung up, hit the intercom, and barked, "Tim. Get in here."

Jocko looked older. He still had the old fire in the belly, but his belly now hung a little farther over his belt. His jowls had grown, making him look even more like a bulldog.

"Tough break at the *Fog*," McKenzie said with uncharacteristic sympathy. "Ruffen's an ass. You want to work at a real paper, I need a managing editor."

Ed was touched. "Is that why you asked me to stop by? To offer me a job?"

"Who offered a job?" a malicious grin worked its way across Jocko's face. "I just said I need an M.E. You want to apply, ask Melissa for an application. Maybe you'll get an interview. Maybe not."

Ed was still groping for a snappy comeback when Tim stepped cat-like into the office. "Hey, Ed, you okay?" He placed a brotherly hand on his friend's shoulder. "What happened?"

Ed shrugged. "The usual. Insubordination. Seems I'm not a team player."

"You never were," McKenzie quipped.

"No, not that," Tim continued, "what happened to *your house?* We heard it got taken apart board by board."

"Oh that." Ed felt suddenly vulnerable. His life was a mess and everyone seemed to know it. "Saves me having a garage sale."

"Nothing stolen. Everything trashed." Jocko observed. "Someone doesn't like you."

"Maybe," Ed replied, struggling to appear nonchalant. "Or maybe some kids at Mission High just got carried away. How'd you hear about it?"

"Oh, you know," Tim smiled, "sources." His eyes sparkled. Ed could tell Tim had been anticipating this moment.

"Let me guess. You have some shut-in who monitors the police band and feeds you anything that sounds vaguely juicy."

Tim nodded, deflated.

"Tell him," Jocko said.

Tim brightened. He flipped open his reporter's pad. "The cops have a tentative ID on the shooter at Theater Artaud. Brian "Baldy" Jessburger, a two-bit hood who's done time all over the state."

"Baldy?" Ed flashed on the man poking around his car on 50.

"Shaves his head. A prison thing. Aryan Brotherhood."

"Got a description?"

"Better." Tim held out a wire photo from the Department of Corrections. The guy from 50, definitely, and a good bet for the shooter at Theater Artaud.

"No one knows about this except us," Jocko said smugly, "and we can't print it."

"Why not?"

"Our deal with the source," Tim explained.

"Who?"

"Confidential," Tim said.

Ed's blood pressure rose. "Come on. You called me down here to tease me?"

"A deal's a deal," Jocko retorted.

"Cut the shit, guys," Ed didn't realize he was yelling until his throat protested. "This Nazi prick is trying to kill me. Where'd you get his ID?"

Tim looked at Jocko, who nodded almost imperceptibly. "A cousin of mine works in Consumer Fraud. She's dating a guy in Homicide."

Ed turned down the volume. "They have a line on him?"

"On parole after doing a nickel for some barroom brawl. Had a job washing dishes at a cafe in Meyers."

"Where's that?"

"Five miles west of South Tahoe."

"Thanks." Ed nodded to them as he stepped toward the door.

"What are you going to do?" Tim asked.

"What else? Go up there."

"What about the M.E. job?" Jocko called after him.

But Ed didn't hear him. He was on the street running toward the 'Stang.

38

Ed made one stop on the way up to Tahoe—the El Dorado County Probation Department located in the county building in Placerville. A Gold Rush town on Highway 50 in the Sierra foothills, Placerville once boasted the only jail and courthouse between Sacramento and the diggings. But the jail didn't get much use. The judges handed down so many death sentences that the place was known as Hangtown until the transcontinental railroad came through and Union Pacific, conscious of public relations, prevailed on the locals to change the burg's name. Down by the highway, Placerville was wall-to-wall McDonalds, Burger Kings, and Taco Bells. The historic part of town sat back a ways on higher ground.

The County Building was an enormous Victorian with towers, turrets, and wrought-iron trim. It reminded Ed of the house on *The Addams Family*, except that the building was beautifully maintained and surrounded by mature fruit trees. It sat on a grassy hilltop studded with carefully tended monuments to the native sons who had fallen in the Civil War, the Spanish-American, the two World Wars, Korea, and Vietnam. A piece of World War I artillery stood by the steps pointing toward the river valley.

The Probation Department was on the second floor. Ed took the stairs two at a time.

"Jessburger … Jessburger … Brian. …" The receptionist was a young, sunburned strawberry-blond with thick glasses. "Mr. Heckendorf is his P.O. Down the hall, left."

Mel Heckendorf occupied a grimy little office that hadn't been painted since Truman was president. He looked like he belonged in Fish and

Game. He wore a flannel shirt, jeans, and hiking boots, and had a weathered face covered with rust-colored hair and a bushy chestnut beard. Ed flashed his *Foghorn* ID.

Heckendorf sighed. "SFPD called me yesterday. Seems Brian really put his foot in it this time."

"Killed two people in San Francisco."

The probation officer shook his head as he dug out the file. "Can't say I'm surprised. Brian's a bad apple. Always has been. This time around he didn't last two months before he skipped."

"You mean he missed his appointment with you?"

"Correct-o-mundo, which violates his parole, which puts him back in prison. Not that anyone expected him to walk the straight and narrow."

"So what happened when he didn't show?"

"I sent a form to the Judge. Judge issued a warrant. But he hasn't been picked up far as I know."

"I understand he was washing dishes in Meyers."

"For a few weeks. Then he got a job as a groundskeeper-handyman."

"For who?"

"Some company that manages guest houses around Tahoe."

Ed's jaw clenched. "Thanks."

39

Ed pushed the speed limit over Echo Summit and skidded down the steep winding grade into Tahoe Basin, past Meyers, then up a mountainside to Heavenly Vista and the chalet where he'd stayed with Julie. The place was locked up tight. A sign on the gate referred interested parties to a management company on Ski Run Boulevard. Ed drove back down the hill. He found the office halfway up to Heavenly Valley, housed in an A-frame dolled up with chintzy faux-Swiss doo-dads, the place where he and Julie had picked up the keys.

"It's like I told the cops," a chunky middle-aged woman informed him as she took a long drag on a cigarette. "Jessburger worked there a couple weeks, then left. No notice. No phone call. Nothing." She had a round, bronze face with long black hair tied in two braids. Native American, Ed guessed. She wore a shapeless dress and an equally shapeless down vest. The ashtray on her desk was full of butts.

"Cops? From here? Or someplace else? San Francisco?"

"I don't know. Cops."

"Did you hire him?"

"No. Some guy called and told me he'd be working there and living in the maid's quarters. Said I should give him keys."

"You catch his name?"

"No. Just said he was from MRD—"

"MRD?"

"Mountain Resort Development, Inc. They own the place."

"You have a contact at MRD?"

"Nope. All we do is book reservations, hand out keys, and call the cleaning service after the caretaker deals with the owner."

"Did you know Jessburger was an ex-con?"

"Not until the cops told me. I mean, I had suspicions. The shaved head. The homemade tattoos. He wasn't no Boy Scout."

"And you're sure you don't remember the name of the guy from MRD? Don't you have any files on the place? The name of anyone who manages it?"

She shrugged. "Look, we book close to two hundred places. Some, we deal with the owners and handle the maintenance. Others we don't. That one, all we do is book it, hand out keys, and call the cleaning service after."

Ed drove into town, had potato pancakes at IHOP, then walked the two blocks to Harvey's and hit the pay phone in the hotel lobby. Mountain Resort Development, Inc. was not listed in the Tahoe area, nor in Reno, Las Vegas, Sacramento, San Francisco, the eight other Bay Area counties, Los Angeles, or San Diego.

But someone had to pay the taxes on the chalet. Ed drove back over the mountain to Placerville. The Assessor's office was on the first floor of the County Building. Ed gave the address and asked for the tax records. The clerk was a skinny, sullen man. A button on his sport coat said: Abortion is Murder. He fished out the file and handed it to Ed.

The taxes had been paid on time every time by MRD, Inc., a California corporation using certified checks drawn on a bank in Chicago. There were no names, no phone numbers. Which meant he had nothing.

Someone had to have pulled permits to build the place. The Building Department was down the hill in a quaint brick building with a brass plaque bolted beside the door. It was on the National Register of Historical Landmarks, the old Pony Express office. A pregnant woman who looked about nine months gone with twins presented Ed with the file.

The chalet had been built in 1968. There was a surveyor's report, a soils report, a geologist's report, an engineer's report, architectural plans, utility permits, water and sewage hook-up permits, and a form identifying the general contractor as one Henry Tinsmith.

Ed asked if he could see the local phone book. With an effort, the pregnant woman waddled to a shelf and lumbered back with it. There was no listing for a Henry but a Louise Tinsmith lived in Pollock Pines. Ed already knew, but he made the call anyway. He guessed right: Henry's widow said he'd been dead six years.

40

Striking out in Placerville left Ed with only one alternative, the Department of Corporations in Sacramento. If he gunned it, he could get there before it closed, then listen to the World Series on the way home.

The 'Stang flew down 50. The mountains ruined radio reception, so he listened to an old cassette, Dylan's *Highway 61 Revisited*. The tape ended on the outskirts of Sacramento. Ed ejected the tape, which triggered the radio. Ninety-odd miles from San Francisco, KFOG was laced with static, which destroyed the Kinks' "Rock 'n Roll Fantasy."

He was about to reach for another cassette when the DJ read a news bulletin: Two bodies had been fished out of the Bay by the old wharf in China Basin. The police said one was Brian Jessburger, wanted for the shootings of a San Francisco actor and lighting designer. The other was Chester Gilchrist, Jr., son of the *Foghorn* publisher, wanted for the murders of California Museum director Gregory Murtinson and his family's former chauffeur.

Suddenly, Ed felt nauseous. He swerved to the right, ran off the pavement, and almost off the shoulder into a ditch. He slammed on the brakes and screeched to a stop—heart racing, palms sweating, mind on fire. He was too far from San Francisco to pick up all-news KCBS. He twirled the radio dial. No closer station offered more than the headline he'd just heard. Getting a grip, he got back on the road, then spied a sign for a Shell station at the next exit. He pulled in, found the pay phone, called the *Defender*, and asked for Tim.

"I just heard." Ed was suddenly aware that he was panting and that his armpits felt spongy.

"All hell's breaking loose. Hang on." Tim barked at someone to position the TVs to face him, and to turn up the radio.

"I'm in Sacramento. What gives?"

"It's still pretty sketchy. KGO says Chet had a suicide note in his pocket. Channel 2 says the cops found a .38 with a silencer in the mud near the bodies. KCBS says Jessburger's hands were bound and he was shot between the eyes, execution-style."

"Jesus."

"It looks like murder-suicide: Chet shot Jessburger, then killed himself." Tim sighed: "All I wanted was to go home early and watch the Series. Now I'll be here all night."

Ed wanted to speak, but his mouth wouldn't work. He was the one reporter who'd bent over backward to give Chet the benefit of the doubt—even when a body turned up in his living room. Now this. He'd been a fool blinded by friendship. He felt disgusted. He deserved to be fired from the *Horn*, not for insubordination—for stupidity.

"I'll lay odds," Tim continued, "that it was the same gun that killed Murtinson and Cabral."

"So, everyone's saying Chet must have hired Jessburger to settle some old scores. Then Jessburger got out of control, so Chet killed him, then shot himself."

"You got it."

The pay-phone handset felt greasy. A hot wind blew into Ed's face. Out on 80, 18-wheelers roared by. Ed swallowed hard. It still didn't add up. Chet had no motive to kill Murtinson. Where did Wardell-Gardener fit in? And if Chet hired Jessburger, why would he have him kill the actor? On the other hand, life isn't neat and tidy. All the evidence was circumstantial, but it all pointed at Chet.

"Any evidence of a struggle? Any time-of-death estimate?"

"Ed, hold on." Tim covered the mouthpiece. All Ed heard was unintelligible mumbling. Then Tim came back on.

"Look, Ed, I'm watching three TV stations at once, plus we've got KGO and KCBS on, plus our guy just called in from China Basin. I gotta go. When you coming back?"

"Now."

There was no point visiting the Department of Corporations. Chet was dead. Ed flashed on Laura and Old Man Gilchrist, on what they must be going through. He recalled the emptiness he felt when Diane moved back to Grass Valley, the hurt and guilt when Julie ditched him.

He thought about two little girls in the Excelsior who no longer had a father. He wanted to drink himself into a stupor and forget how to feel pain. Instead, he slid back into the driver's seat and headed home.

He ignored the speed limit, hugged the left lane, and drove into the late afternoon sun, passing everything in sight like they were covered wagons and he was in Indianapolis looking for the checkered flag. West of Davis, the radio reception improved. He stayed glued to KCBS.

The note found on Chet's body said, "Please forgive me. I never wanted to hurt anyone. The drugs made me crazy. Tell Laura I love her."

That old teen-death song from the early '60s began playing in Ed's mind: "Tell Laura I love her. Tell Laura I need her. Tell Laura not to cry. My love for her will never die." Who sang it? Roger Miller? No. J. Frank Wilson? No, That was "Last Kiss." Then from the subterranean depths of adolescent make-out-party memories, it came to him: Ray Peterson.

But Ed felt no joy at conjuring the singer's name. If Chet had conned him, he was one gullible SOB. If not, he was no better off. Either way, he'd broken the cardinal rule of journalism: Keep your stories at arm's length. Friendship had compromised his judgment.

Just west of the Nut Tree, in between interviews from the Coliseum with Roger Craig and Tony LaRussa, there was another bulletin. The preliminary coroner's report showed heroin in both Chet's and Jessburger's bloodstreams. *The drugs made me crazy.*

"Fuck you, Chet," Ed said aloud, slapping the steering wheel hard, hurting his hand. I trusted you. I believed you. You prick. Still, though, something didn't smell quite right.

Ed imagined a coffin being lowered into the ground, with Laura and the Old Man dressed in black, taking turns with the shovel. Tears welled up in his eyes. Chet was dead, and they never even had burritos at La Cumbre.

The Game started as Ed rocketed through Vallejo. The A's wasted no time putting two runs on the board. Meanwhile, Dave Stewart struck out one Giant after another.

More bulletins: The gun appeared to be the same one used in the Murtinson and Cabral murders. Then Harrigan came on: "In light of the suicide note and other physical evidence," the detective said, "it appears that Chet Gilchrist was behind the murders of Gregory Murtinson, Juan Cabral, and the two men killed at Theatre Artaud. Brian Jessburger pulled the trigger, but it appears he was taking orders from Chet Gilchrist, who subsequently killed him."

"What about motive?" the reporter asked. "Why did Gilchrist want so many people dead?"

"We still don't know," Harrigan conceded, "but we're working on it."

The Bay Bridge was backed up through the Maze. It was dusk by the time Ed pulled into Dolores Terrace. The Giants were down four-zip in the top of the eighth. The cats meowed for dinner. And a water change. And a box change. As Ed returned from carrying the old litter out to the garbage, he noticed his new phone machine blinking. He had one message—from Old Man Gilchrist, asking him to call his private line no matter how late he got in.

Ed trembled as he dialed. What do you say to a father who has just lost a son? A son who had so much going for him? A son who—?

Gilchrist answered on the first ring. Ed expressed condolences and Gilchrist thanked him politely, automatically, without any discernible emotion. The man was deep in shock. "I'd like to see you in my office first thing in the morning."

"Haven't you heard? Ron fired me."

"Yes, but in light of recent events, I'm rehiring you—that is, if you're interested."

"What time?"

"Eight thirty."

"I'll be there."

He was still minus a television, so he turned on the shower radio. It was over. The A's won it 5-0 on Stewart's five-hitter and homers by Parker and Weiss. The color guy said it was like watching men play boys.

41

Gilchrist looked haggard. His hair seemed whiter, his face thinner and more deeply lined. His hands trembled. But his voice did not: "I mourned my son 10 years ago," he said, gazing off into space somewhere above Ed's head. Behind the Old Man, beyond the Old Mint, the construction crane hoisted a huge steel I-beam up a good 20 stories. "I lost Chet to drugs. I *hate* drugs. I wish I could drop a *hydrogen bomb* on every place on Earth that produces the opium poppy." He paused, collected himself. "Then Chet disappeared, and I lost him altogether. I was convinced he was dead. I had vivid dreams in which Laura telephoned and gave me the news. For years, I read all the stories and watched all the TV shows about the heroin problem, hoping I'd see a picture of him. I didn't care what shape he was in or the depths of his degradation. I just wanted to know he was alive. All the while, I was convinced he was dead.

"Then, out of the blue, he contacts me. Not only off heroin, but with a career in journalism and a Pulitzer Prize! I couldn't believe it. For weeks, I went around pinching myself. My mouth ached from smiling. The Governor pardoned him. He came home. He was mature, affectionate, truly the prodigal son. It felt too good to be true. And it was.

"I'm going to see the Handgun Initiative through to election day, and then ... I don't know ... maybe take Irene and the kids and go away for a while. I've always wanted to hike the Andes, see the Great Wall of China ... I'd like to do those things while I'm still physically able ..." His voice trailed off. His chin dropped to his chest and he massaged the bridge of his nose with his thumb and finger.

Then he raised his eyes and drilled deep into Ed's. "I want you to write Chet's story. All of it. I don't want anyone anywhere ever whispering that the *Foghorn* was weak on … *this* … because it cast my son or me in a bad light. I've told the entire Editorial Board that I want no misguided attempts to spare my feelings. Chet would have wanted it this way. So write Chet's story and don't pull any punches. Is that clear?"

"Perfectly," Ed replied. He shifted in the leather chair. "But what about Ron? And Gus? And Walt? Are they all right with this? With me … coming back?"

"That's somewhat complicated. I have a long-standing commitment to Walt not to get involved in personnel matters in the newsroom. But you know this story better than anyone and it's *critical* that our coverage be above reproach. So you're rehired at the salary you were making— but on a freelance basis. When your story runs, assuming you do the kind of job I know you're capable of, I will recommend full reinstatement. But that's Walt's decision. Not mine. Understand?"

It was a generous offer. Sure, Ed knew the story best. But there were a good half-dozen reporters downstairs who'd been working the story since before he got fired. They were doing a competent job. Was the Old Man being sentimental about Ed's friendship with Chet? If so, it was a side of Gilchrist he'd never seen.

"Yes. I understand."

Gilchrist nodded. The meeting was over. Ed rose from his chair.

"Wait. One more thing: The—" Gilchrist took a breath. "—funeral." He had trouble articulating the word. He sighed, closed his eyes, and rubbed them. When he reopened them, they glistened with tears. "We're having a small, very private, graveside service. In view of your friendship with Chet, I'd like you to attend."

"Of course," Ed replied. "Is it on the record or off?"

Gilchrist regarded him quizzically.

"The story. You want me to include it? Or leave it out?"

"It's your story. It's entirely up to you. Like I said: Pull no punches."

• • •

It felt surreal to enter the newsroom. His cube was still there, his desk untouched, right down to the dark residue in the coffee cup sitting by his screen. His old login and password still worked. Reporters and editors floated by, ribbed him about his "vacation."

The coffee was as rank as ever. As he stirred in white powder, the sports writer-union rep sidled up to him. "You're one lucky SOB, Ed. But the sword's still over your head. Be careful. Don't turn your back on Ron."

Sitting in his cube staring at his screen, a familiar voice asked, "How was the vacation?" Ruffen. Ed whirled around. In one hand, his editor held a coffee mug, in the other, an Egg McMuffin oozing yellow glop.

Ed took a breath. "Look, Ron, I know I can be … difficult. But someone *was* trying to kill me—and maybe *still is*."

Their eyes met. Ruffen took a sip from his mug. "Yeah. And if you don't get a Pulitzer nomination for the Chet story, someone *will* kill you—*me*. We got a tip that Jessburger and Cabral did time together at San Q. Chet probably met Jessburger through Cabral. See where that takes you."

"Right."

Ruffen waddled away. I'll look into it, Ed thought, but later.

Ed walked the long six blocks to the Hall of Justice, along the way dodging a few homeless beggars under the Central Skyway. It was a warm fall afternoon, the best time of year in the City by the Bay. A light breeze blew down from Twin Peaks, taking the edge off the sun.

The coroner's office was in the basement. Ed showed his press card and asked to view the bodies.

He was referred to the media-relations officer. "You're a day late. Everyone else was here yesterday: the networks, all the papers, *Time*, *Newsweek*, everyone. Biggest thing since White shot Moscone and Milk."

He handed Ed a press release summarizing the coroner's findings. Cause of death: gunshot wounds, both very close range, Jessburger's in the forehead, Chet's in the temple, presumably self-inflicted. Heroin in the blood of both deceased. More in Chet's.

"I'd like to see the bodies."

"I'm sorry," the press liaison apologized, "but that's impossible."

"Why?"

"Regulations. If I let one reporter down there, I have to let everyone."

"But no one else is here. You just said they all came and went yesterday. I've been down there before, on other stories."

"Sorry. Only next of kin are allowed to—"

"Fine. I was sent here by Chet's—Mr. Gilchrist's—next of kin, his father, Chester Worthington—"

"I know who he is."

"Then I'm sure you can appreciate that if I call him and mention your lack of cooperation, he'll call the Chief and you'll get a call ordering you to take me to the morgue. But if you just take me down there now, no one ties your shorts in a knot. I get to see the bodies either way."

The media-relations guy glared at him, and didn't budge.

"Look," Ed said, more conciliatory, "this is more than just a story for me. Chet was a close friend. I just want to say goodbye. I won't reveal that I saw his body. No one else in the media will ever know. I just want to say goodbye to my friend. Please."

The press guy picked up his phone and a young black deputy coroner in an immaculate white lab coat escorted Ed down. The morgue was one place he'd never get used to. The cold was numbing, the glare blinding, the smell revolting.

The deputy pulled a drawer open. Jessburger lay naked, blue, waxy, and unreal, a big swastika tattooed on one pec. He'd been shot at close range between the eyes. Even after a day in the freezer, the wound looked raw and angry. His face was largely intact, but the back of his head was gone.

The deputy pointed at the entry wound. "The entry side stays together. But the eggs get scrambled. The exit wound takes a lot of stuff with it."

Ed stared at him, the shape of his head, the simian curve of his shoulders. He was the skinhead nosing around the 'Stang on Highway 50. He was the shooter at Theatre Artaud.

When the deputy pulled the other drawer open, Ed had to swallow hard to keep from vomiting. The left side of Chet's head had been blown away.

"Shot himself in the right temple."

Ed felt an urgent need for fresh air.

42

Chet's funeral took place on a grassy knoll by a jacaranda tree above the small creek that meandered through Junipero Serra Memorial Garden in Colma, the place San Francisco's old money preferred for their final rest. It was a warm October morning, with big pillowy clouds rolling across a bright blue sky from the coastal hills past San Bruno Mountain to the East Bay, a perfect day to be outdoors, a day much better for baseball than for a funeral. Game Two was set to go that afternoon in Oakland. But one Giants fan would never see his team again.

Ed walked up to the glistening walnut casket, perched on a stand atop the hole under a canopy-covered platform with two dozen folding chairs and several huge vases of flowers. Chet's mother, Margaret, was buried a few yards away under an enormous stone ringed by well-tended flowers.

An engine purred. Ed turned and watched a limousine pull up and discharge Chet's father, his wife, and their young sons, plus Laura, and her sister, Rosemary, all of them in black, the women with black veils. A second limo held a half-dozen people Ed didn't recognize, presumably relatives, followed by a few cars with people Ed recognized from the elevator as big guns in Gilcorp.

The Old Man stood stooped and grim. Irene dabbed her eyes. Their boys shifted feet uncomfortably. Chet was their half-brother, but they'd just met him, didn't know him. By the time the eldest was born, Chet was already in Alaska. Laura sobbed loudly through the brief service.

The minister didn't mention the circumstances or even talk about Chet much. Instead, he read two psalms touting faith in God as the answer to the great mysteries of life, then ad-libbed a while on the inexplicable nature of life and death, sanctity and sin, kindness and cruelty, and the way people choose among them.

Then a professionally solemn attendant hit a button and the casket slowly descended. Worth stepped forward, reached resolutely for the shovel, and drizzled a spadeful of dirt into the hole. Afterward, he lingered a moment, went weak in the knees, and needed the shovel to steady himself. The minister grabbed his elbow and the attendant helped him back to his seat. Then the others filed forward and took their turns. All except Laura, who couldn't do it. She groaned at the graveside, and for one scary moment, Ed thought she might throw herself in. Then her sister led her sobbing back to her seat.

After the service, Ed expressed his condolences to his publisher, whose patrician breeding carried him through the ordeal dry-eyed. Then he embraced Laura, still sobbing, her face contorted in grief. Between moans, she thanked him for his friendship and for believing in Chet long after most other people had given up on him. Ed mumbled the usual, "If there's anything I can do …" Laura hugged him, then turned and disappeared into the gloom of the limousine, with Rosemary following grimly behind her.

• • •

The Golden Gate Bridge was an orange jewel shimmering in the sun against a backdrop of wind-whipped clouds. The bridge's walkway was packed with tourists wielding cameras. A thousand sailboats dotted the Bay. KFOG seemed to be in a San Francisco mood. Just as Ed passed the south tower, the DJ segued from the Starship's "We Built This City," into Otis Redding's "Dock of the Bay."

Ed took the exit for the Richmond-San Rafael Bridge, then turned off at the rutted road that led to a gate studded with razor-wire, the outer perimeter of San Quentin. A burly guard checked his press credential, his driver's license, and appointment, then opened the gate and waved him through. Fifty yards in, another guard ran him through the same drill, then waved him through another massive gate that led into the huge stone fortress.

A Department of Corrections functionary picked him up at Reception and led him through a warren of narrow windowless hallways illuminated by exposed bulbs and into the office of an associate warden, who fished through a file cabinet, pulled some paper, and explained that Juan Cabral and Brian Jessburger had been assigned to cells in the same block, D Block, had lived there for two years, and might have known one another.

"Might have?" Ed asked. "How many men in that block?"

The associate warden looked to be in his late forties. He had sand-colored hair going to gray, a big frame going to flab, an acne-scarred face, and a nose that looked like it had been broken more than once. "Maybe a hundred."

"They eat together? Exercise together?"

The associate warden nodded.

"Why wouldn't they have known each other?"

"Because," his tone bordered on exasperation, "Cabral was Mexican Mafia and Jessburger was Aryan Brotherhood. They don't mix much."

"They mix at all?"

"Very little."

"They have cellmates?"

"No. All singles on D Block. It's for hard cases."

"Would it be possible for me to talk with a few of their friends?"

"Prisoners don't have friends."

"Well, some inmates who knew them?"

"Sorry. Department regs prohibit that."

"What about guys from that block who've been released. Can I get in touch with any of them?"

"I don't know. Can you?"

"What I mean is: Do you keep track of where they go? Halfway houses? Parole officers?"

"Not us. You'll have to talk to Sacramento."

• • •

At the Front Page, Ed had just paid for a Byline, a turkey and Swiss on whole wheat with everything except onions, when he was paged. He picked up one of the house phones. "Rosenberg."

It was the operator with a call from Laura's sister, Rosemary. "I hate to bother you—"

"No bother at all. How's Laura holding up?"

"Not well. I gave her Valium. She's resting. But she asked me to call you."

"Something I can do?"

"Maybe. When we got back from the funeral, she had a call from a lawyer. I talked to him. It was very strange."

"What was?"

"He said he had a package for Laura—from Chet's mother."

"*What?* Margaret's been dead for years."

"The lawyer said the package was for Chet, but—"

"What's in it?"

"I don't know. He wouldn't say. He wants Laura to come down to his office to accept it. In person."

"How did this lawyer come by a package from Chet's mother?"

"He said she left it with him for safe keeping, with instructions to give it to Chet on his 30th birthday or 10 years after her death, whichever came second. But when Chet turned 30, he was gone, and the lawyer sort of forgot about it until—"

"Until all the press around Chet's death jogged his memory."

"Right."

"Did you get the lawyer's name?"

"Trawlings. Averill Trawlings."

Ed knew the name. The guy was no ambulance chaser. He was a honcho at Trawlings, Starrett & Melville, a financial-district firm that represented movers and shakers.

"You want me to call him? Collect the package?"

"Oh, would you? Laura's in no shape to go. But the lawyer said she should come right away."

Yeah, Ed thought, so he can send the final bill.

"I'll call him and get back to you."

"Thank you."

Averill Trawlings sounded like he was pushing 90. He had a thin raspy voice, but mentally, he was all there. Yes, he had the package. Yes, it was from Chet's mother. No, it could not be mailed or messengered to Laura or picked up by anyone else. Margaret had given specific instructions that he was to hand it personally to Chet, but given California's community property statutes, Laura would suffice.

"What's in the package?"

"I wouldn't know. It's sealed. And that's not your concern. It concerns only Mrs. Gilchrist."

Ed explained that Mrs. Gilchrist was seriously indisposed, in fact, beside herself, and that she'd asked him to pick up the package for her. Trawlings was sorry, but his instructions were clear: From his hand to Chet's or in this case, his wife's.

"What if Laura calls or faxes you allowing you to release the package to me?"

"I'm sorry. I'm bound by my long friendship with Margaret and by the Code of Professional Conduct to place it in her hand myself."

"Really? Well, suppose I call the Board of Professional Conduct at the State Bar and mention that you failed to contact Chet weeks ago—"

Trawlings hung up on him.

• • •

The next morning, Laura opened her door and embraced Ed, nuzzling her cheek into his chest.

"You sure you're up for this?" he asked. She looked frail. Her eyes were sunken, her face deeply lined. Her hair hung limp around her shoulders. "Whatever's in this package, it's waited a long time. It can wait a little longer."

She shook her head. "No. Chet and his mother were very close. I want to get it. For his sake."

Ed helped Laura into the 'Stang just as KFOG launched into "10 at 10," 10 great songs from one great year. There were sound effects of a wheel of fortune spinning, then a fanfare announcing the year, 1963. The opener was "He's So Fine" by that girl group. … Who?

"You remember who sang this?" Ed asked, irritated that he didn't recall. But Laura was a mummy beside him.

Halfway to downtown, "It's My Party" came on, and again Ed couldn't remember the singer. At Leavenworth, the radio played "Twist and Shout," which allowed him to recover some musical self-respect: the Isley Brothers. And as he pulled into the lot beneath the Bank of America building, the original "Louie, Louie" came on, another easy one: The Kingsmen.

On the thirty-eighth floor, Averill Trawlings occupied a large corner office with a view from the Marin headlands past Alcatraz to Berkeley. Trawlings was younger than he sounded on the phone, maybe seventy. He could have passed for one of the Seven Dwarfs. He was short and plump, with a full head of longish white hair. He handed Laura a bulging padded envelope stapled shut and sealed with shipping tape. "Your mother-in-law gave this to me, oh, maybe a year or so before she ... passed on. Quite frankly, I forgot all about it until the news of your husband's. ... At dinner, my wife said she was glad Margaret hadn't lived to ... you know ... That's when I remembered."

Trawlings handed Laura a scissors. "Would you like to have some privacy? I could—"

"No, thank you," Laura murmured, fumbling with the package, then giving it and the scissors to Ed, who snipped it open.

Out fell an old Bible. A few pages in the front were folded in on themselves. They listed six generations of Margaret's family, names, birth and death dates, the spouses they'd brought into the family, and their children, a pyramid of procreation. It all looked pretty standard—except at the very end, where Margaret Melinda Gilchrist married her second cousin, Chester Worthington Gilchrist, III, and had a son, Chester Worthington Gilchrist, IV. Next to that entry, circled in red ink were four sets of initials—M.M.G., C.W.G. III, C.W.G. IV, and G.R.M.—and next to each set of initials, a single capital letter, A, B, or O.

Laura looked at the notations, then from Trawlings to Ed. "Who's G.R.M.? And what do these letters mean?"

"I haven't the foggiest," the lawyer said.

"Me either," Ed lied. "May I see it a moment?" He committed the initials and letters to memory, then closed the Bible and handed it to Laura. "Weird."

She whispered. "I'd like to go home now."

Ed scooted around a cable car on California as KFOG played a live version of "Tenth Avenue Freezeout" from one of Bruce's shows at Winterland. When they pulled up in front of Laura's building, she apologized for taking him on such a wild goose chase. "Nothing makes sense anymore," she sighed, "so why should this?"

"No need to apologize. It was no trouble. Meanwhile, there's something I've been meaning to ask you: What was the name of the Gilchrist's cook again? The one who helped raise Chet? Mendoza?"

"Melendez. Rosa Melendez. Why?"

"Oh, you know, I'm writing Chet's story. I thought maybe she could reminisce about him as a boy. You said he got in touch with her when he won the Pulitzer."

"Yes, he called her."

"And then Cabral contacted him."

"Yes, Rosa was sick with emphysema and Chet gave her our secret phone number, and she gave it to Cabral."

"Do you recall where she lives?"

"No, Chet never said. But I assume it's somewhere in the Bay Area. Maybe Worth knows.

"Yeah, I'll ask him."

"Oh, and one more thing: Wasn't Chet left-handed?"

"Yes. But he bats either way. He's very proud of that." Then Laura realized she'd used the present tense, and began to cry. She leaned toward Ed, who held her as she let go for a while. When she was finished, she climbed out of the car and trudged up the walk. She moved like an old woman.

As Ed drove off, he noted that the white van with the curtained windows was still parked across the street.

43

Ed dialed the *Defender*. When Tim came on the line, he leaned deep into the sound-deadening corner of his cube and spoke softly. "You want to make good money on a one-day freelance reporting job?"

"Sure. What? And how much?"

Ed named a figure he knew was about a week's pay at Jocko's little sweatshop.

"You're on," Tim said with glee. "What do I have to do?"

"Let's deal with the 'when' first. I need you to do this tomorrow. It'll take all day."

"Uh, okay. I can take tomorrow off. Now what's the job?"

"Drive to Sacramento to the State Department of Corporations and check the ownership and contact information for a company called Mountain Resort Development, Inc. It might be listed under MRD, Inc., so check that, too. Chances are it's owned by another corporation. I need you to follow the paper as far back as you can, and give me every name, address, and phone number of every person you come across."

"Got it. What's this all about?"

"I'm not sure yet. Just a hunch I have. But one worth checking out."

"A hunch about Chet?"

"You've got a future in journalism."

Tim laughed. "Don't get me wrong, Ed. I can use the money. But why not just call the *Horn's* Sacramento bureau and have them do it?"

"Because I need this done very quietly. So not a word to anyone. Not Jocko. Not even Kim. Okay?"

"And what about me? Do I get to find out why I'm chasing all this paper?"

310   Michael Castleman

"As soon as I can tell you, I will."

"But not now."

"Correct. I'm sorry this has to be so hush-hush, but it does. You still willing to spend tomorrow on this and not tell anyone?"

"Why not?"

"Thanks, Tim. I really appreciate it."

Ed pulled out the phone books for the nine Bay Area counties. The "Melendez" list came to 141 names. No Rosas. Seven R's, none of them old ladies with emphysema. Then he tried the Registrars of Voters for the nine counties, with the same result: No elderly women. Next he called a credit bureau. No one named Rosa Melendez with a birthdate before 1940 in the nine counties had any credit cards. He was out of luck.

Then he had an inspiration. The *Foghorn* subscriber list. She worked for the Gilchrists for years. She had to subscribe. He called Circulation and had them run the name. No Rosa Melendez. What about the complementary sub list? Nothing.

Maybe she was dead. That happens with emphysema. More likely, she remarried and changed her name. ...

Ed filled his coffee cup and finished paging through the day's paper. Toward the end of the Metro section, nestled down low in the gutter was a small headline: Wharf Hotel to Allow Union Vote. It seemed that one of the newer hotels on Fisherman's Wharf had finally decided to obey the law. Four years after San Francisco's largest union, Local 2 of the Hotel and Restaurant Employees and Bartenders Union, had petitioned the National Labor Relations Board, the hotel was finally willing to allow its workers to vote on union representation. It was your typical POS story with predictable quotes from the union president and hotel management.

Ed was about to turn the page when a thought occurred to him. From what Laura said, Rosa Melendez was now too old and infirm to be whipping up nouvelle cuisine in a restaurant kitchen. But maybe she'd done some restaurant cooking after leaving the Gilchrists. He dialed Local 2.

The union had no retirees named Rosa Melendez. Just one person by that name, a 34-year-old, part-time banquet waitress at the Hilton.

Demoralized and hungry, Ed decided to get some fresh air and eat lunch somewhere other than at the Front Page. He wandered north, crossed Market, and without consciously planning it, wound up in the seedy little neighborhood a few blocks west of Union Square where new hotels were pushing out the peep shows and massage parlors. Before him stood the huge tower of the San Francisco Hilton, its first 15 stories swaddled in scaffolding. A sign said they were renovating 300 rooms and adding a gym, restaurant, bar, banquet rooms, and an International Business Service Center, whatever that was.

There was a sweet little Thai place around the corner. Just the thought of their lime chicken salad with garlic peanut sauce usually made Ed salivate. But not today. He felt drawn to the hotel. He dodged an Airporter van and made for the bank of gleaming brass-and-glass doors. A bellman directed him to the banquet kitchen. It was in full-court press, a half-dozen cooks churning out shrimp-stuffed chicken breasts with wild rice and asparagus for two hundred Toyota dealers. He flashed his press card at the banquet manager, an Indian kid who looked fresh out of hotel school. Yes, Rosie was working the lunch. Ed could see her after she served dessert and coffee. The kid directed him to the bar.

Two Calistogas, a bowl of munchies, and an episode of *Days of Our Lives* later, Rosa Melendez tapped Ed on the shoulder. She reminded him of Frida Kahlo, except that her long black hair was piled on top of her head, and she wore large gold hoop earrings and blood-red lipstick. "You the reporter? Deepak said you were asking for me."

"Sorry to bother you, Ms. Melendez. This is a real shot in the dark. But by any chance are you related to the Rosa Melendez who used to cook for the family that owns the *Foghorn?*"

"She's my mother."

Ed had to suppress the urge to throw his arms around her. "Your mother? *Fantastic!* I'm a friend of Chet Gilchrist's."

Rosa looked away and sighed. "Terrible what happened to him. We used to play together as kids. My mom was like a mother to him. She was very upset when he got into trouble years ago and more upset when he ran away. She's been taking it very hard these past few days. None of us can believe that Cookie would—" She left the sentence unfinished.

"Cookie?"

"That's what we always called him. Chet was Cookie, and I was Candy."

"How well did you know Chet?"

"Real well when we were little kids. We were together a lot. But less as we got older and he went off to boarding school. My mom left the Gilchrists when I was in tenth grade. I don't think I saw him after that."

"Where does your mother live?"

"Daly City."

"She's not in the phone book, or registered to vote, or even on the *Foghorn* subscriber list."

"That's because she remarried. Her name's Cartagena now."

Daly City, on the ocean just south of San Francisco, had two dubious distinctions. It was the home of Matthews TV & Stereo, whose radio commercials Ed loved to hate. And its ridgetop homes were the inspiration for Malvina Reynolds' song "Little Boxes." Driving out Mission, it seemed to Ed they weren't all made of ticky tacky. But close.

Rosa Melendez Cartagena lived in a well-kept bungalow in a foggy canyon near Serramonte Shopping Center. Mr. Cartagena answered the door and ushered Ed into the living room where Rosa was watching *The Price Is Right.* She had tubes running from her nostrils to an oxygen tank on a small hand truck. It was an effort for her to raise her hand to shake his.

But she was eager to talk, albeit slowly and with many breaks. Margaret Gilchrist may have been a doyenne of high society, but away from the cocktail parties, she was a beast, an alcoholic addicted to diet and sleeping pills who abused her husband, neglected her son, and destroyed herself. It was no wonder Cookie got into trouble. Rosa had done the best she could, but a spirited boy needs a mother's love, and Cookie never got much, which is why he went astray.

Then Ed took her hand and told her that Chet had never been a heroin addict. Rosa's dark eyes widened in amazement and she clutched her hands to her heart. "Then Juan was right? What he told me is true?"

"By Juan, you mean your cousin, Juan Cabral, right?"

"Yes."

"Rosa, this is very important. What did Juan tell you?"

Two hours later, Ed parked at Serramonte Mall and found a pay phone by the Mervyn's. He dialed Harrigan's number, and by some miracle, the desk sergeant said he was there.

"What do you want?" Harrigan snorted.

"It's about Chet Gilchrist."

"What about him?"

"I don't think he did it."

Silence. Then Harrigan sighed, "The trouble with you is you *don't think.*"

"Look, I—"

"No, *you* look. I got four open files screaming for arrests—including the Symphony guy's wife." Ingrid Solvytin, 27, new bride of the first clarinetist, had been found raped and stabbed to death behind the Opera House after the Symphony performance two nights earlier. "The Gilchrist case is closed. End of story."

"What would it take to reopen it?"

"Jesus, Rosenbaum. I don't believe you."

"What would it take?"

"A signed confession."

"How about a taped confession?"

But Harrigan hung up without answering before Ed could correct him on the last name.

Back in the 'Stang, he drove the half-mile to Matthews and bought a microcassette recorder with a tiny lapel mike.

At home that evening, he was in the middle of a roast chicken breast with spicy guacamole on a French roll from the Front Page, when Tim called.

"You find anything?"

"What you predicted. Corporations stacked one on top of another."

Ed grabbed a pad and pen. "Shoot."

"Okay. Mountain Resort Development, Inc., of Truckee is owned by California Land Management, Inc., of San Diego, which is owned by Real Property Trust, Inc., of Oxnard, which is owned by Sierra Resorts, Inc. of Wilmington, Delaware."

"Delaware. Shit." Delaware was where you registered a corporation if you wanted to keep its ownership as secret as possible. "Did you get any names?"

"No directors or shareholders. Just a bunch of lawyers."

"Their names?"

Tim read the list. The lawyer who filed the papers on MRD was from San Diego. The lawyer for California Land Management was in Chicago. Real Property Trust, Inc., was represented by a lawyer in Seattle. And the lawyer for Sierra Resorts was in New York.

"Great work, Tim. I'm writing your check as we speak. You want me to mail it? Or stick it under my doormat for you to pick up?"

"You can mail it. You need anything else?"

"Not at the moment."

"Well, you know where to find me."

"Thanks, man. Great job. Oh, and about the M.E. job at the *Defender*: Tell Jocko I got rehired. Seems I was only on vacation after all."

44

With Game Three of the World Series scheduled for that afternoon at Candlestick and the Giants down two games to none, the newsroom sizzled with anticipation and anxiety. Someone hung a huge Giants banner across the coffee alcove. Giants caps seemed to sprout from every head. The Sports writers held court and joked about scalping their choice seats, then watching the game on TV. The *Foghorn's* handful of A's fans laid low. Deep down, few people expected the Giants to win the Series. Any way you sliced it, the A's were the better team. But with the Bay Bridge Series crossing to the Giants' yard, the smart money was betting the home team would take one or two.

When he wasn't loitering around the Sports cubes, listening to KNBR's pre-game chatter, or munching on the tray of orange-and-black-iced donuts courtesy of the Style editor, Ed worked his way through the paper's old files on Chet's arrests and flight, his mother's life and death, and anything else the Archive had under "Gilchrist."

He also called UCSF Medical Center and asked a public information officer to put him in touch with a geneticist.

Then he tackled the lawyers on Tim's list. He knew what they'd give him: *bupkis*, as his grandfather used to say, Yiddish for "nothing." Which was why he initially asked for their secretaries, hoping to luck out on a first-day bimbo who didn't know enough not to pull the file. But no. All the secretaries were sphinxes and all the lawyers had the same reflexive line: "That's privileged information. You are, of course, free to file suit to pierce the veil. But if you do, we will oppose you vigorously, and we will prevail." Of all the crap that filled reporters' ears, Ed hated lawyer crap the most. Any idiot could see that Mountain Resort Development, Inc., and all the other corporations were shells set up for the sole purpose of obscuring ownership from nosy schmucks like him. Each corporation was probably nothing more than a few pieces of paper mouldering in some long-forgotten file. Ed wondered what it must feel like to have a privileged relationship with a phony corporation. Did it keep these shysters warm at night?

By mid-afternoon, he'd reached three of the four attorneys. Only one to go, the New Yorker. It was after hours back East, but the way New Yorkers work, someone was bound to be there. Ed dialed 212, then hung up. Did he really want to put himself through this? New York lawyers prided themselves on being the surliest on Earth. He flashed on that old joke about a rube's first visit to Manhattan. His watch stops, so he asks a native, "Excuse me, sir, do you have the time—or should I just go fuck myself?" But Ed believed in crossing his Ts, and he'd paid Tim good money to ferret out the bozo's name, Kenneth Hampstead, and his number. He steeled himself, then dialed. A woman with a lilting Caribbean accent answered. Between her "Good evening" and "How may I direct your call?" she sing-songed the name of the firm. It was all Ed needed to hear.

• • •

Up on the fifth floor, the Old Man's secretary buzzed Ed through the redwood doors. The security guard, now familiar with him, didn't get up, just pointed him down the hall toward the inner sanctum.

Gilchrist was on the phone, leaning way back in his chair, legs up on his big desk crossed at the ankles. He was being interviewed by someone about the Handgun Control Initiative. He motioned Ed to the buttery leather chair he'd warmed on previous visits.

Gilchrist sat up and hung up. He looked like a cat who'd just finished a bowl of milk. "A pre-interview for *Sixty Minutes*." As he named the show, his voice dropped a reverential half-octave. "Seems our little initiative has captured the fancy of the national media. Ed Bradley is coming out next week to do a segment that will air ten days before the election. Excellent timing for us."

Gilchrist rubbed his temples. "You know," he said, suddenly somber, "before Gregory's death, the polls had us losing 60-40. Now, with all the … handgun killings, we're ahead 55-45." He closed his eyes. When he reopened them, they glistened with stifled tears. "Chet was a drug addict and a murderer. My pain and anger and disappointment over the mess he made of his life will be with me till the day I die. But it looks like the initiative is going to win because of him. I consider it his dying gift, and it comforts me a little."

Gilchrist gazed down at his desktop and ran his fingers through his silver hair. Then he looked up, forcing himself to brighten. "So tell me, Ed, how is your story coming? Any new insights into my son?"

"Several," Ed replied, shifting in his chair, "starting with this: *He wasn't your son, was he*?"

Gilchrist's lips slowly curled into the kind of smile a crocodile flashes as it waddles into a river, heading for a meal. He pressed a button on his desk, and gazed into his computer screen. "Very interesting. I see you're carrying a tape recorder—and a gun."

Ed went wide-eyed.

Gilchrist leaned back regally in his chair. His voice was calm. "This office is equipped with state-of-the-art surveillance electronics. I can understand a reporter carrying a tape recorder. But not a gun." He spread his palms and raised his eyebrows in a gesture that asked why.

Ed stared into cold reptilian eyes. "Serial killers make me nervous. Try any shit, and I swear, I'll shoot you just like you shot Chet and everyone else." Ed patted his jacket pocket, drawing sustenance from the presence of the .38.

Gilchrist chuckled. "Oh, I doubt that." He touched his finger pads to their opposite numbers, and flexed them, a spider doing push-ups on a wall mirror. "We both know you don't have the nerve. And if, by some act of colossal stupidity, you pull that trigger, what would happen? You'd get life, maybe even death—"

"But you'd be punished—"

"—and you'd never get your questions answered—"

"—but Chet would be avenged."

"—No he wouldn't. No one would listen to a word you had to say. You'd be dismissed as a disgruntled ex-employee who went crazy—"

"But you *rehired* me."

"No I didn't. In deference to your friendship with *my son,* I brought you back on a temporary, part-time, freelance basis to write his story. But you demanded full reinstatement. I refused. You couldn't handle it. You snapped, and shot me. That's how the world would see it."

The intercom buzzed. Gilchrist told his secretary to hold his calls.

Ed's mouth went dry and his armpits went wet. A weapon is only as threatening as the will to use it, and the Old Man was right: He didn't have the will. The .38 felt leaden in his pocket. He'd thought this through. He'd pegged Gilchrist for a coward. He would flash his iron and the Old Man would crack, answer his questions to save his miserable hide, then surrender to the police. But Gilchrist was made of stronger stuff. Ed's plan now appeared inane. He felt outmaneuvered, powerless.

"So here's what we're going to do," Gilchrist explained. "First, you give me your tape recorder. Keep the gun for all I care. Next, you tell me what you know—what you *think* you know. Then, I'll answer your questions. And then you'll answer mine. All very civilized."

Ed's breath came in shallow gulps. "Then what?"

"Then we come to an arrangement, you and I."

"What kind of arrangement?"

"A financial arrangement. A generous one."

"And if I refuse?"

Gilchrist pressed a button on his desk. Off to his right, Ed heard a loud click. "I've sealed the door. You can't leave unless I let you."

Ed squirmed. "Maybe I should just shoot you. God knows you deserve it." He reached into his jacket pocket.

"You see this button?" Gilchrist pointed to a red disk on the arm of his chair. "It calls security. They're armed. They'll find you threatening me with a gun. They might shoot you. They might not. Either way, you get charged with aggravated assault, a felony that carries mandatory prison time. Last election, the district attorney prostrated himself for my endorsement. He won't cut you any deals. You might make some wild accusations. In reply, I simply suggest that, despite my generous offer of freelance work, you couldn't handle getting fired. You had a nervous breakdown. No one will believe a word you say. You'll wind up in the mental ward at Vacaville, so drugged that you won't be able to find your own genitals in the shower."

Ed held his breath.

"Now, give me the tape. Tell me what you've discovered. I'll answer your questions. Then you answer mine."

Ed didn't move.

"Hand it over, and we can have our conversation." Gilchrist's crocodile eyes bored into Ed's. "Refuse, and I press the button—and we both get to see if you have the nerve."

Ed sat still.

"Last chance. I'm not asking for the gun. Just the tape. You're a better reporter than I thought you were. But you're short a few details. I bet you want your questions answered. And I bet you'd like to be rich."

Ed heaved a sigh. His eyes darted from Gilchrist's smug face out the window to the Old Mint and back to the red button on the arm of Old Man's chair. Ed mumbled, "All right." He reached under his jacket lapel and unhooked the tiny microphone, then pulled the microcassette recorder out of his breast pocket.

"Toss me the cassette."

Ed popped it out and slid it across the big desk. Gilchrist dropped it into the paper shredder. The machine made a brief grating noise. A shower of tiny brown confetti fluttered into the can.

Gilchrist smiled, the crocodile returned to the riverbank with a full belly, "Now, let's see just how good a reporter you are." He leaned back in his chair ready to be entertained.

Ed shifted uncomfortably in his. This was so different from how he'd planned it. But the Old Man was right. He had questions he wanted answered. He took a breath: "Your first wife," he began tentatively, "Chet's mother, Margaret, was … difficult—"

"Difficult? Ha! She made Lady Macbeth look like Mother Teresa."

"She was an alcoholic addicted to barbiturates. She delighted in reminding you that she was the Gilchrist with the money, while you were the poor relation. When she got pissed, she called you 'church mouse.'"

"Very impressive. Where'd you dig that up?"

"None of your business." No way he was going to tell this prick about Rosa.

Gilchrist pursed his lips down to pencil lines, then smiled. "Rosa. It has to be Rosa. She was the only one who saw Margaret … at her worst. I thought she died."

Ed didn't take the bait. Instead he continued: "You took Margaret's abuse for years, but eventually, after you consolidated control over Gilcorp, you decided to arrange a little 'accident.' You waited until she was good and snockered one night, then you drowned her in the swimming pool in Hillsborough. It was all so simple. You ducked out immediately after to a meeting at the Golden State Club, which gave you a bomb-proof alibi backed up by the biggest names in Bay Area money. You even did it on a Wednesday, the servants' night off. They were all supposed to be out. But you didn't know that Juan Cabral was in his apartment above the carriage house. He was ill with a stomach virus. He heard the commotion, saw you drag Margaret out of the house, and push her into the pool. He watched you jump in after her and hold her under until she stopped kicking."

"Very good. Go on."

"A few weeks later, Cabral quit his job and tried to blackmail you. To shut him up, you set him up for a heroin bust. He started singing, telling the cops you'd drowned your wife, but it was his word against yours and no one was about to believe a Mexican junkie against one of the Bay Area's leading lights, not to mention that you had a golden alibi."

"I also had the paper and … *influence* with other media. It wasn't difficult to make sure that Juan's accusations were ignored."

"So Margaret's death was ruled an accident. She'd been taking pills and drinking, and the poor thing fell into the pool. You played the bereaved widower. Publicly, you even made a show of trying to rehabilitate Cabral. You got him into a diversion program, which made you look like a saint. When he got out, you set him up again. But the second time, not even his devoted former employer could save him from prison."

Gilchrist smiled, a rattlesnake sunning on a warm rock. "He was a fool. I offered him an arrangement. He could have returned to Mexico a rich man. But he was greedy and stupid, so I had to fall back on Plan B. I hope you don't make the same mistake. Go on."

"Everything went so smoothly. Even Cabral's blackmail attempt turned out to have a silver lining. You'd always hated Chet. He wasn't your son. His parents were Margaret and Murtinson, and you despised both of them. But as Margaret's son, Chet—not you or your children—stood to inherit Gilcorp. With Margaret out of the way, you felt free to move against him. So you set him up for his two heroin busts and everyone assumed the evil Mexican had led the sheltered rich kid astray. Of course, you played the devoted father. You bailed him out, put him in rehab, and looked so anguished on TV. But it was all your doing. Chet never used heroin, did he?"

Gilchrist's smile broadened. It was still reptilian, but a human emotion had bubbled up beside it. What was it? Ed wondered. The Old Man was riveted to his every word. But his smile conveyed more than just fascination. Then Ed realized what Gilchrist was feeling. *Pride.* He'd created a masterpiece of manipulation, but for years, he'd had to keep it to himself. No one knew. Now, finally, someone did—and he liked it.

"No," Gilchrist said. "Chet never used heroin. Neither, to my knowledge, did Cabral."

"I thought so."

Gilchrist gave a slight nod.

"Chet was thunderstruck by his first arrest. He wasn't a user, but there was enough heroin in his bedroom to make him look like a major dealer. In rehab, he was Mr. Denial, a classic junkie move and one that convinced all the counselors that he was seriously strung out. The more vociferous his denials, the more they came down on him and the longer they kept him. Finally, he realized that to get released, he had to play the addict. It worked, but it put him on the record as one. Three weeks after he got out, you set him up again. Chet's second arrest just about unhinged him. He took a swing at one of the arresting officers. The others beat him up and hauled him down to Bryant Street in chains. He knew he'd been set up. He figured Calderone was behind it. They'd almost come to blows over Laura, and in revenge, Chet threatened he'd get Overland to drop *Full Disclosure*, which would have killed it. Again, you played the distraught father, but inside, you must have been yukking it up."

Gilchrist smiled. "Yes, Chet's feud with Calderone came in quite handy. Not only that, but after Chet threatened to have Overland cut Calderone off, we demanded better terms to carry his magazine and he had no choice but to accept."

"You're one sick fuck."

Gilchrist bridled. "And you're a sanctimonious little shit—but a surprisingly good investigator. Go on."

Suddenly, Ed didn't want to. The more he revealed, the less power he had. But he also wanted the Old Man to know just how good he was. And he had questions he wanted answered. He took a deep breath: "Everyone figured Chet would get another shot at rehab, not 20 to life. But you'd endorsed a bunch of Republicans and the Dems trounced your guys. The district attorney, the mayor, the attorney general, and the governor were all your political enemies and they decided to make an example of Chet. But even their vindictiveness had a silver lining. Chet jumped bail and disappeared. You figured he was out of your hair for good."

Gilchrist nodded. "That was my hope."

"Too bad you didn't know that Rosa and Cabral were cousins."

"Were they?" Gilchrist stared off into space.

"Cabral told her how you killed Margaret and what you did to him. She didn't believe a word of it. She was completely loyal to you."

"I'm not surprised. I was very good to her and her daughter."

"But Cabral kept writing her from prison retelling the story in letter after letter. She never really believed Cabral—until I showed up at her door."

"Where is she now?"

"You think I'd tell you?"

"I have no wish to harm her. I want to help her."

"Sure you do—right into her grave."

Gilchrist stared curare-tipped darts at him.

Ed continued: "After Chet won the Pulitzer, he wanted to share the news with the closest thing to a loving parent he'd ever known, so he called Rosa. She put Cabral in touch with him. Cabral told him about Margaret's death and how you set him up after he tried to blackmail you. Chet put two and two together and figured you'd set him up, too."

"Possibly. But he never confronted me. When he got in touch, he was the loving son, abjectly apologetic for running away and embarrassing me."

"What did he say?"

"Just that he wanted to come home. He said he was willing to go to prison for the drug charges."

"But you didn't want him in prison. You wanted him dead. It was the only way to retain control of Gilcorp and pass it on to your kids with Irene. Margaret's father's will was quite clear—the company passed from him to Margaret to Chet, unless, of course, they were deceased, in which case, it passed to you."

"Correct."

"So you pulled strings. This time around, the D.A., the A.G., and the governor were all your boys, and here was Chet, the Prodigal with the Pulitzer, so you collected on a few campaign promises and got him off."

"Correct again."

"But why did you wait so long? Why did you bother to set Chet up for the drug busts? Why didn't you just kill him way back when?"

Gilchrist shrugged, palms up. "In retrospect, I should have. But I was young. I hadn't met Irene. I didn't have children and wasn't thinking about corporate succession. I thought the stigma of drug addiction and the humiliation of a prison record would be enough to keep Chet out of my hair."

"So, by getting the drug charges dropped and sparing him prison, you were lulling Chet into a false sense of security."

"Correct."

"So you could have him killed."

Another palms-up shrug, along with a sly smile.

"And while you were at it, you figured it was the perfect time to settle your old score with Gregory Murtinson."

Gilchrist nodded. "Very good."

"You started with Murtinson because he was Chet's real father."

A smile and a nod. "I must say, I'm impressed you discovered that."

"Spare me. Did Chet know?"

"No, I don't believe so, though Gregory never did much to hide it, doting on him as he did. How did you find out?"

"A note in Margaret's family Bible. She gave it to Averill Trawlings before she—before you *killed her*—with instructions to give it to Chet on his thirtieth birthday."

"Averill. I'll be damned."

"But by the time Chet hit thirty, he was long gone and Trawlings forgot all about it until the news of Chet's death jogged his memory. He gave the Bible to Laura a few days ago. It listed all your initials and blood types. The blood types proved you couldn't have been Chet's father and that Murtinson was. Except that Murtinson was gay. How did that work?"

Gilchrist crossed his legs and resettled himself in his chair, the raconteur. "Gregory was seeing a psychiatrist who was trying to 'cure' his homosexuality. This doctor urged him to date women and have sex with them. Gregory didn't want to. He'd already seen his first marriage collapse in scandal over his … orientation. Women did nothing for him sexually. But it was the early '50s. The psychiatrist was adamant. Gregory was desperate. He told Margaret about his 'homework,' and as his close friend, she volunteered. She said it was horrible for both of them. But she got pregnant."

"And that's how the two of you wound up getting married."

"She wouldn't hear of getting rid of it, so she needed a husband in a hurry. I was available. We were second cousins, but as you know, my side of the Gilchrists had no money. Physically, I found Margaret repulsive. But I wanted her money, her newspaper, her social standing. So we struck a bargain. I made her son legitimate and she made me rich and powerful."

"And miserable."

He rolled his eyes. "You have no idea. Drowning was too good for her."

"How did you set up the heroin busts?" Ed asked. "Where'd you get the heroin?"

Gilchrist smiled broadly, the artist expounding on his masterpiece. "For a man in my position, nothing is impossible, and few things are even difficult. You'd be surprised how many very rich men enjoy heroin— less for the high, more for the thrill. Most skirt the edges of addiction. A few actually are addicted. But their money shields them from the depravity people associate with the drug. The addicts I know function quite well. My source is worth, oh, probably $500 million. I'm sure you've heard of him. He owns businesses all over the world. He imports it himself, on his own corporate jet. Flies to Bangkok several times a year. He's financed several projects for the Thai government. When you have his kind of clout, customs officials become very … accommodating." Another broad grin. Gilchrist was enjoying this.

"But your heroin escapades came back to haunt you."

"I wouldn't say that. Juan's and Chet's … misfortunes brought me a great deal of public sympathy, and 10 years of peace. When they resurfaced, it wasn't difficult to arrange … recent events."

"Weren't you worried that Chet would reveal your role in Margaret's death and the heroin business?"

Gilchrist chuckled. "Don't be silly. Juan tried that and got nowhere. And Chet had no evidence tying his legal problems to me. He blamed Ted Calderone."

"What about Jessburger? How'd you get him to do your dirty work?"

"Quite easily. As far as the public is concerned, business empires like Gilcorp run with the help of lawyers, PR people, and political influence. But privately, they also resort to … other means. A man I know has helped … quiet some labor problems for me over the years. He introduced me to a colleague of his, who introduced me to Jessburger. Once the connection was made, it was simply a matter of money."

"So you had him start with Murtinson because he was Chet's father."

Another quick laugh. "Oh, there was more to it than that. You said it yourself: I hated Gregory, hated him my whole life. When we were young, I was the poor relation, and he was the ultimate snob. He wouldn't have anything to do with me. His attitude never changed, even after I married Margaret and joined the board of the Golden State Club—which, incidentally, he secretly tried to block—and built Gilcorp into a financial powerhouse that made his lousy $50 million look like pocket change. None of my accomplishments mattered. I was always beneath him. So I wanted *him* beneath *me*—six feet beneath. In addition, of course, Chet loved him. I knew he would be distraught about Gregory's death, which would give me more room to put … other plans into action."

"So stealing the paintings, making Murtinson's murder look like an art theft, that was all your idea."

Another smile. "Of course. I especially wanted the Rembrandt. It was Gregory's most prized possession. Spoils of war."

"But it's so well known. You can't sell it."

Gilchrist chortled smugly. "I wouldn't think of trying. The Rembrandt and the Degas are both in storage—very secure, climate-controlled storage. A few years from now, I plan to announce that the thieves contacted me, that I ransomed the paintings for, oh, say, $6 million in cash—small untraceable bills. I present them as gifts to the California Museum and become the toast of the art world. Then I write off the ransom, which I never actually paid, and I see my tax bill drop more than $2 million."

"You son of a bitch. Is there any angle you haven't figured?"

Gilchrist flashed a toothy grin. "By the way, thanks for mentioning that Jessburger dropped the Picasso. Saved me some aggravation."

"What about Scott Gardener, the actor who played Wardell? Why the big ruse about the Lost Gold?"

"To distract Chet even more. As you know, he was obsessed with it. With a little help from the actor, I used the Lost Gold to lure Chet out of the party. Jessburger drove him away, never to bother me again."

"So Chet never went back to Anchorage."

"Of course not. I kept him so drugged, he was barely breathing. Jessburger went, using his identification."

That was why the air-charter people couldn't identify Chet from photographs.

"And Jessburger killed Cabral there, and planted heroin on him."

Gilchrist nodded. "Correct."

"And then you killed Jessburger and Chet and dumped their bodies in the Bay."

"I would have preferred not dirtying my hands, but I had no choice. Chet's 'suicide note' played quite well, don't you think?"

Ed glared at him. "And when I started getting a little too close for comfort, you had Jessburger try to kill me, too."

"*Absolutely not.* You were *never* my target."

"Oh really? Highway 50? Theatre Artaud? They don't ring a bell?"

Gilchrist's stare burned into Ed's retinas. "Like I said: You were never *my* target."

"What's *that* supposed to mean?"

"Let's just say that Brian didn't like seeing his girlfriend in bed with a Jew."

Ed felt like he'd been kicked in the ribs. That scumbag *and Julie?* Could it be possible? No, Ed decided, no way. "Bullshit. She didn't even know him."

Gilchrist smiled, again the crocodile wading back into the river, eyeing his next meal. "On the contrary. *You* didn't know *her.* Our Julie was quite an interesting specimen—"

"'Was?' *Was?* What have you done with her?" Ed reached into his jacket pocket and felt cold steel. At that moment, he almost had the nerve.

Gilchrist held up a hand as if to say: Who me? "I haven't done *any-thing* with her. She quit the paper and left town, if you recall. I have no idea where she is, but I seriously doubt she'll ever be back."

"And why not?"

"Because she got in over her head. When she realized it, she didn't see any other way out."

"What are you talking about?"

Gilchrist licked his lips. He was enjoying himself. "I'm saying that one can enjoy sex, very imaginative sex, as Julie did, but realize that it's gotten out of control."

Ed didn't like where this was heading. "I don't follow you."

"Julie and I had an enjoyable affair for over a year. Then within the last few months, at my request, she had a torrid go with our esteemed Governor, after which she fell for a violent ex-con, and then for you. Then she got shot. I think she decided it was time for a fresh start."

Ed felt something regurgitate up his throat and burn it. During the ride home from Tahoe, Julie had used those very words, "fresh start."

Gilchrist licked his lips. "Our Julie was very talented at public relations. But she was at her best in private, on her knees. She was quite adept at fellatio. Did she do that for you?"

Ed's heart raced. He felt faint. "I don't believe a word of this."

"No? Didn't you ever wonder how I managed to get Chet pardoned? I had lawyers, of course, a dozen of the best. But I also had something else—a video of the governor cavorting in that special bed out in the greenhouse with—"

"You're lying!" Ed's stomach churned. He felt ill. Julie said she'd spent some weekends with "friends" at the chalet. But the person Gilchrist was describing was not the Julie he knew. Or maybe the Old Man was right. Perhaps he never really knew her.

"Come on, Rosenberg," Gilchrist sneered. "Grow up. How do you think the system works?"

"I *thought* your old political enemies made an example of Chet to get back at you, and then the new governor, your political ally, did you a favor and pardoned him."

"Oh, he did. But it didn't hurt to have a video of his head between a black woman's legs."

"I don't believe you. Show me the tape."

"Sorry. It's been returned to the governor who, presumably, has destroyed it."

"Honor in sexual blackmail. Is that it?"

"Precisely. The governor isn't speaking to me at the moment. But I'll endorse him for re-election and contribute generously to his campaign. In a few years, we'll meet at Bohemian Grove and laugh about this."

Ed recalled that old saying: The rich are different. Now he understood what it meant.

"I took Julie up to the chalet some months ago, ostensibly to coordinate a ski weekend for the governor. But I thought he might fancy her, and he did. Very much. I told her that our own sex would be enhanced if she had a fling with him, then told me all about it. The greenhouse is particularly cozy when it's all covered with snow. Soon after, Julie returned to the chalet to prepare for a weekend with top advertisers. I'd just hired Jessburger. But until I needed him, I kept him in the caretaker's apartment there. Like so many women attracted to the rich and powerful, Julie also had a weakness for dangerous men. When I found out about their affair, I ordered them both to break it off. I didn't want Jessburger preoccupied when I had other chores that required his undivided attention. I don't think Julie knew Jessburger was up there the weekend you two were. But he was, and he saw his girlfriend with you, which was bad enough. Then he learned your name. In his view, you polluted Julie, so you both had to die."

"If he was such a Nazi, why would he fuck a black woman?"

"Isn't it obvious? To exercise power over her. Like a plantation owner with the slaves. Lucky for you he wasn't a good shot."

"So we were targets!"

"*His*. Not *mine*. He went after you totally on his own. I had nothing to do with it. When I heard about it, I *ordered* him to stay away from both of you. I had no quarrel with you, and certainly none with Julie. Later, in a meeting here, when you mentioned that you intended to interview Scott Gardener, I ordered Brian to eliminate him before he could speak with you. I also specifically told him *not* to go after you."

"But he didn't listen."

"That's right. So I decided to alter the terms of our agreement. He was supposed to receive his fee and disappear. But I changed my mind—"

"And killed him along with Chet."

"There was no other way."

Ed could think of a few, but kept his mouth shut. They both shifted in their chairs. Ed's eyes found Gilchrist's. They held no hate, no fear, no contrition, just a mixture of smugness and pride.

Ed felt dizzy. He was seated in the same chair he'd occupied several times since snagging the Coin Collection story. The Old Mint still rose up behind Gilchrist, a mountain of gray granite. This time, however, he and his publisher were not discussing the Reilly Double Eagle, but seven murders—Margaret, Murtinson, Cabral, Jessburger, the actor, the lighting designer, and Chet—as if they were two buddies at a Giants game reviewing the batting order. Could Julie have fucked the Governor as a favor to Gilchrist? Could she have fallen for Jessburger? Could he have decided on his own to kill her and her Jewish boyfriend? Ed had no idea. He ached to poke holes in Gilchrist's story. But he couldn't. It neatly explained all the facts. Julie *was* unusual. Maybe she had a fling with Jessburger. Despite the gun in his pocket, the Old Man really didn't seem angry with him or the least bit vindictive. Maybe Jessburger had acted on his own. Ed didn't know what to think.

"So," Gilchrist ventured, arching an eyebrow, "how did you zero in on me?"

In Gilchrist's eyes, Ed saw the glassy stare of a snake. Bile rose in his belly. Suddenly, he detested the man, despised what he had, what he'd done, and his arrogant certainty that he was above the law. But oddly, he also felt something else—a sense of obligation. He'd answered all of Ed's questions. Now it was Ed's turn to answer his. Ed was surprised to realize he wanted to, that something compelled him. *Pride*. "Process of elimination."

"Yes …?"

Ed took a deep breath: "From the moment Foxsen fingered Chet as having been at Murtinson's, I didn't believe—didn't *want to* believe—that he was the killer. The Chet I knew was a gentle soul, a scholar who couldn't hurt a fly, especially having just been pardoned after 10 years on the run. And I never really believed he was a heroin addict. I know: People with money can be junkies and still function and no one knows. But I just didn't see Chet slipping down that hole. Laura was adamant that he never used. Calderone didn't believe it. I just couldn't see it.

"But it was impossible *not* to be suspicious of him. The morning after Murtinson's murder, Chet conveniently 'forgot' to tell me he'd been over there. And when Cabral turned up dead in his living room carrying heroin—you engineered that one quite well—I was ready to believe Chet was the killer. Laura sensed it and threw me out of the house. But on reflection, even with Cabral dead in Anchorage by the same gun that killed Murtinson, I just couldn't see the Chet I knew as a murderer.

"So I focused on Larry Foxsen. He was in Seacliff the night Murtinson got it. He and Murtinson had a stormy relationship, and not long before he was killed, Murtinson stole a lover from Foxsen. Jealousy is a classic motive for murder. With Murtinson dead and his connections in the art world buried along with him, Foxsen stood to become a lot more important to the Museum's acquisitions program, and make more money, which added to his motive. He also had contact with the actor, who approached him about mounting a search for the Lost Gold. He fit the description of the man who stole Chet's thesis from Stanford. And his security guard is enough of a thug to have been the trigger man. But Foxsen had no motive to kill Cabral, no motive to kill Chet, and no connection to Mountain Resort Development and Jessburger. Without them, he couldn't be the one.

"Which pointed me to Ted Calderone. He's sleazy enough to have been the mastermind. He had a strong motive for killing Murtinson—the bundle he lost in that libel suit. He also lost Laura to Chet, which gave him a motive to kill Chet and set him up for killing Murtinson. For a while, I thought his bodyguard was the shooter on Highway 50. He also had contact with Cabral. But from what I saw, Calderone didn't hold a grudge against Chet. At the party, he greeted Chet and Laura cordially—and *they* were rude to *him*. When I got a good look at the shooter at Theatre Artaud, it wasn't Calderone's man. If Calderone was the killer, he wouldn't have revealed his connection to Cabral. He had no connection to Jessburger. It made no sense for him to have arranged the shooting on 50 the day after I visited him. And when I confronted him with my suspicions, he said something that made a lot of sense—"

"What?"

"'If I wanted you dead, I wouldn't fuck it up.'"

Gilchrist nodded, a cobra mesmerized by the flute.

"At that point, I didn't know what to think. I got a line on Jessburger's identity and was in the middle of chasing it down when he and Chet turned up dead. At that point, it was almost impossible *not* to think Chet was the killer. Things seemed to fit so neatly, and his so-called suicide note was very damning. All the media were screaming he was the one. I almost bought it."

"Why didn't you?"

"Several reasons. One was the fact that Chet had no motive to kill Murtinson. Murtinson doted on him, and Chet loved him. Everyone said he didn't need a motive, that he was a crazy junkie, and that was enough. But he certainly wasn't crazy. And I never believed he was a junkie.

"Then I saw Chet's body. He was shot in the right temple. It blew off the left half of his skull. But Chet was *left-handed*. To commit suicide, he would have used his dominant hand and shot himself in the *left* temple. When I saw his body, the 'suicide' started looking like murder."

Gilchrist sighed as if to say: Silly me. "You know, I completely forgot he was left-handed."

"Then there was Margaret's Bible—"

"Leave it to Maggie," Gilchrist said ruefully, "to screw me from beyond the grave."

"Sons sometimes kill fathers, but fathers don't kill sons. Then I learned he wasn't your son.

"Then there was the theft of Chet's thesis from Stanford. The woman in the Truman Room described the thief to me. It sounded like Foxsen. But on reflection, it could just as easily have been you. Why'd you do it?"

"To distract you. To keep you focused on the Lost Gold."

"Just like you did with Chet."

Another palms-up shrug. "You were a coin collector."

"Rosa filled in more of the puzzle. Then there was Jessburger. When I learned that the police had ID'ed him as the shooter at Theatre Artaud, I traced him up to the chalet, and eventually traced Mountain Resort Development to you."

"How?"

"All those shell corporations eventually led back to Foster Hitchens, your law firm in New York."

"How did you know FH represented me?"

"You told me a few weeks ago, when I did my first piece on the Coin Collection donation. I asked you how much of a tax deduction you planned to take. You referred me to Armand Hitchens."

Gilchrist sighed. "Ah yes. I knew I should have taken those corporations off-shore. But I never got around to it, never thought anyone would— Anything else?"

"Your not quite rehiring me. It didn't make sense. Other reporters could have written Chet's story. Even as a friend of Chet's, there was no reason for you to come up with this freelance gig—unless you wanted to keep an eye on me."

"Well done." Gilchrist said. "I'm impressed." He looked at his watch. "I'm due at Candlestick in less than two hours. I'd like to wrap this up."

"Then tell the police what you just told me—"

Gilchrist snorted. "Don't be ridiculous."

"Confession is good for the soul."

"Without the tape, you have nothing. Not one shred of real evidence. Everyone involved is dead, except Rosa, and all she has is second-hand nonsense from a two-time loser who was also her cousin. The DA would laugh her out of his office—even if I didn't own him."

"I could still fuck you. Calderone wants the story."

"Please," Gilchrist guffawed, "Ted Calderone knows two things— naked girls and libel. If you accuse me of *any crime* without solid evidence, your piece is libelous. You were fired. That establishes malice. Calderone would never publish your diatribe—especially after you get arrested for dealing cocaine."

Ed started. "*What*?!"

"You heard me. Several ounces of pharmaceutical-grade cocaine are hidden in your house at this very moment, along with a ledger of your transactions going back, I believe, three years. You're quite the dealer—and you're one call to the police away from 20 to life."

"Bull*shit*."

"Not at all. I'm sure you recall the uninvited guest who … rearranged your things. From what Jessburger said, he wreaked havoc. He also left a little something behind."

Ed's heart raced. His jaw clenched. He had trouble breathing. "You mother*fucker*."

Gilchrist chuckled. "You know, Ed, our nation's drug laws are really quite wonderful. They're so counter-productive and so widely flouted by such a large proportion of the population that just about everyone is prepared to believe that anyone might be in deep. You have a reputation as a loose cannon. After your arrest, everyone in the newsroom will chalk it up to cocaine. They'll believe you were a dealer. Everyone will."

Ed pulled out the revolver and pointed it at Gilchrist's chest. "I have *had it* with you."

Gilchrist waved a hand dismissively. "Please. We already know you don't have the nerve."

"Wrong." Ed felt his finger tighten against the trigger. He knew what it meant, but at that moment, he didn't care.

Gilchrist saw murder in Ed's eyes. "Wait!" He held up a hand, and said, "$2 million."

Ed squeezed a little more. His finger was a hair away from the firing point.

"All right: $2.5 million. But that's my final offer."

Ed backed off the trigger, but kept the gun trained on Gilchrist's chest.

"You were never my target. *Never*." He was pleading. "I had the cocaine planted as insurance. To persuade you to negotiate, if it came to that. Now it has. I could have called the police anytime. But I didn't. Here's my offer: You take the money. Then you leave the country—and *never return*. Paris is a wonderful place to be rich. London. Rome. Rio. Hong Kong. And with $2.5 million, you'd be rich."

"So … take the money and run."

"No. Take it and *live.* No matter what you do, I'm in the clear. Your story is entirely hearsay peddled by a disgruntled ex-employee with an ax to grind. The police won't believe a word of it, and Calderone won't print it. No one will. That leaves you with two choices: Shoot me, or take the money and expatriate. If you shoot me, you go to prison. Once the Aryan Brotherhood learns your name, you won't last long. I'll see to it. On the other hand, if you take the money, you live happily ever after."

"But with a very guilty conscience."

"Why? For what they did to me, they deserved to die. All of them. In my position, you would have done the same."

Ed flashed on two fatherless little girls.

Gilchrist waved a hand. "So what'll it be? Life—a short life—in prison. Or a long one living in the lap of luxury? It doesn't strike me as a difficult decision."

"What if I take the money, then stick around?"

Gilchrist sighed. "There are other Jessburgers."

"You have $2.5 mil lying around?"

"Of course not. But it's just a phone call away. My private banker can cut a certified check for the full amount."

"Private banker?"

Gilchrist smiled, the iguana on the sunny rock. "Epicenter Capital Management. They don't touch people worth less than a $100 million. I'm worth close to ten times that. If I want a check, they cut it."

"And you'd make the call now? From here?"

"Just say the word."

It was life-changing money. Ed lowered the gun. "All right. But no bullshit. I still have the gun—and I'm prepared to use it."

"Of course." Gilchrist leaned forward and punched a single button on his phone console. "Beatrice. This is Worth Gilchrist. Put me through to Sullivan … Henry? Worth. I need a check immediately, payable to Edward Rosenberg, R-O-S-E-N-B-E-R-G, in the amount of $2.5 million … Half hour?" He looked at Ed. "Fine. Mr. Rosenberg and I will stop by to pick it up." He hung up. "We have a deal. Congratulations. You're rich. Shake?" He held out his hand.

Ed didn't move. "No thanks."

Gilchrist looked irked. He dropped his hand and sat back down. "I'll call my chauffeur to take us over there. It's on Sansome near Market."

"No way I'm going in your car."

"Why not?"

"I don't want to be 'taken for a ride.'"

"You've got the gun."

"Who knows what you've got built into your limo."

"You've seen too many James Bond movies."

"Let's walk."

"I'd rather not. I have arthritis in my knee."

"Then a cab."

Gilchrist looked at his watch. "This time of day, it would take too long to get picked up. I'm due at Candlestick. The Mayor's box."

"Then Muni."

A pained expression crossed Gilchrist's face. "I *don't* ride Muni."

"Then BART."

Gilchrist considered the idea. "All right." He looked at his watch and punched a button on his phone console. "I'm going to arrange to be picked up after our business is concluded. With any luck," he said brightly, "I'll get to the game by the second inning."

45

It was the beginning of rush hour, but the streets were nearly deserted. The Game, Ed realized. Everyone had gone home early to watch the World Series. It was a great afternoon for baseball: cloudless blue sky, temperature in the '60s, and just a hint of breeze. Ed could almost hear the prayers being offered up from North Beach to Lake Merced. Go Giants.

Side by side, Ed and Gilchrist crossed Mission and walked up Fifth toward Market. The Old Man limped slightly on his bum knee, which slowed them down some. Neither spoke. At Powell, by the cable car turnaround, they took the escalator down two levels, past Muni to the BART station.

The platform was virtually empty, just a small knot of commuters at the far end, several with their noses in the *Foghorn*. Ed and Gilchrist stepped to the Inbound side. Below their feet, the brick pavers shone from a recent steam-cleaning. Across the tracks, a billboard offered free checking at San Francisco Federal. Overhead the tiny bulbs of the message monitor flashed the time, 5:00, then an ad for computer classes at UC Extension, and then the news that a Richmond train would arrive in two minutes. Ed stood near the lip of the platform and peered into the dark tunnel that would soon sprout two headlights as the sleek silver train approached.

Gilchrist stood a few feet back, absorbed in massaging his left knee.

Twin beacons appeared in the inky distance and grew steadily larger and brighter. Then came the other harbinger of an arriving train, a blast of wind that blew gum wrappers and other trash around the platform. The monitor flashed RICHMOND. RICHMOND. 10 CAR TRAIN. RICH-

MOND. RICHMOND. The train approached with a high-pitched whine punctuated by two toots of its horn.

The monitor flashed 5:02.

Just then, Ed felt the platform rumble beneath his feet. Vibrations from the train, he thought at first. But no. The rumble grew louder and more powerful. It shook his knees. Up the tracks, the train rushed toward him. But it swayed peculiarly from side to side. Something was wrong. Ed was transfixed by the train, now lurching wildly from side to side, its burnished aluminum skin scraping the platform with an ear-splitting whine, showering sparks. Then he felt the platform rise and fall beneath him, like a wave, like a whip. Like an *earthquake*. A big one.

Down the platform people were running. Someone screamed, "Earthquake!"

The train hurtled into the station, banging grotesquely from side to side, slamming against the platform and the opposite wall. The shaking continued. From overhead, a cloud of white plaster dust rained down.

Out of the corner of his eye, Ed saw movement. Gilchrist. The Old Man lunged furiously at him, his limp miraculously gone. He smashed a shoulder into Ed's side, throwing him off-balance and backward toward the void above the train tracks.

Ed hung in space, teetering on the edge of the platform. The train kept coming. The platform continued to shake. The light fixtures swayed. The billboard bolts snapped, and suddenly the ad for free checking hung akimbo. The train rushed forward, still lurching incongruously from side to side.

Panic spread in a hot wave from Ed's bowels up to his throat. He stopped breathing. Time slowed to a crawl. The train crept steadily toward him. Its headlights were blinding, moving from side to side like a metronome. Ed flailed, trying to regain his balance. He windmilled his arms, but they moved in slow-motion, as if immersed in oatmeal. He tottered at the edge, then fell.

In the nose of the train, the driver's face contorted in horror. Brakes screeched. Orange sparks showered the tracks. But the train kept coming as Ed fell into its path.

Ed's life did not flash before his eyes. Oddly, this irked him. Wasn't that supposed to happen? Instead, Gilchrist's blow dredged up a long-buried memory of a similar hit years earlier at the dojo, when a much younger Tim landed a sidekick hard against his ribs, stunning him. Master Chen leaped to his side and ordered him to breathe, and find his center.

In mid-fall, Ed exhaled forcefully, centered himself, then inhaled. His eyes burned into Gilchrist's. An arthritic knee? A lie to trick him into dropping his guard. "Never *my* target." Another lie, for the same reason.

After shouldering Ed off the platform, Gilchrist pulled back from the lip. But not fast enough. Ed exhaled. He reached out as if fly-casting, hooked the Old Man's sleeve, and reeled it in. The two of them plunged down to the tracks together.

A moment later, the train hurtled over them. There was a scream, then just the whoosh of the train as it slowed to a stop.

46

At 7.1 on the Richter scale, the Loma Prieta was the most destructive earthquake to hit the Bay Area since 1906. Downtown Santa Cruz, near the epicenter, was reduced to rubble, killing a dozen people and injuring scores more. Along the Bay shore in Oakland, landfill liquefied and the Cypress Structure elevated freeway collapsed, claiming 42 lives and injuring hundreds. A section of the Bay Bridge's upper-deck collapsed into the lower, mangling two cars, killing their occupants. In San Francisco's Marina District, a dozens buildings erected on landfill collapsed, claiming more lives, including an infant's when the old brick chimney next door toppled through the roof and crushed him in his crib. And from Gilroy to Santa Rosa and out to the Livermore Valley, what became known as the Pretty Big One shattered windows, cracked roadways, and left supermarkets knee deep in goods thrown off shelves.

When the dust settled, 67 people were dead and 3,757 injured. More than 1,000 homes and 350 businesses were destroyed. Another 23,000 homes and 3,500 businesses sustained substantial damage. Five million people lost power and phone service, most for a day or two, some for up to two weeks. Property damage was estimated at $7.5 billion.

At Candlestick Park, 56,241 Giants and A's fans—and a small army of national media—rode out the shake with no injuries, and then were sent home. Game Three was postponed indefinitely.

When the power failed, KFOG switched to emergency generators and pumped out earthquake music: "Shake" by Otis Redding, "Rock This Town" by the Stray Cats, "I Feel the Earth Move" by Carole King, and "Shake, Rattle, and Roll," by Jerry Lee Lewis.

In the Mission, the quake hit hard in a series of powerful jolts. A dozen old brick buildings failed, killing a half-dozen people. Windows shattered all over the neighborhood. Sidewalks buckled. Utility lines snapped and sparked. Looters hit a few electronics and liquor stores. And with refrigeration gone and everyone afraid to turn on gas stoves, restaurants up and down Mission Street set up outdoor grills, charbroiled everything they had, and sold it cheap before it spoiled.

At the Inner Mission Youth Center, two of the five enormous plate-glass windows in the Games Room shattered like cherry bombs, covering the floor with broken glass. The fifty kids gathered around the TV to watch the World Series panicked. The staff herded everyone out back to the play field, while Jerry sniffed for gas and Arturo checked for structural damage. They found neither, but as a precaution, sent the kids home. The staff swept up and slapped plywood over the broken windows, leaving the Games Room unusually dim from the loss of sunlight. The power was restored the next day. A few days later, the City signed off on the building's soundness. The kids came back, and after hours, Jerry and Ed returned to shooting pool.

"Eleven in the side, kissing the eight." Ed pocketed the shot, but awkwardly. The bulbous bandage around most of his bridge hand made it difficult to aim. "Three in the end." The ball rattled in the gate for a moment, then dropped. "Nine-six combo in the corner."

"Whoa, Ed," Jerry frowned. "You sure about that?" It was a tough shot with two good hands. But with a pound of gauze wrapped around a left hand missing a finger, it seemed beyond reach.

Ed shrugged. "You see anything else?" He placed his white mitten on the felt and lined it up. "Besides, I think I'm getting the hang of Bandage Billiards." He tapped the nine into the six, which rolled home. "Yes!" he exulted, pumping his stick over his head.

"Nice," Jerry said, impressed.

"I feel a pool moniker coming on," Ed said. "Nine-Fingers Rosenberg. I didn't need that pinkie anyway."

"Hey, if you enter some tournaments, maybe you can get BART to sponsor you."

They both laughed.

The train wheel had sliced it off clean. The ER doc merely disinfected the stump, sewed it up, bandaged the hand, and sent him home with a scrip for Vicodin. Gilchrist wasn't as lucky. It took four guys with shovels working twenty yards of track to pick up the pieces.

"Let me ask you something, Jer, in your capacity as a rabbi—"

"An almost rabbi."

"Whatever. Have you ever seen God? I mean, really *seen* Him?" He lined up the seven for a cross-table angle shot.

"No. I've felt the divine presence sometimes at the end of Yom Kippur when I'm hungry and spaced, but I can't say I've ever seen Him—or Her. Who knows if God's even there?"

"I never thought He was," Ed said quietly, "but I don't know. ... Maybe He is. Maybe I saw Him." Ed tapped the cue, which hit the seven too far left of center, for a miss. "He's a light."

"As in 'Let there be ...?'"

"No. More like a ... light bulb."

Jerry was incredulous. "What? Sixty watts? A hundred?"

"I know it sounds crazy—"

"A nightlight? A floodlight?" Jerry smiled. He chalked his cue, leaned over the one and dispatched it into a side pocket.

"Jer, I'm trying to be serious here. He's ... like a ... flashbulb ... like those old flashbulbs when we were kids. A blinding light, then little sparkly after-things."

"Maybe what you saw was the train's headlights." Jerry bagged the nine and twelve in rapid succession. "They're pretty bright."

"No. Not the headlights." Ed looked across the Games Room past the plywood-covered windows to the mural the Art kids had painted of scenes at the Club: basketball, ping pong, ceramics, pool, photography, the computer lab. "It was weird. It all happened so fast. But it felt like slow motion. I was falling off the platform. The train was *right there,* coming *right at me,* brakes squealing, sparks flying, unstoppable. I was terrified. Then my old karate teacher appeared to me and told me to breathe. And I did. Then I grabbed Gilchrist and pulled him down with me. I landed on my shoulder, hard, only it didn't hurt. Gilchrist must have hit his head and been knocked out because he didn't move. The train was on top of us. It was huge. It smelled like grease and steel and ozone. It was like watching a movie. That's when the flashbulb went off. I was blinded. I lost sight of the train. I was floating in space, weightless. I wasn't afraid anymore. Next thing I know, I'm under the lip of the platform with my nose pressed against a big wheel."

Jerry rifled the four into a corner, with enough backspin to line up the cue by the last remaining ball, the five, for an easy corner shot. "I'm no expert, but maybe you did see God."

"I thought I was going to die, but after the flashbulb went off, when I was floating in space, I felt calm and safe and knew I'd live. Weird, huh?"

"Yeah, weird." The five dropped. "But you hear stories like that."

Ed racked the balls.

"What about the finger?" Jerry hit a corner ball lightly, but the pack broke up enough for Ed to run three.

"Damndest thing. It didn't even hurt. I didn't even know about it until the BART guys pulled me out."

Jerry ran three balls, then Ed downed two, then Jerry missed, and Ed ran the remaining seven. "I'm in the zone, Jer. Watch out for Nine-Fingers Rosenberg."

Jerry racked up. "You see the piece in the paper this morning about the family of the guy who got killed at Theatre Artaud?"

Ed played safe, but kicked out a few balls. "Yeah, some mystery man gave them $2 mil."

"Through a lawyer. Like that old show, 'The Millionaire.' What was that rich guy's name?"

"John Beresford Tipton."

"Right. Very *good*, Ed. Who says pot destroys brain cells?"

They shared a smile, then Ed sighed, "I'm glad. They need all the help they can get."

"It *wasn't* your fault." Jerry shot Ed a look that said: And how many times do I have to tell you? He hit the one hard. It zipped into a corner, and the cue ball ricocheted into the pack, which broke up and allowed him to run four more. Then Jerry scratched.

Ed chipped the six into a corner, then coaxed the two into the same pocket. Inside his mitten, his stump began throbbing. He placed the bandage on the felt and lined up the ten for a long, straight corner-to-corner shot, the kind that separates the talkers from the players. It dropped smartly.

"Nice," Jerry said. "You *know* it wasn't your fault, *don't you?*"

Ed pursed his lips. The throbbing was worse. "Yeah ... well ... but there's no getting around the fact that that bullet was meant for me. It's going to be a long time before his widow and daughters have any fun on Father's Day."

"True. It was a horrible, terrible thing. But you can't whip yourself forever."

"I'm trying not to."

"Try harder."

"I'm *trying,* okay? Now can we change the subject, please?" Ed chalked up. He was whipping himself a lot less ever since he handed the lawyer the certified check for $2 million. He laid his mitten on the table and lined up the three for a long angle shot to the far corner. It rolled in.

"Very nice. And now for *my* big news—"

Ed looked up from the table. Jerry had an ear-to-ear grin. "What?"

"The Club isn't closing."

"What?" Ed did his best to feign surprise. "But I thought—"

"An anonymous donor ponied up the $500 K, and the foundation matched it."

"No shit," Ed said. "Congratulations." He lined up the thirteen, but chipped it a little too high.

"Thanks. The million gives us another two years or so—and some buzz in the foundation world. Arturo's already had some calls. We're back from the dead." Jerry pocketed the eight on a long rail shot, then found himself with nothing, and was forced to take a tough combination that missed by a mile.

"That's really great. You guys deserve it. Not to mention that now we can keep playing."

Jerry shot Ed a look. "Funny thing about the anonymous gift, though. It came with strings. We have to have the pool tables professionally leveled and refelted every three months."

"Really. Your donor is my kind of guy."

"You're telling me." Jerry stepped around the table and embraced his old friend.

Ed pushed him away. "What's *that* for?"

"I don't know how you did it." Jerry placed a hand on Ed's shoulder. "And I don't want to know. But thank you. It means a lot to a lot of people."

Ed's chin jutted out and his eyes narrowed. "The fuck you talking about, man?"

"Come on, Eddie. How long have we known each other? You can't bullshit me."

Ed made no reply. He sized up the table and ran four balls, missing on a long cross-table heartbreaker. Jerry put it away and Ed pulled out the triangle.

"You know," Jerry ventured, "the Talmud talks about the different levels of charity. The highest form is the anonymous gift, to do good without recognition."

"Let's keep it that way, shall we?" Ed lifted the triangle off the pack, avoiding his friend's gaze. "Your shot."

47

Ruffen, the C.E., the M.E., the X.E., and a middle-aged woman Ed didn't recognize were all arrayed around the Editorial conference table when he slid into the chair next to City Editor Gus Oberhoffer.

"The cops found the Rembrandt and Degas," Ed announced. Around the table, eyebrows rose expectantly. "In a secret closet in Gilchrist's wine cellar in Hillsborough."

"How?" Ruffen toyed with the oily flesh of his double chin.

"It wasn't easy. On the tape, Gilchrist said the paintings were in 'climate-controlled' storage, which ruled out your typical attic or cellar or storage locker. Harrigan asked the curators at California Museum what kind of climate control would be necessary. They took him to some special room in the basement there, where they store famous paintings. Harrigan decided it felt like a wine cellar, and sent some cops to take Gilchrist's apart. Only his guys didn't find squat. Then Harrigan brought in a forensic architect, who poked around and found a hidden latch that opened a secret panel."

"Forensic architect?" John Gagliano, the Managing Editor, shook his head. "Who ever heard of such a thing?"

"But I thought you said Gilchrist shredded your tape," Gus said, taking a big swig of coffee.

"*One* of them. I had a *second* microcassette recorder."

"That's foresight." Despite himself, Ruffen was impressed.

"More like superstition. I've had bad luck with those things. With only one, I was afraid it might not work. The surveillance registered 'tape recorder,' but not how many. It was a lucky break."

"One of several," Executive Editor Walt French said, looking at Ed's bandaged hand.

"With the paintings found, Harrigan's ready to believe the rest of the tape."

"Every publisher I've ever worked for thought he was God," Gagliano observed, "but Gilchrist was over the top."

"Your tape," French said, "is the reason I asked Ellen Frank to this meeting." He nodded toward the woman. "Ellen is from Leland, Ross, Weintraub, Van der Hout, and White, our libel firm." Frank had fetchingly styled short brown hair, large brown eyes, a creamy complexion, and a resolute jaw, but somehow everything added up to less than the sum of the parts, giving her a severe, dour look despite a rose-colored suit and matching silk blouse. As all eyes converged on her, she crossed her arms over her chest. French addressed her: "Can we go with Rosenberg's tape? Are we on thick ice? Or thin?"

Frank looked from face to face, consciously making eye contact with everyone. She donned wire-rimmed reading glasses and shuffled some papers, reminding Ed of the kindly school marm from the old Our Gang comedies. "I haven't heard the tape or seen a transcript. Without that, I can't give you an official opinion. But based on what I've been told, I'd say you're on comfortably thick ice. The only person you'd accuse of criminal conduct would be Mr. Gilchrist, and you're well-covered—"

"How?" French demanded. "Spell it out."

"Truth is a complete defense. And dead men can't sue for libel."

All the editors nodded and smiled at one another, four men sharing a single thought: Pulitzer Prize.

"So," Gus said, turning to Ed. "When do we get the story?"

Ed looked from one expectant face to the next, then through the glass wall across the newsroom to the cubicle behind whose gray fiberboard half-walls he'd toiled for … how many years now? Four? Five? Six? He couldn't recall. The thought of his cube made him nauseous. "I was fired." He looked at Ruffen, who did it, then at the others, who approved it. "Remember?"

"Oh, for Christ's sake, Ed," French said. "You're reinstated. Back pay. Clean record. Bonus. Everything."

"We have our little spats," Gus added, as contritely as an editor could, "but we're *family*."

Ruffen silently squirmed in his chair.

"I appreciate that," Ed replied. "I really do. But *while* I was fired, I agreed to write the story for Ted Calderone. Signed a contract and everything. Exclusive rights." The contract part wasn't quite true, but Ed thought it would impress the lawyer.

"Calderone?" Ruffen said. "That sleazebag?"

"Fuck him," Gagliano added.

"We can get you out of it," French insisted, glancing at the lawyer. "Can't we?"

Ms. Frank looked dubious.

"Thing is," Ed said softly. "I made a deal. Signed a contract."

"But *Full Disclosure?!* No one reads it for the articles."

"This contract," Oberhoffer probed, "is it exclusive *magazine* rights? Or *exclusive rights?* If it's just a magazine excloo, you can still write it for us and everyone's happy."

"The phrase that sticks in my head is 'exclusive worldwide serial rights,'" Ed lied.

"So, you're *not* going to write it for us?" A look of horror filled French's face.

"I don't see how I can."

The four men stared machine guns at him, again sharing a single thought: You're fired, asshole. Of course, he already was.

"But here's what I *can* do for you," Ed said. "I'll transcribe the tape, and give it to the one reporter who helped get the goods on Gilchrist. He can write the story for you."

"Who?" four voices asked in unison.

"Tim Huang. Writes for the *Defender.*"

"That piece of shit?" Ruffen spat.

"If you give *him* the transcript, the *Defender* gets the story," Gus lamented.

"Not if you hire him," Ed ventured.

"That's *ex*tortion!" Gagliano pounded a fist on the table. "Reporters *don't* make personnel decisions on *this* paper!"

Ed shrugged. "Just a suggestion."

The four men glared at him. "You're burning bridges, Ed," Gus said. "Think about it."

"Hey, I got *fired*, remember? I'd love to write the story for the *Horn*. I really would. But I have rent to pay, so I signed a contract. And now we're stuck with it. Who knew things would turn out this way? Tim's good. He's been on the story since day one."

"You're kissing a Pulitzer goodbye," Ruffen moaned.

"I can't help it. Tim can win it for you."

"We're not throwing our best story in years to some *kid*," Oberhoffer scoffed.

"So *don't* hire him. The *Defender* and *Full Disclosure* get the story, and the *Foghorn* doesn't."

"You fuck," Gagliano sneered.

"Get a grip," French placed a hand on his Managing Editor's arm. "I've read Huang's stuff. He's decent. We could team him up with Miller and Hubig. Besides, we could use more Asian bylines."

"Walt, I can't believe you're—"

"Enough," French said, holding up a palm. Then to Ed: "If we hire Huang, you'll give him the transcript?"

"Soon as I can."

"A complete copy?"

"Yes."

"And you'll let him hear the tape? Compare it with the transcript?"

"Sure."

"And you'll talk to him? He can interview you?"

"Of course."

"And you won't talk to anyone else? I'm thinking the *L.A. Times, New York Times, Washington Post*, the newsweeklies, the wires."

"I haven't said a word since the press conference. A few called, but they know they can't horn in on an exclusive."

The editors nodded in unison. After Gilchrist's death, the paper had arranged a press conference where Ed ran down the highlights. The insatiable media monster had to be fed. But to get the details, the world would have to read the *Horn*. That didn't happen very often, and the editors relished it.

"And if Ron or Gus or I have any questions, you'll talk to us?"

"Of course."

"Then, gentlemen," French clapped his hands together and rubbed them, "I'd say we have ourselves a deal." He was already considering where to display the Pulitzer.

48

When the World Series resumed ten days after the earthquake, Ed and Tim got together on Dolores Terrace for Game Three. They sat on Ed's new burgundy leather sofa and watched his new Trinitron, which stood in his new home entertainment center a shelf away from his new stereo, all courtesy of Twin Peaks Casualty. Tim provided take-out pot stickers, shrimp chow fun, and green beans with garlic black bean sauce. Ed supplied Giants caps, microwave popcorn, peanut M&Ms, and Anchor Steam. The A's methodically obliterated the Giants 13-7 on homers by Canseco, Phillips, Lansford, and two by Dave Henderson. With the victory, the A's led three games to none. The announcer must have said it fifty times: Only two professional teams had ever come back to win a seven-game series after going down three-zip—the 1942 Toronto Maple Leafs over Detroit and the 1975 New York Islanders over Pittsburgh. It had never happened in baseball.

Ed and Tim drowned their disgust in beer, then Ed turned off the TV and handed Tim a sheaf of papers clipped together. "The transcript."

Tim dived in while Ed cleaned up. The new bandage was smaller, but it still made some things awkward, for example, opening CD jewel boxes. Ed fumbled with one of the several dozen he'd bought with the insurance money, *The Raw and the Cooked*, by the Fine Young Cannibals. Bouncy British soul to clean up by. As he puttered around the kitchen, he heard pages flip and every now and then, Tim saying, "Whoa," or "Unreal."

Ed filled his new blue plastic laundry basket with dirty new clothes and trundled down the back stairs. "I'll be across the way in the laundry room. When you're done, we can talk."

Tim nodded and waved, flipping a page, engrossed.

Ed lugged the basket across the courtyard, separated the lights and darks, and pumped a few quarters into the slots. When he returned, Tim was finished, and Rhythm was curled up in his lap. "Amazing. The interview of a lifetime."

"Yeah, and almost my last one." Ed settled into a new chair. Blues jumped into his lap. "Any questions?"

"Several." Tim pulled out a notebook and pen. He was no longer the cub reporter he'd been when they first drove out to cover Murtinson's murder. He was less wide-eyed now, less easily impressed. His hair was cut short and expensively styled in the spikey arrangement popular with young Asian-Americans. No more jeans and denim shirts. Tim looked like he just stepped out of a display at Nordstrom. Was it the new salary? Or Kim's influence? Probably both. "Gilchrist kept saying you didn't have the nerve to shoot him. But when he revealed the planted coke, you threatened him with the gun. How close did you come to pulling the trigger?"

"Not very. Remember, I had the second tape going. I needed him to *think* I might shoot him to keep him talking. So I put on a show, and luckily, he bought it."

"Planting coke was really nasty. You ever find it?"

"No. One of Harrigan's guys came out and looked. Didn't find anything. Personally, I doubt Jessburger did it. I think Gilchrist was just blowing smoke to push me into taking the money and leaving."

"Speaking of the $2.5 mil, you ever get your hands on it?"

Ed chuckled and shook his head. "I tried, believe me. But with the earthquake, and Gilchrist dead, and the media going crazy over it, Epicenter Capital Management wouldn't even talk to me." He snorted in disgust. "Bankers."

Tim tapped his pen on his pad. "You see the piece in the Horn about the family of the guy who got shot at Theatre Artaud? Some unnamed benefactor gave them $2 million."

"Yeah, I saw it. I'm glad. It doesn't replace him, but it helps."

"You wouldn't happen to be that benefactor, would you?"

Ed laughed. "Me? You kidding? First of all, I never got the money. And second, if I did, you think I'd *give it away?*"

Tim's almond eyes narrowed. "I don't know. You were pretty busted up about the guy's death. Would you? "

"Not until the Giants go a whole season undefeated."

"I could call Epicenter."

"Go ahead." The man there had assured Ed that the firm's lips were locked tighter than the vault at the Old Mint.

"But you *were* on your way down there when Gilchrist pushed you in front of the train."

Ed nodded.

"So if you'd gotten the money, you would have taken it?"

"Sure. Why not? It's not every day someone hands me a fortune."

"Would you have left the country?"

"Of course not. I had the tape. I planned to tell Gilchrist I was on my way to Paris, then play it for Harrigan."

"Even with his death threat?"

Ed shrugged. "He'd already tried twice and blown it. Jessburger was dead. I figured he'd be behind bars before he could come up with someone else."

"Speaking of the tape, Ruffen said you'd play it for me."

"Did he?" Ed scratched Blues behind the ears. She began to purr.

"So I could check the transcript against it."

Ed looked perplexed. "Really? That wasn't the deal. I said I'd give you a complete transcript. You have it. It's all there."

Tim's eyes bored into Ed's. They were on the mats again, circling each other, looking to attack, ready to defend. "I appreciate it. And I *really* appreciate everything you did to get me the job at the *Horn*. But Ron *specifically told me* to check the transcript against the tape. Can we play it?"

Ed's lips curled into a sheepish smile. "Sorry, man. Those microcassette players really suck. Right after I finished the transcription, the damn thing conked out."

"Really." Tim rolled the transcript into a tight cylinder, and held it the way Bruce Lee held nunchuk sticks in *Enter the Dragon*.

"You've got the transcript," Ed said soothingly. "It's going to be a hell of a story. Pulitzer material for sure. You've got the big job. You're making real money. Kim must be impressed."

"She is."

Ed popped a few peanut M&M's, chewed them slowly.

"But Ruffen was crystal clear. I need to hear the tape. There's a Radio Shack on Twenty-fourth Street I'll run over there. Pick up a new player."

Ed looked down at Rhythm, curled up into a sleeping ball of fur in

Tim's lap, then at Blues licking a paw in his. This was not going according to plan. Tim was supposed to be so grateful for his new job that he'd accept the transcript—the slightly edited transcript—with no argument. But here he was, being an obnoxious reporter, the ingrate.

"Your reluctance to play the tape wouldn't have anything to do with … the governor and Julie, would it?"

Ed flinched. "The fuck you talking about?"

"That's exactly what I'm talking about: Fucking. Julie and the governor."

Inside the bandage, Ed's stump throbbed. A big drop of sweat coursed its way down his side from his armpit to his kidney.

"You remember Wendy Forray? Used to write for the *Defender*. Now she's at the *Bee*."

"Yeah, I know her. Good reporter."

"She picked up a juicy rumor about how Gilchrist got Chet off."

"Do tell."

"He allegedly videotaped the guv having sex with a young black woman at some vacation place in Tahoe. It's all rumor, of course, so the *Bee* wouldn't touch it. But Forray called Jocko thinking he might be able to do something with it. I'm thinking the black woman was Julie. And that Gilchrist says so on the tape. And that you left that part out of the transcript."

"You're out of your mind."

"Am I? Remember the Handgun dinner? Our double date? Over dinner, Julie mentioned arranging a weekend for Gilchrist and the governor at a place in Tahoe. Said she was there with them. Said they … had fun."

Ed pushed Blues off his lap. His armpits felt soupy. His palms were moist. He wiped them on his jeans, and sighed, "You're a better reporter than I thought."

Tim nodded. "So it *was* Julie."

"Yeah." Ed folded his arms across his chest, girding himself for sparring. "I'm sorry. I didn't want to mislead you. But you're young and hungry. I was afraid you wouldn't give a second thought to dragging Julie through the mud with this."

Tim leaned forward in his chair. "It's not a question of dragging her, Ed. The girl *jumped in* with both feet. I can't believe you. This is incredible stuff. The governor trading a high-profile pardon for a weekend of sex with a babe while his wife is home wiping the kiddies' noses. It could ruin him."

"No way. It might cause a minor stink, but the governor would just deny it, and we have no evidence other than the allegations of a dead serial killer who loved to brag about how he ruled the world."

"What about the video? That would be proof."

Ed rolled his eyes. "Long gone. Come on, Tim. All politicos fuck around. But you don't get elected governor by archiving your flings."

"What about Julie? She could verify—"

"What about her? She's gone. You won't find her. I've looked. Hard."

"But we could place them both in Tahoe—"

"So what? She was doing her job, PR for the paper. He went skiing."

Tim opened his mouth to speak, but Ed cut him off. "Look, Tim, I got you the job. Now I need a favor. Leave Julie out of it." His stump throbbed. His brow furrowed. He stared deep into Tim's almond eyes. "No mention of her with the governor—or with Jessburger."

"*Jessburger?*"

Ed sighed. "Gilchrist said they had a thing, too."

"Julie? With that *Nazi?*"

Ed's face contorted. "I didn't want to believe it." He rubbed his eyes. "But it fits the facts. Jessburger saw Julie at the chalet with me. He got jealous, and opened fire on 50."

"Incredible. And after all that, you're still carrying a torch for her?"

"I don't know," Ed mumbled. "I guess." He kneaded his bandaged hand with his good one. He gazed out the back window across the courtyard that separated his cottage from the apartment building that shared the lot. His laundry must be finished by now. One of the big building's tenants worked in a sheet-metal shop and had decorated the enclosure with whimsical metal planters the size of large ice chests. They were filled with Mexican lavender. He'd also crafted a life-size Tin Man from the *Wizard of Oz,* whose chest opened on a hinge to reveal a heart fashioned from a salvaged oil filter he'd painted with red enamel.

Tim drummed the rolled up transcript against his thigh.

"I just don't want her smeared all over the paper," Ed explained, "I don't want her looking like—" He didn't finish the thought.

"A slut?" Tim suggested.

Ed pursed his lips. "A groupie, a star-fucker, an idiot. Whatever. I just don't want her dragged through the mud."

"Ed, you had a fling with her. Then she almost got you killed. Then she disappeared and hasn't been seen since. You don't owe her a thing." This wasn't coming from Tim Huang, newly jaded Metro reporter. It was coming from a friend.

"Maybe not. But if you do a number on her, she'll never come back."

"And you *want* her back?"

Ed didn't answer.

"You're whipped, man."

"Look who's talking."

Tim shifted in his chair. "That's different. Kim and I have a relationship. A *real* relationship. What do you have with Julie? She used you, and now she's gone."

"Just leave her out of it. *Please.* I'm asking as a friend. You've got a great story without it. Pulitzer stuff. You don't need her. And it's so speculative, Ruffen and the rest of them probably wouldn't let it in anyway."

Tim gazed into his lap. Rhythm awoke and stretched, then scratched herself under the jaw and jumped down to the floor. "Play me the tape."

Ed hauled himself out of his chair and fetched the little player from a drawer in his new desk. He tossed it across the room to Tim, who caught it, and hit the Play button.

They listened in silence. Ed stared out the back window. The lavender bushes trembled in a light breeze. Tim kept shifting in his chair, unable to get comfortable, wrestling with himself.

When it was over, Tim said, "All right. No mention of Julie."

"And not a word to Kim."

"Okay. But about the job, we're even."

"Agreed. Thank you."

49

Sixteenth Street and Valencia had to be one of the scummiest corners in San Francisco. Throughout the 1980s, as gentrification slowly oozed down into other parts of the Mission from Noe Valley and the Castro, 16th and Valencia remained resolutely down and out. Many of the buildings were welfare hotels with one iffy bathroom per floor. Drunks, crazies, and homeless littered the sidewalks, which smelled of cheap wine and body functions. Street corner entrepreneurs with bad teeth hawked used books and records, watches of questionable provenance, and joints. The first of each month, a line snaked out of Money Now Check Cashing. Toward the end of the month, the line formed at the Plasma Donor Center.

But despite its air of privation, 16th and Valencia also boasted two of San Francisco's finest little gems—the Roxie Theater, a small art cinema that showed offbeat movies and served real butter on the popcorn, and La Cumbre, an unassuming taqueria that served the best burritos in the world.

"Two barbecued chicken. Whole black beans, well drained, *por favor.*" Ed told the plump Latina wearing a Giants cap behind the counter. She threw two plate-size tortillas into the steamer and pressed the lever a few times. A thick cloud of vapor rose around her.

"You want cheese?" Only it came out as: *You wan chis?* Her face glistened from proximity to the steamer.

"No cheese," Ed replied.

"Salsa? Hot sauce? Jalapeños?" She scooped two slotted spoonfuls of black beans from the steam table, let them drain, then dumped them on the tortillas followed by spoonfuls of seasoned rice. Then she stuck a barbecue fork into a bin and pulled out two chicken breasts criss-crossed with black grill lines. She chopped them quickly with a cleaver.

"All three," Ed said.

The woman added them, then deftly rolled the results into wrist-sized logs and wrapped them in aluminum foil. "For here or to go?"

"Here."

She plopped the burritos into red plastic baskets. "Chips?" *Sheeps.*

"Please."

The man with the droopy mustache in the green beret at the end of the counter recognized Ed as a regular.

"To drink, bro?"

"One diet Coke. One V-8."

On the wall behind him hung 10 framed certificates bearing the *Defender* logo: "San Francisco's Best Burrito," for the years 1980 through 1989. On the counter next to the cash register were two stacks of newsprint, the latest *Defender*, and the current, much funkier *Mission News*, the neighborhood monthly.

Ed paid the man and wove his way to a wobbly, dark-stained pine table by the wall. He slipped into a high-backed hacienda chair under a huge painting of Mexico's buxom Lady of Revolution, holding high the tricolor flag, leading Zapata's army to victory.

Balancing the tray with his bandaged hand, Ed handed a burrito and the diet Coke to an attractive blonde, whose golden tresses were done up in a French knot. She wore a magnificently embroidered Guatemalan vest over a black cashmere top and black leather pants. Money, but understated.

Laura Gilchrist unwrapped her burrito, and took a large unladylike bite. "Mmmm," she exulted, her mouth too full. "Thish ish *delishish!*"

"You don't want to know how often I pick up dinner here after work."

Laura swallowed. She smiled. "You can't get a decent burrito in the entire state of Alaska."

"Welcome home."

They chewed a few bites in silence, both thinking about the missing member of what was supposed to have been a threesome.

The tables around them filled up: an Irish-looking priest with two Central American-looking nuns, a crew of UPS drivers, an Asian woman and a black man staring dreamily into each other's eyes, two suits who might have been realtors, a couple of young skateboarders with spiked green hair, a few singles reading the *Foghorn* or the *Defender*, some kids in Mission High sweatshirts, and a big Latino family, the mom cradling an infant, the dad carving up a burrito for the three-year-old, the grandparents supervising the rest of the brood. Ed noticed a few of the men notice Laura. Considering her bereavement, she looked pretty good. The deep furrows in her brow and around her mouth had subsided to mere lines. None of the gawkers, Ed realized, had the slightest idea that he was dining with one of the richest women in San Francisco—or for that matter, in the country.

"I owe you an apology," Laura announced solemnly, setting down her burrito and looking Ed in the eye. "I think you know why."

Ed nodded. "No apology necessary. If you'd told me what Cabral told you, it wouldn't have changed anything."

Laura stared into the dark bubbly depths of her Coke. "It wouldn't have saved Chet. But maybe the actor and lighting guy would still be with us. *Oh, God,* I feel so guilty and ashamed." Laura grabbed a napkin, held it to her eyes, and cried. She cried the way rich people do, discreetly. At the next table, three longhairs in paint-smeared T-shirts and overalls noticed, but no one else did.

Ed reached across the table and placed a gentle hand on her arm. "Let me ask you something: Do you think I'm responsible for the lighting guy's death? That bullet was meant for me."

Laura stopped crying and wiped her eyes. "Of course not. You had no idea—"

"Right. And neither did you. If I'm not responsible, you're not either."

She eyed him dubiously. "I still feel I am. I can't shake the feeling."

"Me too. So what do we do?"

She hung her head. "I don't know. Try to make amends, I guess. Somehow."

"Right. Why don't you start by telling me why Cabral came to visit. Last time we discussed it you said he was talking 'paranoid nonsense.' I'm betting he told you that Gilchrist killed Margaret and set him up, and probably Chet, too. Right?"

"Yes." Laura nodded, taking another bite of her burrito.

"But you didn't believe him, which is why you never told me."

"Right. Neither of us believed a word of it. As far as we were concerned, it *was* paranoid nonsense. Margaret's death—all the evidence we knew pointed to an accident. She was drunk, fell in the pool, and drowned. When Juan told us differently in Anchorage, Worth was moving heaven

and earth to get Chet pardoned. He and Chet were in the process of rec-
onciling—or so it seemed. Chet really wanted a decent relationship with
his father—the man he *thought* was his father. As for Worth having anything to do with Chet's arrests, that struck us as ridiculous. We were
convinced Ted was behind them."

"So you guys weren't at all suspicious of the Old Man?"

"No. We were grateful. Worth got Chet pardoned."

"Now, why exactly did you come back?"

"Basically, Chet felt he owed it to his mother."

"But she'd been dead for years."

"Yes, but he adored her. Growing up, Margaret always told him it
was his destiny to take over the business. She used the word so much, he
used to tease her that it was his middle name: Chet Destiny Gilchrist. But
he never wanted the paper or Gilcorp. He felt *embarrassed* about who he
was. He wanted a quiet academic life. He wanted to be a historian, a
scholar."

"But at Stanford, he worked on the *Cardinal*."

"Only because his mother prodded him. He would do just about anything to please her."

"But I thought she was a mess."

"Oh, she was. But Chet had a major blind spot where his mother was
concerned. He saw only her good side, and was in denial about her …
problems. I could never decide if he was being sweet or stupid. When
Margaret died, he was devastated. By then, he was interested in me, and
I was heavily involved with the *Cardinal* so he stuck with it. When we got
together, maybe six months after her death, he announced that he felt
released from his mother's vision of his destiny. He decided to go to grad
school. But then in Alaska, he landed at the *Pioneer*, and much to his surprise—and mine—he fell in love with journalism. As the years passed,
his mother's words kept coming back to him. He started believing that
running the *Horn was* his destiny. Even before the Pulitzer, he'd decided
to return. He would have, too, last year, except that I was dead-set against
it."

"Why?"

"Because it meant prison. I didn't want him spending years behind
bars. I wanted him with me. I wanted children. We had a good life in
Alaska, all things considered. I was ready to put down roots there, commit to our new lives."

"But he insisted on coming back."

"No. He was on the fence. He didn't want prison. But he was willing to go to put his past behind him. He wanted some idea how many years he'd get. His lawyer made inquiries and encouraged him to contact Worth—"

"—Who pulled off the pardon."

"It was a miracle. We couldn't believe it. At that point, there was no reason *not* to come back."

"And no reason to be suspicious of Worth."

"None …" Her lower lip trembled, and a tear coursed down her cheek. She dabbed it with a napkin. "Worth acted so thrilled to hear from us. He was so warm and welcoming. Chet was ecstatic about their reconciliation."

"And the inheritance issue? Worth's kids with Irene? It didn't occur to you that there could be conflict?"

Laura's chin dropped to her chest. She dabbed her eyes with another napkin, then added it to the damp pile in front of her. "Frankly, no. The boys are children. The will was clear. Gilcorp passed to Chet. Worth welcomed us back with open arms. We had no idea he would—"

"But if you weren't suspicious, why did you hire a private investigator to keep your apartment under surveillance?"

Laura's red-rimmed eyes opened wide. "How'd you find out about *that?*"

"I kept noticing the van in front of your building. On a hunch, I ran the plates, traced them to the agency you hired. Of course, they wouldn't talk to me. But a reporter I knew at the *Defender* became a PI. He knew people there, found out they were working for you."

"We were convinced that Ted had planted the heroin. We thought he might try something again." She took the last bite of her burrito, wiped her mouth, and crushed the napkin in her hand. "I should have told you what Cabral told us—"

"Like I said, it wouldn't have mattered. I wouldn't have believed it either—until I linked Jessburger to the Old Man."

"Still. I feel so *stupid.*"

"Don't. You had no way of knowing how evil Gilchrist was."

"I wish I could convince myself of that."

Ed told her what Jerry had been telling him: "Try."

They finished eating. Laura excused herself to the bathroom. When she returned, her make-up was freshened and her face showed no trace of tears.

"So, is the piece in the paper true?" Ed asked. "You're taking over Gilcorp?"

She cocked her head, accusingly. "You doubt the *Horn's* accuracy?"

"Of course. It's a newspaper. And I used to work there."

In spite of herself, Laura laughed. "You're incorrigible."

"That's what my editors always said."

"Yes, Ed, God help me, I'm taking over Gilcorp. Irene's threatening to sue, of course. But I have a lawyer offering her a very generous settlement, which is what she really wants. I hear she's talking about moving to London, getting the kids away from … you know."

The messiness of growing up as the children of a notorious murderer.

"Well, congratulations. Or condolences. I'm not sure which."

"Me neither. Ever since I got together with Chet—" her face clouded for a moment, then she willed the clouds away, "—my life has been one big roller-coaster ride. Now this. It's like a dream."

"You have any idea how to run a billion-dollar corporation?"

"Not really. But I brought on Margaret's attorney, Averill Trawlings, as a special advisor. I trust him. He says I'm learning. Yesterday we had an all-day meeting capped by dinner at Masa's. All the V.P.s, the heads of all the units. Thirty of them. Half flew in from New York and L.A. We had what diplomats would call a 'frank exchange.' This morning, I fired the four who seemed like jerks, gave the other 26 raises, and told them I wanted 10 percent revenue growth annually for the next five years."

"You'll do fine."

"That's what Averill said." She reached across the table and touched his arm. "But I'm concerned about the paper's Editorial side."

"Why?"

"Tell me why I shouldn't be."

"You've got a solid group there. Straight shooters who know their five W's, understand the city, and love the smell of fresh ink."

She looked him in the eye. "But I need someone in the newsroom I can trust. I need you." Her hand found his and squeezed. "What's all this nonsense about you quitting to write for Ted?"

She was a remarkable woman. He hated to disappoint her, but his mind was made up. "I didn't quit. I was fired. When it happened, Calderone made me an excellent offer. I wasn't in a position to refuse.

Now I have a contract to honor."

"Walt told me you gave everything to a new hire from the *Defender*."

"Tim Huang. An old friend who helped with the investigation. He and the vets Ruffen teamed him with will do a fine job for you. A Pulitzer job."

"Good. As ugly as this story is, it's our story and we have to tell it right. What about after you finish your piece for Ted? What then?"

"I don't know. Maybe a book. A few agents have called."

"And after that?"

"No idea."

"Come back to the *Horn*. You can have any job you want. C.E.? M.E.? Name it."

He eyed her. "I thought publishers don't interfere with Editorial."

"Right," Laura retorted. "And Santa slides down the chimney."

They both chuckled.

"Well, it's a very generous offer, Laura. I'm flattered. Really. But I'm not cut out to be an editor. And last time I was in the newsroom, I felt physically ill. I need some time away."

"What about a column? When you're ready to come back."

"That might be fun. When I'm ready to come back."

"You think La Cumbre might be talked into opening a place on Union Street?"

"If a major media mogul financed it, why not?"

Laura blushed. "Oh, God. I'm not used to this."

"Shouldn't take long."

50

"Champagne?" Ted Calderone was grinning from ear to ear. Dressed in khakis and a silver silk turtleneck, he opened a small walnut-veneer refrigerator tucked under the solid walnut bar in his office, which overlooked the corner of Pacific and Columbus at the intersection of Chinatown, North Beach, and Sin City. Across Columbus was a dim sum place that made Ed salivate. Up the hill toward Broadway was Tommaso's Ristorante. Across the street, blinking purple neon proclaimed: Live Nude Girls.

From the refrigerator, Calderone extracted a foil-wrapped bottle. "This calls for D.P. What do you think of this for the cover: 'The Gilchrist File: The Untold Story of Money, Mayhem, and Murder by the Reporter Who Uncovered It.'"

"Has a nice ring."

"With your byline played up big, of course."

"A cover byline is nice." Ed already had a spot picked out on his living room wall for the framed cover.

Calderone worked the cap off slowly. It emerged with a faint burp and no spray. The office reminded Ed of Gilchrist's: major square footage, cool view, oversized desk, bar and conference grouping. But this place was less corporate, more entrepreneurial, more comfortable. Gilchrist had fine art on the walls. Calderone had cover blow-ups that plastic surgeons could use to market implants.

Calderone poured the champagne. "I'm thinking: No boobs on the cover. Just the type. Real big."

"Really?" Ed didn't expect this. *Full Disclosure* buyers *wanted* boobs on the cover. Other things as well. "Why?"

"For the newsstand. To get out of the girlie ghetto and up front with *Time* and *Newsweek*. Marketing and Circulation are projecting an extra two-hundred thousand sell-through."

He handed Ed a crystal flute alive with bubbles. As they touched, the glasses chimed. An extra two-hundred thousand? How nice. In his calculations, Ed had figured only half that.

Full Disclosure had spent its first few years in funky offices ten stories above Mission at Second. But as the magazine's circulation and revenue grew—not to mention its owner's ego—Calderone bought the old brick building on the corner of Pacific and Columbus. Pacific had been the heart of the Barbary Coast, and Calderone reveled in the bawdy past of his new address, though he had no idea of its actual history.

The original occupants were the Sydney Ducks, the gang of British convicts who escaped Australia's penal colonies and arrived in 1850 in the first flush of gold fever with a boatload of lice-infested Mexican whores. They set up a tent bar-brothel in what quickly became known as Sydney Town.

Six years later, after the Second Vigilance Committee hanged the Ducks' leaders and ran the rest out of town, lower Pacific became the Barbary Coast and boasted two dozen ramshackle saloons and brothels that turned "Shanghai" into a verb. A one-eyed gangster out of Chicago, Cyclops Murphy, built what he called a "dance hall" at the corner of Pacific and Columbus, the Dancing Bare. The sign outside depicted a caricature of the bear from the new California state flag doing a jig. Inside, the dancers and waitresses wore next to nothing, and could be taken to the tiny rooms upstairs for fees ranging from 25 cents for Mexicans, Indians, and Chinese to 75 cents for French women and red-heads.

Lower Pacific burned to the ground in 1906. A year later, Titus Graves, a New Orleans ragtime clarinetist who'd played with Buddy Bolden, built a brick saloon on the site, the Promised Land, offering liquor, jazz, dancing, jambalaya, and a few women unobtrusively tucked away upstairs. Similar clubs lined Pacific: the Thalia, Hippodrome, Midway, and Spider Kelly's. But their comparative discretion was not enough for a coalition of clergy, who spent the years after World War I railing against Pacific Avenue's debauchery. Finally, in 1921, the police closed all the clubs and the City decreed that no liquor licenses would ever again be issued along Pacific east of Columbus. This prohibition pushed later generations of exotic dancers, peep shows, and massage parlors up the hill to Broadway and left lower Pacific a quiet backwater that eventually became home to architects, antique dealers, import-export agents, clothing designers, and a magazine that the Ducks, Cyclops Murphy, and Titus Graves would have enjoyed.

"How's the hand?" Calderone asked, ushering Ed to a circular chrome-and-glass conference table by a seismically retrofit brick wall covered with framed awards for investigative reporting and a shelf supporting three Ellies, the shiny copper, Alexander Calder elephant sculptures given to winners of National Magazine Awards.

Ed held up his hand. The doctor had rebandaged him that morning. No more mitten, just some gauze taped over his stump. "I'll live."

"I figure we're a lock for another Ellie." Calderone glanced smugly up at the awards wall.

"I certainly hope so." Ed cleared his throat. "But before I get started, we have a few details to discuss."

Calderone looked at him askance.

"Contract details."

"What?" the publisher grumbled. "I thought we had a deal—$30,000 for 15,000 words, and you keep the book, TV, and movie rights. It's a hell of a deal, and you know it."

Ed leaned forward, poker-faced. "We had a tentative deal. But things have changed."

Calderone didn't like this. He leaned over the table and laced his fingers in front of him. His eyes narrowed. "Changed? How?"

"For one thing, this." Ed held up his bandaged hand. "For another, you're not the only publisher interested in the story."

"No one's offering more than 30 K, are they?"

"I did a little checking with Overland—"

"—the hell for?"

"They split newsstand revenues with you 50-50."

"So?"

"So, you just said you're projecting my piece selling an extra 200,000 copies on the newsstand."

"So?"

"With a cover price of $3.95, you're looking at a windfall of a $1.98 times 200,000. Call it $400,000 in extra revenue from circulation alone—not counting all the extra ad money the buzz over my piece is sure to bring in."

Calderone was silent, seething.

"You can keep all the ad money, your regular newsstand, and half the bonus newsstand. All I want is the other half. $200,000. Half now. Half on acceptance."

"That's fucking extortion!" Calderone pounded the table. Then he shot back in his chair and crossed his arms belligerently over his chest. "No writer shakes me down. *No one.* We had a deal."

"I don't recall signing a contract. I'm ready to sign now. My terms."

"Well, fuck your terms, pal."

"Funny. That's not what *Penthouse* said."

Calderone's face flushed. Through gritted teeth he hissed, "Then sell it to Guccione."

Ed sighed loudly, got up, and strode the five steps to the door without looking back. He turned the knob, pulled the door open, and stepped over the threshold. He grabbed the knob to close it behind him.

"Wait!" Calderone shouted.

Ed stopped.

"All right. Your terms. But no more bullshit. And you sign a contract right here, right now, with a drop-dead delivery date."

Ed stepped back into the office, working to suppress a grin. "Happy to." He returned to the table and sat back down.

Calderone picked up a phone and ordered an underling to prepare the contract and check. "How do I know you won't take the hundred grand and skip town?"

"I guess you'll have to trust me."

Calderone was silent. He wasn't the trusting type.

"By the way," Ed added, "there are two other little details—"

"Now what?" Calderone groaned. "You want my pubic hair?"

"First, any disparaging remarks about my religion and the price doubles."

Calderone laughed. "Rosenberg, you kill me. Fine. And second?"

"The negatives of Laura."

Calderone's eyes narrowed to slits. "No can do, pal. They're gone. Lost. Didn't I tell you?"

Ed shrugged, got up again, and headed for the door. He opened it, closed it behind him, and crossed the large open room where various assistants toiled in cubes surrounded by enormous wall posters of *Full Disclosure* covers. He took the elevator down the four flights to the lobby.

When the double doors opened, he was face-to-face with a security guard. "Mr. Rosenberg? Mr. Calderone wishes you to return to his office. He says he has something for you."

Back upstairs, Calderone's molten eyes said: This is the one and only piece you'll ever write for me, scumbag. His lips said, "Funny thing. A photo assistant found the negatives in our archive. She's getting them. In the meantime, sign these." He placed the contract on the conference table. Calderone had already signed both copies.

Ed perused it, signed both, left one, folded the other, and slipped it into his pocket.

"I've never paid *anywhere near* this much for an article. I'd appreciate your not blabbing it all over creation."

"My lips are sealed."

"They better be."

A knock at the door announced a statuesque young woman in a black skirt that was too short, a black top that was too tight, and black heels that were too high for an office. She presented Calderone with a large manila envelope. "Give it to *him*," Calderone said, motioning to Ed, who opened it, pulled out the plastic strips, held them up to the light, and slid them back inside.

"How do I know this is all of them?"

Calderone flashed an ironic smile. "I guess you'll have to trust me."

51

"Noe Valley" is a misnomer. The neighborhood is actually a hilly plateau carved out of the broad shoulders of Twin Peaks and Diamond Heights, supported by the strong back of the Mission. Along Twenty-fourth, the commercial heart of the neighborhood, Noe Valley slides gently down to the Mission. Elsewhere, the border between the two neighborhoods is marked by two-hundred-foot bluffs. The steepest section is Twenty-second Street between Church and Vicksburg, where the sidewalk is a concrete staircase and the street is one-way, down. The drive is a black diamond ski run. Years ago, at the upper lip of the precipice, the Department of Public Works erected a sign with the understated warning: HILL. Soon after, a graffiti artist crossed it out, and spray-painted: CLIFF. Periodically, the city replaced the sign, but it rarely took more than a few days for CLIFF to reappear.

Jocko McKenzie lived a few doors down from the CLIFF sign in a renovated Victorian, one of a line of about a dozen homes dating from the 1890s. They survived 1906 because they were built on the rock of what the geologists call Goat Hill Escarpment. Ed drove up to Jocko's to attend the pizza party Mr. *Defender* decided to throw in honor of Game 4. It was a raucous beer-drenched affair that overflowed with present and former *Defender* staffers and a sprinkling of leftist activists and City Hall types. The many Giants fans—Jocko most prominent among them—hunkered down on one side of the family room. The handful of A's fans set up on the other, with yellow police tape strung between them. Each side lustily cheered their team and jeered the other—and threw popcorn across the tape. Tim was conspicuously absent. Jocko was steamed by his defection to the *Horn* and didn't invite him.

The A's won handily 9-6, sweeping the Series. Shortly after Dave Stewart was declared the MVP, Ed said his good-byes. He picked some popcorn out of his hair and headed for the 'Stang, parked perpendicular on the steep section of 22nd. The driver's door was on the uphill side. He could barely open it.

KFOG saluted the A's with "We Are the Champions" by Queen, then gave a nod to the Giants with Bob Seger's "Beautiful Loser."

It was a perfect autumn afternoon. Below Ed's windshield, the Mission was a mosaic of bright colors and diverse architecture. Farther east, Potrero Hill raised its rocky head and beyond it, across the Bay east of Oakland, the solitary pyramid of Mt. Diablo punctured the blue horizon.

• • •

Back on Dolores Terrace, Ed opened the envelope Calderone had given him, extracted the yellowed plastic strips, and held them up to the light. He preferred the woman Laura had become to the girl she'd once been.

How to get rid of the negatives? He pulled a scissors out of the lap drawer of his new desk, but then replaced it. The task called for something more … ceremonial. He climbed the back stairs to the flat roof of his cottage where he kept a small hibachi grill, a couple of cheap Costco lounge chairs, and a small shed he'd assembled from a kit that contained charcoal briquettes, a starter chimney, a bundle of old *Foghorns* for kindling, and a few packs of Safeway matches in an old yogurt container. Ed balled up some newsprint, set it in the grill, dropped the negatives on top, shooed away the cats, then struck a match. The paper flared and a few seconds later, the negatives were smoke drifting over the rooftops toward Guerrero.

Ed stretched out in one of the chairs and watched the smoke dissipate. He knew he would write only one piece for Calderone, but felt no regrets. Seeing the look on Ted's face when he handed over the negatives was worth permanent residence on the man's shit list. He could always return to the *Horn*.

Then something about the shed caught his eye. The charcoal. As he recalled, the bag was almost empty, but oddly, it looked almost full. What was in there? He opened it and spied a metal tin, the kind used to package holiday cookies. Jessburger.

Ed opened the tin and pulled out a ziplock bag filled with white powder. From the feel of it, he guessed it weighed three, maybe four ounces. Sold on the street, that much coke would bring major bucks. Some papers were stuffed into the bottom of the tin. They contained cryptic lists of dates, initials, and dollar amounts that made it look like he'd been moving an ounce or two a month for three years, enough "evidence" to land him in San Q until his teeth rotted.

Ed tossed the papers into the grill. They went up in a whoosh of yellow-orange flame. He considered taking a little toot, but thought the better of it. Cocaine had never been his drug. It had been years since he'd done any. Then he remembered. It hadn't been years ... just a few weeks. He'd done some with Julie the night they drove to Tahoe. Then he wanted it even less.

Ed carried the bag down to his bathroom, dumped the contents into the toilet, and flushed, just as the doorbell rang.

"Coming!" Ed yelled, figuring it was the neighbor who'd borrowed his ladder that morning. As he strode through the kitchen, he idly wondered if he should heat a can of black bean soup for dinner or hit La Cumbre.

Through the stained-glass pane, he could see that his caller wasn't holding a ladder. It wasn't the neighbor. It was a woman with bronze ringlet hair. His heart stopped. He wasn't conscious of opening the door.

"Hi." Julie smiled sheepishly, averting her eyes.

"Hi." It was all he could manage to reply. His throat felt as dry as the sand blown across Great Highway.

"Congratulations ... on everything."

"Thanks."

She still looked exotically alluring, but had a deeply furrowed brow he didn't recall. He wanted to reach out and caress her milk-chocolate cheek, but his arm wouldn't move.

They regarded each other silently, then Julie ventured, "Mind if I—?"

In a dream, Ed drew back and gestured into the living room. She stepped past him with her head slightly bowed. She wore white sandals, white jeans, a print blouse with a design that evoked Africa, and a white denim jacket with a giraffe embroidered on each breast pocket. Big gold hoop earrings dangled from her teardrop lobes.

"Nice place," she said. She stood before Ed's new sofa, but didn't sit down.

"Please, sit," Ed managed to say, slowly emerging from disbelief to realize that Julie was, indeed, in his living room only an arm's length away. "Lately, it doesn't feel much like home. Everything's so … new." He couldn't explain any more.

"Tim's series mentioned the burglary."

"Want something to drink? Juice? Beer? Wine? Calistoga?"

"White wine would be nice."

"I think I have some Sauvignon Blanc."

"Great."

Ed poured two glasses, scooped some Kalamata olives into a custard cup, and placed a small block of cheddar cheese and a stack of Ak-Mak crackers on a plate. He carried everything in on a tray, and set it down in front of Julie on his new coffee table. He handed her one glass, took the other, and sat opposite her on his new rocker. He realized his jaw was clenched. An unfamiliar pressure gripped his chest. His stump, just about healed over, throbbed.

Julie raised her glass and met his stare with lips pressed tight. "To you, Ed. I'm so glad you survived."

Ed didn't know what to say. What came out was: "You embroider those giraffes?"

Julie looked down at her jacket. "No. Never had the patience for embroidery. I made the top, though, from cloth my Mom brought back from Kenya a few years ago." She opened the jacket to reveal more of the blouse. It looked smart and fit perfectly. He wanted to undress her, feel her warmth, her heat.

"Nice," Ed said.

"Thanks."

They sipped their wine as KFOG segued from the Yardbirds into "Fortunate Son" by Creedence. Rhythm jumped into Ed's lap. Blues was nowhere in sight.

"How's the arm?"

"Almost better. It aches sometimes, but I can open jars again. How's the hand?"

"On the mend." He held it up, revealing the small residual bandage without mentioning the throbbing. "Down at the pool hall, they now call me Nine-Fingers Rosenberg." Julie smiled, reached for an olive, chewed it slowly. "How was Barbados?" Ed scratched the cat behind the ears and she began to purr.

"I didn't go. I stayed with a girlfriend in D.C. for a while. Since I've been back, I've been house-sitting for some friends in Oakland."

Ed said nothing, just gazed at her, drank her in with his eyes. She was as beautiful as he remembered, no question about that. And as talented, fascinating, and sexy. But who was she, really?

"I finally got up the nerve to see you," Julie began slowly. "I wanted to explain."

He pursed his lips. The reporter in him wanted to pummel her with questions. But he held his tongue.

"I—I was scared. Terrified. That's why I left. You thought those bullets were meant for you. But I knew he was trying to kill me."

"How?" Suddenly, Ed's stomach ached.

"He talked in his sleep. Woke me up a few times. His anger was scary. He talked about … shooting people. And then the …" She shut her eyes tight, as if not seeing might blot out her memories.

"What?"

She shook her head, rubbed her eyes. A tear coursed slowly down her cheek. She took a deep breath and opened her eyes. "The sex. It changed. It was less mutual, more like him taking it." Her head fell into her hands. "Oh, God," she groaned, "I felt so trapped. He'd been so good to me. But then I met you and suddenly I felt so alive and in love, and I wanted it to work—you and me—but …" Her voice trailed off. She cried. Her shoulders shook. Tears fell on the giraffes. Ed wanted to sit beside her, gather her into his arms, hold her, tell her everything was going to be all right. But he couldn't move. If she'd been the target on 50, then he was released from guilt. But he still felt guilty … and given the way she'd disappeared, hurt. He reached for a box of tissues and slid it across the coffee table. She snatched a few and dabbed her eyes, blew her nose.

Ed heaved a sigh. "Of all the crazy weirdness of this whole mess, the one thing I could *not* wrap my mind around was you in bed with Jessburger."

"*What?!*" Julie's jaw dropped and her eyes became eggs, sunny-side up, popping in a hot frying pan. "What are you *talking* about?"

"I pulled some strings to keep that part out of Tim's story, but I know all about you and Jess—"

"What *the hell* are you talking about?" Her face contorted with shock and disbelief. A vein pulsed on the side of her neck. "I was talking about *Worth*. I was *never, ever* involved with—. How could you even *think* such a thing?"

"Because Gilchrist said so. Because it made sense: Your attraction to rich men, Gilchrist and the Governor, and dangerous men, Jessburger."

"No!"

"But you didn't figure on his jealousy. When Jessburger saw us together, he—"

"Stop! *Stop!*" She glared at him. "You are *so wrong!* Let me *explain!*"

Their eyes met. Julie's blazed with anguish. Ed gestured: Go ahead.

Julie shifted on the sofa, gathered herself, folded a leg up under her, and took a deep breath. "If you don't believe *anything else* I say, you've *got to* believe this: I was *never* involved with Jessburger. *Never.* Never met him. Never even *heard* of him—until his body was found with Chet's."

"That's not what Gilchrist said."

"Who are you going to believe? Him? Or me?"

"But you *were* Gilchrist's mistress."

"No. We were lovers, casual lovers. I was *never* his mistress."

"But he gave you fancy jewelry, took you up to Tahoe, set you up to fuck the Governor—on video."

"He never paid my rent and didn't get me my job."

"Splitting hairs, isn't it?"

"Not to me."

A ray of afternoon sun struck her face, highlighting the bronze of her hair, the set of her jaw. KFOG played the Talking Heads' "Take Me to the River."

"I never even *met* Worth until I'd worked at the *Horn* for several months," Julie explained. "The paper was co-hosting a publishing conference in Carmel with the *L.A. Times,* and I went down as part of the crew dealing with all the arrangements. Worth was charming, flattering. I was lonely, hadn't had a date in months. He invited me to his suite for a drink and we wound up in bed. I enjoyed it. You have *any idea* how hard it is to meet a decent man in San Francisco who isn't gay? After that, he took me on some business trips and sometimes we'd meet in a room he kept at the St. Francis. And he gave me some gifts, mostly jewelry—"

"Like the amethyst necklace and earring set you wore to the Handgun dinner."

"Yes. He was very generous."

"He was old enough to be your father."

"So what?"

"So, in my experience, women who get involved with men like that usually have some issues with their own fathers."

Julie gazed at him wide-eyed, but said nothing.

"You said yours was a jazz musician. Played sax with Charles Mingus."

Julie rolled her eyes. "Once, just once, he sat in after hours with Mingus. But that's all. My father tried hard, but never got anywhere in jazz. Left my mother when I was four. I only saw him a few times after that until he died a few years ago."

She ran her fingers through her hair, gathered it, let it fall around her shoulders. "My mother was a young social worker in Greenwich Village. My father was playing sax in Washington Square for tips, and swept her off her feet. She scandalized her family by marrying a black man. They disowned her, said that prayer Jews say when someone dies."

"Kaddish."

"Yeah. He played small clubs—when he worked at all. My mother rarely talks about him, but she's hinted that he fooled around. I have dim memories of them arguing, doors slamming. After he left, Mom couldn't make ends meet. One day—I have vivid memories of this—she took me on the train up to Yonkers to see her parents—"

"The tailor."

"Yes, and my grandmother, who ran the shop while my grandfather sewed in back. They had an apartment above the shop. I remember my grandmother letting us in, the apartment smelling like chicken soup. And I remember my grandfather trying to throw us out, pointing at me, and shouting *schwartze*. You know what that means?"

"Yes," Ed said softly. Yiddish for nigger.

"I remember my grandmother all flustered, yelling at him, pushing him out of the room. Then she gave me a bowl of ice cream. Next thing I know, we're living with them. Mom and I shared their back room. I had a little cot by the window. Out in the courtyard, there was this big tree, a maple, I think. When I was older, I read *A Tree Grows in Brooklyn*. I thought the author got it wrong. The tree grew in Yonkers. Even living with my grandparents, my Mom had a tough time making it. We shared that room until I went to college.

"At first, grandpa had nothing to do with either Mom or me, the black sheep daughter with the *schwartze* child. He was Old World. He had a hard streak. He never completely forgave my mother till the day he died. But my grandmother was a kind woman, doted on me. When we showed up, the neighborhood was changing. By the time I was eight or nine, it was mostly black and Puerto Rican. Having a brown child playing in the front of the shop turned out to be good for business—"

"Your start in PR."

She flashed a quick smile. "In a way. When I was around seven, my grandmother showed me how to sew. I had a flair for it. My grandfather noticed, took me into his sewing room, where I'd been forbidden to go, taught me more, and started paying me to help out. He accepted me, enjoyed teaching me the fine points of sewing—buttonholes, fancy pleats, beading. Almost all of my memories of him are fond ones, especially as I got older. I started making my own clothes. It was the only way Mom could afford to dress me in anything decent. My grandmother used to say, 'Someday, you'll have finery.' When Worth came along, I did."

"But he was married, with kids. That didn't bother you?"

"Why should it?" She shrugged. "If it wasn't me, it would have been someone else. That's how rich men are. And after growing up poor, I liked being a rich man's—"

"—Mistress."

"—*Friend*." She thrust her chin out. "Stop being so *obnoxious* about it. I'm not ashamed. It happens all the time."

Yes, it does, Ed concurred, but why does it have to happen to the woman *I* fall for? "Sorry."

Julie took a sip of wine that was closer to a gulp, and shifted position, brought the other leg up under her. KFOG went into one from the new Paul Simon album, "Call Me Al."

"Then Worth told me that Chet had contacted him and wanted to come back. This was a few months before he returned. That's when things started to change."

"How so?"

"Worth became irritable, distant, preoccupied—and much more sexually demanding. He said he was stressed and needed it to relax."

"And you were happy to oblige."

"Why not? I enjoyed sex with him and he was very good to me. It was a way to be there for him, show him I cared."

"What about the governor?"

Julie blushed and looked away. "You've got to believe me: I had *no idea* we'd be taped. And I had no idea Worth would use the tape—use me—to blackmail the Governor. I didn't find out until after Chet was pardoned."

"He told you?"

She nodded. "Bragged about it. Thought I'd find it amusing. I didn't."

"What happened?"

"He asked me to plan a weekend at the Tahoe place for some 'important people.' He led me to believe there would be a big group, men and women. But at the last minute, it was just the three of us. On the drive up, he said he had this fantasy of me having sex with the Governor and then telling him all about it. It struck me as pretty strange. But he kept talking it up, saying it would be fun, that the Governor was sexy and my doing it would bring us—Worth and me—closer. Well, the Governor *was* sexy. We had some wine and got in the hot tub, and Worth disappeared, and … well—"

"You fucked him in the greenhouse on the motorized bed."

"Yes."

"And you enjoyed it." Ed's heart raced.

"Yes."

"And you told Gilchrist all about it." His jaw clenched.

"Yes."

"Every smarmy detail. Sluts R Us." The moment the words passed his lips, Ed knew he'd gone too far.

Julie's eyes blazed. She jumped from the sofa, and bolted for the door. With a hand on the knob, she whirled around and faced him. "Who *the hell* do you think you are, judging me? I had *no idea* Worth was using me for blackmail. If you could have a fling with—with some movie star, wouldn't you? You know you would. It's fine for men, but not for women? The Governor was charming and sexy. And we were in a setting *you know* is romantic. What was *wrong* with it?"

Nothing, Ed thought. I just don't want to hear about you and other men. "I'm sorry," he said. "Really. I was out of line. Please, sit down. I apologize. *Please.*"

Julie continued to grasp the doorknob as she considered his words.

"I guess I feel jealous. I'm sorry. Please don't go."

She let go of the doorknob, crossed the room, and returned to the sofa.

"Here, let me make you a cheese-and-cracker."

She took it and munched in silence as he cut more cheese slices, lay them on Ak-Mak pieces and topped them with Kalamatas. They both chewed on a few. Neither looked at the other. The twilight deepened. Ed rose and turned on a lamp.

"Got any music?"

Ed switched off the radio and popped an Al Green collection into the CD. Track 1 was "You Ought to Be with Me."

"Great song," Julie said.

"Yeah."

They listened a while in silence. When the first chorus began, Ed asked, "So when did Gilchrist start talking in his sleep?"

"Right before Chet's pardon was made public. We were working on the press release. It got late. He decided to stay at the St. Francis and I joined him."

"What did he say?"

"Mostly nonsense. But some intelligible phrases: 'Shoot them,' 'Kill them,' that sort of thing, and then some names: Gregory Murtinson and Chet … and me."

"So what did you do?"

"Nothing. Everyone has crazy dreams. I didn't take it seriously until Murtinson got killed."

"And then?"

"I didn't know what to think. Everyone thought Chet did it and Worth called me, *begged* me, to do something to deflect suspicion from Chet, and I crashed that press conference … and met you."

"Did you tell him about you and me?"

"Oh, sure. He was all for us getting together. He liked hearing about my … relationships with other men."

"You mean the sex."

She nodded. "Yes. It turned him on. But he wanted to know all about your story, too. Now I know why."

"He was using you to spy on me."

She nodded.

"So you forgot about what he said in his sleep?"

"It just didn't seem real to me. He acted so upset about Murtinson's murder, and so protective of Chet. I couldn't *imagine* him as a killer. People have weird dreams and some say crazy things in their sleep. He was always so nice to me, a real gentleman."

"What about after you got shot? You didn't get suspicious?"

"I did. A little. But I couldn't imagine why he would—"

"To tie up all the loose ends. In his mind, his big mistake was not killing Chet and Cabral the first time around. The second time, he didn't want to leave any unfinished business, and you and I were part of it. I'm convinced he told Jessburger to kill us both."

Julie averted her eyes, looked down into her lap.

"You could have mentioned your suspicions. …"

She wrung her hands, swept her eyes from one corner of the ceiling to another. "I thought about it. But it just seemed so impossible. And I was afraid of how you'd react to learning that I was … with Worth, too." She cupped her hands over her face, rubbed her eyes.

"But you couldn't imagine hanging around, either."

"If I did, I was afraid he might kill me … or that you'd make me want to stay."

He looked into her eyes. They were hypnotic. Part of him was ready to fall for her all over again. Another part wanted nothing to do with her.

"I'll take that as a compliment. But I have to tell you, Julie, the way you left, just disappearing with no word, it hurt."

"I asked you to come with me," she said plaintively.

"I didn't think you were serious. I thought it was the codeine. As far as I knew, you had no reason to run. I never imagined you would. I couldn't believe it when you did."

"I—I couldn't think of any other way out. I was scared. It never occurred to me that your life was in danger. I thought it was only me. And in all my other relationships, I've always been the one who ended them. I have trouble trusting men."

Al Green launched into "I'm So Tired of Being Alone." The cats prowled around, rubbing themselves against Ed's ankles. Julie drained her wine glass. Ed peered at her. Should he let himself go? Or let her go?

"So Worth said I was with Jessburger."

"Yes. And now I know why: To make me think he wasn't trying to kill me."

"I don't understand."

"You said Gilchrist started brooding when Chet called him, that he was on edge. He realized that Plan A hadn't worked, so he opted for Plan B—killing everyone who could possibly threaten him, including you. I bet he sensed your suspicions. Jessburger was doing his dirty work. Once Gilchrist realized that I was putting the puzzle together, he added me to the hit list. When I confronted him, he tried to get me to drop my guard by reassuring me that I *wasn't* on his list. He kept saying I was never his target, that he just wanted me to leave the country. But there was no denying that Jessburger had taken a shot at me at the theater, and at us on 50. He needed to explain that. An affair between you and a jealous Jessburger was the simplest way. Then it would make sense that Jessburger was acting on his own when he went after you and me."

"And you believed him. You believed that I'd be with that ... *creep*."

Ed stared into his lap. "Yes. I did."

"How could you *think that?*"

He glared at her. "You left without a word. I was hurt and pissed, and people were shooting at me. I knew you'd fucked Gilchrist and the governor. Why *not* the Nazi?"

"Because I *didn't*, that's why."

Ed shifted in his chair. Julie pulled her legs out from under her and sat primly on the sofa, hands folded in her lap. "Okay. I believe you." But his words sounded tentative.

"For real? You're not just saying that?"

"I believe you," he repeated, with conviction this time. "I'm sorry I ever thought you—"

"No, I'm sorry," Julie asserted. "Sorry about everything. I know I hurt you. You were good to me. Wonderful. You deserved better." Her eyes were as deep as the ocean. Her eyebrows were crunched together. She leaned forward, her body language communicating pain and regret.

Al Green launched into "Let's Stay Together." The cats chased each other around the room, then Blues reared and hissed, and Rhythm wheeled and scampered into the kitchen.

Julie asked, "Are you ... seeing anyone?"

"No. You?"

"No." She gathered her hair behind her head, then let it go. "Any chance—?"

When Diane left, Ed seriously considered chucking everything and following her back to Grass Valley. But he didn't. Could he get past everything and try again with Julie? "I—I don't know."

"I'd like to try."

"Would you?"

"Yes," She replied without hesitation. She gazed deep into his eyes.

"What we had was special."

"What about your problem trusting men?"

"I'm working on it."

Ed felt powerfully drawn to her. He also felt hesitant. So much had happened in such a short time. Was the Julie he ached for the real woman? Or just a fantasy as Tim had said? "Can I get back to you? I need some time to sort things out."

"Take all the time you need. I'm not going anywhere."

Ed wondered if he could believe her.

December 30, 1994

At 6:30, the mid-winter morning was dark, damp, and raw, with a razor wind slicing down from Twin Peaks. Enrique Xuncax pulled a worn 49ers cap down over a head of dark Mayan hair and sullenly took his place with the two dozen other men hoping for day labor at the corner of Mission and Army in front of the Kelly-Moore Paint store. He nodded at the men he recognized leaning against parked cars and parking meters or squatting at the curb, men from Mexico, Honduras, El Salvador, and the knot from his own country, Guatemala. They weren't as green as he was, but they all looked just as lonely and hungry for work.

Then he noticed his cousin, Carlos Santos, in a ratty Golden State Warriors jacket, and drifted over to him. Carlos was 28, seven years older than he was, and had been in *los Estados,* the States, for six years when his cousin showed up at his rooming house on Shotwell broke and nearly starved after a three-week journey from Santa Cecilia, their village a few coffee plantations south of Lake Atitlán.

"*Buenos días,*" Enrique said.

"*Hola,*" Carlos grunted, sipping steamy liquid from a tall paper cup Enrique recognized as coming from a coffee shop around the corner.

Enrique sighed, not sure what to say. Back home, when you said *Buenos días*, people always answered, *Buenos días*. It was the polite reply. But in this cold cruel country, things were different. Your own cousin didn't think twice about being rude.

An icy gust made Enrique huddle deeper into his two sweatshirts. One was a pullover he'd picked up cheap at Goodwill with Los Lobos emblazoned across the chest. Over it he wore a hooded, zippered, warm-up jacket with mercifully deep pockets that Carlos had given him to survive San Francisco's damp, bone-chilling cold. Enrique had thought California would be warm. But even in the worst of the rainy season, Santa Cecilia was never this frigid.

Carlos nudged him. "*Cafecito*?" Here, have some coffee.

"*Gracias.*" It was Enrique's only breakfast.

Carlos could be brusque, but he was *un familar*, family. He watched out for Enrique. Carlos showed him where to stand to have the best chance of getting work, and protected him when some of the other men, even Guatemalans, tried to push him down Army toward the freeway, where the less skilled laborers congregated. Because he'd been in *los Estados* so long, Carlos knew more English than many of the men, which often meant an invitation up to the back of a pickup truck when *los jefes*, the bosses, pulled up in front of Kelly-Moore. Once selected, Carlos always tried to bring Enrique along, though he was not always successful. Carlos averaged four days of work a week, Enrique maybe three.

Enrique shivered, stamped his feet, and huddled into his sweatshirts. The sidewalk around him was littered with broken glass, bottle caps, cigarette butts, and trash from the McDonald's a few blocks down Mission.

Then, out of the corner of his eye, Enrique spied something *de oro*, gold. He inhaled sharply. Back in Santa Cecilia, his uncle Jorge had always said, "The streets of America are paved in gold. You just bend down and pick it up." His parents scoffed, calling Jorge *un viejito*, an old fool. Enrique was inclined to agree. On a journey with his mother to Sololá to sell her weaving, he'd seen an American movie, *El Terminador*, "The Terminator." The streets of *Estados Unidos* were paved not in gold, but in blacktop and concrete, just like the highways in Guatemala. Perhaps uncle Jorge was a little *loco*. But he was a good man. He'd risked his life to save Enrique's.

The previous spring, Enrique's father had complained about a wage cut at the plantation. Soon after, he disappeared. The priest found his severed head impaled on a stake in *la plaza*. Then Enrique's mother disappeared.

That was when uncle Jorge came for him. He hid him in the underbrush of the ravine near the cemetery, then led him to the Pan American Highway in the middle of the night, stuffed a wad of *quetzales* into his pocket, slung a coil of rope over his shoulder, and told him how to find a train heading north in Huehuetenango, how to lash himself to the undercarriage of one of the cars. Since his arrival in San Francisco, despite himself, Enrique had habitually scanned the ground looking for gold. He'd found one quarter, three dimes, two nickels, and 38 pennies.

Enrique squinted. There on Army Street, he saw *gold*. He had to have it. He would send it to *el tio,* his uncle. He jumped out between two parked cars and lunged for it. A UPS truck swerved, just missing him.

"Quique! Que locuras haces ahí?" Ricky! What are you? Crazy? Carlos called. Enrique ignored him. The gold was still there on the pavement *unos metros,* a few meters, away. Between waves of traffic, he picked it up—and discovered that it was just a piece of gilt-colored foil used to wrap a stick of chewing gum. Dejected, he returned to the curb, dimly aware of eyes on him and Carlos shaking his head, calling him *un tonto,* a dimwit.

A while later, a green van pulled up and the two *gringos* who'd taken Enrique and Carlos and some other men the past few days beckoned them once again. Same deal: $50 cash to dig and sift dirt for the day, no lunch, and no ride home. Silently, the men climbed in. Enrique got a window seat in the back. One *jefe* slammed the sliding door. The other drove down Mission toward *los edificios altos,* the skyscrapers.

Los jefes were *arqueólogos,* archeologists, men who dig up ruins. Enrique was not clear on the details, but from what Carlos said, there was some *ley,* a law, in San Francisco that when a builder excavated a foundation in *el barrio antiguo,* the old city, he had to hire *arqueólogos* to dig up anything valuable. Enrique and the others dug trenches and sifted the dirt for bits of San Francisco history.

What history? Enrique mused bitterly. He understood little of *las instrucciones,* the directions, *los arqueólogos* spoke as they passed out shovels by the strings that marked the trench they were to dig that first morning. But he gathered they were digging up *antiguedades del siglo pasado,* artifacts from the previous century. What fools. *Los gringos* knew nothing of *historia.* His people, the Maya, had built great cities more than 1,000 years ago. The newest church in Santa Cecilia was 250 years old. If *los arqueólogos* wanted *historia,* they should visit Guatemala. Instead they paid lousy money to good men with history flowing in their veins to dig up *basura,* trash.

So far, Enrique had unearthed some buttons, a few dozen whiskey bottles, some forks, knives, and spoons, and one odd piece of *basura* that earned him a $10 bonus—a small pipe. Carlos explained that such pipes had been used to smoke *drogas*, opium. It was hard to believe: A bonus for digging up a useless bauble. But in *los Estados*, few things made sense.

To make matters worse, Enrique had learned the previous day that the place where they dug had been *un zona de putas*, a street of whores. He prayed that *sus padres*, his parents, up in heaven would forgive him for the vile compromises necessary to survive in *los Estados Unidos*.

The van bumped down Mission in heavy morning traffic. *El jefe* at the wheel honked at slow pedestrians, and weaved around bicyclists, Muni buses, and double-parked delivery trucks with blinking lights. Under the elevated *carretera*, the freeway, Mission curved to the right and the van entered *el centro*, downtown, where Latino faces became more scarce and *los edificios altos* became plentiful.

Then Enrique heard a loud crash. The van jolted to a sudden stop, throwing him into the seat in front of him. Some of the men around him cursed. An accident up ahead. Enrique couldn't see it, but word spread quickly around the van that a Mercedes had tried to make an illegal left, and crashed into a bus in the middle of the intersection.

"Shit," Enrique heard one of *los jefes* say. It was one of the few English words he knew. "Can you get around it?"

"No way," the other replied. "We're screwed until they clear it."

"We'll still have time to finish the trench," the driver *jefe* ventured.

"Let's hope," the other replied, not so sure.

Enrique had no idea where they were, and didn't care. But without motion, without the feeling of going somewhere, he felt uncomfortably shut in, a feeling made worse by the fact that the pock-marked Salvadoreño next to him was flatulent. To take his mind off his discomfort, Enrique gazed out the window. The building to his right was decorated with a symbol he recognized, *el faro*, the lighthouse, of *El Foghorn*. Its big revolving glass doors seemed to be in perpetual motion as throngs streamed in and out.

From inside *El Foghorn*, three people emerged into what had turned into a chilly but sunny morning: *un chino*, an Asian man, *una negra*, a black woman, and *un gringo*. The *negra* smiled up at the *gringo* and kissed his cheek. He smiled back, and slipped an arm around her waist. With his free hand, he pulled sunglasses out of a pocket and slipped them on. Enrique noticed that he was missing *el meñique*, his pinky.

The three of them jaywalked in front of Enrique's van, headed up some other street, and stopped by the steps of a large gray stone build-ing. Enrique had no idea what it was, but it resembled the newer govern-ment buildings back home, the ones built within the last 150 years. The three met up with *una china,* an Asian woman, who was *embarazada,* preg-nant. She held a microphone and conversed with a man who balanced a big camera on his shoulder. At the curb was a van with KPIX-5 on its side and *un platón,* a microwave dish, on its roof. *El chino* kissed *la china* on the lips. The other two kissed her on the cheek. She opened her coat and showed off her belly to the *negra* and *gringo,* who laughed and smiled at one another.

Up ahead, four *policias* began routing traffic around the accident and the van lurched back into motion. Enrique last glimpsed *la china* setting herself as the cameraman held up three fingers, then two, then one. Enrique did not hear a word of what she said and would not have under-stood if he had. The Old Mint Museum was closing that afternoon. Nei-ther the federal government nor the city wanted to keep it up, so they were abandoning it.

The van made a few turns and passed a place Enrique recognized, *La Plaza Grande,* Union Square. Then it bounced down a big street and turned into a narrow alley filled with stores and well-dressed *gringos.* Enrique noticed the *letrero,* the street sign, Maiden Lane. To him, it was just an-other *calle* whose shops were filled with things he couldn't afford on the way to the hole in the ground where he'd spent the last three days dig-ging up *historia* that wasn't *historia* at all. He had no idea that the little alley had once been one of San Francisco's most notorious thoroughfares, Morton Street. After the earthquake, the city fathers evicted the brothels and rechristened it with a name that evoked their hopes for a more gen-teel metropolis.

Enrique and the others dug and sifted all day. More broken bottles, more utensils, and two finds that earned him bonuses: a bottle of whis-key miraculously intact, and a portion of a Chinese lacquer screen.

But on that particular day, something was different. Fat *gringos* drove huge earth movers into position around the trench diggers, clearly pre-paring to dig much deeper. *Los jefes* drove the men harder than they had, but by the time the afternoon sun dipped below *los edificios* around them, Enrique's crew was barely halfway along the length of trench *los jefes* wanted completed.

One of the *arqueólogos* motioned for Enrique and another man to start digging at the far end. A giant earth mover rumbled to within *unos metros* of them. Enrique watched with a mixture of awe and apprehension as the operator manipulated three stick controls and raised the enormous toothed bucket over their heads. Enrique wondered if he'd be scooped up along with the first load of dirt. He jabbed his shovel into the sandy earth praying that the giant machine would spare him.

After a while, one of *los jefes* called, "All right, you guys, knock it off. We got all we're going to get." The men slung their shovels over their shoulders and began climbing out of the trench and up the ladder to the sidewalk above them.

Just then, Enrique's shovel broke through something, opening up a small subterranean chamber. He was about to call *los arqueólogos*, but they were 20 *metros* away herding the other laborers up and out, and he would never be heard over the rumble of the heavy equipment.

Enrique dropped to one knee and peered into the chamber. It was dark. But off to the left, he caught a glimmer of something *de oro*.

At the other end of the trench, Carlos waved his arm, signaling for Enrique to come quickly. He waved back: *"Ya vengo!"* I'm coming. Next to him, the big earthmover rumbled louder and the huge toothed bucket jerked this way and that, like a horse not yet broken to the bit.

Enrique reached into the chamber. His fingers felt a hard metal disk. *Oro.* He pulled it out. It was clearly *una moneda de oro*, a gold coin, a large one. He took no notice of the date under the Liberty head, nor of the slightly blurred reverse with its "SS" mint mark. All Enrique knew was that this was *oro*. No way would he turn it over to *los jefes*. This was his. He slipped the coin into his pocket and clambered up to Carlos and the others. He would send it to *el tío* Jorge. The *viejito* was right: The streets of America are paved in gold. You just bend down and pick it up.

Afterword

The story of the 1906 earthquake and fire is historically accurate. General Frederick Funston was the U.S. Army commander in San Francisco. Enrico Caruso sang Don Jose in *Carmen* the night of April 17. The Dewey Monument in Union Square survived the earthquake. A herd of cattle escaped from a slaughterhouse in Butchertown and stampeded up Mission Street. The Army sent a squad of men to help protect the Mint. The Fire Department's Captain Jack Brady helped defend it. The Mission Dolores cemetery was used as an infirmary to treat the injured. And months later, Morton Street was rechristened Maiden Lane.

But the story of the lost gold and everyone connected with it is entirely fictional. The Mint Superintendent was not Herbert Walther, but Frank A. Leach, who enjoyed a distinguished and unblemished career. As the fires approached, he and his men along with Captain Brady risked their lives to guard the $200 million in gold in the Mint's vault. Leach never lost a single coin.

Acknowledgments

The longer I write, the more I appreciate the insights of talented editors. *The Lost Gold of San Francisco* benefited tremendously from the generous assistance of several: my wife, Anne Simons, has been critiquing my work for more than 30 years, and has never once flinched when I've asked, "Would you please read this?" My brother, Deke Castleman, put every plot point, character, paragraph, sentence, word, and punctuation mark under his editorial electron microscope. Clyde Leland asked searching questions that helped sharpen several characters and plot points. Elissa Miller and Pedro Arce contributed tremendously to the final section, thanks to their knowledge of Guatemala. Amy Rennert of the Amy Rennert Literary Agency in Tiburon, California, is much more than the consummate agent. As the longtime editor of *San Francisco Focus* magazine, she edited my articles for years. Amy made critical editorial suggestions as the manuscript neared completion.

I also thank the following readers for their support and suggestions: Belle Adler, Betsy Bannerman, Mildred Castleman, Rick Clogher, Frank Colin, Kay Daniels, Nancy Dunn, Florence Edlin, David Goldstein, Larry Gonick, Trisha Hollenberg, DeWayne and Lorna Johnson, Janine Johnson, Debby Krant, Lee Lazar, Lynn Magid Lazar, Jody LeWitter, Philipp Meussig, Meredith Maran, Fred Miller, Charles Piller, Joel Riff, Michael Robinson, Dolly Magarik Rosinsky, Matt Ross, Dan Schuster, Betty Seiden, Paul Selinger, Sid Shaw, Dave Simons, Nissa Simon, Peter Straus, Mildred Toberman, Dana Ullman, Louanne Weston, Bright Winn, and Robin Wolaner.

Many thanks also to Brian Rouff, Laurie Shaw, and Scott Bieser at 21st-Century Publishing. You're bringing publishing into the 21st century.

And thanks to book publicist Anita Halton, of Anita Halton Associates, San Francisco.

I also gratefully acknowledge:

• The San Francisco History Center and Archive at the Main Branch of the San Francisco Public Library.

• "Saving the Mint—From the Inside," by Frank A. Leach in Malcolm E. Barker's *Three Fearful Days: San Francisco Memoirs of the 1906 Earthquake and Fire* (Londonborn Publications, San Francisco, 1998).

• *Denial of Disaster: The Untold Story and Photographs of the San Francisco Earthquake and Fire of 1906* by Gladys Hansen and Emmet Condon (Cameron and Co., San Francisco, 1989).

• *The San Francisco Earthquake* by Gordon Thomas and Max Morgan Witts (Stein & Day, NY, 1971).

• *The Earth Shook, The Sky Burned: America's Great Earthquake and Fire, San Francisco, 1906* by William Bronson (Doubleday, Garden City, NY, 1959).

About the Author

This is Michael Castleman's first novel. For the last thirty years, he has been "one of the nation's top health writers" (*Library Journal*). He is the best-selling author of ten consumer health books, and more than 1,000 newspaper, magazine, and Web articles. He lives in San Francisco with his wife and two children, and passes the Old Mint frequently. Visit www.mcastleman.com or www.thelostgold.com.